To John &
We loved you
Castle - Thanks (?)
a beautiful spot!

TEARS OF

Deceit

Hope you enjoy this strange tale!

REGIS SCHILKEN

Regis H. Schilken

regehschilken@aol.com

Comfort PUBLISHING

For information, address Comfort Publishing, PO Box 6265, Concord, NC 28027. The views expressed in this book are not necessarily those of the publisher.

First printing

Book cover design by
Colin L. Kernes

ISBN: 978-1-935361-56-5
Published by Comfort Publishing, LLC
www.comfortpublishing.com

Printed in the United States of America

To My Wife,

Jennie
For Her Many Years of
Help, Encouragement
And Most of all,
Love!

Vice is a monster of so frightful mien,
As to be hated needs but to be seen;
Yet seen too oft, familiar with her face,
We first endure, then pity, then embrace.

Alexander Pope, 1734

Contents

Content Cont.

01 A Strange Farewell

August 20, 1995—Sunday
6:45 P.M.

"Oh, for Heaven's sake, it's your bid," old Stephen croaked.

"I know when it's my turn. Let me think a minute," said Anthony. "Okay, let's see now ... I bid eight hearts," said Anthony.

The lights in the monks' recreation room blinked ominously. Loud thunder boomed in the distance. Even the monks' card table seemed to vibrate along with the overhead lights.

"This could give us the game," Matthew smiled. "We already have two-hundred fifty."

Matthew kept score for these same monks when they played Contract 500 almost every evening during recreation. It was a bidding game, similar to bridge, but much simpler and much faster. He would miss his friend, Anthony.

"Eight hearts? Hah! We are going to set you, Brother." Exasperated, Stephen cranked, "I pass, but you won't make eight hearts."

Ancient Father Martin was Brother Stephen's partner. Martin was as calm and good-natured as Stephen was impatient and sour. The furious storm continued almost unnoticed as the card game went on.

Anthony picked up the three-card widow. "Hah," was all he said.

1

He discarded three cards, and then laid eight of his ten cards down, face up on the table.

"And here, if either of you two bozos has a higher club or diamond, you might win two tricks. Here's the only two losers I have." He laid down his five of clubs and ten of diamonds right in front of scowling Brother Stephen.

Old Father Martin thumped down the ace of clubs; "Hah! At least you don't git 'em all, now. Do ya, Pal?"

But Anthony's eight-heart bid put him and Matthew over the winning 500-hundred mark for that game.

After their evening meal in the refectory, Father Matthew, Brother Stephen, old Father Martin and Brother Anthony, had dashed across the outside quadrangle in the pounding rain to the recreation room. The wetness on Stephen's robe only added to his foul mood.

"My deal—new game," said Stephen as he picked up the cards, and began to shuffle.

Now, deafening claps of thunder occurred simultaneously with the lightning indicating the strikes were very close.

"I'll be right back. It'll only take a few minutes. If I don't turn off that kiln, my statues will overcook," said Anthony. He pulled his pocket watch from under his robe and glanced at the time. "Be back in just a few minutes."

Brother Stephen glared at him for leaving since revenge was in order after losing the first game of the evening.

As Anthony pushed back his squeaky chair, he motioned for Brother Mark to take his place.

"But just till I get back, Mark!" warned Anthony.

Anthony walked over to the heavy door and pushed hard to open it against the howling wind and blowing rain. The door swung shut behind him.

7:15 P.M.

Anthony had every intention of going back to play cards. For years, this same foursome played together each evening after a hard day of work and prayer. Since Anthony was artistic, his daily job consisted of creating religious articles such as rosary beads and statuary, not only for the monastery, but also for churches and religious stores. In addition, statues and crucifixes were sent to him for refurbishing from all over Pennsylvania and adjoining states.

Yesterday, Anthony finished redoing the heavy oak cross from Saint Paul's Church in nearby Latrobe. It had been hanging since the church was built in 1898. To parishioners this huge life-sized crucifix was a priceless antique, but long years had taken their toll. The colors of the corpus had lost their luster. The wood was dust covered and cracked in places, but artistic Anthony immediately recognized its hidden beauty. Father Kerr, the African-American pastor of Saint Paul's, confided to Brother Anthony that his congregation would not allow him to replace it even though he wanted to.

"With all due respect, Father Kerr, we'd like to have the old crucifix restored if at all possible," a parish spokeswoman had said.

Anthony had meticulously cleaned the Christ figure on the cross until he could glimpse its original faded colors. Then using new hues he carefully repainted it. The dry wood he treated with many coats of linseed oil.

Now, after weeks of artful labor, Brother Anthony had finished the restoration. The cross lay drying in his warm work cellar.

Anthony took great pride in knowing Saint Paul's parishioners would once again see their giant cross hanging in place as the devotional center of their old Gothic church. So when he phoned Pastor Kerr late Saturday afternoon, the priest agreed to pick up the cross the following Monday.

As he hurried across the quadrangle in the rain with his cowl pulled up over his tonsured head, Anthony chuckled to himself thinking about the 500-game he and Matthew had just won, *Brother Stephen sure hates to lose. What a character. He's really a nice guy with a gruff personality.* Then he considered the hours he'd spent before dinner working soft clay into ten-inch statues of Saint Joseph. These he had painted, and after applying a layer of glaze, he'd placed them in his kiln so they would bake into hardened ceramic statues.

Anthony knew every inch of his work area in the building by heart. So, once inside the door, all he needed was the bright red light from the exit sign to find his way to the top of the stairs. He placed one hand on the railing and started down. For a moment, his steps slowed near the bottom. He spotted a very dim light coming from under his workroom door. He paused just long enough to scold himself for leaving lights turned on to waste electricity.

And then it happened!

As he reached out his right hand towards the doorknob, in the darkness, a huge figure emerged from under the steps behind him. It reached around and covered the monk's mouth squealing hideously, "One sound—one tiny noise and you are a dead man. Do you understand me?—Dead!"

Anthony filled with such terror he couldn't have spoken if he wanted to.

The ugly Voice gripped him tightly for several moments to make sure the brother had no impulse to fight back. The shocked man began to tremble.

4

The voice shrieked, "Put your hands on your hips with your elbows facing outward. Remember, not a sound, not a single sound!"

Shaking like a palsied person and fighting nausea, Anthony followed The Voice's deadly orders. He felt two very strong hands slide under both armpits, then up over the back of his neck until they came together in a full-nelson hold. Instinctively, his head bent forward at a painful angle. Now he kicked furiously, aimlessly, and grabbed at the hands behind his neck. The very last thing he felt was excruciating pain until there was a dull snap, one he barely heard. The strong figure waited several moments, then walked backward, dragging the lifeless body.

8:15 P.M.

Unaware of Brother Anthony's demise, the 500-card games continued. More than an hour passed before Father Martin said, "Hey, didn't Anthony say he'd be right back?"

"Never fear," growled Stephen, "when that man gets into his workroom, he forgets everything. His wondrous clay is more important than we are."

"He's missed some good hands," said Matthew. "Looks like four games to two—our favor. Better luck next time, Fellows."

9:45 P.M.

With the card playing over for the evening, Stephen looked around the room for someone to argue with. He knew his opinions were always wanted and certainly correct.

Matthew walked over and started talking with Brother Charles, who had just wandered in. Old Father Martin spied the two men talking.

"Matt, I think we should find Anthony—give him hell for

deserting us," said Stephen.

"Find who?" asked Charles.

"Anthony! That old geezer said he'd be right back. Maybe he got sick over there."

"I'll come with you two," said Brother Charles.

Covering their heads against the rain, the three monks hustled across the quadrangle. Anthony's building appeared deserted. Opening one of the double entrance doors, the three men could see the glow from the exit signs.

"Strange," said Martin, as he crept carefully down the stairs. "His lights aren't on."

Martin turned the knob to Anthony's workroom. "My hearing's not so good, but I can't hear a single sound in there. Can you?"

They listened quietly in the darkness.

"Nothing," said Charles.

Silence! Eerie silence!

They heard only the whistling of the wind blowing through the first floor door as it slowly squeaked shut behind them. They started back up the steps.

"Well, there are two rooms down here and they're both dark. We have Compline in fifteen minutes, so we'll nab him there," whispered Father Matthew noticeably upset.

The three monks returned to the first floor, meandered through the semi lit library and on into the basilica a few minutes before ten o'clock. Pretending to meditate in their assigned stalls, they watched as one-by-one, the brothers and ordained monks filed in and took their places. Brother Anthony never appeared.

10:30 P.M.

Toward the end of Compline the monks chanted, *"Nunc dimittis servum tuum, Domine, secundum verbum tuum in pace"* (Now you may send away your servant in peace, Lord, as you promised).

With these prophetic words, Martin, Matthew, and Charles glanced over at Anthony's empty stall, and then stared at one another.

Usually when Compline was over, the monastery observed a strict code of silence. This lasted until after Matins, the next morning's first hour of prayer at five-thirty.

Tonight however, as the monks filed out in silence to go to their sparse, but comfortable cubicles, Father Matthew and old Father Martin could not hold their tongues.

"Let's buzz by his room and make sure he's all right. It just ain't like him to miss night prayer," said Martin.

The two men left the basilica and entered the dormitory building. They walked to Anthony's room, dreading what they might find.

"Anthony, are you okay?" Martin asked as he knocked on Anthony's door.

Silence.

By now, Mark and Charles and a few others came scurrying to join them. They, too, had noticed Anthony missing at Compline. Father Martin knocked again then pounded on the door. Still no answer.

The monks at Saint Vincent's were not permitted to lock their doors. Father Matthew burst into Anthony's cell. "Anthony, are you all—" But a desk lamp switched on by old Father Martin showed an empty cubicle. The bed had not been touched.

11:15 P.M.

Martin left the other monks chatting as he shuffled down to the monastery's main office on the first floor below the abbot's second floor quarters. After clicking the ALL CALL lever on the intercom system, he made an announcement. It was strange to hear his voice so very late throughout the entirety of the monastery's grounds and buildings on this gloomy, windy, rain-soaked night.

"Brother Anthony! Brother Anthony! Please call or come to the front office. Brother Anthony, if you can hear this message, please call the front office!"

Five, ten, and finally, fifteen minutes passed. Still there was no response!

"We need to fan out and find him," said Martin. "He might be sick—lying unconscious somewhere."

The monks fanned out throughout the monastery searching the favorite places Anthony haunted. No one observed the rule of silence. Even the aged abbot joined the manhunt.

"This makes no sense. One minute he played cards with us, and now he seemed to vaporize," said Matthew.

Brothers and priests exchanged puzzled, anxious looks as they continued their search.

"Well, he must have left the monastery for some reason," suggested one of the searchers. "Do you think he went to Latrobe—"

"I—don't—think—so," interrupted old Father Martin. "Not at this hour and not on a Sunday night."

"I keep hearing him say, 'I'll be right back,'" added Matthew.

Charles looked as bewildered as the others.

Once again, Father Martin led a group back across the quadrangle to Anthony's work building. By now the rain had reduced to a slow, steady drizzle. Switching on the stairway lights, the group went down and invaded Anthony's work studio switching on the lights.

"Look, this kiln is extremely hot; he never shut it down." Bunching together to look through the small, thick oven window, the monks spied the statuary, now reduced to mounds of ashes.

"Why this just ain't right," said Martin. "I don't think Anthony ever got here after leaving our card game!"

02 The Bermuda Quadrangle

August 21, 1995 — Monday
11:00 A.M.

Twenty-four-year-old Latrobe Police Officer, Jim Simmons, and his twenty-three-year -old fiancée, Martie Meyer, a teacher at Latrobe Middle School, were planning a short sensual interlude after having a quick lunch.

The end of Martie's summer break was nearing. It was a beautiful balmy Monday. Jim had arrived at their home around eleven, but knowing he had to be back on patrol by twelve-thirty, the two decided on a quick lunch followed by a few minutes of sensual indulgence.

They were upstairs in their bedroom. Martie had already showered and was just climbing into their king-sized bed. Jim had just walked in from the shower with a terrycloth towel wrapped around his loins.

As luck would have it, Jim's cell phone on the dresser beeped, but not the usual caller tone. Instead, it sounded like the special SOS tone from the police station.

"Damn, Martie, what perfect timing." He lifted the cell phone from the dresser and answered, "Yeah, what's up?"

"You sound angry?"

"Sorry about that," said Jim recognizing Police Chief Romeric's voice.

"Got a problem over at the monastery."

"What's happened?"

"Remember your buddy, Brother Anthony?"

"Yeah, he's a good friend of mine. Why?"

"Not anymore," said the police chief. "At least, not at this moment."

"Anthony's dead?"

"I can't say, but the monastery said he's gone. At least he hasn't been found anywhere."

Noticing the startled look on Jim's face, Martie forgot about their sensual plans and tried to catch the gist of Jim's phone conversation. She heard Anthony's name mentioned. She knew he and Jim were good friends.

"I'm sure he just went out some place. Maybe he's visiting a friend or relative."

"Well, I think you'd better drive over there and investigate. There's one hell of a lot of upset priests and brothers looking for him."

"Has anyone called his sister in Pittsburgh? He might've gone there for a visit. It might be as simple as—"

"Jim, all this happened last night at around six or seven, according to those who saw him last. They waited until this morning thinking that's where he'd gone for some reason. When he didn't return, that's when they phoned his sister."

"And?"

"And, he wasn't there. Now, she is a basket case. She keeps calling our station every half-hour. Until you check this out, I can't offer her much in the way of an explanation."

"Why did the monks wait so long to call?"

"I guess they just didn't want to embarrass him. Didn't want him to think they were, you know, checking up on him. Maybe they thought he snuck out to meet a woman! Who knows?"

"You've got to be kidding; not Anthony. I know him better than that." replied Jim, "But I'll scoot over there. If he did leave, Anthony's the last person I'd expect would desert the monastery. I've always thought he was the ideal monk. Every few weeks, I visit and chat with him. You know, that man is a good listener. He always cheers me up. And, get this, he always beats me at ping pong!"

"Ping pong?

Yeah, the man's an expert and he beats me at pool, too!"

"Sounds like a really likeable guy."

"Look, Chief, I'll get on it right now. I'm really upset about this."

Closing his cell phone, Jim told Martie about the phone call and apologized for interrupting their playful interlude. Martie knew how much Jim liked Brother Anthony. She remembered times when the two went hiking in the mountains together, just to enjoy nature.

"I'll give you a call if I find out anything, Baby. There's got to be a simple explanation. I just can't believe Anthony would just up and leave the monastery. Anyway, let's do tonight what we didn't get the chance to start now."

Jim kissed Martie who held a towel draped down over her breasts.

"I'll be waiting for you, officer," she teased, "I hope everything is all right. Come back without your uniform or towel."

Latrobe covered a geographic area large enough to be recognized as a small city. It was located about three miles north on Route 981 just after it intersected with the four lanes of Route 30 coming from Greensburg. As one turned left off

Route 30 and drove northwest on Route 981, Saint Vincent's Monastery complex sat several hundred yards back from the left side of the highway.

Its old red brick buildings, built by the Benedictine monks who settled there ages ago, dominated the landscape for at least a quarter mile. Particularly noticeable was the large basilica, rounded at one end, and the oversized statue of Saint Benedict planted atop a huge decorated pedestal.

The monastery was affiliated with Saint Vincent College. It was a place of prayer and work where monks could spend their lives praying for the rest of mankind and along with lay professors, teaching college students. Here, the monks farmed 983 lush acres to provide food for themselves by the fruits of their own labors.

It was a serene place where any person could attend church services in the huge basilica used each day and night by the monks. Almost always, they could be heard chanting or seen praying, making it very conducive to meditative prayer. Lay folk often went there just to listen to the Latin chanting during the Canonical hours of the old Roman Catholic Rite.

Some teaching monks were brothers who had taken religious vows: poverty, chastity, and obedience. Others were ordained priests who could celebrate Mass and administer the sacraments, but all lived by their belief in one of two mottoes: *"Ora et labore"* (pray first and then work), or was it *"Labore et ora"* (work first and then pray)? This argument had lasted for centuries.

12:30 P.M.

Within fifteen minutes, Jim stopped his patrol car beside the monks' quarters just across from the quadrangle. Many of them were standing around in small groups talking in hushed tones. Father Martin was the first to reach Jim as he was closing his cruiser door. In great detail, Martin told Jim the story of how Anthony got up from the card table saying he'd be right back, but didn't return. He also explained that Anthony never made it to his workroom.

"Hold on, and slow down," said Jim. "Let me get my pad and take some notes."

He reached into the backseat and retrieved a clipboard holding several sheets of lined paper and began writing. By this time, others had gathered around, each one vying to have his version of last evening's events documented.

Once he had detailed the entire scene on paper, Jim talked a bit longer with Brother Mark who explained how they waited several hours this morning before phoning Anthony's sister in Pittsburgh, only to make the poor woman hysterical and forcing the monastery to call the Latrobe Police Department.

Jim spent most of his afternoon at Saint Vincent's quizzing various monks who were close friends of the missing brother.

"Does he have any enemies? Did he perchance mention to anyone that he was tired of the monastic life? Has he been known to leave Saint Vincent's at other times either day or night without telling someone? Did he have any mental or physical conditions that could explain his disappearance? Did he take drugs of any kind? Had he been seen with any strangers? Had he ever mentioned another woman in his life in addition to his sister?"

After the interviews, Jim walked over to Anthony's basement studio beside the monastery's laundry. Old Father Martin followed close behind. Jim searched for unusual marks on the stairs, walls and floor, for scuff marks, blood, a knot of hair, or for any sign, the slightest hint that a struggle had occurred around Anthony's workroom. Without a clue, he was forced to call Chief Romeric with no helpful information except that Anthony was indeed, gone.

Around five o'clock, he called Martie and explained to her what had happened. "This entire affair is so peculiar it seems more like a practical joke."

"I can't imagine anyone letting a joke go on this long," said Martie. "Even if the man decided to end his religious profession, he'd have told some other person about his plans, especially his own family." Jim had to agree.

"Anyway, see you in a little while so we can mess around this evening."

"I hope that's a promise."

5:30 P.M.

When Jim arrived at home around five-thirty, Martie had already defrosted and cooked two turkey dinners. Since there never was enough in the vegetable portion of the plastic tray, Martie had made her own side dish of green beans covered with melted butter with a hint of garlic. The two sat for quite some time discussing the "evaporation" of Brother Anthony as Jim called it.

"There is something wrong here, Martie, I sense something really evil. I know Anthony wouldn't just walk off."

"I must agree with that. When I think of the times we've had him over here for dinner, the man never lectured us about religion, but there was something about his demeanor—the way he acted, the way he talked—that reminded me of a holy person," Martie replied.

"That holy man knew how to play ping pong. Why, I

remember buying that table in our basement so I could try to beat him when he'd visit."

The two finished their meal still discussing the missing Anthony. As they stood up from the table, Marty asked, "You didn't forget, did you?"

"Me, forget?"

"Well, did you?"

"Hmmm, let's see now. What was I supposed to remember?"

Jim walked around behind Martie, scooped her up in his arms then climbed the stairs to their bedroom.

† † †

In the days and weeks that followed, no one found any helpful clues. That included the Latrobe Police, Officer Jim Simmons, and the monks at Saint Vincent's.

Jim returned to question various monks several times but their stories remained consistent.

Chief Romeric told Jim, "You know, there is no better way to leave than to just pick up and go—no sad good-byes; no explanations; nothing to pack; just leave and start a new life. Sooner or later, he'll show up somewhere."

Jim remained unconvinced. He would miss his friend. This man wouldn't hurt his friends and family by such an idiotic departure. He is the most devout man I know, too good to pull a cruel stunt like that. Still, neither Jim nor Martie could envision the possibility of foul play.

A very brief story appeared in the Latrobe Gazette. It mentioned that a brother was absent from the monastery for no known reason. Also, that he might be considered a missing person.

Anthony's sister had refused to give the Gazette his picture, because she knew how embarrassed her brother might be if he returned to the monastery or came home.

"The monastery is different now, Martie," said Jim after returning from a recent visit.

"How so?"

"A pall of sadness, suspicion, even dread has settled over the place. The monks seem afraid."

"I can understand that."

"Martie, even the most positive-minded monks, and of course, the never positive Stephen, believe Anthony has come to no good end—that he was kidnapped or—or even murdered."

"Either is possible, I guess."

"Monks who used to wander alone to meditate now go about in pairs or small groups. Mark told me they're all afraid they might stumble on Anthony's body in some ungodly, foul-smelling state of decay when they work in the fields and pastures."

"Oh, gross!" said Martie.

Jim found the monastery unnerving. Few monks ever ventured outside after dark. Most used the inside passageways linking the various buildings, rather than walk out across the dreaded quadrangle, which Brother Mark had aptly renamed the "Bermuda Quadrangle."

Days turned into weeks, and then months, and finally, long years. Anthony's disappearance, while never forgotten, became a hazy, faded horror of the past. It took some time for the monastery to return to a more normal routine, but it never completely recovered.

Because Anthony's stall in the basilica remained empty, it was a constant reminder of the nonbeing who might someday reappear.

Brother Mark remained convinced that Anthony's

mysterious disappearance in the "Bermuda Quadrangle" was due to the electrical storm that fateful evening.

"He was vaporized by lightning, plain and simple—body, mind, robe, socks, shoes and shorts—Zap! Poof!"

Old Father Martin may not have had the best theory for the odd disappearance, but he believed it.

"Jim, I think the man was assumed into Heaven without dying just like the Virgin Mary. Z-z-z-i-p!" he would say, as he raised his arm until it extended heavenward.

The Feast of the Assumption would always have a special double meaning for the ancient priest and Officer Simmons.

03 A Leak above the Ceiling

Seven Years Later

August 19, 2002—Monday
8:45 A.M.

Martie and her next door neighbor, Amy, were sitting in Amy's kitchen enjoying a morning cup of coffee. Amy's eight-year-old daughter, Mildred, was still asleep. Amy had recently lost her husband in a battle with cancer so she enjoyed these morning moments to gab about anything, everything or nothing at all. Martie was enjoying the waning days of summer vacation away from the stress of teaching sixth, seventh and eighth graders at Latrobe Middle School. Jim had already gone to work.

"Yes, you heard me right," insisted Amy. "There was water on the floor in the middle of the aisle right under the hanging crucifix. Lots of people saw it not just me."

"So?"

"Martie, I'm telling you that water came from the crucifix."

"Amy, there must have been a leak or something, above the cross. You're making too much of this."

"I don't think so, but I do know that I always sit toward the front of the church and at the end of the pew. I know what I saw. For sure, that water wasn't there when I came in; for sure, it was

21

there when I left."

"But someone might've had water on their shoes. Who knows? How can you be so upset over something so—so trivial? It could've been any number of things."

"But Martie, it didn't rain last night. Remember? It was bone dry outside."

"Even so, then something got spilled there. Maybe someone was carrying a bottle of purified water, took a swig, and dripped some on the floor. You know how health nuts are. They take those bottles everywhere."

"Well, maybe so, but I know I'm remembering correctly; that water was right under the large crucifix suspended above the center aisle, and I saw it."

It had been quite some time since Martie had been inside Saint Paul's Church or any church for that matter, except for the occasional wedding or funeral that required her attendance. She was an atheist some of the time, an agnostic most of the time, and a Christian at Christmastime because she adored the simplistic beauty of the Bethlehem story and its heartwarming pageantry. She did not consider herself a proponent of any organized religion.

Although she had doubts about her faith as a young girl, she had finally turned away from Catholic dogma during her freshman year at the University of Pittsburgh. After several years of contemplating what she'd been taught by nuns, priests, and her parents, Martie had begun to question her faith. *Why would a God allow his or her son or daughter or any other messenger for that matter, to travel to earth to be killed as reparation for sin. Come on now! An act that heinous would represent humankind's greatest sin ever, certainly not an act of atonement. No, the idea of a crucified savior is perversely illogical.*

22

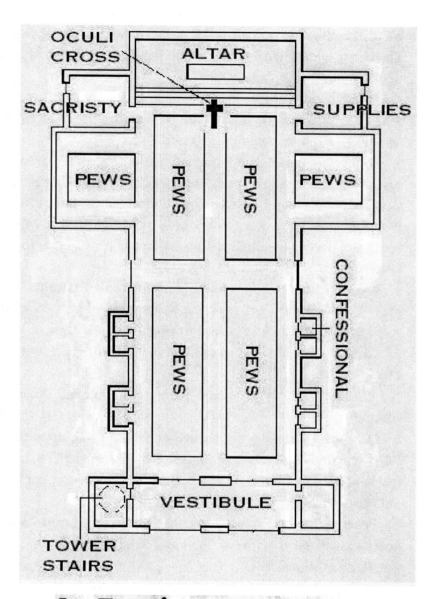

OCULI
CROSS

ALTAR

SACRISTY

SUPPLIES

PEWS

PEWS

PEWS

PEWS

CONFESSIONAL

PEWS

PEWS

VESTIBULE

TOWER
STAIRS

St. Paul's from above

She recalled one of the last times many years ago when she went to confession and shared her doubts with a young priest. The young curate had listened to her questions and then offered up the following explanation.

"Martie, our Creator loves us all so much He sent his Son, Jesus Christ, to be crucified as the perfect sacrifice to atone for any sin any human could ever commit."

What that priest said exploded her entire cortex, front to back, side to side. She had not been back to church since. So, the large heavy wooden crucifix suspended in Saint Paul's Church that Amy was so concerned about symbolized all that Martie could not accept about Christian dogma that preached savior killing.

"So why did you stop going to church? Don't you want God's grace?" asked Amy, not realizing the myriad of anti-religious sentiments that had just rushed through Martie's head.

"Amy," she said, "it's too difficult to explain right now and I must be going."

"It's not that late," said Amy who enjoyed Martie's company.

"I've got to make a shopping list to keep me on track or I'll overspend and ruin my budget for this week. You know teachers in most big cities get a halfway decent salary, but here in Latrobe, hah!"

Because Jim had a huge appetite, she always planned a few special meals for the two of them and skimped on those when she dined all alone.

"Talk to you later," said Amy as she watched Martie put her coffee cup in the top dishwasher bin. As her friend walked through the door, Amy teased, "I'll be sure to let you know what happens next week at church."

"Great. Can't wait. Take notes. Make a recording, take pictures," she said aloud, but was hoping Amy would forget all about it.

† † †

As one enters Latrobe by driving past Saint Vincent's Monastery on Route 981, the highway splits. The left leg remains 981 running up through the business center of the city and on through the cultural area as Main Street, then out through various neighborhoods and small suburbs. The right leg of the split becomes Saint Paul Street.

Standing at the corner of the third side street, Sanctus Street, one would see Old Saint Paul's Gothic Church. Even today it is an inspiring edifice. Its two spires, one on each side of the double main doors, rise to a height of one-hundred-twenty-five feet. Each is topped with a metal crucifix grounded as a lightning rod and years of decorative pigeon droppings. The interior of the church is two-hundred-twenty-five feet long from the massive front doors to the far wall behind the main altar. The altar has been moved out thirty feet from its original position so the priest can stand behind it and face Catholic worshippers.

There are two side aisles, each containing two confessional boxes. On each side of the church near the front are two transepts where the pews face toward the center, perpendicular to the main aisle. These two transepts give the church its traditional cross shape if viewed from the air. Both transepts also contain a number of vigil lights. The donation to light one of these candles is normally five dollars, and it burns for about eight hours. It is believed that if a candle is lighted and a prayer said, that petition stays before the Lord God as long as the candle continues to burn.

August 25, 2002—Sunday
7:00 P.M.

Amy left her house twenty minutes early taking little Mildred with her. She wanted to grab a pew nearest the place where the water had been found on the floor during the previous week's Benediction ceremony. Other churchgoers entered and they, too, anchored themselves in the end pew positions as close to the suspended crucifix as possible. Professor Bob Troft, an usher who always volunteered as the seating authority during any important ceremony, attempted in vain to get these cemented-in anchorites to slide inward so that others who wished to sit in the same pews did not have to climb over. To him, these disobedient ignoramuses were crude, rude, and uncultured.

Hushed whispers could be heard among those present who, like Amy, had seen the water on the floor last week. Before the actual Benediction ceremony began, Mrs. Reed played the ancient pipe organ in the background as worshippers entered the church and took seats. When Father Paul Kerr, pastor of Saint Paul's, walked out of the sacristy behind an altar boy wearing huge, untied, oversized, clopping tennis shoes that blinked with red lights as he walked, the congregation stood and joined in singing the hymn "Come, Holy Ghost" while the organ played.

Following the hymn, another altar boy brought out a white cope, an additional vestment he placed over the kneeling priest's shoulders. Father Kerr pulled it around and over his brown arms like a shawl, hooking it under his chin to keep it in place.

Standing up, he climbed the three steps to the altar, opened the tabernacle, which contained the sacred wafers of bread, and placed one host into the center of the sunburst-like monstrance. Now worshippers could see the wafer through a small glass window, believing it to be the body of Jesus Christ himself under

26

the appearances of bread.

Of course, Amy paid little attention to the actual Benediction ceremony. She stared at the floor as did those in the pews near her. Her mind was wound like a clock spring. As the organist intoned the Latin hymn, *"O Salutaris Hostia"* (O Saving Victim), the congregation started to sing. First, one small water drop, then another fell to the floor just as they had done the previous Sunday. Hushed whispers could be heard as a few anchorites nearest the crucifix spotted the droplets.

Next, the altar boy brought out the incense thurible. Father Kerr had returned to the bottom of the altar steps where he placed incense inside the burner on the red-hot charcoal. Kneeling down, he swung the thurible outward and back, outward and back several times, so that thick, fragrant clouds of frankincense and copal swirled up toward the altar and around the wafer in the monstrance.

So sincere was this priest and so strong his faith that no doubt existed in his mind. He was paying homage to the same Jesus Christ who walked the earth over two-thousand years ago. He stepped back up to the altar, draped the ends of the cope to cover his hands then lifted the golden monstrance high and turned so all present could see and adore the sacred wafer.

By this time, the seven or eight drops that had fallen under the crucifix began to congeal into a very tiny water blot on the polished church floor.

Returning to his kneeling position at the foot of the altar, Father Kerr led a prayer while the congregation repeated what he'd just intoned: "Blessed be God."

"Blessed be God," responded worshippers.

"Blessed be His Holy Name."

"Blessed be His Holy Name."

"Blessed be Jesus Christ, true God and true Man," intoned Kerr.

"Blessed be Jesus Christ, true God and true Man," the congregation responded.

And so the ceremony continued until the prayer was over, the Eucharistic wafer returned to its tabernacle home, and all present sang the final hymn, "Holy God, We Praise Thy Name." Those who had witnessed the droplets sang loudest of all.

By now the dripping had stopped, and as the priest left the sanctuary following the tennis-shoed boy, those nearest the suspended crucifix left their pews and gathered around the tiny water blot on the floor. They kept their distance as if afraid to get too close. Amy, of course, was right there in the front line standing mesmerized. Yawning Mildred wanted to go home.

Hearing the tumult of voices from his church, Father Kerr left the sacristy and came to see if someone had fallen ill where the small crowd had gathered in the center aisle.

"Father," said Amy as the pastor approached, "the water, that water, right there on the floor—" Before she could finish her sentence, others began to speak out.

"It came from the crucifix, Father. We saw it happen. It came from the eyes."

"Yes, I was sitting right there and I saw the drops fall," said one astonished man.

"So did I," repeated Amy, "and the same thing happened last week."

Skeptical Kerr, trying to calm the group which was by now quite boisterous, said loud enough for all to hear, "There must be a leak of some kind. Maybe the old roof is bad, or some plumbing. Who knows, this is an old building. I doubt if came from the *Oculi*."

"Oculi?"

"Eyes," said Father Kerr. "That is the Latin word for eyes."

"But Father, it's not raining outside so it can't be the roof."

"Well, it rained hard a few days ago. Maybe it took this long for the rainwater to soak through the plaster; this church is so old anything is possible."

While talking he pointed his finger to an area of the high, Gothic ceiling far above the crucifix. Then he knelt down and touched the water.

"It has no odor and it looks and feels like regular water. I'll have Ed Bristol check the building."

Mr. Bristol, Saint Paul's custodian, was looking on from the vestibule and had heard Father Kerr's comment. He and the priest had been best friends since childhood.

Although he was referred to as a custodian, Mr. Ed Bristol was Saint Paul's caretaker and general manager. He was also a jack-of-all-trades who took care of the plumbing and heating, figured out electrical problems, and solved just about any crisis that arose. He had assumed the responsibility for replenishing burnt-out vigil candles and collecting the money from various offering boxes stationed around the church.

Because of their long relationship, Father Kerr trusted him to act as the treasurer for the church's meager bank account. On Thursday evenings at six o'clock, Bristol would lock the church doors after permitting a commercial cleaning crew to enter. They mopped and waxed floors, cleaned and polished the hardwood and pews, and maintained the restrooms.

Sisters Margaret and Lucy took care of cleaning their own convent building, while Mrs. Pierce, Mr. Bristol, and even Pastor Kerr, maintained the rectory. The small elementary school required little servicing since it had been closed for several years. The two nuns who ran an after school latchkey program used just two of the schools abandoned classrooms.

As the church emptied, Bob Troft came up the center aisle and began asserting his authority by shooing curious onlookers toward the doors. And when Father Kerr mimicked Bob Troft's dismissal hand and arm gestures, the small crowd began to disperse. Before leaving, a few people including Amy, walked over to the wet spot on the floor, reached down and touched it, and then made the sign of the cross. Little Mildred did the same as her mother although she hadn't the foggiest notion why.

When Amy walked by Mr. Bristol in the vestibule, she asked him, "Ed, do you think the water came in through the ceiling?"

"It's hard to say."

"I mean, if it did, could that be dangerous?"

"Not if the ceiling stays up there."

"But what if it falls?"

"Not a good place to sit then, is it?" grinned Ed.

8:45 P.M.

As Amy walked home from Saint Paul's with Mildred, the word "miracle" kept creeping into her thoughts. Father Kerr's meager "leak" explanation did nothing to dissuade her belief. Before reaching her house, she stopped at Jim and Martie's home to tell them about the mysterious water.

"Slow down, slow down," Jim said, "tell me exactly what you saw." Amy recounted the events at church while bored Mildred stood beside Jim, holding his arm.

"I sat at the end of a pew almost under the suspended crucifix along with others who had witnessed the droplets last week."

"And?" replied Martie.

"It wasn't until the bread wafer was exposed that the tears began to fall."

"Come now, Amy. You're sure they came from the crucifix?"

"Yes, Jim, I'm sure. The man in the pew behind me was thoughtful enough to bring his flashlight this week. I'm telling you the water came from the Oculi." Amy felt very knowledgeable using Kerr's Latin word.

"Oculi?" questioned Jim and Martie almost at the same time.

"The eyes," said Amy, "that's what Pastor Kerr called them. Oculi is Latin for eyes," he said.

"Go on."

"Well, it appeared the droplets were coming from the eyes. It was uncanny. I mean, it spooked me and those around me."

Jim asked, "So what did your pastor say?"

"He came out after service to see what the fuss was all about. When we pointed out the water on the floor, he dismissed it as a leak in the roof or in a water pipe. He said the custodian would check it out tomorrow morning."

"Well, that's reasonable," replied Martie.

"But I think you're overreacting, Amy. There is always some logical explanation for these kinds of happenings. What I'm saying is that crucified plaster figures don't cry. Do you know what I mean?" said Jim. "They're not real Amy, the figures are fake ... painted plaster ... no tear glands ... can't weep."

"Jim, you can laugh if you want and the same goes for you, Martie, but I know what I saw, and it was very convincing. It has me rattled. That cross has been hanging for years and years and then all of a sudden this, this, this miracle thing happens."

"If it is water, then it's a trick or an illusion of some kind.

31

Someone has tampered with that cross. I think you should forget your ideas about miracles until Father Kerr has it all checked out. You know him, he'll get to the bottom of things," added Martie.

"Well," Amy paused, "you could be right. No sense getting fired up and then finding a reasonable explanation. Anyway, I've got to go next door and get Mildred to bed. I know she's tired."

Mildred just smiled at the three of them because she enjoyed staying up late with adults, and even though she was sleepy, she adored being nearby Officer Jim; Jim shared the little tot's feelings because he and Martie had no children of their own. Mildred had no idea why her mother was so curious about the water in the church, or why she had put her hand in it, and then made the sign of the cross.

Before leaving, Amy pressed, "Martie, Jim, please, ple-e-ease go with me next Sunday?"

"Amy, you know I'm not a churchgoer," Jim responded.

"Yes, but Benediction lasts about forty minutes, often less than that if there is no sermon. Now, I know you're not a practicing Catholic but come anyway, if for no other reason than to help me find out what's going on."

Martie thought for a few more seconds and then, because Amy was her close friend, she reluctantly said, "I'll go." Jim just rolled his eyes and said nothing more.

August 28, 2002—Wednesday
12:00 P.M.

"It's funny," said Jim as he flopped down a newspaper on the kitchen counter. "The story about the tears is wildfire throughout Latrobe. Did you see this clip in the Gazette?"

"No. What's it say?" asked Martie, her hands busy as she

prepared some tuna sandwiches for lunch."

"It's a short blurb saying something about tiny water drops appearing under the old crucifix and that Pastor Kerr is having the roof checked. According to this article, the water amounted to five or six drops."

"... Just enough to fire-up religious fanatics."

"Amazing how fast the bizarre spreads," replied Jim, "I heard Mildred and her little friends talking about it while playing out front this morning."

Martie had also heard them talking about going back to school next week which reminded her that she would soon resume her teaching role. As much as she loved her job, she hated to see the calm, relaxing summer vacation drawing to a close.

"Tomorrow and Friday are in-service days at school," she told Jim. "These two days are planned for us by our principal who mailed me this flyer outlining tomorrow and Friday's activities. It sounds kind of interesting," she said handing Jim the typed flyer.

He glanced through it commenting, "Martie, I can imagine you up there giving these presentations. A lot of these topics are things you do with your students every day."

They enjoyed their lunch together, but Jim had to leave early to take part in a hearing about a brawl the night before at Prevacids Grill. The local judge would hear the case around two o'clock. Jim had been one of the first officers to arrive at the scene.

"Love you, Beautiful," he said hurrying down the front walk. "I love you, too! Be waiting for you."

04 A Time for Us

Martie had always wanted to be a teacher. She enjoyed school from her earliest kindergarten days. Whereas a lot of tots have an initial separation problem when mom first leaves them with a schoolteacher and walks out the classroom door, Martie's reaction had been to say, *"Bye, Mom,"* and then run off to play with the other kids.

Mrs. Flynn, Martie's first teacher at Belmar Grade School in the Homewood section of Pittsburgh, reported to Mrs. Meyer that her daughter was a delight that first day of school because she could get kids who missed their moms to stop crying.

"She can do it when I can't," reported Mrs. Flynn. "Your daughter should take my place."

During grade school, Martie loved playing teacher with the other neighborhood children unless one of her playmates acted as teacher. Then she delighted in telling that little teacher how to act and what to say and do. She was a precocious little girl. When she wasn't teacher, she'd become bored and walk indoors to read.

Martie's modest family home had been on Kedron Street about one block from Belmar Grade School. Her father, a gentle, quiet man who liked model trains, was now about fifty-six and drove a bus for the Port Authority of Pittsburgh.

When Martie entered Westinghouse High School, her

mother began working as an assistant in Homewood Library at the corner of Hamilton and Lang Avenues. She would walk to and from the library each day, a distance of eight blocks, claiming the walk was her thirty minutes of daily exercise.

An A-B student, Martie enjoyed doing research, then writing term papers and essays. Since her mother worked at Homewood Library, mom carried home books for Martie to read or use for reports. It was natural for her to major in education at the University of Pittsburgh but joining a sorority was out of the question; too much group thinking, too much agreeing. Martie liked to make her own decisions about life, religion, and sex. She could never have conformed to the demands of a women's group.

Upon graduation from the university, the Latrobe School District hired Martie as a middle school teacher. As a result, she rented a small, two-bedroom home on Elm Street to be near her job. Certified to teach math or science, she usually taught both subjects. Several middle school teachers had informed her that sixth, seventh, and eighth graders were difficult: disrespectful, hard to understand, hormonally electrified and bratty. But Martie didn't believe that hand-me-down tripe.

Martie was a democratic teacher. At the beginning of each year, she'd explain the rules and then ask her students, "Should I teach first each day, and then give you five minutes to goof off at the end of the period, or vice versa?" Then the class would vote to see which three nights of the week they "wanted" homework. This atmosphere created a cooperative classroom mood for the entire school year. Most importantly, she loved her job and students sensed it; best of all, they enjoyed learning from her and she knew it.

Although Martie was not quickly swayed in many things,

she could become infatuated with every sharp-looking, well-defined male she saw, be he in a suit, a uniform, swimming gear, a photograph, a calendar, Playgirl, or his birthday suit. When Officer Simmons was around, she preferred him dressed in the latter.

✝ ✝ ✝

In 1993, two weeks before the end of the school year, Martie phoned the Latrobe Police Department requesting that an officer come to the school to talk with students who might someday consider police or detective work as a career. When dark-haired Officer Jim Simmons walked in, Martie could not concentrate. Jim was tall, broad-shouldered with a thick neck, and to her delight, immaculately dressed in his attractive uniform. While the students adored Jim's smooth, deep-voiced delivery as he walked up and down between their desks, Martie wondered, *What would he look like undressed. Is he smooth all over? Is he hairy? Does he wear sexy jockeys or boxers.*

She was still staring at his overall physique when the students began clapping, and Officer Jim prepared to leave. Embarrassed because she had been so preoccupied that she hadn't the faintest notion of what he'd said, she covered her faux pas by asking Nancy Brainerd to sum up what the officer had told them.

When Nancy finished elucidating, Martie said, "Class, I think we owe Officer Simmons a big thank you for coming today and spending time with us. Let's give him another round of applause before he leaves."

Instead of clapping, it seemed like every hand in the classroom began waving at the same time. *I must have missed something important.* Embarrassed, she addressed another pupil, "What is it Emmett?"

"Officer Simmons said that if you take us out to the parking lot, he'll let us sit in his cruiser, didn't you, officer?"

"Yeeeesssss!" said all the kids in unison.

"Did you mean right now, officer?" Martie asked.

"Sure. Why not?"

"YEAAAAH!" erupted thirty-two children but much louder this time. Jim told the first row of students to stand against the wall, followed by the second row behind then the third and so on until the line went almost around the room.

"Are you ready, Ms. Meyer?" Jim thought, *these kids love this teacher. I can feel it.* This fascinated him. *She's a very attractive woman. I wouldn't mind sitting in her class.*

"Ah-h, why of course—yes, I'm ready."

"Then, would you bring up the rear behind the last student over there?"

"Oh, yes I will—you want me at the rear." She could barely speak.

Here she stood at the end of the line of students, following this hunk that had taken over her classroom and thought nothing of it. When the group reached the police car, Officer Jim told everyone to stay in line but to stand tall and erect like they were officers, because they were going to get inside. He opened all four cruiser doors and had three students slide across the backseat from the driver's side. They could see the cage-like heavy metal grating between the front and rear seats.

"This is like being in jail," one of the students said.

Then Simmons sat in the driver's seat, turned on all the flashing lights and the police radio. Next, he allowed the pupil in the right rear passenger seat to move up into the front while the next person in line slid in behind Jim. Since there were thirty-two students waiting in line, to keep all of them from getting restless, Jim let each one sit next to him in the front seat for ten seconds. He gave each a turn pushing the siren button bringing about a short but loud wail. In a little under ten minutes, the entire class finished. Ms. Meyer took her turn sliding along the backseat like her students and then up front beside Officer Jim. *Hm-m*, he thought, *what delicate fingers and just a hint of perfume.*

"Thank you, students," said Jim. "Stop and visit me at the police station, but not because you've done something wrong. You, too, Ms. Meyer," but he was thinking, *You can visit me any time. I'd like to get to know you.*

The kids laughed. Jim got into his cruiser and drove out of the parking lot. Ms. Meyer led her class back into school but could not get the officer out of her thoughts. Her brain remained jostled for the rest of that period and for the next one as well. Little did she know Jim was obsessing about her at the same time.

After dismissal, she phoned the precinct and asked for Officer Jim. She left her home phone number when told he was out on a call.

"Nothing serious, I hope?" she asked.

"Just an accident, that's all."

"He was in an accident?"

"No, no, Miss, he had to go to the scene of an accident."

"Oh-h, thank God."

When Jim called her home, she thanked him again for visiting her students, and never one to be bashful, she said, "I'd like to repay you with dinner if you could come over sometime— sometime soon, perhaps?" She had seen no wedding ring on his finger when he visited her classroom, a ring she looked for the instant she decided he was an attractive male with a delicious physique. He was thinking, *Wow, this is great; I was trying to think of an excuse for phoning her.*

Jim responded, "Okay, how about tomorrow night?"

"Tomorrow night?" she repeated.

"Ms. Meyer, would tomorrow night be a good night for dinner?" he asked. *Gee, maybe she wasn't serious after all!*

"Yes, why yes, that would be wonderful. Um, how about six?"

"Great, I'm off duty at five-thirty tomorrow, so I'll be over around six o'clock."

"Around six?"

"Ms. Meyer, didn't you just say six would be a good time for dinner?"

"Yes, yes, that I did. Then, six it is," she said, flustered—happy he could not see her embarrassment. "That would be terrific. See you tomorrow."

"Great, I'll be there." *But I don't know where she lives—*

Martie started to hang up the phone, but heard, "Wait, wait, wait, hold on a minute. I don't know your address."

Martie calmed down enough to give him directions. *I'm a terrible conversationalist,* he thought. *What will I ever say during a whole dinner? Nothing too stupid, I hope.*

After their first, awkward dinner together Martie and Jim began seeing one another more frequently: movies in Latrobe and Greensburg, plays in Ligonier, and good food. Jim enjoyed attending school programs and students loved seeing him there.

In summer, they picnicked, hiked, and swam together. One day in July they went to a swimming hole Jim had used since childhood. In actuality it was a section of Loyalhanna Creek, well hidden in a forested area where the water deepened from its normal five to six-inch flow into a much deeper spot he had estimated at six or seven feet.

Jim had climbed high up on a rock at the water's edge saying, "Martie, let's jump in."

"And get wet?"

"Uh-h, is that a question or a statement of fact?"

"Jim, I mean we'll get all wet."

"So?"

"Well, uh-h—"

"I have a great idea," he said. She looked up to see him stripping. He glanced down and watched her disrobe until she stood naked with the bright-yellow sunlight dancing around her face as it played through the moving oak leaves. *I think the gods brought me this woman.*

He saw that Martie was tanned, but not all over. He could easily see those areas that had been covered by bathing attire. She was beautiful: long, shiny, brown hair; expressive, smiling face that highlighted her tanned cheekbones; lips that suggested the tiniest pout—wanting to be kissed, maybe begging to be kissed; fine legs and a beautiful firm bottom. While she stood naked looking up at him, his eyes kept wandering back to her face.

What a prize I've found! Am I a lucky man, or what? he thought.

He was standing there eyeing her from top to bottom, not thinking of his own nakedness when she called, "Hey, police officer, stop parading around with a weapon like that. Why you could be arrested for indecent ex—"

Jim jumped, pulled his knees to his chest, then plummeted down into the creek so that a huge, concussive swath of cold water splashed up over her. She leaped in beside him, but came up coughing. He held her tenderly until she stopped, then he smiled and kissed her. She held on to his neck for quite sometime. They spent the entire afternoon enjoying the water, the filtered sunshine, the fun of being together, the beginning of an intimate, loving relationship. *This is one person I'd hate to lose—ever!*

† † †

Up to this date, Jim had been living in his own rented apartment on the outskirts of Latrobe. He would go home after they had made love. But on this particular night, he knew he felt very different. *I don't want a home of my own. My home is here. This is where I want to stay, to be with her, to live with her, to laugh and love with her.* The CD played, "When I fall in love—it will be forever."

"Martie, I love you. I want to stay here—to live with you—not just tonight—forever."

"Jim, that's a long, long time—and I'd enjoy spending all of it beside you."

From that night on almost eight years ago, Although they never married, in their conversations, each referred to the other as husband or wife.

05 Media Uproar

September 8, 2002—Sunday
10:00 A.M.

Jim called Martie's phone mid-morning. "Are you and Amy still going to Benediction tonight?"

"Yes, why?"

"So am I!"

"Ah, so the religion bug has stung you after all these years."

"Nah. Chief Romeric asked me to go to Saint Paul's with him. Says Father Kerr phoned, claiming the media wants to record the Benediction ceremony. Kerr forbade it, but the media insisted on being there. Romeric pledged he and I would stand guard. So-o-o, I'll be there. See you tonight, beautiful."

Martie laughed at how quickly Saint Paul's Sunday ceremony had become big time news not just in Latrobe, but in Greensburg and some of the Pittsburgh stations as well.

6:45 P.M.

Amy, Mildred, and Martie, walked down Saint Paul Street toward the church, Martie told Amy about Jim's phone message. "Yes," said Amy barely containing her own excitement. Can you believe how big this, this miracle—" she noticed the frown on Martie's face, "well this, this event, is becoming?"

Media vans had already parked near the church when the

threesome got there. Some vehicles sat up on the yellow-lined curb at the bottom of the steps leading to the church's main entrance. High telescoping antennas arose from the tops of some vans. Their very bright halogen lights cast a surreal glow on the church steps and the crowd.

Jim stood at the door and turned away reporters, photographers and local TV personalities and their camera crews. He had arranged with Father Kerr to open just one front door, locking all other entrances. Worshippers who had come for the Benediction service filed by Jim one by one as seats were available.

Jim refused to engage in any kind of conversation or debate. But the media kept pushing him. Things were getting a bit hectic just as Chief Romeric arrived with red lights flashing followed by two enormous local tow trucks. So many people were in the street that Romeric had to slow to a crawl to allow them time to move aside.

The chief stopped near the first illegally parked van belonging to a Pittsburgh crew and got out of his SUV. He walked over to the first tow truck, and ordered it to back in and lift the van as if to tow it away. By now the crowd had moved back leaving a safe distance between themselves and the heavy vehicles. Because of the flashing lights of the two police cruisers and the tow trucks and the eerie brightness of the elevated media lights, the scene looked much like an accident or a fire had happened. This ruckus brought out most of the neighborhood seeking the source of all the excitement.

When the Pittsburgh media noticed their van being hoisted, they dashed to the tow truck and implored its driver to pardon them. As if following police orders, the driver continued lifting the van after sending them to Romeric. Although he never planned on towing the vehicle, the chief gave its owners a difficult time while they pleaded.

When he figured they'd had enough, he said, "Okay, but move it right now. Move it around to the church parking lot. And I do mean now!" His stern voice and quick actions restored immediate order. Other media crews hustled to move their vehicles off the street and curbing.

8:00 P.M.

The Benediction service began when Mrs. Reed played "Come, Holy Ghost," and then while the congregation sang, Father Kerr entered the sanctuary, following two adult women acolytes, one of whom was carrying the incense thurible. Kerr wore white vestments and appeared distracted by all the commotion he could still hear outside the church's main entrance.

Kerr took his place in front of the three steps leading to the altar flanked on each side by his two women attendants. Benediction continued as usual. As if on cue, when the congregation started singing *"O Salutaris Hostia,"* first one drop of water fell from the crucifix, then another. Worshippers began pointing to the floor, some twisting themselves into awkward contortions to gawk around others blocking their view. Father Kerr could hear the commotion as it grew louder and louder.

"Look, there it is!"

"Where?" asked one person.

"See? Right there!"

"Look there on the floor!" said another

"Oh, it's just a small drop or two," remarked several people at once.

"I know, but look where it's coming from," said a man shining a powerful flashlight.

A small boy asked, "Is the ceiling leaking, Dad?"

"No, no! The cross, the cross," said the man to his young son.

"Where?"

"Look up there at the eyes! Do you see, now?"

"Oh, good Lord, look! It is the eyes, the Oculi!" people began to say.

"The Oculi are weeping!" people cried.

"But you can hardly see it," added her husband.

Another man joined in. "But I see them, too. Look up there," he said pointing. "A drop seems to be forming right now under the left eye."

Father Kerr could not ignore the growing commotion any longer. He left his place at the altar steps where he had been kneeling and walked down toward the middle aisle. As he came near the very tiny wet spot on the floor, people started to leave their pews to follow.

Kerr turned, held up both hands and motioned them to stop. "Please!" was all he said; very calmly, "Please."

He stopped while everyone returned to their pews. Alone he stood under the cross and gazed upward. The man with the flashlight shined it directly on the corpus' eyes. It became evident to Kerr that the eyes were the source of the drops of water. He watched a tiny droplet begin to form, and then grow in size.

He waited several moments until the drop fell. Mesmerized he stared upward at the Oculi. Then with complete dignity, he folded his hands, walked back to his place at the foot of the altar and resumed the ceremony. People stayed in their pews.

Like sharks, the media had a feeding frenzy as the congregation left the church, interviewing as many eyewitnesses as possible. It took some time for the church to empty.

Like a hefty Steeler running back, Amy ran interference for tiny Mildred, elbowing her way through the throng in an effort to reach the media with her opinions. Martie followed clinging to Mildred's other arm. She waved at Jim as she went by.

He called over the confusion, "Is Amy wearing shoulder pads?"

The few tiny drops Martie had seen baffled her keen sense of observation. She had been sitting very near when she saw the first few drops—maybe six or seven. She had also seen the look on the pastor's face when he noticed them. The man appeared awed.

9:15 P.M.

Martie hurried home and within the hour, Jim arrived. He appeared tired. The events of the entire evening, especially the rudeness of some of the media, overwhelmed him.

"They just wouldn't take no for an answer," he said. "It was going to get ugly until Romeric arrived and pretended to tow away their vans."

"Smart man."

"Well, it distracted them for a while. Once the ceremony began, everybody calmed down. That priest's holy aura had a lot to do with it. He reminds me of paintings of Christ standing with his arms extended. His parishioners surely love him."

"I saw all the confusion as we were leaving," said Martie.

"The media was having a field day by that time. Can you imagine the stories in the newspapers tomorrow morning?"

"I can see Amy and Mildred on TV giving their accounts."

"I'm glad the usher—what's his name?"

"Professor Troft."

"He said he'd help solve this thing. The man is a bit arrogant, but he is intelligent and knows a lot of brilliant people at the university," Jim said.

"I know you stood in the back, but I saw the drops."

"And?"

"I've got to be honest with you."

"Oh?"

"They were very convincing. It could be easy to believe."

"And they were forming at the eyes before falling?"

"It looked that way to me and a lot of others. One man had a flashlight."

"Were there a lot?"

"No, just a few drops. But I saw them, Jim, I—saw—them and so did Kerr."

"Well?

"At first he had a smirk on his face as if it was all a bunch of hooey. But as he stood there and watched a drop form and then fall to the floor, he shook his head in disbelief."

"And you, Martie, what do you think?"

"You know me, Jim, I'd be the last person to fess up to a miracle, but if it's a trick, it's reeeeally clever. I find myself not believing but I know what I saw. I stood right there—and I saw."

"Well, now we both know what all the excitement is about." Jim shook his head and said, "It's too much for me to think about tonight. I'm tired."

Both started for their bedroom and prepared for some much needed sleep.

"Ah-h-h!" said Jim as he closed his eyes, "Quite a night! You're all I need to help me relax, Baby."

In spite of all their earlier excitement both fell asleep in record time.

06 The Voice from Behind

September 15, 2002—Sunday
10:00 P.M.

By the following week, broadcasters on radio and TV interviewed actual witnesses, ministers, and experts in the paranormal and supernatural, including astrologers. At the same time, Father Kerr's Sunday Mass sermon still included remarks about jumping to conclusions. Even though he felt there was some rational explanation, occasionally he slipped and used the words "unnatural happening" since he had no hard evidence to prove otherwise.

After the Benediction ceremony that evening, while people drifted about the church praying and lighting candles, Professor Troft and Father Kerr dragged up an old wooden ladder from the sacristy stairway that led to the church basement. As they opened it under the cross, people gathered around to watch in silence. The ladder was twelve-feet high, but Troft stood on the eleventh step, so he could lean his shins against the very top to maintain balance.

"If nothing else, this crucifix is dusty," said Troft.

"Well, no one ever gets up there to dust it or clean it. But from down here, who notices?"

"Shall I wipe it off now?" asked Troft.

"Heavens no, Ed! I don't want anyone to touch it until it's

been examined."

"I don't see anything unusual," said Troft. "There's some residue under the eyes where the water has dried up. There are no signs to indicate your cross has been touched for years. Actually, there are a few cobwebs," he started to reach out, "that I'll just wipe—"

"No, don't touch them. Leave everything just the way it is," said Kerr looking over his bifocals. "Bishop Mallory doesn't want it messed with without his permission so that's what we'll do."

"I'll borrow some sophisticated scanning equipment from the university and bring it over tomorrow evening. We can examine it without touching it."

"Terrific," said Kerr, "I need a logical explanation, and the sooner, the better." The two men returned the ladder to its storage space along the sacristy stairway.

"I'll call you tomorrow and we'll have a look around six or seven o'clock. I'll bring some university people with me."

Troft left the church via the side door facing the parking lot. Lately, cars belonging to the faithful, the media, or just curiosity seekers visiting the church always filled the lot. As he climbed into his driver's seat, Troft did not notice that his right rear passenger window had been shattered. He buckled his seat belt, and started the engine. After backing out from his space, and then turning toward the street, he stopped to look for oncoming vehicles.

From behind his seat, a huge, claw-like hand reached around and covered Troft's nose and mouth, clamping his head back against the seat's headrest. An unearthly, high-pitched voice warned, "Don't—make—a—single—sound. Don't even attempt to struggle. And whatever you do, don't try to look back here.

Do you understand me?"

Troft was dumbfounded. *I can't breathe. I can't even move my head or mouth to answer.* He pulled hard trying to free his mouth.

The Voice shrieked, "I take your silence to mean you heard me. Toot your horn if you understa"—*hoooonk!* Troft's lungs were screaming for fresh air. "Good, now I want you to drive over toward the cemetery at Saint Vincent's Monastery. You'll feel me touching your shoulder. Start driving and don't dare call out or turn your head around."

I'm going to pass out. I need air. I see dark spots forming—

The Voice allowed Troft to breathe. Engulfed in a frenzy of shock, Troft had no idea whether the creature behind him was armed with a knife or a gun or some other tortuous killing instrument. Its voice sounded fiendish, Hell-like. Since he had always been a superstitious sort and was scared shitless, he drove as he was told, imagining Lucifer himself was riding in the rear seat.

Just before making a right turn onto the road that looped around the monastery buildings, The Voice once more shrieked, "Pull over onto the grass right here." Troft could feel the diabolical creature breathing on his neck hairs. Wracked with panic, he pulled over and stopped where grass and gravel met. Again The Voice covered his mouth and nose as it jerked his head back sharply, harder than the first time. Desperately, Troft tried to pull the hand away to get air.

"Stop messing in my affairs. What goes on at Saint Paul's is a battle between me and God. Stop—messing—NOW! Honk if you underst"—*hoooonk!*

"Now, get out worm—walk in front of this car then get down

on your hands and knees and crawl straight up towards the monastery cemetery. Whatever you do, whatever happens, do—not—turn—around."

Once released and soaked with beads of perspiration, Troft sucked in fresh air. With no hesitation, he climbed out, walked in front of his auto and dropped to all fours. Like a scared dog, he began crawling up the short rise into the monastery property as if caught in a hypnotic trance. Within seconds, he heard his car door slam shut, followed a few seconds later by what sounded like a loud—*POW!* Instinct forced him to the ground curled up like a fetus. He waited several seconds. *I ... I don't feel any pain. I think I'm okay. Please don't let that creature come to get me. What was that loud noise I heard. Should I look?* He managed a slight glimpse around then continued crawling. *What is that bright orange glow I see in the glass of those buildings over there?* Lightheaded because his breathing was so quick and so shallow, he thought, *I smell smoke, lots of it.* He crawled ten, fifteen, twenty yards until he passed a wide elm tree. He scurried behind it, then peeked around its side toward his automobile. The shrill, haunting wail of sirens pierced the night.

"Holy shit, that's my SUV. It's on fire!" he cried aloud.

07 The Police Scanner

September 17, 2002—Tuesday
8:00 P.M.

"Thanks for your help managing the crowds and the media Sunday night," said Father Kerr over the phone to Jim, "Sometimes they are hard to deal with, a bit pushy, perhaps."

"Glad to help," replied Jim. *They were a little more than pushy Sunday night,* he thought.

"Let me ask you something, Jim, since you deal with a lot of mysterious cases, what do you think about this whole situation."

"Father, I'm not much of a miracle believer nor am I a practicing Catholic."

"You acted Christian-like last Sunday with all those impatient media people haranguing you."

"Just doing my job. By the way, my wife Martie was there."

"Oh? And what did she think?"

"To be quite honest, she was stunned, she's not a miracle believer either but what she saw troubled her. "

"Jim, I've never experienced anything like this in all my years as a priest. I don't know what to make of it."

"You sound as puzzled as Martie. She was amazed by it, possessed by it." *Actually, she was rather convinced,* he thought to himself.

"Well, like you and Martie, I'm very skeptical that this is divine intervention of some sort. I was hoping you could investigate a bit for me."

"I'm just a police officer. Are you sure your custodian has checked for leaks of some kind?"

"Certain. More than just once."

"But, Father, police don't investigate church affairs. You know that whole thing about separation of church and state."

"I know that," said Kerr, "but the longer this matter goes on, the more difficult it will be to stop. Almost everyone in the parish believes a miracle happens here. My church is jammed with curiosity seekers all day long. They'd stay all night if I let them."

"I wouldn't know where to start," declared Jim. "Have you had any recent break-ins or, or gee whiz, I don't even know what questions to ask?"

"None that I know of. I try to lock up each night around eleven o'clock and Ed Bristol locks up at six o'clock on Thursdays after letting in the cleaning crew. Neither of us has noticed things missing, and no one's broken in."

"Did you or Ed see any person lurking around that made you feel kind of, you know, suspicious?"

"Not really. Some of the homeless folks hang around and I feed them. Sometimes I invite them into the kitchen for a meal that Mrs. Pierce cooks."

"On a regular basis?"

"Well, yes, particularly in the winter. Sometimes every night but they come to the parish house side door near the breezeway."

"And none look suspicious in any way?"

"To be honest, some of these folks seem drugged out

mentally. I can't imagine any of them being involved."

"Jeez, Father, I don't know how I can help you."

"Look at it this way, if someone altered our crucifix without my permission or Bishop Mallory's wouldn't that be regarded as a police issue?"

"How so?"

"Property damage. That crucifix is Saint Paul's Church private property. It's a property issue, not religious."

"Clever, Father, because in that sense you're right. Tell you what. Let me talk to Chief Romeric about your 'private property' concerns. He's got a logical, legal mind for odd cases, and by far this is the oddest mystery I've ever dealt with." Jim began to chuckle, "I mean, what would I look for: fingerprints, batteries, hidden water tanks, spirits, water guns?"

"Don't be funny, Jim. There must be something, some trick, some gimmick that makes those tears. My biggest problem is that Bishop Mallory has written me a letter stating he does not want the cross taken down. He says we can examine it in place, but he won't permit us to take it down and mess with it. I think he believes that Christ's eyes are crying and I can't prove otherwise."

"Well, maybe he's right and we're wrong," suggested Jim. "But just the same, I'll ask the chief to come over with me since you mentioned the private property issue. Do you have a ladder that will reach the crucifix?"

"Yes, Troft and I used it last week. It's lying along the sacristy stairs."

"So, you two have already checked out the cross?"

"That's just it, we did."

"And?"

"It seemed normal to both of us: very dusty. That's exactly

why I need another opinion."

"Okay, I'll talk with Romeric. If the cross is gimmicked, there has to be something we can spot."

I hope I can convince him, he thought.

Father Kerr sounded somewhat relieved. "Jim, this is serious. Please, don't take this lightly. My rectory phone rings all the time with questions I can't answer. I dread meeting parishioners because all they want to hear about is the weeping crucifix. Everyone knows it's been hanging there many years. If it was messed with, wouldn't that be obvious? Look, closely, Jim. You'll see the dust and cobwebs, too."

"May I ask you a very personal question, Father?"

"Go ahead."

"Why don't you believe?"

A strange silence followed as if Kerr had been thrown a left hook.

"Why? Why I just don't have the faith. There is a philosophical treatise that says a thing can only act according to its nature. Is it in the nature of plaster images to produce tears? Know what I mean? It's that simple."

"You mean you don't believe just yet?"

"I mean that I'm convinced that Saint Paul's is not a place for miracles to start happening. It's not Fatima or Lourdes. For some unexplainable reason, I'm suspicious that treachery is involved here—some clever, diabolical deceit."

"Wow," said Jim, "Yet, there isn't a shred of evidence to prove your suspicions. No evil is being done that I can see, except that your church must be getting rich by now with all the donations." *What if it is a supernatural occurrence?* he pondered. *Wouldn't that be something!*

"Well, will you help me check out the crucifix first? Troft

56

promised to bring some kind of sophisticated scanning device yesterday evening, but the man never showed."

"Maybe he just got busy and forgot."

"Troft? Never. That fellow does exactly what he says, especially if he's the center of attention. I'll have to give him a call."

"Good, because if anyone can help, he and his university colleagues can—ah-h provided there's a solution."

Kerr didn't know what to say. He looked over the top of his bifocals, "Bye, Jim."

September 18, 2002—Wednesday
7:00 P.M.

Jim and Chief Romeric met in the rectory around seven o'clock and proceeded to the church with Kerr. Romeric and Tim dragged up the same heavy ladder used by Troft.

Even though there were no scheduled ceremonies during weekday evenings, more and more people visited the old church. They sat or knelt in their pews: some meditating, some praying on rosary beads, some reading from a prayer book, many gawking about to see what was going on, many lighting vigil candles. Needless to say, the noise from the three-man ladder crew brought all eyes front and center.

Ed Bristol, who had been changing the additional vigil candles that had been added daily, was just as efficiently emptying the donation boxes into a metal box marked "Offerings." The box was bolted to a large wooden dolly. He hurried over to the group. "What's going on?" he asked.

"I've asked the police to examine the crucifix with me," answered Kerr.

"If you're planning on lifting it down, it looks mighty heavy.

Do you need my help?"

"Ed," replied Kerr, "For heaven's sake! You know we can't take it down."

"We're just dusting it for fingerprints, or gimmicks, or what not," replied Jim.

Ed Bristol said, "If you need my help, give a yell."

"Sure," said Romeric. With that, the chief climbed the eleven steps.

"How long did you say this thing's been up here?" he asked.

"As long as I can remember," said the custodian who started walking back towards his Offerings cart.

"That's true," Kerr cut in, "many years ago, I took it to Saint Vincent's Monastery. It had been hanging so long that the oak and the Christ figure were no longer attractive to look at. I wanted to get rid of it altogether until one of the monks over there repainted the Christ figure and re-stained the wood. The cross has been the focal point of this Gothic church since it was first built. Mmmm ... I'd say it hasn't been touched since that time unless it's been messed with, somehow."

"You know you've got a nice black spider living up here?" said Romeric.

"No, I didn't notice. Don't you wonder how it ever got up there?"

Jim added, "That damn thing must have come all the way down one of the cables."

"Amazing, how could a tiny spider have that much energy or web."

First the chief examined the wood with a magnifying glass without ever touching it. Then he looked at the dust-covered figure and the large metal hooks in each cross arm. Long, steel cables that anchored the cross to the arched Gothic ceiling were connected to the hooks. They, too, were covered with many years of dust. Cobwebs ran from the cables down to the wood of the cross and to various parts of the crucified corpus.

"Father," said Chief Romeric, "I'm sorry, but there are no areas that have been touched, at least not recently. The dust and cobwebs haven't been disturbed. We could brush off the dust and then check for prints, but—but doesn't that seem rather pointless?"

"Well then, just leave it be," muttered Kerr very disheartened. "So in your professional opinion, there are no clues of any kind to show it has been taken down or altered in any way?"

From atop the ladder, Romeric said, "In my opinion, it hasn't been touched for a long time—a very long time. What can I say?"

He checked the eyes last by holding his magnifying glass very close as if to peer into them. "The pupils alone are like glass disks about three-quarters of an inch in diameter. If the light hits them just right, it looks like I can see into them and they look hollow. The eyes seem larger than human eyes but so is the figure. These are about the size of ping pong balls. The only thing I see that's recent ... the only thing," said Romeric, "is residue from water that forms on or around the eyes. Other than that, I'd say this cross is clean."

"Oh! For heaven's sake! Let me take a look," said Kerr.

The chief scampered down and held the ladder while Kerr climbed up holding up his cassock with one hand and steadying himself with the other. Jim handed up the magnifying glass and Kerr took a long look.

"It's dusty all right. Looks just like it did when it was rehung, but many years dirtier. The eyes always did look hollow—haunting, actually. I remember staring at them when I brought the cross back from the monastery. Any suggestions?"

"I have an idea," said Romeric. "You know those X-ray devices that the airports use?"

"Yes."

"I think equipment like that is in order here. It could X-ray the crucifix without touching it yet it all seems pointless, doesn't it?"

"But how could something get in there," asked the custodian who overheard the remark from a side aisle.

"I haven't the faintest idea. I guess it doesn't make much sense, does it, Ed?"

"Not to me," Ed Bristol stated.

"Do you think you could locate a machine like that?" asked the priest.

"You're in luck, actually. I have one in the rear of my SUV. We use it to inspect suspicious packages for bombs. I'll go out and get it."

By now, word had somehow gotten out that the police were examining the holy cross. First a few curious worshippers gathered around the scanning group. Then it seemed that additional parishioners started to arrive. A media van once again parked along the yellow line up on the curb. Before they advanced even part-way up the aisle with their recording paraphernalia, Jim met them with his hands extended from his sides.

"I'm sorry, but Father Kerr and Bishop Mallory want no media coverage of the crucifix," he said sternly.

When Father Kerr came down the aisle waving his arms as if shooing them away, the media, who had inched closer and closer, retreated to the vestibule and then outside. Kerr's imposing figure stood alone in the center of the church's double doors as if daring them to pass his lowered but outstretched arms. Much to the media's delight, he explained what was going on and agreed to make a statement after the chief's examination. They should just wait in the church vestibule. This satisfied them.

9:00 P.M.

Romeric walked back in with his X-ray equipment; all eyes were upon him as he mounted the ladder. To worshippers watching from the pews, it appeared as if he was taking close up pictures of the wooden cross, the corpus of Christ, and particularly the Oculi.

To Father Kerr, he said, "This shouldn't take more than five or ten minutes." Romeric scanned the eyes many times without touching the crucifix or leave marks on it. "I must admit," he said, "this is the first time in my long police career that I've used this device in a church or to X-ray a crucifix." He worked saying very little.

When Romeric finished, he climbed down the ladder stood a minute and addressed the pastor. "Father Kerr, there is nothing in the wood or in the corpus that I can see that could cause tears—no tanks, no pipes, no batteries, no—nothing. There are bunches of wires that run up and down inside the body. They extend out into the legs and arms and head, but I'm sure they're for support because on a corpus this size, something would have to reinforce the heavy plaster. This is no small statue. Know what I mean?"

"I do," said Kerr. "Will you all come with me. I want to show you something. It'll take but a few minutes."

He led them to the rectory basement. In one of the large closets, there stood a five foot tall statue of the Virgin Mary. Her left arm had been cracked loose and separated a bit from her body but remained strongly attached. It was easy to see the wire mesh holding the statue together.

"Ah, now I see what you mean," said Jim.

"That's just what I thought they were," added Romeric. "You know there are powerful scanners that could give you a layer by layer look at your crucifix, but I doubt they'll find anything different than we just did. I'm thinking that the cross would have to be taken down to use those scanners."

"Well, that's out of the question," said Kerr. As all walked back to the church, Pastor Kerr had little to say other than to thank Romeric for his examination. Observers in the pews heard the chief's comments. They began to buzz among themselves. Kerr shook his head then walked back to talk with reporters in the vestibule. The custodian came over to help Jim carry the heavy ladder back to the sacristy stairway. Romeric walked out to his SUV and drove away.

"This is certainly an interesting turn of events," said Jim to the custodian.

"Wow, you're not kidding. You know that crucifix has brought a lot of needed money to our church. Since I'm the caretaker, that money can be put to good use. Our furnace needs replaced, and even though it isn't leaking, our roof needs some attention, not to mention our old school building and the convent where the two nuns live. You know Bishop Mallory was talking about closing this parish not long ago. Now, parents are clamoring to have the elementary school reopened."

"Is that right?" Jim asked.

Bristol replied, "I doubt that will happen before next September."

"Hmmm ... I didn't know. But I am curious, Ed, what do you make of all this? Is it real? Is it a miracle? Is it fakery of some kind?"

"Look, Jim, if it's fakery and I'm hoping it isn't, the perpetrator must be very clever. I know magicians can perform a lot of clever illusions on TV with special gimmickry, but these tears happen right here in front of us. No mirrors, no black boxes, no sleeves." he grinned.

"And no magician," added Jim.

They met Kerr in the sacristy.

"You know, earlier today I received a phone call from Rome. Imagine that ... from the Holy City? An *Advocatus Diaboli* ... a Father McCarthy, is coming to investigate this whole affair. Well, after the police chief's scans, at least I can explain to him what we've been doing. He can take over the investigation."

"Advocatus Diaboli?" asked Jim, looking at Kerr.

"Supporter of the Devil," explained the pastor. Rome gives that ignominious name to the person who attempts to disprove alleged supernatural incidents."

"By the way," said Jim, "Martie's interested in your after-school program. She'd really like to help out. She's great with kids."

"If she's that generous, Sisters Margaret and Lucy would love to have her. Each day around three-thirty they open two classrooms. They keep the kids busy until their parents pick them up around dinnertime. She could work with the older students who need help with homework. Any time she has would be appreciated. If she could stop by tomorrow, I'll have Margaret and Lucy talk with her."

Although one month had passed since the first tears appeared, attendance at the Sunday night Benediction service had increased so dramatically that there were no more seats available inside the Church in spite of Dr. Troft's attempts to prove that two human entities can occupy the very same pew space at the very same time. During the initial weeks, placing folding chairs in the side aisles against the church walls, provided extra seats. Now the overflowing crowd had no recourse. They were forced to stand in the vestibule and outside the building's main doors on the sidewalk and street.

08 An Advocate of the Devil

September 27, 2002—Friday
8:00 P.M.

Days and nights had become much cooler. Father Kerr was busy in the rectory jotting down notes for Sunday's sermon. There was a sharp rap on the door. He was quick to answer it. "Hello, come on in," he said in a cheerful voice. "How can I help you? Are you collecting?" It was then he noticed his visitor was wearing a collar. "Oh, sorry Reverend, I didn't see your collar at first. What can I do for you?"

"Well, now, Fawther—Fawther Paul Kerr is it not?" said the newcomer with a noticeable Irish brogue.

"Why yes, that's me. And you are?"

"Fawther McCarthy, all the way from Rome, I am. Now, the question is, how can I help you? Is it not?"

"Well, glory be! I was expecting someone with a pitchfork and horns, especially with the despicable title *Advocatus Diaboli*. You've caught me by surprise unless you have a devil's tail tucked in somewhere," laughed Kerr.

"No, 'tis not the devil himself, it 'tisn't, but I do have a wee bit o' the devil in me."

"Well, take off your jacket and make yourself at home because I'm glad you're here. We've been expecting you; your room is ready. Believe me, you are welcome. I've been under a lot of stress lately with this, this so-called miracle thing going on."

By this time, the housekeeper, Mrs. Pierce, had walked in and was about to take the Irish priest's jacket.

"Mrs. Pierce meet Father McCarthy. He's just arrived from Rome."

"Aw! Now, how do ye, me fair young lassie?" he inquired in his same pleasant, smooth brogue.

Mrs. Pierce answered with a genuine grin, "Oh, I'm doing just grand. Father Kerr treats me wonderfully, but it's him I'm worried about."

"And can I ask ye why my dear woman?"

"He doesn't believe. He's seen the tears, but he keeps telling his parishioners there is a logical explanation," teased Mrs. Pierce with a grin.

"Ah, for shame, Fawther. A doubtin' Thomas if ever there was," he teased. "Sounds a wee bit like you've already done me job, does it not?"

"Can I make you some dinner, Father? There are lots of goodies in the refrigerator," said Pierce.

"No Lassie, I had a most tasty dinner at McDonald's somewhere near Erwin. Sounds a bit like Erin, doesn't it now?" he said with an impish twinkle in his eye.

"But I wouldn't turn down a nip of the Devil's drink, now would I, just to warm meself a bit."

Mrs. Pierce replied, "Well, you and Father Kerr can do your nipping in the parlor. I'm sure he'll show you were it is. I'm just finishing up before going home. It was nice meeting you, Father." The housekeeper left the room and the two priests walked into the front parlor that Father Kerr used as his office.

"'Tis a fyne lassie ye have, Fawther Kerr, and I'll bet she's a bit of a good cook, too. Isn't that so?"

"She has been very helpful around here, Father. This has become an overwhelmingly busy place." Father Kerr handed McCarthy a hefty scotch.

"Well now, will ye tell me a wee bit about your miracle? Just a brief synopsis. I'm a wee bit tired, I am. I've been traveling most o' the day you know."

"What I'm about to tell you is a very brief synopsis. It's all the information I have. That's why I need help."

"Hm-m-m."

Kerr was very brief and to the point. He was finished within minutes.

"Well, for heavens sake, 'tis more than a wee bit of a puzzle, 'twould seem."

"Yes, and here is my problem. My gut instinct won't let me believe that divine intervention is taking place right here at my old church. I just can't believe it."

"Well, well, now, Fawther, ye seem to have a real problem. Do you not?"

"I do and it's serious!"

"Can ye show me the cross if you're not too tired?"

"Right now?"

"If ye don't mynd."

The two priests walked through the breezeway to the church, through the sacristy, across the front of the altar and down the center aisle about fifteen feet. McCarthy walked right under the crucifix without noticing it suspended above his head. People were milling about. Turning around and pointing upward, Kerr said, "Up there, Father, right up there is what's causing all this talk about the supernatural."

McCarthy took his time staring up at the cross. "H-m-m.

"Tis a sad corpus indeed. Does not look so old, Fawther."

"Oh, but it is. It's as old as this church building. That's what's so mysterious. Why would it suddenly become a miraculous cross?"

"Ah now, Fawther, 'tis my job it is to help dispel the mystery unless it is truly God's intervention. The Catholic church could stand a good miracle right now, I would think; wouldn't you, with all the scandals here in America tearing Catholicism apart, creating doubters by the thousands. 'Tis rather sad is it not?"

"That it is. Sometimes I feel that people see my collar and think I'm some kind of weirdo. Anyway, that's a whole other issue. You have a difficult job ahead of you. Something just bothers my conscience about the suddenness of this—this miracle."

"And now, what would that be, may I ask?"

"Why, it's the sheer quantity of money—tons of it—dumping into my church treasury."

"Mm," was McCarthy's only response!

The two priests walked back to the rectory. Mrs. Pierce had gone but was thoughtful enough to have turned down the bed covers in both priests' rooms and had left several chocolates beside the lamps on their nightstands.

"We'll talk more about this tomorrow," said Kerr while showing McCarthy to his room. "But I am glad you're here, and do make yourself at home. In that bottom dresser drawer, right over there, is a bit of the nip if you can't go to sleep."

"Well now, 'tis awfully nice of you, Fawther, but I think me travels have left me sleepy enough. See you in the mornin' now."

"Good night, and my the Lord be with you," said Kerr and he walked out of McCarthy's room and into his own. He picked up

68

a copy of *Tears of Deceit*, and sat down to read.

September 29, 2002—Sunday
5:30 P.M.

Saint Paul's was filling up with expectant churchgoers. Tears had fallen last week, but barely a drop or two. Some worshippers thought that maybe the tearing was coming to an end. For the first few Sundays, the drops appeared each week, but then they became more sporadic. A week, sometimes two or three weeks, might intervene before the next incident. It seemed Father Kerr was right. Since no one knew which Sunday would be "miraculous," pilgrims kept coming and coming—hoping. And the money kept flowing and flowing into collection baskets, offering boxes, special masses to be said, and general donations from those wealthy Latrobe-ites and others who were looking for a worthy, tax-deductible cause. Father Kerr predicted that even if the droplets stopped, pilgrims would keep coming to his church shrine just like they do at Lourdes and Fatima.

Kerr had argued with the bishop that the crucifix should be removed and scientifically examined. But Bishop Mallory had replied, *"Quod Deus vult,* Whatever God wishes, in my diocese, my son. And it will remain so. God knows what is going on here, so we need not concern ourselves with the obvious. So far, there are no signs that these events are anything but divine intervention, so I don't intend to fool with that holy cross."

8:00 P.M.

Jim had given Father Kerr two slides with which to collect a tear sample. Mrs. Reed again played various classical pieces from seven o'clock until the intonation of "Come, Holy Ghost" just as the ceremony commenced at eight. While the two priests stood in the sacristy watching the crowd gather, Dr. Troft walked in. He appeared particularly unnerved when Father Kerr introduced him to the papal delegate. Kerr was visibly annoyed at seeing him.

"Troft teaches at the University of Pittsburgh extension campus just outside Latrobe." Kerr glared at him, dismayed by the man's broken promise. "He had promised to bring some special scanning equipment the Monday before last." Kerr's frown deepened, "So what happened? Where were you, Professor, after your great promises to help?"

Troft was very embarrassed by Kerr's harangue and the fact that he omitted to address him as Dr. Troft. He shook Father McCarthy's hand, then replied, "I'm sorry, Father McCarthy, and Father Kerr, but the equipment I wanted to bring is in Pittsburgh at the main Oakland campus. I'm not sure when it will be available." Troft was remembering his night of terror when his car was set ablaze by The Voice, the inhuman sounding creature that warned him to stop interfering. His face paled noticeably.

Kerr chimed in, "Troft, we've already had the police scan it. But if you can bring something more powerful, bring it this week."

"But—but I'm not certain I can bring any scanners. Sorry to let you down." He prepared to exit the sacristy.

"Now, wait just a minute here," chided Kerr. "First you tell me one thing, and now you're telling me something different. Do you want to help or not?"

"No—I mean, I can't help." He turned and started for the exit.

"Stop, Professor. What's wrong? What happened? What on earth or in Hell is going on with you? You act like you've seen a ghost or the Devil, himself."

"The—the Devil—from Hell?" gasped Troft, his face aghast at the word "Devil."

Then McCarthy spoke out, trying to put him at ease. "So, ye' feel a wee bit troubled, Laddie?"

"I'm afraid I can't help—I, I think you'd better look elsewhere for assistance."

Kerr was dumbfounded at Troft's words.

"Why? Why are you so nervous? Are you ill? You didn't come to usher last week either."

"No, no, I didn't. I just didn't have the time."

"Ah-h, well," said McCarthy noting Troft's severe discomfort, "don't worry, all in good time, we'll find our answers, we will. But can ye answer another question for me?"

"No, I'm not so sure," hesitated Troft.

"Oh, for heaven's sake, Troft, he hasn't asked you yet."

McCarthy went on, "If perchance we can collect a tiny tear sample tonight, now do ye think your university could analyze it for us?"

"Oh, no, I'm afraid that wouldn't be possible. No! I don't know too, too many people in that, that department," he stammered, but fooled neither McCarthy nor Kerr.

"What are you talking about? You know everyone on campus. Tell me what happened. What's the matter with you?" Kerr knew the man was lying through his teeth. Now he looked sickly, petrified.

Troft nervously spouted, "I'm so sorry. I've got a busy schedule tomorrow. I'm heading home right now. I won't be here for the ceremony. Good night." He rushed out of the sacristy before either priest could question him further.

"Tis almost eight it is. I'd better get started, Fawther."

"Yes, it is. I can't promise you'll see anything tonight. We never know about the water drops."

Father McCarthy lined up to begin the Benediction ceremony. Tonight's procession from the sacristy to the altar was a bit different. Father McCarthy followed two adult acolytes in new choir robes led by the altar boy with the huge, blinking tennis shoes leading the way with a processional cross.

As the service began, Kerr walked to the rear of the church then proceeded up the narrow spiral staircase to the choir loft where Mrs. Reed played while the congregation sang. He rarely came up here, but he thought it would be an interesting perch from which to watch the ceremony tonight.

McCarthy wore the same white vestments Kerr had worn on so many previous Sunday evenings. The Papal Delegate placed the white, flat, sacred wafer inside the golden monstrance high atop the altar for adoration by the faithful then returned to his kneeling position at the bottom of the altar steps. While the faithful sang *"O Salutaris Hostia,* (O Saving Victim)," a few tiny drops began to form, until first one, and then another fell from the Oculi to the aisle floor.

"Oh my God, look!" cried one woman out loud pointing to the cross."

"It's happening," cried another! "Look, the Oculi are crying."

"Jesus, Mary and Joseph, I can't believe this," said another. The cries grew into loud talking as people craned their necks and bodies for a glimpse. The tiniest blot of water was collecting on the church floor. Seeing disorder breaking out, Father Kerr left the choir loft, hurried down the steps then started up the center aisle. Distracted Father McCarthy turned to see people pointing, staring, some leaving their pews. He stood up, left the altar steps, and hurried down toward the spot where people had gathered.

Without uttering a single word, Kerr waved curious onlookers back to their pews as he came up the aisle. People obeyed so that the two clerics met alone under the crucifix at the same moment. McCarthy wasted no time. From under his vestments, he pulled out the two slides given to him by Kerr in the sacristy. As he reached down to dip a slide into the tiny puddle on the floor, a drop splashed directly on his slide. The priest jerked his head upward and glanced at the crucifix. He set the other slide on top the first, trapping the drop between them. These he handed to Kerr along with some balled up plastic wrap.

The pastor wrapped the slides to keep the tear from evaporating. McCarthy looked upward. He gazed at the crucifix long enough to watch a tear form, held up his opened hands and arms as if to receive a supernatural gift, and stood entranced. Kerr walked back the way he had come. After several moments when he realized that all were staring, McCarthy regained his composure, put his hands together and started toward the sanctuary. By this time, all singing had stopped, but Mrs. Reed continued to play until Father McCarthy was in place. The ceremony proceeded as calmly as possible after an apparent episode of divine intervention. Father McCarthy, with his lilting Irish-tenor voice, joined with the congregation in singing the final hymn.

"I saw it with me own eyes, I did," said an awed McCarthy in the sacristy. "Never, never, never in my entire sixty-six years of existence have I seen the likes of it, now have I. What's to be said? It all seemed so real, did it not?"

"Now—NOW you have some idea why this parish is abuzz with two words: Oculi and miracle."

"Fawther, standing there under the Lord himself did truly seem miraculous, it did. But now I must keep me head about meself, mustn't I."

September 30, 2002—Monday
9:00 A.M.

Kerr phoned Jim explaining how Dr. Troft had done a complete about-face refusing to help him.

"You wouldn't believe it, Jim, It was as if he was another person. I know I lost my cool with him, but he deserved it."

"Oh?"

"First, he backed out of his promise to bring another scanner. Now, you know how much he likes doing anything that will make him the focus of attention."

"You're right about that."

"But now he literally ran out of the sacristy when I cornered him."

"Now here is a weird question. Do you suppose he's somehow mixed up in all this—whatever it is?"

"Jim, that man looked panicky; irrational might be a better word. His voice trembled while he talked. When McCarthy asked him to have a tear sample analyzed, he refused. Said he doesn't know the right people at the university. Now, that's pure bull crap. Troft makes his importance known to everyone."

"I'll call him. Meanwhile, I know a few folks at Carnegie Mellon. They'll probably jump at the chance to help if I explain the situation. We'll work around Troft until we find out why he changed his mind. I'll stop by for the tear sample and have it analyzed either in our police lab or over at the hospital. Just keep it covered so it can't evaporate."

"Thanks a lot, Jim."

10:00 A.M.

When Professor Troft answered the phone at his campus office, he sounded like he always did.

"Professor Troft here," he chirped.

"This is Jim Simmons. Beautiful day, isn't it?"

"It most certainly is. Good day for a nice hike in the woods."

"Sounds like you're in good spirits."

"I am. I love days like this. Reminds me of spring."

"Well, good. I just finished talking with Father Kerr who tells me that you've quit on him. Is that true?"

"Mm ... why ... yes, ah-h ... yes, that's very, very true," he stammered.

"He said you were stressed out and worried about something."

"He did?"

"Yes."

"Listen, Jim, my schedule is overloaded this semester. I've got a lot of things on my mind. That's all."

"Is that so?" Jim asked sarcastically.

Troft did not catch the mockery. "I am so busy here that I just don't have time to get involved with such trivial things."

Jim baited him. "No problem, Bob. Give me the name of one of your less important technical people. I'll call and use you as a reference—"

"Oh, good Lord! No!" Troft almost shouted. Then he quickly rephrased, "Um ... what I mean is no ... please ... Jim, don't do that. Everyone of us is busy here ... tied up with a lot of new grants, new research projects—"

"Cut the crap, Troft! Cut it! I know you're bull shittin' me," said Jim, "and you and I both know it. Now, tell me how are you involved in all this?"

"Involved? Me?"

"You heard me."

"I'm not involved. How dare you insin—"

"Listen here, I'm not insinuating anything, and don't you dare hang up on me or I'll be over there in twenty minutes and hunt your ass down."

"Hell, I'm not involved at all!" replied Troft, his voice beginning to break as it got louder. "I love that old church. That's why I help out there all the time. I wouldn't deliberately hurt Kerr or my friends over there. Good grief, Pastor Kerr is the nicest man I know." Troft sounded on the verge of tears.

"Well, you've cut that holy man to the heart. You've hurt him."

"Oh—geez, I'm really sorry! It wasn't some—"

"Sorry, nothing. I want you to talk to me."

"I can't talk. I'm sorry about Kerr. I gotta go."

"What do you mean you can't talk? You've got a tongue."

"I didn't want to hurt him, Jim. Tell him I didn't mean it," sobbed Troft. "But I must be getting back to work now, so—"

"Professor, now you listen to me," he interrupted, "You are my friend and I sense you need help. Tell me, are you afraid?" There was quite a pause on the line as if Troft was fighting his own thoughts. Jim could hear Troft sniffing and blowing his nose.

"Why yes, yes I am!" he blurted, "terrified actually—but I must be going—"

"Can't you tell me about it?"

"No—I—"

"What do you mean 'No?' No isn't an option here."

"Jim, I'm afraid it would find out. I'm going to hang up—"

76

"Don't you dare. What it? What it?" Then Jim warned a second time. "Troft, if you dare click off I'll—"

"Jim, listen to me, I don't want to die. Just leave me alone, please. Leave me be. Now, I've got to go."

"Look Troft, I might be one of the few people who can help you. Talk to me."

"I can't talk about—it. I'm scared shitless, Jim. Really scared. It was just awful—evil."

"Troft, I'm driving over there so we talk."

"NO, no, please don't come here," he cried.

"Look, I'm gonna help you!"

"You can't! No one can."

"Bob Troft, you have my word as a friend that what you say to me, I'll never repeat—never."

"I hear you, but—" the terrified man sniffled.

"Not to Kerr, not to Martie, not in a court of law without your permission. But please, please help me. Do you understand? I need your help."

There was a long hesitation. A distraught voice whispered, "Have you heard about my car?"

"No."

"It was set afire."

"What?"

"It was burned."

"Are you all right? Were you hurt?"

"Physically, I'm okay, but sometimes I feel like my nerves are breaking down."

"Were you in a wreck?"

"No."

"Then how did the fire start?"

"I can't talk about that," he choked up again, "because of,

because of, of The Voice."

"What voice?"

"It told me to get out."

"What?"

"The Voice made me get out and crawl up towards the monastery cemetery."

"When did all this happen?"

"On Sunday night, it was September 15. I'll never forget that date. The police were there."

"I didn't read that report. A fellow officer told me about a car fire, but I never dreamed it was yours."

Troft began to loosen up. "Jim, it was ungodly. It was a Hellish experience. Just awful—I don't want to die."

"What do you mean die? What on earth happened?"

"It was the hideous voice—The Voice in my backseat."

"Oh, come now!"

"No, it's the truth." Dr. Troft described the horror of September 15. His voice trembled as he talked faster and faster.

When he finished, Jim said, "That's incredible. No wonder you're afraid, but why? Did The Voice give you a reason?"

"Yes," Troft could hardly utter the words. His voice was a mere whimper. "It told me, 'What goes on at Saint Paul's is a battle between me and God!'"

"Holy shit!"

"It's all true, Jim; that's what it said to me."

"It?'"

"Jim, The Voice sounded inhuman, and whatever covered my mouth? Why, it was huge, and powerful. I couldn't breathe! I'm scared to go anywhere near that church or Kerr or that investigator from Rome. What am I to do, Jim?" cried Troft.

"I think you should stay clear of the matter after what you just said. Now listen, I give you my word I won't repeat anything you just told me to anyone, but I will try to solve this—this damnable puzzle."

"Okay," sniffed Troft, "but things are out of control."

"So, what did you report to the police?"

"That my dashboard started to smoke, so I pulled over and went for help at the monastery. When I looked back, my car was on fire."

"Now listen, Professor, McCarthy and Kerr still want the crucifix scanned more scientifically. I'll contact people not associated with Pitt for help. I'll make it clear that McCarthy and I are behind the scanning. You'll not be mentioned. We have a terrific secretary at the bureau that will know just the right people to call. That should keep you safe and out of the picture. No wonder you're terrified. Hang in there."

"You know, Jim, just talking about it has made me feel a lot better. But I'll keep taking my pills."

October 7, 2002—Monday
10:00 A.M

"Good morning, gentlemen. Come inside, have a seat and make yourselves comfortable," said the bishop. "I'll be with you in just a moment—Too much coffee already."

Bishop Mallory started down the hall to the restroom. His office was not lavishly decorated, but displayed those pictures and decrees on its walls that were important to the bishop and his status in the Roman Church. An oil painting depicting Christ rising from the sepulcher, hung just behind the bishop's desk. On another wall was a much larger framed photograph of Saint Paul's Church, and beside it, a huge photograph of the famous

Oculi Crucifix.

"Very interesting," remarked Kerr pointing to the two photos hanging side by side. "I'm sure I already know how Joseph Mallory feels about Saint Paul's."

"Indeed, indeed," winked McCarthy, "'tis so, my friend!"

When the bishop returned, he chose to sit in an easy chair rather than behind his huge oak desk. Kerr introduced Father McCarthy and then the three engaged in small talk for a few moments.

"Now for the business at hand," said Mallory.

"Your Excellency," said McCarthy, "Rome has sent me to help determine the authenticity of this mystery. But 'twould help me with my job, it would, if we could take down the crucifix and examine it at close range."

Bishop Joseph bristled at the remark. "If Romeric's scan gave no hint of deceit either in the cross or in the crucified figure, why scan it again?" Then he looked directly at Kerr and asked, "Did the X-rays from the police scan not penetrate all the way through?"

"Yes, they did," Kerr answered.

"And?"

Kerr could only be honest. "There was nothing very unusual."

McCarthy spoke up again, "But, Your Excellency, there are more powerful scanners—"

"So tell me, what do you need to see? Is it the molecules— the atoms, the electrons whirling in orbit? The equipment used by Chief Romeric is as accurate as that used in airports. Am I correct in that assumption?"

Kerr answered, "Yes, that you are."

"And do we not trust our lives to what those scanners show every time we board a plane?"

"Well, right you are about that," said McCarthy.

"What I don't understand is why scan the cross at all. These happenings, these mysterious incidences, must have a cause, but I think the cause is outside the crucifix. So why scan its insides when there isn't a single clue to suggest fraud. Nothing! No, I'm afraid I must insist that the cross remain where it is. I'm not one to question what the Lord has done."

Kerr asked, "If perchance fraud is eventually detected, would that not be embarrassing to this entire diocese?"

Mallory responded sternly, "As bishop, I'm not afraid, you see." His face slowly changed to a grin. "You may use whatever you wish, but I don't want the cross taken. Removing it for study would be a slap to God's face because there are no circumstances to warrant a more detailed analysis. I'm not worried about becoming America's joke as you put it. Your studies will eventually discover the correct answer. I already have it!"

October 7, 2002—Monday
1:00 A.M.

Father McCarthy could not fall asleep on this particular Monday night. He had been at Saint Paul's for ten days now and had nothing to report to Rome. *It was a mind-boggling experience I had, a'standin' there under that cross. It seemed so uplifting. But, come now, McCarthy you can't let your mind jump to untested conclusions regardless what your heart feels.* He paced his room attempting to dream up various gimmicks that could cause the tears. Even with his scientific background, he was stymied. He knew the church had needed funds just to remain open. Now, it was wealthy, and in all probability would become the richest parish in the Greensburg diocese as a result of the Oculi.

He considered the various people he had met since arriving at Saint Paul's that could be involved in some kind of duplicitous scheme, but there was no evidence of a scheme to begin with. His mind went around and around trying to find some thread, some trail, any fragmented clue he might investigate.

When I examined other miraculous claims, they always involved some type of cure for the human body, they did. Now in those cases, I had X-rays, medical records, doctors' and nurses' logs, hospital reports. Doctors and nurses helped me examine and compare them. But here in this old church, this is the first time in me life that I've tried to establish the validity of an ongoing, supernatural event and I am miffed, I truly am!

He dressed then crept downstairs where he removed the keys from the hook near the rectory side door and walked over into the church. The building was deserted. He sat in the middle aisle near the crucifix and stared at it. The quiet darkness of the church, lit by the flickering wicks of hundreds, many hundreds of vigil candles, was inspiring. For a long, long time he sat thinking, staring, thinking, staring at the candles, pondering. While meditating, or daydreaming, or a combination of both, he decided on a simple plan that might indicate whether anything or anyone passed through the church after it was locked each night.

11:30 A.M.

McCarthy drove into downtown Latrobe and purchased several spools of thin, black thread along with a package of thumbtacks. Near bedtime that evening, he approached the pastor.

"Would ye mind, now Fawther, if I lock up the church each

evenin' so I can sit and pray a wee bit when it's empty? Makes for much better sleep having the Lord on me mind the last thing each day, it does."

"No, I wouldn't mind at all. Maybe I can tuck in early some evenings."

"I know how you feel, I do; truly I do."

"I'm assuming you don't need company," said Kerr.

"A big boy I am, now Fawther—not afraid of the dark."

Kerr went upstairs. McCarthy took the keys and walked back into the church. He was alone. In the vestibule of the locked building, he knelt down by the door to the choir loft. He pushed thumbtacks into the wood on each side of the doorjamb about two inches from the floor. To these he tied a black thread from one tack to the other.

Methodically, he did the same to the door leading into the baptismal area on the opposite side of the building. Next, he closed the swinging vestibule doors, put tacks at their bottoms, and again threaded them. From there, he booby trapped both side exit doors, and the doors leading into the supply room on one side of the sanctuary and into the sacristy on the opposite side. Last of all, he tied a black thread across the steps leading from the sacristy to the church basement then walked back to the rectory and retired for the night. *Now, I'll know if something goes bumpin' about in the night.* He knew his detection method was primitive, but he had to start somewhere. Just before dozing off, he set his alarm for five-thirty.

October 8, 2002—Tuesday
5:45 A.M.

The Advocatus Diaboli reached over to his night stand to shut off his alarm, then climbed out of bed and dressed. Down the steps he hurried as softly as possible. He grabbed the keys and hurried over to the church to check his threads. Every single one was still in place. *Now if Satan himself entered this old church, then his spiritual substance would pass harmlessly right through the threads, wouldn't they. Only one time in me past have I been involved in a case where a demon possessed a little girl's human soul. But, I'm thinkin', maybe the cause of the tearing crucifix is the demonic possession of a material object. Now that would warrant the Rite of Exorcism. I will just have to wait to find out, I will.*

09 The University Scan

October 10, 2002—Thursday,
6:30 P.M.

After the building had been closed to worshippers at six o'clock, a van pulled up and parked outside the main entrance behind the cleaners' van. Kerr was already inside with McCarthy and Ed Bristol. Noticeably absent was Professor Troft. Two no-fooling-around scientists from the University of Pittsburgh carried in a device that looked much like a large video recorder. "Will that disturb the crucifix in any way?" asked Kerr.

"Not at all," said the woman from the University. We won't have to touch it."

"Good. That's what our bishop ordered."

Together the group walked up the center aisle stopping just under the cross. Handing their heavy scanner to Ed Bristol, the two scientists went back outside. The next sound was that of squeaky rolling wheels coming up the middle aisle. The woman researcher took the scanner and attached it to an arm on top of the rolling cart. The other researcher pushed a button on a handheld remote. Then the arm with a camera attached began to rise from the cart's center on an expanding accordion-like device.

"Well, I'll be damned. Would you look at that," said Ed.

"And look at this, Mr. Bristol said the young man, we can

see what is happening on this tiny remote down here."

The woman stopped the scanner directly in front of the cross. By adjusting several knobs, the image transmitted to the video screen became clear so that those standing in the aisle could view what the lens of the camera was seeing. The other examiner looked up at the cross and grinned. "So this is the famous crucifix we've all heard so much about?"

"It 'tis indeed," said McCarthy faking indignity. "You sound a bit disappointed, you do."

"I expected something different—more mysterious, I guess; something modern that could be manufactured and gimmicked."

"Nope," said Kerr. "This is it. You are looking at the one, the only, Oculi cross."

"And it cries?" grinned the woman poking fun at the absurd.

Kerr answered curtly, "Laugh if you like. Let's just say that something makes it appear to cry."

"Drops actually fall?"

Kerr again answered brusquely, "That's exactly what I'm telling you, young man, and that's exactly why you're here to find out exactly what's causing this bizarre phenomenon."

The male researcher commented, "You know, that's pretty hard to believe."

"Tell us about it," added Jim. The man looked at the serious faces of those around him.

"But none of you is joking, right?"

Kerr's glare burned into the researchers head. "We don't know where it comes from, sir. You are going to tell us."

McCarthy added, "The water seems to form around the bottom of the eyes and drops, it does. I caught some of it on me slide. Truly, I did now."

It appeared from the two embarrassed examiner's expressions that neither gave credence to the tear story. Nevertheless, they went about their business as scientific professionals. "Okay," joked one. "Let's find out what's inside JC to make him cry."

"What if they find nothing? Then will the bishop let us take down the cross?" asked Ed.

McCarthy answered, "I'm afraid this is it, I am."

"With the magnetic imaging camera, you can see various layers of the body and the crucifix," said Jim, "Is that right?"

"Yep," said one of the researchers who now appeared delighted to be scanning a "miracle" crucifix. "We'll find out what's going on."

For the better part of an hour, the twosome scanned the wood; they scanned the outstretched arms; they scanned the legs and the entire body top to bottom.

Meticulously, they scanned the eyes. "We can see residue under the eyes as if water had been dripping from there," said the woman. "But there is no water now, and for sure, there is no water inside."

All was recorded by the computer that sat beside a large monitor on the cart.

7:45 P.M.

When the examiners finished, they lowered their camera and removed it from the cart. Ed held it and commented, "Boy, I'll bet this cost a bundle."

"Well," said Father Kerr, "Nothing looked odd on this monitor."

"What can you two tell us?" asked McCarthy directing his question to the examiners.

Both began shaking their heads. They looked concerned, their faces puzzled. "Not a lot more than you already know. Your cross looks normal to us."

Ed Bristol helped the two scientists reload their truck. Then he locked the church doors and started his monotonous but lucrative routine of emptying donation boxes while Sisters Margaret and Lucy replenished the spent candles. Kerr and McCarthy helped with this chore chit-chatting about the scan they had witnessed.

When all were finished, Bristol locked the church for the night and walked back into the rectory with the two priests. Before leaving, he drank a can of beer while McCarthy and Kerr had their scotch. As soon as Ed left for the evening and Kerr had retired, McCarthy went through his secret, nightly routine setting his black thread booby traps. It did not take long because the thumbtacks remained in place. He merely had to retie his threads each evening that got snapped during the day.

October 11, 2002—Friday
5:45 A.M.

A sleepy McCarthy discovered that the threads tying both sets of vestibule doors had been broken, including one leading into the storage room to the right of the church sanctuary.

At breakfast, he asked who besides the custodian would have a key to the main doors of the church.

"Me," said Kerr, "mine is the one hanging on that ring next to the side door. It's the one you use when you lock up each night."

"Oh, so 'tis. I was wondering what all those other keys are for."

"Well, one of them opens the door to the baptismal font,

another opens both side doors, and that very old key opens the door to those infernal stairs leading to the choir loft. The smallest key, as you already know, opens the tabernacle on the main altar."

"Would you be willing to say who else has keys?"

"Mrs. Reed and I use the keys I just mentioned, but she may have others. Ed has keys and so does Sister Margaret. She has a set just like mine. Troft also has a key to all the doors," answered Kerr. "Why do you ask?"

"A curious Irishman, I am," answered McCarthy, "just part of me job, 'tis. Did you by any chance go back inside the church last evening, or maybe during the night?"

"Father, I did my meditating in bed. Why? Is there something wrong?"

"Curiosity, that's all or an over-active imagination; just checking things out."

I know something was in that church last night.

10 A Mental Connection

It was evening, and the two researchers from the Carnegie Mellon University who had done the recent scan were back in the rectory parlor. They had phoned Kerr asking him to set up a small meeting. He had invited Martie and Jim since both shared his skepticism.

Kerr introduced Martie to Father McCarthy who was his usual winsome self. "'Tis nice to meet the two of you, it 'tis. Fawther Kerr has told me about both of you, now. Let's see if I remember correctly. You're Martie Meyer, are you not? A wonderful teacher, I hear. At the middle school, am I right? Ah-h the patience of Job you must have to deal with so many energetic children each day." Then he extended his hand to Jim. "And you're the mighty officer that I've seen helping us handle the Sunday night crowds, now, am I right?"

"I don't know about wonderful, but I am the officer," smiled Jim.

McCarthy looked at Martie and Jim, "Well now, may the Lord bless ye both."

Realizing the woman researcher wanted to speak, all grew silent. "I phoned Pastor Kerr because we want to apologize for making fun of your cross and your beliefs last Thursday. We

91

must have seemed very rude. Obviously, this is important to you; and from what we've been hearing from the media, maybe to the entire world."

"Think nothing of it," said Kerr.

"When we re-examined the scans we took, we noticed some things that might be very interesting to all of you."

The young man extended a portable screen. "We've made slides to show you."

Martie and Jim both leaned forward so they could see the screen more easily. "From what your Pastor told me about the police scan, you already know those crisscross lines are for reinforcement. If you were wondering whether this Christ figure is the original, we definitely think it is. Under the new paint lays the old over the original sealed plaster. The figure is at least as old as your church."

"Hm," muttered the custodian.

"The hand nails are real. They go through the hands and into the wood. We did some other research to find that the usual way the corpus is mounted to the wood is with large bolts embedded in the plaster of the corpus' back. They are long enough to extend right on through the center beam of wood so that washers and bolts anchor the figure in place. On those crosses, the nails are mere plaster projections. Now your Oculi Christ figure is mounted with both back bolts and real hand nails. Yet the nails through the feet are fake. That is item one."

"Mm," said Kerr. "Anthony must have been very careful when he pried out those nails without marking or cracking the plaster."

Anthony—Anthony! Something distant—even slightly strange—clicked in Jim Simmons' mind when Kerr mentioned the name Anthony. He had been paying strict attention to the report until this point. Then his thoughts changed. *Why, I remember investigating the disappearance of my good friend, Brother Anthony.* He knew the brother was very talented, but did not know he had redone this cross. The others at the table noticed the startled look on Jim's face. *Anthony,* Jim thought, *Brother Anthony did this remarkable work at least seven years ago.*

The male researcher added, "Whoever repainted it—"

"Anthony, a Brother Anthony repainted it," inserted Kerr again. The scientist finished his sentence.

"—must have built a special jig, or used clamps to hold the body while working on it."

"Makes sense to me," said Martie.

Then the woman continued. "Now, about the eyes," she said. "The eyes are a bit unusual. They appear to be glass when you look at them with the naked eye. But on closer examination, we think they are hollow metal orbs attached to glass fronts. The cornea and pupil are glass."

"You know, I knew they were hollow when the cross was taken down," interrupted Kerr. "I swear it looked like I could see into them if the light was just right. I'll bet that the original artist deliberately made tiny eyeballs, covered them with ceramic glass then fired them in an oven."

"Sounds too complicated," said Martie, "for a plaster statue."

"I wouldn't be so sure, Martie. My own chalice was made using a similar process. The red enameled outside is bonded with the metal below it. It looks like glass."

Jim asked, "How large would those metal spheres be?"

The female researcher looked at the screen and pointed with her red laser. "Just a little more than one inch in diameter. As you can see, the orbs are larger than the glass corneas, much like human eyes." She clicked off her pointer. "Most statues I've ever seen have glass eyes embedded in the plaster and that's it. These are more like the eyes on a good China baby doll."

Jim, who had been thinking of his old friend Anthony who disappeared seven years prior, quipped, "So we have nothing conclusive here, just the fact that the eyes are rounded metal balls with glass fronts."

"Sorry, but that's about it," said the woman.

"Do either of you have any conceivable theory," asked Martie, "as to the source of the water because I've seen it happen. There must be someth—"

"We had our camera one inch in front of each eye while we did the scanning. The eyes appear to be much more oval in shape than spheroid, maybe more egg shaped. As the camera layered through the eye, it first picked up the glass and the metal then it showed the sphere was hollow."

"Now, tell us this would ye, lassie," asked McCarthy, "in your professional judgment, did you discover anything—anything at all that ye think could cause the water to form inside those eyes?"

Both researchers shook their heads, and almost as one voice replied, "No, Father, I'm sorry. We didn't. Nothing that we saw in our scans could produce water—nothing that we know of!"

Then the woman added, "In fact, if water formed inside the spheres, there would be no way for it to get out."

The room fell silent. All sat stunned. Each person looked around at the expressions on the faces of everyone else. Martie had convinced herself that *there was some tricky reservoir inside the wood of the cross that the police scanner had missed.* In his own mind, Jim thought *the water might be running down through the suspension cables. But if that were so how did it get to the eyes when there was not a hint of hidden plumbing?* Kerr was now mystified. His chair remained tipped back on two legs; he frowned deeply turning his head from side to side. Sitting beside him, Ed Bristol beamed, thrilled to death with the report because he handled the church's treasury. McCarthy maintained his red-faced, Irish smile thinking *a hefty nip of scotch, maybe two, might be in order before he flew to Rome the next day to file his initial report.*

When the others had left, Father McCarthy took Mr. Ed Bristol aside and asked, "I was wondering if ye would answer a question for me?"

"Sure, Father. I'll try. Ask away."

"Would you by any chance have gone back into the church after we locked it last Thursday?"

Ed Bristol looked a bit perplexed, "Don't know that I did, but let me think a minute." He stood quietly. "No, as I recall, after the cleaning crew was finished, I'm certain I locked up and went home. In fact, we all left together. I had a beer in the rectory with you and Paul."

"Oh, 'tis right you are. But have ye ever been suspicious that someone or something has been inside your church during the night?"

"No."

"And would you know if Dr. Troft still has keys to the church?" McCarthy asked.

"I don't know. Why all the questions?"

"Just a bit curious, I am. It's me nature."

"So you still don't believe in the 'miracle?'" asked Bristol.

"'Tis not a matter of belief, laddie," smiled McCarthy. "'Tis me job to find proof one-way or the other. But the report was rather convincing, was it not?"

"Sold me," said Ed Bristol.

9:30 P.M.

On their walk home, Jim mentioned Father Kerr's comment about Anthony refinishing the crucifix. "I wonder what date that was?" Jim asked, somewhat to himself and somewhat to Martie, thinking, *It had to have been around August 21, because if I remember correctly, that's the date when Romeric sent me over there to investigate.*

"Let's call Kerr and ask him if he remembers."

"Know what?"

"No, but you're going to tell me anyway."

"Let's just walk back to the rectory and talk to him. It's just a short distance from here."

Ed Bristol answered the rectory door since Mrs. Pierce had gone home. "Can I help you with something?" he asked.

"Maybe both of you can."

"Step inside. Paul's still chatting. I'll get him for you." Within a few moments, Ed Bristol brought the priest to the front door.

"We'd like to ask you a question that bugged us on our walk home," said Jim.

"Come right on in. Let's sit in the front room."

"Oh, we can't stay; just one quick question."

"That's what Ed said; so, out with it."

"Well you mentioned Brother Anthony a bit earlier. Was this the same brother who disappeared from Saint Vincent Monastery?" asked Jim.

"Yes, it was," said Kerr bluntly.

"You know, that monk and I were good friends."

"Wow, I'm sorry. He did marvelous work. I was shocked when I heard he'd left. He and I had talked several times. He'd give me a progress report. Once, he invited me to drive over to see how I liked his work. Believe me, when I took the crucifix to him, it had no real beauty to it. But when I saw the semi-finished Christ figure, it was lifelike ... I mean, haunting. I had no idea the brother was even thinking of leaving."

Martie commented, "Anthony left, or disappeared, on the night of August 20th. Do I have that right Tim?"

"Exactly."

"Did you pick up the finished cross and bring it here, Father?"

"Yes."

"Do you by any remote chance recall what day that was?"

"No. But I do remember being in a rush; didn't talk to many people. When there were no lights in Anthony's work area, I walked upstairs through the monks' recreation room and over to the main office. A Brother Charles said Anthony was not available at the moment, but that he could help me get the cross. I drove around to Anthony's work area, then he and I and two younger monks carried it to my van and I drove back here. That cross is very heavy."

Kerr turned to Ed Bristol. "Ed, do you recall the date I picked up the cross?"

He thought for a minute then replied, "No, but I remember that was the day I took your car in for inspection."

"That's right."

Ed stood statue still and shook his head. "Can't remember back that far, but I know it was a hot August day."

"Wait just a minute, I'll be right back." Kerr excused himself. Within a few minutes, he walked back into the room with a folded pink sheet.

"August 21. That's the day," remarked Kerr. "Monday,

August 21, 1995. Here is the receipt for my car inspection. Cost me four new ti—" Kerr stopped without finishing his sentence. A look of utter shock came over his face as it dawned on him what had happened. "I picked up that crucifix the day after Anthony left Saint Vincent's. Right?"

"Yes!"

Jim added, "I was there most of that afternoon interviewing the monks. What time did you get there?"

"Around noon. The place was very quiet, and I was in such a hurry that the only persons I talked to were Brother Charles and two younger monks."

"Incredible," said Jim, "you were leaving and I was just arriving."

Astonished, Kerr said, "You know, the place did seem a bit odd now that I think back."

"How so?"

"Well normally, some of the brothers or priests come over to talk with me, but no one did."

"Hunh," muttered Martie.

Ed Bristol said, "According to the newspapers, no one knows what happened to him."

"Jim added, "His family has never heard from him—no message, no letter, no note, no phone call."

"Good grief," was all Kerr could say, but his face had a haunted look about it.

11 A Nasty Wound

October 17, 2002—Thursday
9:00 P.M.

The cleaners had finished, a multitude of burnt candles had been replaced, and Mrs. Reed was done practicing new organ pieces. Kerr and McCarthy left with Ed who locked up the building for the night.

"Sleep well, Fathers," said Ed as he walked to his truck. "See you tomorrow."

"Sure thing," said Kerr.

The two priests entered the rectory where Mrs. Pierce had left freshly baked cookies on the kitchen table. Father McCarthy stuck one large sugar cookie in his mouth stretching his jowls sideways until he bit the cookie in half. He carried the entire dish into the front room while Kerr poured their nightly devil's drink then they sat and chatted.

Finally, Kerr yawned, "Well, I'm going to turn in. See you in the morning."

"And a good night to you, Fawther," replied McCarthy, his mouth filled with cookie. "These are delicious—Truly tasty!"

During the next half-hour, he ate several more before leaving for the church hoping that what broke his threads last Thursday might do so again. But tonight he would lie in wait and not tie his threads. In the very last pew where he could rest his head back against the vestibule wall, he sat, staring at the Oculi crucifix attempting to meditate. McCarthy wanted to believe, but would not allow it. He closed his eyes and prayed for guidance for himself and for those around him knowing that his report to Rome could have resounding effects on Christendom. Then he swiftly dropped off to sleep.

He wasn't sure how much time had passed, but he awoke to a soft squeaking sound. *Maybe I imagined it*, he thought, but as he became wide awake it was obvious that *someone or something was behind him in the vestibule. Should I call out?* Instead, he slid down on his side in the pew, hoping he could see without being seen.

A shadowy darkness pushed open the vestibule doors and started up the right side aisle. He watched the dark moving silhouette against the backdrop of glowing candle wicks. Although the shadow appeared man-like as it entered the storage area across the sanctuary from the sacristy, still he wasn't sure.

With his curiosity aroused, after hearing strange unrecognizable sounds, he left his pew, stooped very low, and started toward the front by sneaking up the center aisle. *I've got to get meself a bit closer.* His black cassock helped hide him in the shadows. It never passed through the priest's mind that an intruder might be armed; instead, he thought, *I want to see whatever it is with me own eyes.* Every ten feet, the papal delegate scooted into a pew and listened, ready to duck low. Still he heard the strange sounds from the storage room.

He got down on his hands and knees and crawled closer, ever closer. When he was fifteen pews from the front, he moved part way into a pew and lifted his head. *I only see a shadowy outline on the open storeroom door. Who or whatever is in there must have a powerful light. I'll just have to get closer.*

When he stooped to back out of the pew, he placed his hand on a kneeler and accidentally knocked it down. With a loud—*thump*—it hit the floor. The sounds in the storage room stopped. Several moments of silence passed. Then from the storage room doorway, a blinding light began to scan the entire body of the church. It missed McCarthy's head ducked below the end of a pew.

A high-pitched, unnatural voice shrieked, "Who's there?" McCarthy did not just feel, but he heard his heart thumping. "I know someone's out there, I heard you, so show yourself, NOW," shouted the irate voice.

Silence—silence.

The priest stayed low and waited. "All right, then I'll hunt you down. Don't even think I won't," laughed the voice hideously. The dark figure left the storage area and started down the right side aisle shining the beam through and then under each pew. McCarthy remained hidden in the center aisle behind a pew end.

This downed kneeler will be a sure giveaway to me hiding place. He watched the light beam as it came closer—still closer. It would soon light up the downed kneeler. McCarthy reached into his pocket, pulled out a quarter, and as hard as he could, he pitched it toward the storage room door. The coin hit the door then ricocheted off several objects inside before landing on the floor spinning like a top.

"A luck-o-the-Irish pitch if 'er there was," he whispered to himself.

The light beam turned as the dark figure hastened back toward the storage room. McCarthy reached around the pew end and ever so gently lifted the kneeler to its upright position. The spinning coin clinked against some object, fell on its side, rotated around and around on its edge and then came to a rest.

"You can't fool me," called The Voice again. It sounded wrathful—fiendish! "I know you're still in here—Devil's Quarry!" it laughed, "that's what you are, as good as dead."

The figure started down the side aisle a second time, once again peering above and under each pew.

"I'll put you in Hell tonight with the rest of my demons."

But McCarthy crawled up toward the sanctuary from one pew end to the next every time his position was in shadow. When he reached the first pew, he crossed the center aisle, then crawled along the front left pew. *Just maybe I can sneak across the side aisle and escape through the sacristy exit door.*

But The Voice was too clever; it crossed just as swiftly through the very pew where McCarthy had been sleeping and started coming up the left side aisle where it would intersect the crawling priest.

"I'm still coming. The hunt's almost over and I know right where you are," screamed the vicious voice.

I can't make it to the sacristy unseen. I've been cut off, I have. If I'm to take a chance, it must be now, while that ugly Voice is still near the rear. Any kind of distraction might keep me alive if the intruder is armed. From his kneeling position, the brave priest turned his head toward the opposite side of the church, cupped his hands to his mouth like a megaphone, and while turning his head he shouted, "Patrick be with me." The sound echoed around the inside of the church while the light beam traveled in all directions. *Here goes nothing.* McCarthy stood and dashed for the sacristy.

But he was not quick enough. The light beamed in his direction along with a—*thupp.* A shell slammed into the muscle of his left thigh searing him with pain. *I can't go down now. Surely I'll be a dead man.* He spun into and through the sacristy. Pain ripped through his entire leg. He could hear The Voice running up the aisle. *It's coming fast, Saint Patrick help me.* Still, he hopped toward the exit door, but as he passed the open breaker panel box on the wall, he flipped on the church's interior light switches with both hands.

Crashing through the door, he staggered across the breezeway leading to the rectory holding his bleeding leg with both hands, fully expecting a hail of bullets to drill into his back.

Meekly he said aloud, "Into Thy hands I commend me spirit, Lord, truly I do."

The bullets never came. Forcibly slamming and locking the rectory door behind him, McCarthy peered through a side window. Nothing followed. The lights in the church switched off one by one. It was only then that he looked down at his blood-soaked trouser leg. His strength sapped, trembling, the papal delegate slid down the wall to the floor.

"McCarthy? McCarthy? Is that you down there?" called Kerr from the top of the stairs after hearing the door slamming shut. The pastor didn't wait for an answer. He bounded down the steps calling, "McCarthy, is that—"

A very weak voice answered from its sitting position in the kitchen, "Yes, yes 'tis. And I do need your help, Fawther, I surely do."

12 Ancient Father Martin

October 18, 2002—Friday
3:00 P.M.

Martie phoned the papal delegate for the results of the analysis of the tear sample collected at last Sunday's Benediction. McCarthy asked her to come to the rectory. She knew nothing about the shooting on Thursday night, although Jim had read the police report when he reached the Borough Building that morning and had tried to phone her at school. Since she had already gone up to her classroom, he left his message with the school secretary. The hassled woman had scribbled Jim's message on a piece of notepaper and placed it in Martie's mailbox. Thus, she missed Jim's message as she hurried out of the school.

The two priests were sitting in the right front parlor when she arrived. At once Martie noticed the crutches sitting by McCarthy's chair. "What on earth happened to you?" Martie exclaimed.

"Nothing so serious, lassie, but first, does me pipe smoke bother you?" When she answered yes, McCarthy set down his meerschaum pipe and all three walked across the front hall and into the left parlor.

"I hate to be fussy," said Martie. "But I try to stay away from cigarette and pipe smoke or anything like it because I tend to get bronchitis. Thanks for your consideration."

"Ah-h, don't mention it, me dear. 'Tis another nasty habit of mine."

"Now," said Martie, "why on earth are you using crutches?"

"'Tis not serious, Lassie. 'Tis truly me leg, it 'tis. Would you believe I was shot in the church last night?"

"WHAT!" Martie's eyes turned to saucers. Her jaw dropped. She shook her head in disbelief. "NO!"

"It's true," said Kerr. Then he glanced at McCarthy. "But maybe you should tell your story."

Martie received an abbreviated version of what had occurred. McCarthy omitted any mention of booby traps or his falling asleep in the rear of the church. The entire time the priest spoke, Martie held her hand to her mouth. "I can't believe this!" Martie gasped. "Satan is loose here. Are you okay? Have you been to the hospital?"

"Father Kerr assures me I'm not dead and gone yet!" he joked.

"This is incredible."

"What saved Father's life was this; he turned on the church lights as he came crashing through the sacristy. When the police got here, the church was dim and empty."

"Are you in pain?"

"T'would take a hail of bullets to kill this Irishman, mind you. I'm a wee bit sore, I am." Martie just sat there, her eyes still saucer-like. "Went in about here," he touched the general area, "and was taken out the same way, I guess."

"Father has been going over there late at night to sit and meditate a bit, but he uses the side door. What makes this interesting is that after the shooting, all the church doors were locked when the police got here," said Kerr. "It's as if this prowler appeared inside the building out of nowhere."

"You are one lucky Irishman. Seems violence is everywhere." She thought for a moment. "But wait, if the church was locked, then how did this thing, this intruder get in?"

"Maybe he followed me in or was hiding in there when we locked up earlier."

"Well jeez, if the Oculi is not a miracle, the fact that you're still alive is!"

Changing the subject away from himself, McCarthy inquired, "I understand you called about the water sample I took, am I right?"

"Yes, I did," replied Martie.

"I have here the report Latrobe Hospital sent from its lab that analyzed the tear sample," said Father McCarthy.

"Anything?"

"Just this, my young lass; the water had no sodium at all, not a trace. Tears contain some salt, now don't they. Just like human sweat contains salt. This water was more like distilled water, it was."

Kerr interjected, "Now, when the press and tabloids get hold of that, I can just see the headlines, 'Miracle Tears Not Human.' Then the next edition's headline will be, 'OCULI Tears, Divine!' Then they'll explain how this makes sense because one wouldn't expect Christ to have normal human tears."

"Oh? And why not, Fawther?" kidded McCarthy. "Christ was both human and divine—a Hypostatic Union, I dare say. So I'd think his tears could be just like everyone else's. Don't you agree?"

"I agree," said Martie, "Even though hypostatic means nothing to me."

Kerr hesitated for a moment then nodded agreement with

the other two.

Martie asked, "I just don't understand why Bishop Mallory is so opposed to examining the crucifix in a laboratory. Why is he being so difficult?"

"Ah, my dear lassie, believers seem to feel that non-believers should just, how do you say it? 'Bug off?' Did I get that right? Kerr. And Mallory seems to agree with them, now doesn't he?"

"Martie," interjected Kerr, "A bishop has the power to enforce his judgment in his diocese unless Rome directs otherwise. He has been to Saint Paul's several times since all of this started. In his heart of hearts he believes the tears are real. That's all there is too it. He doesn't want to go on record as a doubting Thomas."

"In due time, my child," grinned McCarthy, "In due time. But you know, the biggest issue for me right now is, without evidence to the contrary, Joseph Mallory might be right."

October 19, 2002—Saturday
10:15 A.M.

The couple was finishing a relaxed breakfast after discussing the wounding of McCarthy.

"Wow, the man's lucky," added Martie. "Can you imagine the headlines, 'POPE'S DELEGATE MURDERED INVESTIGATING OCULI MIRACLE!'"

Jim shook his head and sighed about the outrageousness of it all. Since the mention of Brother Anthony's name by Father Kerr still upset him, he drove over to Saint Vincent's Monastery hoping to ask a few questions about the long-absent monk. There were concerns Jim had about his missing friend that continued to haunt him. Brother Mark was the first person Jim met as he walked across the "Bermuda" quadrangle around one-thirty.

"Hello there, Brother Mark."

"Hi, Mr. Simmons."

"Jim—Call me Jim."

"Okay, thinking of joining the order are you?" teased Mark.

"No, just wandering around enjoying the fall weather," said Jim.

"Same here. Come on, we'll walk just a bit; I need the exercise." Jim joined him in his fast-paced walk around the huge square. "Mind if I ask you a question or two?"

"Not at all. Anything serious?"

"Not sure. I was never satisfied with the explanation that Brother Anthony just got up and left this place. Were you?" asked Jim.

"Never, he was not that kind of man."

"He and I used to chat when my psyche was in turmoil. And do you know I always came away from here feeling better. He had a special empathy for other people and their problems."

"That was Anthony all right. He was a terrific person who loved his card games."

"The evening he disappeared, is there anything, even the slightest thing you can remember that was different about him, or the monastery, or any of the other monks?"

"Honestly? Nothing. Nothing I can remember. But I do recall the night was rather stormy. The thunder and lightning were fierce."

"How about the next morning? Was anything amiss or out of place?" There was a long, thoughtful pause.

"Nope, nothing that I recall. Gee, it seems so long ago, Jim, but I don't remember anything weird except that the man was gone. We stood around like idiots not knowing what to do. Every one of us was shocked. For days, we talked about him, expecting him to reappear in his basilica stall; well, you know the rest."

"See any suspicious strangers?"

"Jeez, I wish I could help by saying yes, but I can't. I feel bad, but I just can't remember anything odd." By this time they had gone around the quadrangle twice.

"Is old Father Martin still around?"

"Sure. He's a bit hard of hearing, but he's still alive and doing well. Wish I could say the same for Anthony," commented Mark. "Anyway, Martin doesn't work much even though he still tries. Probably find him in the basilica."

"Thanks, Mark, see you around." Jim veered off to the basilica and slowed his pace. When he walked inside, old Father Martin was sitting in his stall. Jim walked into the stall next to his and sat down, but the old priest was slumped forward a bit, snoring softly. "Father Martin, Father Martin," whispered Jim. The aged priest continued to snore, but stirred a bit. Jim held his very thin arm and shook it. "Father Martin, Father Martin, it's m—"

"*ET CUM SPIRITU TUO*," sang the old priest out loud, frantically opening his prayer book thinking he had missed a response. Then he noticed Jim sitting beside him.

"Sorry to wake you, Father," apologized Jim.

"Wake me! Wake me? You think I was sleeping? Not me, pal. I don't sleep during prayer time. I may meditate deeply, but I don't sleep. Besides, it's the middle of the day—isn't it?"

"Yes, it is."

"Where is everyone?"

"I think they're out doing chores."

"Geez, they all left without me."

"Do you think you could answer a few questions for me?"

"Will it take long? I should be out working with the rest of them geezers."

"It'll only take a few minutes."

"About what? My memory's not what it used to be, Mr. Simmons."

"Jim, call me Jim."

"Okay, Mr. Simmons, whatever you say, pal."

"Do you remember the day when Anthony left?"

"Anthony?" He thought a moment. "Anthony? He was my best friend. I miss him a lot. By god, don't tell me he's returned to earth?"

"No, but I'd like to ask you a few questions about the day he left?"

"My memory is not as good as it used to be, Mr. Simmons."

"You can call me Jim, Father Martin."

"Okay, Mr. Simmons." Jim was beginning to wonder if Father Martin remembered Anthony or just pretended to.

"The night Anthony disappeared, do you remember anything strange, different, kind of unusual about the monastery, or any of the other monks?"

"There are a lot of strange people around here," answered Father Martin.

"How about the day Anthony disappeared?"

"Some were strange then, too."

"What did you notice that was unusual or different?"

"Talk about strange, I'm the strangest bird of all. Look how old I am and I'm still above ground." Now Jim wondered if he was truly wasting his time.

"What about the next day. Was anything different?"

"Yes."

"What was it?"

"I told you. Anthony was missing."

"Did you help search for him?" asked Jim.

"Sure, but we couldn't find him; we looked everywhere. I even looked under his cot. Nope, no Anthony. He was such a good man. I miss him—I miss him a whole lot. I think he just assumed himself into Heaven, you know, without dying. He walked out and z-z-z-z-zip," the monk made an upward motion with his hand smacking Jim's chin. "Oops, sorry, Mr. Simmons, didn't mean to get fresh."

"Jim, Father Martin, call me Jim."

"Okay, Mr. Simmons, I'll call you Jim."

"Well, you've been a big help, Father," said Jim as he prepared to leave.

"But I couldn't do my laundry that day." said Father Martin.

"You couldn't do your laundry?" asked Jim,

"You know you sound a bit like a parrot."

"What do you mean?"

"Well, you repeat yourself," said the priest.

"I repeat myself?"

"There, you just did it again."

"Oh, sorry."

"Nope, Anthony and I used to go over every Monday morning to do our laundry together. He used the first machine, I used the second."

"You used the second machine, but why couldn't you do your laundry?" aked Jim.

"Because my dryer was broken, and I didn't have the heart to use Anthony's since he wasn't there. It just didn't seem right."

Jim really wanted to leave, but to appear interested in what the old priest was saying he asked, "So your dryer was broken?"

"You seem to repeat things a lot, Mr. Simmons. Parrots do that," said old Father Martin.

"Sorry. What was wrong with your dryer?"

"Didn't you just ask me that?"

"Oops."

"Don't know except that the tub you put your clothes in was sitting on top of the dryer along with an 'Out Of Order' sign. I couldn't open the door, either. It was jammed, so I left. I thought I'd wait for Anthony to come back.

"How long did you wait, Father," continued Jim.

"My memory is not as good as it used to be Mr. Simmons, but, let's see, I did my washing that same day."

"So, the broken machine, as you called it, your broken dryer had been repaired?"

"Did you repeat yourself again?" asked Martin. "Maybe you should see a ventriloquist."

"Sorry." Jim was sure he meant psychiatrist.

"No, there was a new dryer where the old one used to sit. The broken one had been hauled away. The tub was gone, too."

"That's interesting," said Jim.

"It's dull, if you ask me. I'd better get back to my prayers, if you don't mind, Mr. Simmons," said Father Martin. "I need to get the hell out of here and go to work. What will the abbot think?"

"Thanks again, Father," said Jim.

"Kneel down," said Martin. "You need my blessing. Maybe it'll keep you from repeating yourself."

Jim got down on one knee. Father Martin placed his prayer book aside, then placed both feeble hands on Jim's bowed head, *"Benedicat te, omnipotens Deus, Pater, et Filius, et"* (May Almighty God bless you, Father, Son and)—ah—wait a minute,

I know there's someone else, I'm missing someone here, um, well, whoever it is, bless you. Amen."

After that blessing, Jim stood, and started to walk out of the stall area when old Father Martin called, "See you, Jim, pal!"

13 Phillip Versus Walsh

November 2, 2002—Saturday
10:00 A.M.

Father McCarthy continued to lock the church each night after meditating for a short time under the Oculi crucifix. The police and Jim Simmons reasoned that on the night Father McCarthy had been wounded no valuable items had been stolen because the thief had become involved with hunting down McCarthy, and had fled to hide his identity. The golden vessels used in church services remained safely hidden in the sacristy along with vestments, incense, and other ministerial paraphernalia. The thief had hunted in the wrong room.

But McCarthy knew that whoever shot him was most probably that same person who tripped his booby traps the week prior to the shooting. *What's strange is nothing was stolen. And why on earth would any thief waste time hunting through the same storage room he had already searched. Whatever he's looking for is still hidden, that must be it.*

He had arranged to fly back to Rome to discuss his experience and the entire Oculi miracle with fellow investigators. Delegates who had worked with paranormal or supernatural occurrences might help him work out some plan of action before returning to Saint Paul's Church. His flight out of Pittsburgh Airport was departing at three-thirty this afternoon. Since he'd be expected to give a report on arrival in Rome, he and Bishop Mallory, along with Father Kerr and Jim Simmons, were sitting in the front office of Saint Paul's discussing what the Advocatus Diaboli would report.

"Well, Fawther Kerr, we never did get our trip into Pittsburgh, now did we? Well, well, we'll just have to make a day of it when I return. Can I count on that, now?"

"If he doesn't find the time, then I'll go with you," said the bishop.

"You're twisting my arm," teased Kerr.

"So, Father McCarthy," said Kerr a bit exasperated, "what will you put in your report?"

"Well, Fawther, I've puzzled over that question for several days now, I have. But I think I should be as honest as possible, so I will. Now is that not the best thing to do? My report will say that at this point in time after examining the evidence we have, there is no little reason to suspect that the mysterious tearing is not some form of divine intervention."

"Interesting comment," said the bishop. "Seems like you can interpret that statement two ways."

"So it does, doesn't it," said McCarthy with a twinkle in his eye.

"Clever," said Kerr. "Double negatives always confuse people."

Later that afternoon, the Advocatus Diaboli flew back to Rome unsettled with what he had seen, but for now satisfied with his report; Bishop Joseph Mallory continued to rely on his faith; Father Kerr's convictions remained skeptical. Like Jim, Martie did not know what to believe.

November 8, 2002—Friday
11:30 A.M.

Much to Father Kerr's surprise, the bishop assigned two younger priests to assist him with the ministry of Saint Paul's Church because of the hordes of people visiting the place. Kerr had been hoping for assistance, but never expected two curates. Now he would have more time to spend among his parishioners. Father Walsh arrived on Friday; Father Phillip the next day.

Father Walsh was a rotund young man of thirty, who had wished to enter the priesthood since childhood. He was born and raised in Pittsburgh's Lawrenceville neighborhood and had attended Catholic grade school. More often than not, he arrived for physical education classes at Central Catholic High School bearing a note from his mother excusing him from participating in gym class.

Not an athlete, he was an excellent cook whose physique suggested a little too much tasting during food preparation and too much consumption during mealtime. He tended to be a talkative priest who could spend an entire afternoon engaged in endless chitchat. But a bore, he was not. He possessed a small collection of operatic CDs, which he'd play in his room when not otherwise occupied. He preferred to listen to music or read rather than walk outside or indulge in any kind of strenuous exercise.

Father Kerr instantly liked the priest and so did his housekeeper. She and Walsh often chatted over their favorite recipes. He loved to help in the kitchen wearing a huge white apron that barely tied when draped around his girth. He claimed Mrs. Pierce showed him how to cook yet she claimed the very opposite. Father Walsh was intrigued by the ongoing Oculi incidents and could often be seen sitting in the church near the suspended cross meditating. He knew of Father Kerr's mental reservations, but he had none. He had seen the drops and he believed.

November 9, 2002—Saturday
7:40 P.M.

Father Phillip presented himself to Saint Paul's the very next evening. He was short, noticeably muscular and physically fit. He was twenty-six, his face somewhat boyish-looking but handsome. He could be considered the antonym for Father Walsh. He began each day with a three mile run regardless of weather conditions, knowing that he would run two to three miles later in the same day when possible. When he arrived at St. Martin's, the trunk of his car was not only filled with clothing and valuables, but a heavy barbell set he used at least two or three times each week. The man was strong both mentally and bodily.

Father Phillip had been raised in Greensburg, but had won a scholarship to Duquesne University in Pittsburgh where he majored in philosophy and theology. He was a natural for the priesthood. Father Phillip tried to befriend Ed Bristol, but found him somewhat difficult. For whatever reason, the custodian seemed to resent the virile, boyish-looking, priest. Phillip thought that perhaps his appearance brought back some ugly, negative memories for the hard working custodian.

Phillip was a big eater but he ate only those foods that he felt kept him strong and mentally alert. A quiet fellow who occupied his mind with philosophical issues and then submitted his ideas to various journals for publication, he avoided the Oculi mystery.

His was a world of intellectual reasoning, of logical order, of philosophical discourse. He believed that the logic of Thomas Aquinas wedded to Aristotle's ancient philosophy was the right way to interpret existence, life, and religious doctrine. Saint Paul's crucifix interfered with natural law, with logic, with cause and effect, and with common sense. Like Father Walsh, he had watched the droplets fall, but advocated his pastor's belief that an answer would eventually be found. The Oculi mystery was not worth troubling over.

Father Kerr divided his overloaded weekly schedule into thirds. Now he would have time to visit homes, counsel those who sought help, create more meaningful sermons, plan for the eventual reopening of the elementary school, and relax like a normal person. Like Phillip, Kerr liked reading for recreation. He loved history, particularly Civil War history. But he also liked historical fiction, science fiction, biographies and mystery stories. So now, it befuddled him to be living inside a mystery that no one seemed capable of solving. The mystery intrigued him; worried him; confounded him; and possessed him.

Saint Paul's remained a national news story. At Ed Bristol's urging, Father Kerr permitted several TV stations, using telescopic cameras, to record an actual Benediction ceremony. Crews carried cameras up the dangerous spiraling stairs to the choir loft where programs were recorded at a great distance. Regardless of how good or bad each station recorded, edited, and then broadcast what they had seen happen, each program was an immediate hit. CNTV did an entire Sunday night, sixty-minute special they aptly titled, The Oculi Incident, and promised more updates. The program spent fifteen minutes describing the critical attributes necessary to validate a miracle, fifteen minutes showing places in the world where miracles had been validated, and fifteen minutes showing a shortened version of an actual Benediction service at Saint Paul's with the tearing eyes clearly visible using telephoto lenses. The program was punctuated with interview clips of a host of people and their opinions about the validity of the apparent supernatural intervention.

Of course, the more publicity Saint Paul's received, the larger the crowds grew. Tourists seemed drawn to Latrobe as if the church was a huge electro-people-magnet. Father Walsh kept a small notebook in his pocket where he jotted down the various states he'd seen on license plates in the church parking lot at any given time.

On the hall wall leading to the rectory kitchen, he asked the custodian to hang a cork bulletin board to which a large map of the United States was attached. The board was three-feet high and four-feet wide. Then Walsh would stick straight pins with large colored round tops into those states recorded in his notebook. The map at this time had sixteen states pinned.

Mrs. Pierce joined in the project. She began keeping her own notebook, and anytime the parking lot looked very busy, she would walk out to peruse license plates and make notes, then return and enter pins for any new states on the wall map. Father Phillip had no time for such foolishness.

There were many days when tour buses brought a hundred or more curiosity seekers from Virginia, West Virginia, Ohio, New York, and even more distant areas. Ed Bristol had noted that on one particular Friday, he counted twelve different buses between ten in the morning and seven in the evening. Father Kerr had agreed with him that a small voluntary donation of three dollars per person was perfectly in order to help offset the cost of maintaining the church because it was experiencing more wear and tear since August than at any other time in its long history. Kerr could then use this money for the poor and indigent.

Donations flooded the church's offering boxes and collection baskets during all five Sunday Masses. Before the mystery began, Kerr barely managed to pay for Saint Paul's upkeep. Now a new heating and air conditioning system had been installed in the drafty old building. Insulating glass was added over the tall stained glass windows to keep heat from escaping in winter, and cool air inside during hot summer months. A sandblasting company cleaned the exterior and interior stone, while paint contractors restored Saint Paul's interior to its former beauty. It was a slow and expensive process, but everyone involved thought the updates were worth the cost.

When the church was first constructed in 1898, much of the exposed wood was stained a red mahogany to amplify the natural beauty of the wood. The wood trimming the edges of the towering columns on the side walls, and the arches supporting the high vaulted ceiling, were painted with various hues of deep blue alternating with gold relief. In spite of his beliefs, Father Kerr was thrilled to watch the church returning to its pristine glory and so were his proud parishioners.

14　The Light in the Window

November 12, 2002—Tuesday
4:30 P.M.

Because the elementary school had been closed for some time, only two nuns remained at Saint Paul's convent, Sisters Margaret and Lucy. Martie had befriended these two women back in September, helping them entertain and teach children in Saint Paul's latchkey program. She offered the sisters the use of her automobile on those occasions when they needed special transportation. She particularly liked Lucy. It seemed that everyone in the parish loved the woman. Her smile and unexpected, sometimes flighty remarks, made Martie want to chuckle the minute she was present.

At the produce department of a supermarket on Main Street, Martie met Sister Lucy who was shopping with Margaret. Lucy's traditional long black habit and veil starkly contrasted with Margaret's contemporary outfit: white blouse, gray skirt, black shoes, and exposed hair.

Martie and the two sisters talked for a few minutes. "Isn't it wonderful that the Almighty has allowed the Oculi miracle to happen?" said Lucy. Martie could not help herself; she began to grin.

"I guess that's a good sign," was all she could say.

"To my way of thinking there is a rebirth of faith in our whole diocese. I remember in school when the nuns told us about the cures over at Lourdes and Fatima. Those places seemed so very far away. I knew I'd never see them."

"I remember that, too," smiled Martie.

With a puzzled look on her face, Lucy said, "Why don't churches pay to send all their injured and crippled Catholics over there? The Lord would have to cure some of them, don'tcha think?"

Martie had no response. She uttered, "Mm," and stifled a grin. Lucy reached over, picked up a very ripe pear from a display, took a bite and began chewing.

"But now we can witness a miracle for ourselves. It's strange how irregular the miracle days have become. I think our Creator must know that too much of Heaven would be boring to us earthlings. Wow, these are great pears." Serious Sister Margaret rolled her eyes and said nothing."

Laughing to herself at the use of the word "earthlings," and the fact that Lucy stood there munching a pear she had not paid for, Martie attempted to change the subject because she started to laugh. "By the way Sister Margaret, how are all the latchkey kids doing. I've missed a few days?"

"They're doing fine. The older children have asked me about you. You seem to have a special way with them."

Sister Lucy turned the subject matter back to the mystery. "Did you know that I go to Benediction every week just hoping the miracle will happen? The waiting is just so, so, so invigorating, isn't it Sister Margaret?" Margaret looked exasperated and did not respond. She did not share Lucy's enthusiasm for the miracle or the pear-munching.

To relieve the tension, Martie said, "Um, I guess it could be.

These are strange times and strange happenings."

Margaret interjected, "Well, there is shopping to do, Lucy. We'd better see to it."

"You know," continued Lucy, "We have a secret. I get goose bumps just thinking about it." Margaret looked annoyed because Lucy went right on talking. She had finished her pear.

"A secret?" grinned Martie not knowing what to expect.

"Well, you know how the Oculi cry some Sundays at Benediction?"

"Yes."

"Well, here is something just as mysterious. Last Thursday night, Margaret and I saw light flashes in that teeny tiny rose window way up at the end of the church; you know, the one facing the convent? It was as if the Holy Trinity was up there, all three persons at the same time." Martie could barely control herself. Margaret was growing more impatient by the minute.

But Lucy's comment bothered Martie. "Wait, that window is high above the ceiling of the main church. Light can't reach it from the inside."

"I know said Lucy. That's why it has to be something very special."

"In fact, I didn't know it was a window. I thought it was just a stone decoration."

"So did we," smiled Sister Lucy. It looks like stone from the convent window."

"And you saw it, too?" said Martie turning to Margaret.

"Yes, I have to admit I did. But I think it's just reflected light from automobiles or streetlights and we shouldn't be concerned, and we should be shopping."

"Did you ever see the light before?" Martie asked?

"Oh, yes," said Lucy, "just a few times."

"Did you notice it before the mystery began?"

"We weren't looking for it."

"That's odd," said Martie.

"I know. I'm sure it has something to do with the Holy Spirit. Isn't this just a wonderful time to be a Catholic, especially to be a nun and to bear witness!" replied Lucy.

Martie was overwhelmed with the nun's obvious sincerity, and her own curiosity about the light flashes.

"Good grief, Sister, that is very exciting. I'd love to see what causes those lights. They may help my disbelief!" Now Margaret glared at both of them.

"Tell you what. Here's what we'll do," said Lucy. "The very next time it happens ... the very, very next time ... I'll phone you so you can hurry over to see for yourself. You only live a block or so down the street from here. Right?"

"Yes."

Now, Margaret took Lucy by the arm and started off with her, "Lucy, let's get moving or we'll never get finished. Goodbye Martie, and Lucy will call you about those lights. Oh, and Martie, do come over whenever you can to help after school. We love having you."

"I'll do that."

6:30 P.M.

Later, while they were sitting in their dining room eating the frozen dinners Jim had prepared, Martie mentioned Sister Lucy's comments about the flashes of light. "It must be a reflection of some kind," said Jim. "Why? What are you thinking?"

"I'm thinking that maybe someone was up there; the window must be glass because if they saw light, it must have penetrated from some inside source—I can't imagine reflected light from the

126

street reaching up there. I've heard that Mrs. Reed sometimes practices new organ pieces on Thursday evenings, but I doubt it was her."

"Why not call and ask?"

When Mrs. Reed answered, Martie explained where the nuns had seen the lights and asked if she'd seen light or been up to the church attic recently.

"I like to practice on Thursdays while the church is being cleaned. But those stairs leading up to the organ console and the choir loft are steep and very dangerous. I've never gone up beyond the choir loft because those steps give me the creeps."

"Have you ever heard anyone up there?" asked Martie.

"Martie, whenever those pipes are playing, someone could use a jackhammer right beside me and I wouldn't be able to hear it. The organ console faces the rear of the church. I can't see the choir-loft door. In fact, the only way I can see what's going on in the building is through a large mirror attached above all the organ keys." Martie thanked her for the information.

"Jim, why would there be a space above the ceiling anyway?"

"I think all high churches are built with one. I know over at Saint Vincent's Basilica there are no long, dangling chandeliers of any kind. Instead, there are very large spotlights recessed in the ceiling itself. To access them, I'm positive the monks walk through a space above the ceiling. It wouldn't make sense to build scaffolding just to replace a burned out light bulb. But other than checking the ceiling and wiring from above, I can't imagine why anyone would go up there."

"I asked Sister Lucy to phone me the next time she sees the flashes."

"Do you plan on going over there?"

"Jim, you know me. Lucy has piqued my curiosity."

"Well, I'll go with you when she calls." When Martie walked into the kitchen, Jim took out his cell phone and dialed their home phone number. The phone on the kitchen wall rang.

"Hello, Martie Meyer here."

"Hi there, beautiful, I've been watching you," Jim said in his deepest voice.

"What? Who is this?"

"I've been watching you, and I think you're beautiful. I can see your back end from the dining room."

Martie immediately hung up and walked back into the dining room with a big grin on her face. "So what's it to you, Officer Simmons?"

"Hey, I can see the front now, and it's a beautiful face." Martie stood about six feet from Jim's chair and began a slow sensual body movement in time with the music on the radio.

"I wonder if this reminds the man I love of anything?" said Martie.

15 A Spiral Tunnel of Death

November 14, 2002—Thursday
7:15 P.M.

Jim had night duty. Martie was sitting at her computer terminal creating tomorrow's science quiz. True to her word, a very excited Sister Lucy called.

"I've seen the flashes," she exclaimed. "Just a few moments ago. Hurry! Hurry over!"

Martie hurried down the short block. Within minutes she was beside Sister Lucy.

"Wow! That was fast. You must have been on your way when I called."

Martie shook here head violently as if to rid her mind of Lucy's comment. Now the two women stood looking upward from a second floor convent window. Every once in a while, there did seem to be just a burst of light from the high, rose window. They were sure of it.

"Do you have a key for the church?" asked Martie.

"Oh, we mustn't go over there now. If this is a work of the Spirit, we shouldn't meddle."

"Sister," said Martie, "there is nothing to be afraid of. We may be blessed by going."

"Well, only if you think it wouldn't be a sin or anything. I've been dying to go up there. Maybe we'll have an apparition—see some saints or martyrs or angels with real wings. Margaret can give us her keys."

Under the circumstances, Martie paid little attention to the nun's bizarre religious comments because of her own curiosity. She let Sister Lucy lead the way with one bright flashlight while she followed behind with a smaller light from her purse. After unlocking the side door opposite the sacristy, they entered and walked through the supply room, then down the aisle toward the vestibule. There was little need for artificial light; the entire church was aglow with thousands of burning candles.

"Isn't this just the way church should be?" asked Sister Lucy. "Heaven must be something like this. If it's not, I'd rather not go there." Both could smell the ever-present odor of incense in the air.

Again, Martie had nothing to add to sister's soulful sentiment, but it did seem rather beautiful and peaceful. Then the realization of how many dollars were going up in smoke, compared to her meager teacher's salary from the Latrobe School District, brought back reality.

Although the nun's black habit appeared as a shadow, on the contrary, Martie's yellow sweatshirt and blue jeans were more noticeable if anyone had been hiding. "Most of these are newer keys," said Lucy, "but one of these old tarnished ones might open this old fashioned lock. Shine your light here so I can see." She tried the oldest key first, and with some jiggling, it unlocked the gate leading to the steep, circular stairway that led up to the organ loft, and then on up to the high recesses far above. The staircase was not wide enough for two people to walk side by side because the innermost edge of each stair tread was only one-inch wide while the width of the outer edge was about twelve-inches. The steps were quite hazardous unless one walked along the outside edge, holding the railing that spiraled upward at the same steep angle as the stairs.

Although candles lit the church body, there were no lights of any kind in this stair tower. Since it was dark outside, the tower windows were useless. As Martie stepped into the absolute blackness of the tower, she began to doubt the wisdom of their action. When they had climbed to the choir loft entrance, Lucy said, "Stop a minute. I think I hear noises up there. Isn't this exciting?" She shined her light upward. Martie felt a stabbing pang of fear. She lost her nerve.

"This isn't such a good idea after all," she protested. "Let's forget it. We can come up here during daylight."

"But we might not see the flashes then."

"I think Sister Margaret is right, the lights are just reflections from passing autos or trucks." Martie was scared now.

"But we're so close," said Lucy as if she was prepared for the beatific vision itself. "It might be something very beautiful." On up the steps she climbed with Martie following many steps behind. Martie could just make out the very back of Sister Lucy's flowing black habit as she vanished around the upward spiral.

"Wait, wait for me. I'm coming," said Martie. "Lucy, let's get down out of here. I'm frightened."

The very next thing Martie heard was a very loud thump followed by a louder bang! Instantly, she aimed her light up around the last spiral to watch Sister Lucy teetering on the top step, her arms flailing at nothing, trying to regain her balance.

"Lucy," screamed Martie.

But it was useless. As if in slow motion, Lucy began falling backward—completely backward. She shrieked loud with terror. The handrail along the outside wall was beyond her grasp. There was nothing to stop her fall except the empty spiral that twisted like a deadly snake down into the darkness below.

It felt perverse to watch, but Martie could do nothing. Lucy toppled backward grasping nothing but air. The back of her head slammed the sharp metal edge of the step where Martie was standing. For a brief second, the nun was inverted; her injured head at least eight steps below her own feet. She screamed in pain.

Blood splattered from under her veil then her feet came down arched over her head, so that she began to tumble in awkward backward somersaults down the innermost spiral of the staircase where the steps were narrowest. It was like a death chute. It happened so fast that all Martie could manage was one quick grab for the toppling nun's habit, yet she ripped loose only a bloody headpiece as Lucy tumbled down, down, down into the darkness far below.

After her first shriek of pain, the second was that of unspeakable terror. The third somewhat muffled. There was no fourth, or any other sound, except that of a body tumbling, cracking, and coming to rest many spirals below. For a merciful second or two, the unconscious body stopped, propped sideways along a step, at the choir loft landing, but then gravity once again claimed the unconscious woman, until her twisted body began tumbling down the last spirals to the very bottom.

In abject horror, Martie turned and raced down the outside edge of the steps never letting go of the railing as it slid through her hand. She screamed as she went, "Lucy, Lucy—LUCY." As she stepped down around the last spiral, she could see the battered, broken body of Sister Lucy. The nun's head was turned almost backward and tucked down under one of her armpits. One arm bent back at the elbow, out of its socket, twisted behind the lifeless head. One leg was broken so hideously below the knee that Martie could see the jagged edges. Sister's blood had already begun to form a puddle on the floor, her open eyes staring at nothing. Instinctively, Martie screamed, "HELP! Help! Please, please someone, anyone—help me, help me!"

She dashed back through the church and the sacristy and across to the rectory. She pelted the door with both fists. When Kerr answered, and she exploded with, "Call 911, now. NOW! Sister Lucy is badly hurt! Kerr dialed for help as he ran over to the church following Martie. Father Phillip close behind, turned on lights as he ran past the breaker box. The three gaped in horror as they viewed the twisted corpse of Sister Lucy at the bottom of the deadly staircase.

"Oh, my, oh, my good God. What on earth happened?" cried Kerr as Phillip put his arm around the pastor to support him. Then Father Kerr reached down and held the nun's lifeless untwisted hand in his own. He knelt down beside her and cried. He knew help was useless. Sister Lucy was gone from this world.

Through his own tears, Kerr closed the staring, vacant eyes. Phillip knelt beside Kerr supporting his arm. After several moments of shocked silence, Kerr raised his hand over the lifeless form: *"Benedicat te, Omnipotens Deus; atque in pace eius nunc semper requiescas"* (May Almighty God bless you and now rest in his peace forever).

Within a very few minutes, Jim Simmons screeched to a halt in his police car followed by an EMS van. "Sister's lying over here," a shattered Kerr said as Jim and the ambulance crew hurried in with their lifesaving equipment. Through his tears he managed, "You won't need any of that; the holy woman is dead. She's gone. She's gone to her Maker."

Regardless, Jim and the ambulance crew hurried inside the

stair tower. It was their job. One look, however, told them Sister Lucy was beyond hope. She had no pulse and couldn't possibly breathe with her head twisted as it was. As Jim turned away from the corpse, he was dumbfounded to spot Martie sitting with her head in her hands in the last church pew. Jim said nothing, but climbed into the pew, sat down, and put his arm around Martie. He could feel her weeping. He listened to the ambulance personnel talking as they lifted the lifeless body to a stretcher then carried Lucy out to their vehicle.

All was silent. Ever so slowly, grieving Kerr walked past Martie and Jim. He wept openly into his red handkerchief. Finally, Martie barely uttered, "She fell. She—fell. She fell all the way down that horrible metal staircase." She paused. "It's just too awful to describe. I kept hearing her tumble, cracking, breaking, down, down like a broken doll. I'll never ever forget the sound, never!"

It was a long time before they left the church. Father had gone to the convent to inform Sister Margaret of the tragedy—Phillip to the rectory to inform Father Walsh. Walsh was always an emotional man. He had talked with Sister Lucy on many, many occasions. The two enjoyed one another's company. He often said Lucy brought out the silliness in him because he always knew what to expect: the unexpected. Walsh was devastated at the loss of someone he possibly thought of as his dearest friend. Phillip tried to console him, but the big man grieved openly, bitterly and for a very long time.

10:20 P.M.

At home that evening, it took Martie quite a while to explain the specifics of Sister Lucy's death. She would start her story, then cry, then restart, and then stop to think. She kept wiping her tears and retelling the same story.

"Jim," she sobbed. "I know I saw flashes of light. Poor Lucy thought if we went up there, she might see an apparition because of all this business about the cross far below."

Martie's composure began to return only when she had no tears left.

November 17, 2002—Sunday
3:30 A.M.

Three days had passed since the heartbreaking death of Sister Lucy. Martie continued to grieve over the nun's demise and her personal belief that somehow she was at fault for encouraging Lucy to investigate the church attic. She was up most of Thursday night, and was in no mental condition to go into her classroom on Friday and teach, so she took a personal leave day.

Jim continued to console her and so did Amy, but it would take time for Martie's psyche to heal. Although she was not a true believer, somehow Father Kerr's words seemed to comfort her. "Marty," he'd said, "the woman was good; she was kind; she was indeed holy; and she is with her Maker, the One she had pledged her life to. She has now met Him face to face."

By Sunday afternoon, she was feeling much better after having spent time preparing for the next day's lessons. It distracted her. She was extremely creative and enjoyed making puzzles and worksheets.

"You know, Jim, I think Kerr is right. Lucy is happier now. Regardless of my own beliefs, she wanted to go up there because she thought she might see angels, or saints, or the Holy Spirit. So I'm sure she's enjoying those visions right now, even though she died hideously."

"The woman did have faith."

"Can you just imagine her walking around in Heaven keeping everyone in stitches?"

"I can."

"I have to admit that she was a bit flighty, but she never knew it."

"Martie, I have a couple of questions to ask you about what happened, but I don't want to upset you. When you feel emotionally ready, let me know."

"I feel pretty good. If you upset me, I'll tell you."

Jim began, "Can we go back to your story for a minute. You said you heard a loud noise, but did you see anything that caused it?"

"No, I was too far down the steps in the shadows. All I know is that right before she lost her balance, there was a noise."

"What about a door? Was there a door at the very top?"

"Yes, but when I shined my light up there, Sister was already losing her balance. The door to the attic, or whatever that Hellish area is called, was shut." Jim sat for a moment without saying anything. A very serious look came over his face. It took on an almost tortured look. For a moment, Martie was distracted from her own worries.

"Jim, what's the matter? What's wrong?"

"I was just thinking about what you said right after the accident."

"Which was?"

"You said you heard loud noises when Sister lost her balance? Just one noise?"

"No, I think there were two. I'm not really sure. I thought it was Lucy pulling on the door. Maybe it was stuck or something."

"I'm just wondering about that. Martie, if that door opens outward, what you heard might've been someone opening the door so hard that it knocked Lucy off balance."

Marty's mouth dropped open. She covered it with the back of her hand. "But when I flashed my light up there, the door was shut," said the alarmed woman.

"The other noise you heard might've been the door getting yanked shut. Whoever was up there did not want to be seen."

There was a long pause while Martie thought about Jim's statement. As the weight of Jim's supposition impressed itself on her mind, she cried, "Oh, no, you just can't be right. Why, why would anyone ever do a thing like that? No. How could a person still be human and do that to someone?"

"If there's a God, then she or he knows the answer to that question." said Jim, "You know as well as I do, Martie, there are a lot of crazed people in this world."

"No, you're wrong; that's too hard to believe. I mean, no, no," said Martie shaking her head. "No one would ever be that evil; how could you even think that?"

Silence followed as both their minds continued examining what Jim had just said. Then Martie's face became frighteningly serious. She looked at Jim as if they were both having the same thought.

"Father McCarthy," she said. "Father McCarthy." Maybe the person up there shot Father McCarthy and—"

"—was hiding up there." Jim finished Martie's sentence. "Not only that, if that person killed to keep their identity hidden then you may be in danger."

"But if I didn't see a face, I doubt he, or she saw mine."

"But that person would've known there were two of you. And whoever it was either stayed hidden up there, or made their escape in the confusion following Lucy's fall. When you ran down the staircase and through the church for help, they could've been hiding anywhere and seen your face, the others, and mine, even while the two of us sat in the church pew afterward."

"Oh, no, Jim, it just can't be like that! You've got to be wrong," gasped Martie. "It just doesn't make any sense. McCarthy was shot at by an unknown person who had been in the storage room. Your own police department said it must've been a thief looking for sacred vessels but was on the wrong side of the church. Some unknown person in the attic killed Lucy. Do you think some disturbed creature haunts the church like the Phantom of the Opera, or that maybe the place is possessed by Lucifer?"

"I thought you didn't believe in religion."

"I'm not sure anymore."

16　Blackness in the Church Attic

November 18, 2002—Monday
9:15 P.M.

By Monday Martie had recovered enough to return to school. Jim was patrolling Latrobe and decided to phone Kerr from his cruiser for two reasons. First, he wished to see if the priest's spirits had improved because he had grown to like the man and was worried about him. Second, he wanted to visit the church attic. He remained mute about the possibility that Lucy may have been pushed off balance.

The priest was depressed and said to Jim, "Sometimes I wonder how God could let such an evil accident happen. I mean, why create a world and allow evil? Who will ever forget 9/11, or Hiroshima, or—Oh, well—Lucy is with God now. I should be happy for her sake."

"I can't imagine the grief you feel, but I wish I could help in some way. My wife was crazy about Lucy. They became close friends through the school. She was a lovely person, just like you are."

Jim walked over, put both arms around the priest and held him.

"You are one of God's chosen ones," he said to the pastor restraining his own emotions. This is indeed a holy man.

After a moment or two, they separated and Kerr said, "I'll

be okay, Jim, we must go on, you know. I've always preached to others that the Almighty gives us the strength to go on, and he will. But thanks for your empathy. I know Martie and Lucy climbed up there because they saw light flashes through that high rose window. You know, Jim, I'd like to have Ed install a spotlight up there to illuminate that window in memory of Sister Lucy. What do you think?"

"That's a wonderful gesture, Father. I think all your parishioners would appreciate that."

"As much as I hate the thought, I think I'd like to climb up there just to see what would be involved. Do you think I'm being morbid?"

I'd like to look around there too, thought Jim

"Believe it or not, I came over to ask you for a key so I could take a peek." He remembered Martie's comments. "Maybe we'll find a Phantom waiting for us."

"I know you're kidding, but maybe ghosts do live up there," joked Kerr.

"Now you're jagging me, Padre. I just wanted to see if there are any visible clues with the crucifix mystery."

"Your curiosity's got the best of you. Sure," said Kerr, "I know one of these old keys opens that lock." He unhooked a ring of keys that were hung over a nail by the rectory's side door, and they walked to the church. The pastor used the old skeleton key to open the lock to the tower stairs.

Lucy's bloodstains had been scrubbed clean, but there was the lingering smell of disinfectant in the air. *Good Lord,* thought Jim as they started their climb. *Now I can see that if you lost your balance, you could careen all the way to the bottom. These steps are like a long narrow tube.*

"That poor woman," Kerr said aloud. "Just watch your step."

Several small tower windows provided the only natural light for the staircase. Jim led the way. He counted at least three complete spiral turns before they reached the small landing that led across to the choir loft and organ. From there, he counted six additional spirals before reaching the very top step. Directly across from it was a narrow door twenty-six inches or less in width, opening into the attic.

Damn! It does open outward, he thought. *How gruesome. Murder is a real possibility.* To enter the attic, one had to remain on the first or second step from the top so the narrow door could clear when pulled open.

It was as dark as an unlit bank vault when Jim peered inside. If there was any light at all coming through the decorative rose window at the far end, it was hardly evident at this end. He had brought along his automobile's powerful flashlight. He clicked it on and the two stood waiting for their eyes to adjust to the dark surroundings.

Running the length of the attic was a three-foot wide catwalk with a railing on the left side. The walkway was suspended above, and was part of, the superstructure that made up the high vaulted ceiling.

"Isn't it remarkable that this old lath and plaster has stayed in place all of these years."

"I'll say," said Jim, "Looks awful heavy to me. Those stone arches obviously keep all up here."

"Look how those boards down there run all the way from one side to the other right under this catwalk. They don't seem to be connected to anything. I wonder what they were for?" asked Kerr.

"I'll bet they were left by stone masons who walked on them when they tied in the arches for the suspended ceiling," said

Jim. "Notice how they sit on the stone archways and not directly on the lath or plaster."

"Remarkable," Kerr added. "Can't imagine standing on them without a ceiling in place. I wonder what it looks like inside the ceiling of Notre Dame, or Chartres, or some of the other cathedrals that have been standing for centuries. A few years ago, I had the chance to say Mass in Saint Paul's Cathedral in Pittsburgh. Beautiful place: graceful Gothic columns, nice high uplifted ceiling, very powerful organ."

Jim beamed his light at the electric wires that ran the entire length of the attic up and over each archway before dipping down into the hollows of the arches.

"Those cables must power the lights; look how heavy those bars are where the wires disappear down through the ceiling. Each one of those lights with their long chains must weigh several hundred pounds. You know, when I was a kid and went to church, I used to imagine what would happen if one of those chains broke loose."

"Gross thought," said Kerr. "Ghastly." Feeling very uneasy in this gloomy place, he added, "It's really creepy in here."

As they walked toward the far end facing the convent, they could see the rose window for what it was. From below and outside, it looked rather intricate and ornate, but here on the inside, its thick glass was dull and covered with dust. Cobwebs and spider webs crisscrossed its entire three-foot diameter.

"It will be very beautiful when it's lit," said Kerr. "But now I can see why people thought it was stone and not glass. But for the life of me, I can't imagine what Lucy and Martie would've mistaken as flashes of light? I don't see any possible thing that could've caused them."

He paused for a moment, then said, "Unless someone was

here. But why would anyone enter at night after the church was locked?"

He paused a second time, "The only people I can think of would be Dr. Troft or Ed or Lord knows who. I can't remember Mrs. Reed ever asking to come up here."

"Maybe what they saw really was a reflection," said Jim, even though he doubted it. Because Father Kerr had no flashlight, Jim was obligated to shine his along the catwalk so both men could see. When he approximated that they were above the front, center aisle, he focused his beam on the ceiling hunting the supports for the cables that held the suspended cross. The thick layer of dust made it difficult to locate the exact spots. "Funny," he said to Kerr, "I can't see the places where the supports for the cables are."

"I'm sure they're covered with dust like everything else. Well, I've seen enough. Besides, this place has a very strange odor. Let's get down out of here."

Jim sensed Kerr growing ill-at-ease wanting to leave. As the two continued their return trip toward the attic door they'd left ajar, Jim stopped and shined his light one last time toward the opposite end. Both men followed the light beam to the rose window that was just as dim as before.

WHAM—slammed the attic door loud enough to cause both men to jerk and twist around in that direction. Jim turned so fast that his outstretched hand hit Father Kerr's arm. Down went the flashlight. Both grabbed for it, easing its fall but it landed on the catwalk. Terribly shaken, Father Kerr reached down to retrieve it but in the darkness, his nervous fingers pushed it over the edge of the catwalk. It landed with a soft cushioned sound somewhere below and disappeared.

"Damn," said Kerr nervously, "I'm sorry—"

"Just a light, but I can't see a thing."

"Me neither." Holding on to one another for support, neither man knew how frightened the other was. The door remained closed forcing them to feel their way back through the blackness. Kerr thought he heard footfalls retreating down the metal staircase, but said nothing about them.

"Boy, that scared the hell out of me," said Jim. "Excuse the French."

"Scared the living shit out of me," exclaimed Kerr, "and that's plain English. Geez, I'm really sorry about your light."

"Hey, it's okay. Don't worry about it. It's replaceable, we aren't. Let's just hope that door will open when we get there. This would not be my kind of place to break out of."

"What in blazes caused that to happen?"

"Probably the dev—"

"Christ, Simmons, stop kidding. That scared me. Do you suppose someone—"

"Maybe a draft blew it shut, that's all." But he couldn't help thinking, *how could a draft ever reach this place?*

"Maybe someone or some *thing* slammed that door and he, she, or it may still be in here—in here in the dark with us. How in the hell could fresh air blow up into this godforsaken dead space?" asked Kerr. "And I'm sure I heard footsteps or something outside that door! Merciful Jesus, someone or some thing might be crouched anywhere in this inky blackness, or just outside the door. Waiting—just waiting to pounce on us."

Shit, I hope he's not right, thought Jim, *but I did hear something, too. I'm sure of it.* "I think everything is okay," said Jim, attempting to calm himself and the terrified pastor.

The two men slid their right hands along the rough, wooden railing with Kerr in the lead. He extended his left arm and hand out in front to avoid colliding with the door or anything else that might be in the way. The priest was shaking and sweating profusely now. To keep from colliding with Kerr, Jim held out his arm and walked so close behind him that his outstretched fingers touched Kerr's back. "I can't imagine what those two women saw that enticed them to come up here," he said. "It's such a creepy place and that odor—"

"You're right on both counts, Father, but once you get that window lit up, this place might not appear so formidable. Maybe a few lights along this catwalk might not be a bad idea either."

The two men crept along. "I can feel the door now, Jim," He turned the knob and pushed. The knob turned easily, but the door refused to budge. He tried again and yet again. No luck! "You try, Jim, it seems to be stuck. It must have locked when it slammed shut."

Jim moved around in front of the priest, then turned the knob and pushed hard. "Either it's stuck, or some thing is blocking it," cried Jim. *For sure someone is or was in here. Something solid like a piece of two-by-four must be wedged between the door and the low staircase railing,* thought Jim.

"Or someone!" said Kerr trembling. "This is a nightmare from Hell. Let me try again." This time, when he pushed very hard, the door opened just a bit then shut again when he bounced off it. "It moved a little that time. Since the damn door is so narrow, you stand to the side and turn the knob, Jim. I'll throw my full weight against it."

"Okay, but be careful, Father. Bones break." Jim stepped aside and turned the doorknob. Kerr stood back about three feet, turned sideways, stooped down and charged forward throwing his weight against the door with his right shoulder. There was a loud—*crack*—as the door swung open. But Kerr could not stop

145

his forward momentum. His body hurtled across the narrow top step and folded over the knee high railing but he could not stoop low enough or fast enough to grab it. Jim snatched the back of Kerr's cassock and caught the very bottom near the hem. Still, the priest's body plummeted over. The spirals rushed up to his eyes as if through an adjusting telescopic lens.

Instinctively, the pastor extended both hands to break his fall and protect his head. But he never hit the staircase steps. Instead, one side of his forehead slammed against the center pier of the staircase making a bleeding gash. Jim's grip had stopped his fall. Jim wedged his feet against the short railing and shouted, "Father, I've got you, I've got you. You're okay, you're not going to fall." Kerr was completely inverted.

"Jesus, God Almighty," cried Kerr. "Just don't let go or I'll surely meet Lucy in a few seconds. What in hell am I going to do? I'm upside down."

"Part of your cassock is down over your head because I'm holding this other end. Right?"

"Yes."

"Take that part and use it to pull yourself around in a large arc until you're upright. Can you do that?"

"I don't know."

"Do it anyway."

Kerr didn't answer, but Jim could feel him tugging mightily. A short time passed before he could see Father Kerr's head as his hands continued up the cassock's hem closer and closer to the part that folded over the short railing. As Kerr pulled, Jim kept pushing with both feet against the railing. The priest was struggling mightily because the nearer he got to an upright position, the more his body weight wanted to pull him down and out of the arms of his cassock. Inch by inch, he worked his way up toward the railing until with one huge lunge, he grasped it with one hand.

"Don't—let—go, Jim! Please, please just hold on to me. I don't know that I have the strength to get my other arm and hand up there," said the priest out of breath from his struggle.

"You can do it, Father. You can. Do it for Lucy!" With that thought, Kerr stretched his body out just enough to grab the railing with his other hand.

"Jim, I—I can't hang on. I'm just too tired. My muscles won't hold me anymore. I'm going to fall!"

"No, you're not. Father, you're almost here. Just hold on long enough for me to grab your wrists. But I've got to let go for a second. Okay, are you ready?"

"Oh, do it very fast, please? I'm losing my grip right now! Please!" yelled the terrified priest. "My hands are slip—" Jim took his feet off the low railing, dropped the priest's garment, leaned forward and grabbed Kerr's forearms in one smooth motion.

"I've got your wrists. Now, one hand at a time, let go of the railing and then turn each hand and grab my wrists." Kerr responded instantly. With all his strength, Jim pulled up and back very hard and sat down at the same time. This catapulted Father Kerr upward so he could get one knee, and then the other, on the ledge under the railing. But Jim continued pulling till the pastor toppled all the way over landing on top him. Both lay in a heap in the narrow attic doorway.

"Whew! that was the closest I've ever come to the afterlife." The blood from Father Kerr's head dripped down onto Jim's face.

"Shit, you're bleeding!"

"I hit my head on the center pier of the staircase when I did that trapeze act. Sorry about that," apologized Kerr. He wiped the blood from Jim's face as best he could, then stood up and moved back toward the attic door so Jim could get to his feet.

In the dim light, Jim looked at the priest's raised wound. "There's a nasty lump forming, but I don't think the gash is too serious. Let's get down to the rectory and take a look. It's just too dark in here to see. Those tiny tower windows aren't worth the powder to blow them all to Hell."

"Wait. I—I just need a minute to get my strength back." Kerr stood shaking his head. "For a while there, I really thought I'd be visiting Saint Pete. It's no wonder Lucy died tumbling from up here. Jesus, I was scared. May God and all His angels, saints, and martyrs and, and—and plants, and animals—and, and all living things including bugs, thank you for what you did," sputtered Kerr. He reached out and gave Jim a huge bear hug.

Jim ripped off his shirt without unbuttoning it and forced Kerr to wipe his head and face. "It may not be the cleanest, but it will due for now."

"Now," said Kerr smiling and regaining some composure. "Now, I owe you two things: my life and a new white shirt."

"What on earth do you think blocked that door?" asked Jim.

"I swear I heard something falling down the staircase just as I did my aerial act. In fact, I could hear it tumbling while I hung there. I'll bet it's at the bottom of the stairs. As we go down, we can take a look. The biggest question is how did it get there? And why?" Father Kerr continued to hold Jim's torn shirt against his bleeding forehead.

"It was a scare tactic," answered Jim, "It was done to scare us. Someone did not want us up here—"

"Someone or some *thing*," interrupted Kerr. "The ugly

creature could've been Lucifer himself, claiming another victim!" He couldn't help but think of McCarthy and Lucy.

"Well, he struck out this time."

Cautiously, they descended looking for any sign indicating what had been propped against the door. At the very bottom, they found nothing. Nothing at all. So not to cause a commotion since they knew there would be many visitors in the church body, the two men waited in the stair tower until the vestibule was empty, then quickly darted out through the main double doors, scurrying around the side of the church unobserved.

Mrs. Pierce was frantic at the site of them coming through the side door near her kitchen. Kerr was holding Jim's blood-soaked shirt to his forehead, his filthy cassock disheveled. Jim had blood smeared across his face and chest. Both were covered with layers of attic dust stuck to their perspiration. Before Mrs. Pierce could speak, Kerr held up his hand to calm her. "It's nothing serious, Mrs. Pierce. Jim and I were up in the church attic to see about lighting that stained glass window as a memorial to Sister Lucy."

"But I'll call 911 for help. You—you—why both of you look awful! All that blood—and—and—"

"Heavens no, it's just a scalp wound. I bumped my head then fell in the dust along with Jim here who gave me his clean shirt. He and I are going upstairs to clean up. Be down in a jiffy." Mrs. Pierce stood in shock, her mouth agape, as the two men walked past her down the hall and disappeared up the rectory stairs.

Using a wet washcloth, Jim tenderly washed the dried blood and dust from Father Kerr's forehead and face. The wound was just as Kerr had told Mrs. Pierce: a scalp lesion on top of a raised lump. At once, they heard a rap on the door. Mrs. Pierce yelled, "I've set a pan of ice by your door, Father. Wrap the cubes in a wet washcloth and hold it against that bump."

"Thank you! Thanks!" said Kerr opening the door just as Mrs. Pierce was going down the hall. "Thanks a lot." For a good fifteen minutes, Kerr did what she said then he showered, dressed and applied the ice again. Jim washed his face and hands while he waited for Kerr who had given him a fresh tee shirt to wear. The two men then sat in the front office with an ice cold beverage, discussing what had happened and, what if anything, could or should be done. Jim pledged to return to check for clues and fingerprints. Kerr somehow felt his search would be in vain.

12:30 P.M.

Upon leaving, Jim retrieved a second, powerful flashlight from his cruiser trunk and searched the bottom of the staircase. To his dismay, he found nothing. As he climbed the staircase, he focused his beam on each step looking for some hint, some broken wood piece, any indication of what had been wedged between the door and the railing. As he rounded the top spiral, he could see the blood that had been dripping from Kerr's scalp wound onto the steps. On the attic door was a wide scrape mark where whatever had been wedged against it, had slid upward with the outward thrust of Kerr's body.

Jim thought, *Whoever, or whatever, blocked that door is one smart cookie. Whatever was here is gone now. I don't see even a splinter, if it was wood.*

November 19, 2002—Tuesday
8:30 A.M.

Ed Bristol could not believe Kerr's injury. He volunteered to go with Jim and another officer to recheck the attic and the stairway for clues since he knew the area well from checking for

150

leaks. He stayed behind to clean bloodstains from the floor and the staircase after Kerr and Jim left.

November 28, 2002—Thursday
Thanksgiving Day

Martie had invited her parents for Thanksgiving along with Amy and Mildred. Amy's folks lived in Buffalo, New York, but an early winter storm along the Great Lakes Snow Belt prevented them from driving to Latrobe. While Amy was disappointed, Mildred was particularly happy because she could spend more time with Jim. Even though there was an exciting football game on TV, Jim enjoyed entertaining his young guest. After playing simple board games, and then jacks, Jim asked Mildred to read him a story from one of her books. Amy was afraid Mildred was being pesky, but Jim didn't seem to mind at all. When the tot grew tired she sat beside him and stared at the TV until she fell sound asleep, curled up against him. Martie's parents liked Jim, especially his fondness for children. Several times they alluded that it would be nice if they were grandparents. Jim paid them no mind, but Martie glared at their implications.

At Saint Paul's Rectory, Mrs. Pierce had the day off. Father Walsh was delighted to prepare a complete Thanksgiving dinner at noon. Instead of traditional turkey, he baked Cornish hens for Kerr, Phillip and himself. Of course he cooked a little too much of everything. Afterward, the three men relaxed to watch football, but slowly their conversation turned to the alleged miracle.

Father Kerr reminded the two curates of a thesis in one of his philosophy books back in his seminary days. "*Actio in distans absolute repugnant*" (Nothing can move or occur without cause), I learned in Philosophy One, so teleologically speaking,

151

there must be some explanation. There has to be a cause."

Father Walsh continued to accept the miracle and adored being a curate in a parish where so much excitement continued to build. He loved discussing it with parishioners. Father Phillip, on the other hand, seemed upset—skeptical about the entire affair.

"I think Bishop Mallory's wrong," he said. "I don't know why. Plaster and glass just don't cry."

"Why? Why do you say that? questioned Walsh. "Why? Listen to what you just said. You actually defined what a miracle is—something outside of nature—yet when it happens, you don't believe it. It's like living in contradiction with yourself."

"I know, and that bothers me—a lot; more than you think, Walsh. I'm beginning to think I'm the one that's unreasonable, but my faith just isn't as strong as yours."

Their conversations went on. Interesting—yes. Mind boggling—totally. Conclusive—no.

17 A Voice in Confession

November 30, 2002—Saturday
3:45 P.M.

With so many tourists and with parish membership at an all-time high, Father Kerr and both of his younger curates heard confessions every Saturday from three to five o'clock in the afternoon, and then from six to eight in the evening. On this particular Saturday, the pews outside all three priests' confessionals were already lined with people. "Must have been an enjoyable week," joked Phillip to Walsh as they walked into the church with heads bowed attempting not to make eye contact with penitents. Father Kerr walked a few steps behind. Kerr crossed to the far side of the building then walked straight to his confessional cubicle.

The confessionals at Saint Paul's consisted of two small attached cubicles, each having its own door. The priest sat in one cubicle while the person wishing to confess entered the adjacent one and either sat, stood or knelt while telling their sins. Although a wall separated the two booths, a ten-inch square opening existed between them, covered with a heavy cloth and dark screen. Thus, neither priest nor penitent could see one another. The priest could give absolution if he felt the sinner pledged not to recommit the same sins, was genuinely contrite, and was willing to do penance. Generally, Father Kerr sat bent over a bit, leaning toward the screen on his right with his elbow propped on a small ledge, and his forehead resting on the palm of his hand or his folded knuckles.

Good Catholics were encouraged to confess as often as they felt necessary, but were obligated to confess once each year. On this particular Saturday in early December, Father Kerr was in no way prepared for what he was about to hear when the next person entered his confessional cubicle. At first the person knelt down and was silent.

"Go ahead, please, I'm listening," said Kerr.

Silence.

"Is anyone there? If so, go ahead, please."

An eerie, falsetto-like voice asked, "Father, is it true a priest can't reveal what he hears in confession?"

Kerr was unnerved by the shrieking voice but replied, "Yes, that's true. Are you worried about something?"

"Well, yes. But first, I want to know if you can talk to other priests about what you've heard in confession."

Kerr answered, "I cannot under any circumstances mention anything that is said between you and me to another human being. What is said in here goes no further than this confessional. There are two crossed keys carved into the wood above your door on the outside. They symbolize that what we discuss is locked in here, forever. Now, do you still wish to confess?"

"Yes, Father. It's been several years since my last confession."

"Go on."

Nervously, The Voice shrieked, "I killed someone."

Father Kerr continued sitting in his same position. He blinked his eyes shut.

"Was it an accident?"

"Yes, bu—"

"If it was an accident, then you're not guilty."

"But the accident was my fault."

"Look, if you hit someone with your car by accident, indeed you've killed someone, but you are not guilty in God's eyes."

"That's not the way it was," said the squealing voice.

"Can you tell me what happened so I can help you?" asked Kerr even though The Voice irritated him.

"Father, I caused the accident, hoping the woman would fall."

After a long, thoughtful pause, Kerr queried, "So you pushed her down knowing she'd probably die."

"Well, sort of."

"Was it a high place like a roof or a cliff?"

"It was at the top of a staircase. I never touched her though." There was a long period of silence. Kerr's brain was making electro-chemical connections between what he'd just heard and Sister Lucy's horrifying fall. When Kerr did not respond, The Voice asked, "Are you still there?" Kerr was so astounded that he sat like a statue. He knew he had to respond.

"But you said you didn't touch her."

"No, Father, I waited until I heard her just outside the door where I was hiding, then opened it hoping to knock her off balance."

"And—and you did that?"

"She tumbled backward, all the way down to the bottom and died."

No words came to the pastor's mouth. He sat very still, sweating, his forehead still against his knuckles. Unconsciously, his left hand balled into a tight fist. Many seconds passed as he pictured Lucy's crumpled corpse. He could see the jagged bones from her compound leg fracture.

"Father. I killed a nun!"

Kerr could not talk. He wanted to scream in anger, to cry out, to strike out, to harm this, this evil creature, this thing—in revenge. His hands had balled into fists, his eyes shut, his teeth clenched, his faced screwed into an ugly, purpled, silent fit of rage.

Painfully, he recalled the keys he had just spoken about carved in the ancient mahogany above the confessional. There was nothing he could do, nothing. He could never tell another soul, ever.

Then the murderous voice asked, "Father Kerr, will you give me absolution?"

Other emotions took over; the fists uncoiled, his hands reached for tissues. Kerr was sobbing to himself. One tissue wiped his forehead. The other he raised to wipe his eyes and nose. He pictured the face of dead Lucy.

In a distraught, shaken voice, Kerr managed to say, "To—to—to receive absolution and be forgiven, first you must be sorry"—He paused, sniffled, wiped his nose several times, took a very deep breath and continued—"truly sorry. You must be able to tell me you'll never kill again."

A long pause.

"Can you do that?"

This time, there was a very, very long pause. The Voice was thinking while Father Kerr wept to himself.

"Father, I feel bad the nun died, and I hope I don't have to murder again."

"*WHAT!* What did you just say?" he yelled so loud that penitents waiting outside heard him.

"I—I hope I don't have to kill again."

Silence—utter silence.

Kerr could not think. He could not believe what he had just heard.

"Are telling me you intend to kill again?"

"I don't know right now," shrieked The Voice, "it depends on you."

Kerr wanted to yell, to scream, to grab this horrible, indecent creature.

"Then—your—God—can't—forgive—you. It's that plain—it's that simple, it's that damnable. You—need—to—get—help! You need to get help now! Do it today, before it's too late and you kill a second time. Hear me? Do you understand what I'm saying?"

Silence.

"You need to get help from a professional, a psychiatrist who can help you right now. Do you understand me?"

"I hear you!"

"I am going to slide a card under my door. I know this doctor will see you as soon as you tell him Father Kerr sent you. You must phone right now and go there for help." Again there was a pause.

"Father, I don't want your card."

The Pastor knew he was going to be sick; he took out his red handkerchief and tried to take long, deep breaths to keep from vomiting. He was convinced Lucifer himself was on the other side of the screen, inches from his face.

"What—I—want—is—money." The evil voice creaked on, enunciating each syllable, "I saw that televised production 'The Oculi Incident,' and I'll bet that show brought in lots of cash."

Father Kerr sat aghast keeping his mouth fully covered, trying to keep what was left of his lunch where it belonged.

"Now, listen to everything I say, so I won't have to kill again."

157

The priest's nausea was overwhelming, but Kerr managed to keep swallowing.

"I need ten-thousand dollars right away because of some bills I got. Write out a check for that amount to the Homeless Relief Fund. Stick it in an envelope then go to 237 Second Street this coming Wednesday. That house is empty and up for sale. Put the envelope in the mailbox. Just in case you forget, I'll send these instructions in Monday's mail. I need you to do this for several weeks. So, each week you'll put the check in a different location."

Not just speechless, Kerr felt numb. The priest could not have forced a word from his cotton dry mouth if he wanted to.

"You know I've killed before, and I'd like not to kill again, but that depends on you. So see that the check reaches 237 Second Street by this Wednesday. And most important, I want you to change the password to your church bank fund to '1Satan1' so no one can see that account but you; and of course, don't tell anyone the new password. I hope this is all very clear. Now, since I'd like to be sorry for what I'm doing, give me absolution."

Father Kerr raised both hands and placed them on the screen opposite the fiendish head. He wanted to reach through and squash it, crush it, destroy it. He was convinced it was Satan himself. Barely containing a formidable wrath, Father Kerr began to speak very slowly.

"Nunc et semper Lucifer i ad ignes inferni" (Go! Burn in the fires of Hell forever, Lucifer!)

Having no idea what the priest said, The Voice said, "Thank you, Father," and walked out of the cubicle. In the corner of his confessional booth, the priest kept a small, tin waste can. He could not hold back any longer; he grabbed the can and retched furiously.

A woman who had entered and was waiting to confess asked loudly, "Father Kerr, Father Kerr, do you need help?"

Without waiting for an answer, she left her cubicle and opened Kerr's door. He was slumped over in his seat holding the can on his lap.

"Father, I'll get some help." With that, she turned and hurried away.

Penitents in pews stared at the open confessional door. In spite of the putrid vomit stench, several adults came to comfort Kerr. Children, of course, scrambled away.

"I'm—I'm okay," he said to those who gathered around; "—must've been something I ate—just don't call an ambulance —please—I feel better now."

He stood up trembling, did the best he could to wipe off the front of his cassock, apologized for the awful mess, then picked up his trash can and walked toward the sacristy. Several people walked along on each side of him supporting his arms. As he reached the sacristy, Mrs. Pierce was already there. Having heard the commotion, Father Walsh left his confessional.

"What on earth happened?" asked Mrs. Pierce. She turned to Walsh. "Go get your car. We'll take him to the emergency room."

"No, no, NO! Stop everyone. Maybe I have the flu or something. But I'm fine, I'd just like to go over and shower. I feel much better now."

Frightened Mrs. Pierce persisted, "I'll call your doctor and explain."

"No, for heaven's sake, no. I just got sick like a little school kid and threw up."

With that authoritative, almost annoyed statement, Kerr

walked over to the rectory. His penitents moved back to Father Phillip's confessional. When Father Walsh could not locate the custodian, he rolled out a bucket and a mop from the utility room and cleaned up. A strong disinfectant covered the stench of vomit.

It was impossible for Kerr to stop obsessing about the satanic voice. *Why it was like some maniacal force so near my own head. I can't imagine anyone being that evil. And now, now the worst travesty of all, the fiend wants church money, or, or he'll kill again.* Kerr pictured all the new monies pouring into church coffers as desecrated lucre, contaminated by this satanic creature's desire for it. *What if this, this so called Oculi miracle really is a scheme of the Underworld incarnate, not our Heavenly Father!*

Alerted by loud pounding the pastor stepped out of the shower, pulled on his robe, walked over and opened his bedroom door. "It's just me, Father," said a worried Mrs. Pierce. "I wanted to make sure you're all right. Are you?"

"Yes. Thanks for your concern. Yes. Maybe I'll rest up a bit before coming down. Maybe you could even hold my phone calls for a few hours."

As soon as Pierce left, Kerr heard other footsteps approaching his room. It was Phillip, trailed by Walsh.

"You gave us quite a scare," said Walsh. "And we all agree that you should go and have a complete physical. Get your ticker checked out. Make sure you're okay."

"For real, I'm quite okay. I feel fine now."

"But puking for no reason can be a symptom of many conditions," said Father Phillip.

"Fathers, listen to me. I—know—why—I—got sick."

Phillip and Walsh looked at one another as if they understood.

Reluctantly, the two priests turned and walked away.

Phillip stared at Walsh and said, "We'll never know what happened in his confessional today."

The Pastor lay down across his bed in a bathrobe and wept bitterly.

December 10, 2002—Tuesday
9:00 A.M.

Kerr sat in the front parlor with the door shut. He began rethinking all he'd been taught in the seminary about the sacrament of Penance. He tried to think of ways to stop the madness that engulfed him. But deep in is heart, he could not escape his belief in the Seal of Confession. Events of the past months rolled through his mind.

"Father, Father Kerr, didn't you hear me?" asked Mrs. Pierce. Would you like your morning cup of coffee?" Pierce worried that maybe the pastor had suffered a stroke that had affected his hearing, until he answered, "I'd love to have some. Did the mail come yet?"

"Yes, I'll bring it."

First she brought in a tray containing a cup of steaming coffee, a sugar bowl and spoon, and a miniature cream pitcher. Returning to the hall, she gathered up the mail that had fallen through the door slot, squared it off and sat it beside his coffee tray.

"I'll be in the kitchen if you need anything else."

"Thank you."

As he sifted through the pile of mail, an envelope with no return address caught his eye. He ripped it open. Inside he found a folded sheet of paper addressed:

The Homeless Relief Fund
237 Second Street
Latrobe, PA 15650

Father Kerr switched on his computer and waited while it booted up. When he arrived at the AOL home page, he called Mrs. Pierce. *Darn, I'm so nervous I've forgotten how to get from AOL to the church bank account. I hope she remembers.*

"Up here, Father, where it says 'My Favorites.'"

"Oh, yes. Now, I remember."

As the menu unfolded, he slid the cursor down to "Latrobe City Bank" and clicked. Before long the bank's home page opened. Then he clicked "My Account," and once again plugged in his social security number and his Latin password "*semper.*" Mrs. Pierce looked over his shoulder. "I'd like to change my password," he said. "The bank recommends I do it often. I've forgotten how to do that."

"Well, how about clicking over here." She pointed to another box on the screen that simply said, "Change Password."

"Geez, I didn't even see that box." As the screen asked for his old password, Kerr said, "Mrs. Pierce, would you mind heating up my coffee? I know I can handle the rest of this."

As soon as she left he typed in "*semper,*" then in the new password box, he typed "1Satan1". Below it, he typed "1Satan1" in the confirmation box and clicked "Change." He brought up the church's account, looked it over, exited and signed off. Mrs. Pierce brought in his coffee just as he was getting out his checkbook ledger.

"Here you are, Father. This should pick up your spirits a bit."

"We all have our down days, Mrs. Pierce, I'm okay. Your coffee will definitely make me feel better." As she left again,

Kerr wrote out a check for ten-thousand dollars to the Homeless Relief Fund, and placed it in a plain, white envelope. He put it face down on top of his desk, and then wrote "WEDNESDAY" on it with a red marker in very large letters.

From the kitchen, Mrs. Pierce called, "Come get something to eat. Your breakfast is ready."

"I'm not hungry, Mrs. Pierce. I just can't eat!"

18 A Guilty Stare

Each Wednesday, Father Kerr celebrated the eight o'clock morning Mass. He had exchanged with Phillip claiming he had urgent business to attend to each Wednesday for the next few weeks. Phillip was more than happy to help the pastor who had become quite sullen, quiet, even depressed. He had talked to both Mrs. Pierce and Father Walsh about the dramatic change in Kerr's demeanor. The pastor looked gaunt, acted withdrawn, and barely ate even though Mrs. Pierce tempted his palate by preparing his favorite meals. "I'm just not in the mood to eat," he would say. "I think I might have a stomach virus or something."

At 237 Second Street, a realtor's sign hung on a post in the yard. It was in front of a large, well-kept, newly painted home, an attractive piece of real estate. After parking by the curb, the priest sat a moment. Then with utter determination he mounted the eight steps to the porch and deposited the envelope containing the ten-thousand-dollar blackmail check into the mailbox on the right side of the entrance door. As he walked back to his automobile, a next-door neighbor popped her head out and called over to him. "Hello, Reverend. Those folks moved out several weeks ago."

165

Without an explanation for why he'd be up on the porch, Kerr said, "I wondered why there was no answer." He feigned interest by asking, "Do you know where they moved?"

"Yes, they were good friends of ours. We still keep in contact with one another. They moved to Chester, Virginia. Would you like their new address?"

"Yes, that would be helpful." He walked back up on the porch and reopened the mailbox as if to retrieve what he had left there, just in case the neighbor had seen him drop the envelope in the mail slot. He took nothing out, but reached into his inside suit pocket as if replacing something. By this time, the woman next door brought out a card on which she'd written an address. He thanked her, walked over to his car and drove away.

December 16, 2002—Monday
4:00 P.M.

Jim picked up Martie after school because they wanted to stop at Ed's appliance store to ask about their washing machine. For the past few days, it had been making disturbing noises, and this morning, it did nothing but sit and hum. It would fill with water, but would not agitate, empty, or spin. The clothes just sat in the dirty water. Martie wanted to ask Ed about servicing the old machine or perhaps buying a new one since theirs was nine years old.

In addition to being the custodian for Saint Paul's parish, Ed Bristol owned and operated a successful appliance store on Main Street in Latrobe. One of the reasons Kerr had first hired him was his adeptness at fixing things and Kerr's church was in dire need of repair. With little money, Ed Bristol had done his best to keep the old parish buildings functioning.

While driving to Ed's Appliance Store, Martie called ahead to make sure he was there, but was told he was down at the church. Jim parked outside while Martie walked in. "I'll be just a few minutes," she said, walking away from the cruiser.

Inside, a large number of people were scattered about in pews near the middle aisle: parishioners, tourists, and curiosity seekers who had decided to visit the church because they were passing through on the Pennsylvania Turnpike. Latrobe was about twenty-four miles northeast of the toll road, so a side trip to see the famous crucifix was well worth the effort.

Some people knelt. Some sat in pews and stared at the suspended cross. Everyone who visited for the first time would walk to the front center aisle to look down at the floor where the droplets had collected. A clean white linen handkerchief had been placed over the spot. To Catholics who'd sat in these pews and bore witness to the tears, this was hallowed ground.

Upon entering, Martie saw Bristol working across the church in one of its transepts. These were now lined with so many rows of candles that it was difficult to occupy any but the first few pews. Large votive lights started at floor level and then rose on tiers, until they stood eight deep, each row rising a few inches above the one in front.

The lower part of the sanctuary and the entire main vestibule were likewise filled with the flickering candles. A double row lined the outside walls along both sides of the church except where the confessionals booths interrupted them. The effect of all the dancing flames was spectacular. Bristol would work his way around the church collecting monies as he went. If it wasn't for the daily assistance of Sister Margaret, Father Walsh and Phillip working with a handful of parishioners, his task would have been hopeless. Father Walsh relished the job. He liked being in the church near the crucifix. Phillip despised this chore. It was a thorn to real ministry and it interrupted mindful reading and study.

Anchored to the floor in several conspicuous places were large "Offering" receptacles with signs suggesting a five-dollar donation for the "Free" candles. The custodian had a four wheeled cart that stood eight inches off the floor with a warehouse dolly handle at one end. Bolted to the cart was a steel case with a slot on top into which he and the volunteers dumped money from the offering boxes. Ushers did the same during Sunday Mass collections. The slot was large enough to allow coins and bills to fall through, but not a hand. Painted on each side of the box was the word "Offerings." The size and bulk of the monstrous repository suggested it would be very hard to steal.

Ed was hard at work when Martie walked over to him and whispered, "Hello, Ed, I need to talk to you. Got a minute?"

"Sure, hang on a second."

He reinserted the door of the Donations Box he had emptied, locked it in place then stood up several inches taller than Martie.

"This place keeps me quite busy. So what seems to be the problem?"

"My washer is broken."

"Your washer? That's it? You just want me to fix your washer?"

Martie smiled, "Should there be something else? Am I missing something here?"

Ed shrugged off his initial response. "No, no, so tell me, what doesn't it do?" he asked.

"For starters, it doesn't do anything. I put in a load of soiled clothes this morning, added soap, set the dials and went upstairs to finish dressing for school. When I came back down expecting to put things in the dryer, the washing machine was still filled with water, and the clothes were just sitting there."

Ed thought for a moment. "Could be a number of things. How old is it?"

"At least nine years."

"Well, Martie, I'd have to come over and have a look. I don't get to my store like I used to, let alone make service calls."

"If you can't make it, I'll try to find someone else."

"No, no," said Ed, "but how about this? I have a clever young fellow who runs my store for me. I can get Andre to stop over. He's a mechanical whiz."

"Well, if it's no bother—"

"He'll come over," insisted Bristol. "What time can you be there tomorrow?"

"I finish school around three-thirty, so if he's there around four that would be great."

"Andre is a smart young man. You'll like him."

"Ed, just a bit ago, you seemed apprehensive when I said I needed to talk with you. Am I right?"

"I don't know. I'm not sure where you're coming from." Ed's mood turned serious.

"You sounded surprised that all I wanted was to have my washer fixed."

"Oh, I thought maybe you were going to ask me some questions about that horrible stairway because of poor Sister Lucy."

Martie was taken aback, "Sister Lucy?" Surprised, she gasped audibly and covered her mouth with her hand.

"Sister Lucy, yes! I understand you were with her when she fell down the stairs."

"Yes, God bless her. But Ed, why would I be asking you about her?"

"Because as the custodian, I knew that staircase was not in good condition. The steps are hazardous. There needs to be a handrail running up the inside. I feel bad about that." Then he locked his eyes on hers in a way that made her uncomfortable. "I'm curious, Martie, what were you and Lucy doing way up there anyway? I had locked the church for the night."

Feeling guilty, Martie was caught off guard. She averted the huge man's gaze and shook her head while tears welled in her eyes. "Lucy thought she might see an apparition. She thought maybe there were angels up there, maybe even the Holy Spirit."

"And you believed her?"

"Well no, Ed. Actually, we thought we saw flashes of light in that rose win—" A flood of tears rolled down Martie's face as the dreadful accident flashed through her mind.

"Geez, I'm sorry Martie." He quit staring at her and looked down, and then back at Martie's sad face. She had taken out a tissue and was drying her cheeks. "It must have been an awful experience for you. I didn't mean to appear rude. I'm sorry; really I am."

"It's okay, Ed," she said, wiping her nose with a tissue.

"But listen, the next time, ask me first and we'll go up during daylight."

"I won't ever go up there again. I can promise you that." Martie then changed the subject back to the original reason for approaching Ed. "So this fellow, Andre, will be coming tomorrow at four?"

"Yep, I'll make sure of it."

Martie sniffed, "Thanks, Ed. Sorry about the tears," and left the building.

Once back in Jim's cruiser, Martie explained the gist of her brief visit with the custodian.

"Jim, I can't explain it, but that man made me feel bad."

"Hey, Babe, look at me." He lifted her chin and turned her face toward his. "You were crying. What happened?"

"Ed asked why Lucy and I were up on those stairs, I felt really stupid—and guilty."

"I'm sorry, Honey. I should have gone in instead of you."

"Jim, now how would you know he'd ask about that? I just never expected it. I'm probably supersensitive because of Lucy's death."

"Nevertheless, Ed is big enough to frighten anyone."

"No, it's just me. Ed is Kerr's friend. I shouldn't have been so sensitive. That's a woman for you."

19 A Vietnam File

Martie's interpretation of her conversation last night with Ed, bothered Jim. He also knew his wife was very sensitive about anything dealing with Lucy's death. He knew that deep inside, her feelings remained in turmoil.

Jim had heard of Kerr's deepening sadness and depression. Since he was patrolling the streets of Latrobe in the area near Saint Paul's Church, he decided to visit Kerr. The two men stood in the front hall.

"I've got to be honest with you, Father," said Jim, "People are worried. You've been very down and I've been wondering about that. You look like you're losing weight."

"I have been blue lately, very blue."

"Father Kerr, as a friend and as a police officer, if I'm to help, I need you to level with me."

"Well?"

"Do you by any chance know more about what's been happening around here than you've been telling me? Are there things I should know abou—"

Without thinking, the priest burst out, "Damn, it's just that I hope you catch that murdering monster." Jim stood rock still.

"What? What did you say, Father?" Kerr realized what he'd

said and tried to cover.

"Sorry, didn't mean to cuss."

"No, no, that's not what I meant. Did you say 'murder?'" pressed Jim, "I don't remember saying anything about murder. Shit, Father, what aren't telling me?"

Kerr decided to be as honest as possible. "There are things priests can't reveal, even under pain of death."

Jim caught on. He knew the priest was referring to confession because he used to be a practicing Catholic.

"Tell me this. Is it possible that a murderer confessed to you?" asked Jim. "Can't you at least tell me that?"

Kerr was cornered. He could answer neither yes or no.

Quickly, he said, "Jim, we need to talk about something else."

Holy hell, thought Jim, *what kind of deadly secrets is this man hiding? It's no wonder he's depressed.* Jim knew there was no sense prying, but the pastor's response truly unnerved him.

Then Kerr changed the subject. "Jim, I've told you what I can. What bothers me most is, when those drops appear, I become more and more mystified. Each time I leave the altar and go down and stand beneath that cross, I see a crying statue. It's like looking at a magic trick over and over again."

"With no magician!"

"Let me tell you a short story," started Kerr. "A few years ago, I watched a magician perform on a small platform set up at the convention center in downtown Pittsburgh. His act was to attract people into the General Motors' exhibit area. He'd perform a bit, and then quit so the crowd that had gathered around him would mull around the new cars.

"He had these solid rings. I counted them with him, as did the crowd. There were nine, shiny, solid, steel rings. I saw them with my own eyes. Yet, I watched him connect and disconnect them at will right in front of me. I was five feet away, maybe less, and frustrated. He handed two connected rings to me and asked, 'Would you take these apart for me, please?'

"I tried mind you. I hunted for some kind of tiny crack so I could unhook them. After a moment, this magician took the same two rings, asked me to hold one of them, and slid the other one away—disconnected. I was standing right there; I saw it happen; I knew I'd been had; it seemed impossible; he did it.

"So, I returned again and again to the same ten-minute performance. I watched; I saw; but to this day—to this very day, I don't understand. And I know that magician wasn't performing any miracle. Now, that's how I feel about the tearing crucifix. I've seen those drops form. Impossible, yet it continues to happen and I don't believe it. It's a gut reaction."

Changing the topic a bit, Jim asked, "What kind of person is Ed Bristol? He upset Martie by making her feel guilty about going up the attic steps. I'm just curious about his background."

"Jim, when he applied for the job as custodian fifteen years ago, I pitied him because of the years he had spent in Vietnam. I knew he had his appliance business here in Latrobe. He had plenty of customers and I'm sure he has a respectable income, now. He has a small home and car, plus a business truck. When he interviewed, he seemed keenly interested in working here as caretaker. It was as if he needed to be around the church for some reason, maybe some spiritual shot in the arm after our defeat in Vietnam."

"Hmmmm."

"But, you know what? Talking with him, I felt guilty because while he was spilling his guts facing guerrillas, I chose the safe route—to study for the priesthood—rather than volunteer to serve my country."

"I knew he was your friend."

"When the Vietnam conflict broke out in '55, we were seven years old. We used to play soldiers as kids, running and chasing each other like we were battling the enemy. We piled up rocks and wood for our make believe fort. Behind it, we dug a foxhole to flop down into. It was only a couple inches deep. Our parents discussed the war, but we didn't understand it. Who would've dreamed that twelve years later in 1967, we'd sit and discuss US involvement in that war.

"Then one evening while we sat in front of the TV watching draft numbers get picked, as luck would have it, Ed's number was picked. Again and again I squeaked by. I even thought about enlisting, but entered Saint Vincent's Seminary instead. Would I have served if my number had been picked? Sure, just like Ed. But my luck held and I copped out."

"What do you mean copped out? What kind of talk is that?"

"My inspiration was to become a Catholic priest. Even as a kid, I wanted to bring Christ's message to the world. That Man preached peace, justice, love. He desired to bring about a brotherhood of mankind. This was an awesome task for Christ, but that's what I wanted for my life's work, too. I believed in Him and His message that all may be one. Nam was opposed to that Man's message of love and unity."

"Father, what you do outweighs your feelings about not serving your country. You are serving for a lifetime; Ed served for a few years."

"Jim, when Ed came back, he was a changed man. He was anxious, suspicious of others extremely aggressive; often very depressed. He was suffering, mentally. When he interviewed, I thought working around Saint Paul's might ease some of his pain. Heaven only knows what horrors he went through while I was safely studying at Saint Vincent's Monastery. He told me he received a Purple Heart, but he has never mentioned his injury or the atrocities of war."

After hearing Kerr's story, Jim sat for quite some time in utter silence. The priest stared downward. Jim said, "You are too hard on yourself, Father. Think of the number of people you've touched and helped toward a better life, a better understanding of themselves. You didn't 'cop out' as you put it. I think you are a one-of-a-kind person, a good, solid man who has given his life to help others find the peace Christ preached about. There is no way I could ever walk in your shoes."

Kerr raised his head a bit. "Thanks, Jim, I needed that. If you only knew how much I needed to hear that."

10:45 A.M.

Officer Simmons dialed Henry Collins, who worked at the Federal Building in downtown Pittsburgh. In the past, Henry had called several times for favors, knowing that Jim was an encyclopedia with police procedural matters, a good resource for knowing how to snip red tape. Now, Jim phoned to ask his friend a favor.

"Hello?" answered Henry on the second ring, "Collins here."

"Henry, Baby," said Jim, "good to hear your voice. How you doing down there?"

"Question is, how you doing up there with all that e-y-e stuff going on? Everyone seems to be talking about it. One of our secretaries drove up to Latrobe for a Sunday service last week. She had to listen to the ceremony through a loudspeaker. She was outside in the street.

"It's true, Henry. Every Sunday, miracle hysteria breaks out and droves of people arrive. We've had chartered buses come during the early afternoon filled with people who sit for hours just to make sure they have an inside seat."

"Maybe I should come up there. You could let me in just so Saint Paul's would have its minority quota," teased Henry.

"Hey, smartass! Latrobe is a highly integrated place. It just so happens that on the tour bus I told you about, well, half were blacks," said Jim.

"You're shittin' me, man!" exclaimed Henry. "I used to think only white people were crazy. Anyway, what can I do for you?"

"Can you do a background check on a former Vietnam army veteran?"

"Is he part of your mystery?"

"No, just checking him out. His name is Ed Bristol. I know he served in Vietnam around 1970. B-r-i-s-t-o-l. Got that?"

"Tell you what, I'll get on it this afternoon and call you tomorrow because I have a conference to attend in about ten minutes."

"Great. Thanks," said Jim. "Be waiting to hear from you."

"Will call. And solve that Oculi mystery. Earn your money, man."

December 18, 2002—Wednesday
9:40 A.M.

Henry phoned the following morning. "Jim, this Ed Bristol fellow has quite an interesting file. Any chance of you driving down to look it over?"

"You sound secretive," said Jim.

"Well, I'm not supposed to dig into personal records, or release information. I'd rather discuss the matter with you in person."

"Fair enough. I'll ask the chief if I can drive down this afternoon. How does two o'clock sound?"

Henry said, "I'll make it work, buddy. I owe you a few anyway."

After the chief okayed his trip, Jim left a message on Martie's voice mail telling her where he'd gone. He left his cruiser in the Federal Building garage and rode the elevator to the fifteenth floor.

"Well, look at him would you, all dressed up in a uniform," said Henry. "And me in my short sleeves and jeans. Anyway, nice to see you, Jim. "

"Pleasure's mine." Henry led the way through an area sectioned into cubicles, each with someone working at a computer terminal. "Wow, a busy place you got here."

At an office in the back, he tapped lightly on the glass door. Jim saw the man inside motion them to come in.

"Brant, this is a friend of mine from mysterious Latrobe, Jim Simmons," said Henry.

Brant Hardy vigorously shook Jim's hand then sat down in a chair next to Jim's. He did not resemble a person double Jim's age.

"Jim, Brant served with Bristol, so I'll leave you two here and get back to work," said Henry, "maybe I'll get home on time for a change."

"Have a seat, Officer Simmons; Henry told me what you were looking for."

"Jim, Brant, just call me Jim."

"Sure."

"Back in '74, Ed and I and another man named Schaler all served in the same unit. I was terrified. Combat was much different than combat training. We were scared shitless as our copter lowered to the ground, nudging it for just a few seconds. All around us we could hear the sound of gunfire and exploding shells. Bullets actually hit out chopper—*ping-zing, ping-zing.* I can still hear them.

"When we were ordered out, Ed, Schaler and I ran pell-mell hunting shelter: tree trunks, large boulders, clumps of rocks, or mere shallow dips in the earth. Everywhere there was noise and the pinging of striking bullets. We lost sight of Schaler but Ed and I ran alongside a much smaller lad. Like the rest of us, he was terrified.

Not even a minute had passed before a deafening concussion overwhelmed us. For a few seconds, I couldn't see. Dust and chunks of slimy, red, gooey, dripping matter that had once been the body of the lad running beside us, covered us. We wiped our eyes, but then I saw a large bloodstain below Ed's waistline. He tripped, fell to the ground and rolled as we'd been taught, slamming against a huge boulder. The leg he tripped over belonged to a second, youthful body lying face up.

"'Schaler; holy shit man, you've been hit,' shouted Ed above the torrent of deadly noises all around us. The downed soldier didn't answer. 'Christ, you've got a gash in your skull.' Ignoring the pain in his abdomen, Ed pulled Schaler toward him and then looked up to see the chopper dropping from the sky.

"Shit, the bird's been hit, I shouted; it's coming down right on us. But the courageous chopper pilot had never left the area. He had seen what happened. Ed picked up unconscious Schaler and dashed for the lowering chopper. A bullet ripped through my right foot but we kept moving. Ed started to stumble badly so I did my best to help him reach the chopper. Since he was too weak to lift Schaler inside, I hopped aboard and held onto unconscious Schaler lying atop Ed's arms. The chopper became airborne. The pilot had already lifted at top speed and was flying away from the killing field."

Jim could say nothing.

"To make a long story short," Brant went on, "the three of us survived." Schaler had suffered a concussion and a severed leg artery; shrapnel damaged Ed's groin area so badly that Surgeons removed his testicles. My foot, thankfully, healed more quickly. The bullet went straight through flesh and bone without breaking any bones. I was lucky." Brant fell silent as if he had just relived the horrible memory.

"Was that it for you three?"

"We were supposed to go stateside but Ed refused; said he was going back to kill enemy—just kill and kill and make them suffer. Not just for what happened to him, but because he felt the vaporized body of the little GI running with us, saved our lives. He had taken the full brunt of a land mine."

"Did you three stay in contact after the war?"

"For a while we did, but you know how it is, over time, I gradually lost contact with Schaler and Ed—maybe a Christmas card each year. Schaler and Ed stayed close friends." Brant grinned. "I remember those two lying in their hospital beds concocting the most outlandish get-rich schemes. They used to make me laugh."

"Did any of you get counseling after the war?"

"Not really. Ed could have used it."

"How so?"

"The war changed Ed's personality. He became bitter, reckless, hateful. During the few times we got together, Ed talked like a man haunted with death. He refused to marry. He wasn't impotent, mind you, just sterile—knew he could never have kids."

"Wow," said Jim. "You've painted more of a picture for me than I asked for. I can't imagine what I'd've done in combat. The three of you had terrific courage and I admire you—I thank you for that."

6:30 P.M.

That evening after dinner, Jim had explained his visit to the Federal Building earlier in the day.

Martie said, "Since neither of us was around when that war started. I must confess I don't know much about it."

"Well, Brant served in that conflict. He talked to me about events that still haunt him today. It must've been a horrifying experience! From some of the things Brant said, I'd believe Ed Bristol could be a dangerous person. Now, I didn't ask much about Schaler. Brant said that he wanted to be a scientist, and that he had a brilliant mind."

"So, what are you thinking?"

"Crazy thoughts like I wonder if Ed Bristol and Schaler ever teamed up together? Brant said they intended to stay friends. I wonder if they did."

Jim sat thoughtfully silent for a few moments before adding, "I also wonder what nightmarish, confessed secrets Father Kerr must be living with?"

"Jim, your day has been much too long." Martie pouted her lips sensually, "If you come to bed with me, I know I can massage your stress away. There's plenty of baby oil in there."

"Yummie! I'd love a nice back rub."

"You think that's all I'm going to rub?" asked Martie.

20 Death of a Washer

Christmas was Martie's favorite holiday. She decorated their home with a variety of snowmen she had accumulated over the years. Jim purchased a huge, eight-foot high, blow-up, illuminated snowman for their front yard as an addition to her collection. It was the largest in the neighborhood. Martie insisted they have a real Christmas tree, because she liked the pine smell, and each year it was a different challenge to decorate. She would light it with hundreds of tiny, white bulbs. She also placed a single, white candle in each window facing Elm Street.

She and Jim had a very private, sensual, holiday together. That morning, Jim awoke before Martie and prepared breakfast. It consisted of scrambled eggs, sausage, pieces of rye toast, coffee, and a small bowl of mandarin oranges, all of which he carried in on a large, silver tray. He placed the tray between the two of them on the bed, and they devoured everything.

Since it snowed a bit the day before, they took a drive through some of the back roads between Latrobe and Ligonier enjoying the quiet, serene, beauty of the snow covered countryside. They parked near the stream where they had jumped in to swim naked several years ago. Christmas tunes played on the radio. For a few moments, they stood along the stream's edge embracing.

Jim said, "You're not thinking what I'm thinking, are you?" They stopped embracing and backed away from the icy stream.

"Don't even think about it, Jim Simmons. Don't you dare! You're not throwing me in there."

"I promise I won't if you promise, too."

The heavy snow squalls caused driving to became more treacherous than fun, so they returned home. As soon as they removed all of their wet outerwear and changed clothes, they lit the gas logs and sat by their Christmas tree.

Martie continued reading a mystery novel she had started several days earlier. Jim continued working on the daily Latrobe Gazette crossword puzzle while music played in the background. For whatever reason, Martie walked to the basement, noticed a pile of dirty laundry and put it in the washing machine. She had gone back upstairs when they both heard a loud squealing sound coming from downstairs.

"Oh, it's just that old washer, Jim, It's been making that noise a lot lately."

But the squeal was followed by a noxious burning smell. By the time they descended the steps, thick, acrid smoke was pouring from the rear of the washer. Although it had just been repaired a week ago, the old machine just sat there smoking. It had served Martie well before Jim moved in, and for quite some time afterward doing double duty.

But the young man Ed Bristol had sent to repair it last week had told Martie, "Ms. Meyer, this machine is on its last legs. I've replaced the worn drive belt, but that funny odor you sense in the basement is coming from the motor coils. If this machine had three feet, two of them would already be in the grave. The motor is overheating and one day soon, it will *fry* and *die*." She recalled the young man laughing at his own poetic rhyming.

"I guess that's the end of it, Martie."

"She's lasted a long, long time, but you know, tomorrow may be a good day to buy a new one. Everyone who is anyone goes shopping the day after Christmas looking for bargains."

"Great idea. Let's walk to Bristol's and look at his washers? Maybe that young fellow who was so comical will wait on us."

December 26, 2002—Thursday
10:15 A.M.

Jim and Martie walked down to Ed's Appliance Store hunting their bargain. Schools were closed for the week, and Jim had the day off. It was snowing and the spirit of the Christmas season lingered. Martie was hoping the big man himself wouldn't be in his store for two reasons: she was leery of him after their conversation two Monday's ago, and she wanted the young repairman who had serviced her old machine to get credit for a sale.

As they first entered the store, Andre, the young African-American walked up and said, "Happy holidays! May she rest in peace?"

Jim bowed his head and reverently said, "She's passed! She's passed on to another life. Got any after Christmas bargains?"

"Well, we may not have bargain basement prices, but our washers are good machines. Take for example this one over here is $394.89. It has three cycles: regular, wash-n-wear and delicate. You can select a low, medium or high water level. It has self-leveling, rear legs; and it will chime when your wash is done," said Andre. A machine to the right of the one Andre just described actually looked like its twin. Price tag: $489.95.

"How come this one's so much more?" asked Martie, comparing the two.

"Um, this one comes with a three-pronged plug," roared

185

the young man as he watched the expressions on their faces. "Yep, that one there has a two-pronged plug, this one here has three!"

"So, would we need an adapter for the cheaper one?" asked Jim playing along with the hilarious, young man.

Martie joined in the fun, "I'll bet that adapter costs as much as the difference between the two machines."

"You got it, they're damn expensive, especially the shipping freight." With that remark, the threesome laughed hysterically. "Seriously, folks, this one has a much larger washtub and an industrial, heavy-duty motor. That's the real difference."

"Now, over here—"

But just as Andre was about to show them other models, Mr. Bristol came out from the backroom. He had heard the laughter. As soon as he entered the showroom, Andre's demeanor changed. His face became very serious, and his good-natured smile evaporated.

"I'll take it from here," said Ed. Andre left for the workroom in back. "Well, do you want to look around by yourselves or can I point out the different features each machine has?"

"Actually," said Martie, "I like the very first machine Andre showed us. Can you deliver it?"

"Sure thing; how else would it get there," quipped Bristol. "There will be a slight delivery charge."

"Fine," sighed Martie as if she hadn't sensed the sarcasm in Bristol's remark.

When Ed walked behind his counter to write up the bill, Martie whispered to Jim, "This man could learn some social skills from that young fellow who's got an adorable sense of humor."

"Agreed!"

Martie's check for $438.63 included the Pennsylvania sales tax of seven percent, plus the twenty-dollar delivery fee. She handed the check to Ed Bristol, who carefully scrutinized it.

"I'll have my boy deliver it tomorrow morning if that's okay with you folks?"

Martie just couldn't help herself, "A boy? Jim, did you see a boy in here? Ed, how could a young boy deliver that heavy machine?"

"I'm talking about Andre. He was waiting on you before I came in."

Then she grinned. "Oh, Andre, you know he's a delightful *man*." She deliberately stressed the word. "What a great sense of humor that man has. Thank that man for us, will you Ed?"

"I will. And, thanks for the business." Martie doubted Ed Bristol would thank Andre.

I wonder—thought Jim, *I wouldn't want to start a fuss, but it's worth a try."*

As they were about to leave, Jim threw out a fishhook to Ed Bristol, "By the way, how's your friend Schaler these days?"

Unfortunately, Ed was so focused on arranging his cash register and looking over Martie's check, so he only half-way heard Jim's comment at first. Then, as if a hammer had slammed his chin from below and had snapped his head upward, Ed stood there, his mouth clamped shut, his eyes locked on Jim's. After a moment of complete silence, which made all three of them edgy, Ed asked, "What—did—you—say?"

As he walked out from behind his counter, his normally stolid face appeared flushed.

"I'm sure he's fine, but I haven't seen him for quite a while. We were close friends back in our army days," he quipped, as if to hide his discomfort. Without another word, he walked into the backroom.

"Merry Christmas, and thanks, Andre," sang Martie in her cheeriest voice.

With a slight nod and smile, they walked out into the snow, closing the door behind them quietly.

10:45 A.M.

Both waited until they were clear of the store before speaking. Martie spoke first.

"Did you see that reaction?"

"Sure did—I was just fishing, but the bait must have had a nasty taste. He seemed upset."

"Upset? First he looked like he'd seen a ghost, then as his face reddened, he looked almost angry."

Jim said, "Schaler's name struck a sour chord somewhere in his brain."

"Last week after you came back from Pittsburgh, I remember you mentioning that Ed and Schaler, and that other fellow you talked with, were all pals in combat during the Vietnam war."

"You've got a good memory, Martie. The other man was Brant Hardy."

The two did some other bargain shopping. Just about every store in downtown Latrobe had some kind of after Christmas sale. By the time they arrived home, Martie's car trunk was filled with marked down items. She bought several new skirts, blouses, pantsuits, and some items needed for school.

Jim had purchased several pairs of Dockers and jeans. From the Latrobe Hobby Store, he bought two boxcars and two oil tankers to go with one of his freight trains. During the time since he and Martie moved in together, Jim had built an O-gauge train layout in their finished basement den. It was four feet wide and twelve feet long.

That afternoon, they disconnected their old washer, and with the aid of a dolly, Jim and Martie managed to get it through the basement door and out onto the driveway where they parked it for easy pickup when the new washer woud arrive tomorrow.

"I hope Ed doesn't deliver it since you won't be here," said Martie. "Something about that man is creepy. I hope Andre brings it."

December 27, 2002—Friday
9:15 A.M.

The following morning Martie got her wish. It was a cloudless day, but still bitter cold outside. The sun on the snow made the day dazzling bright. Martie sat by her Christmas tree enjoying the holiday break perusing a magazine. The telephone rang and when Martie picked it up, a cheerful voice said, "I'm about to deliver, if you don't mind playing midwife, I'll be right over with your new baby."

"I'll put on some hot water," joked Martie. Within fifteen minutes, a small delivery truck parked in her driveway. With little effort, Andre slid the washer onto the tailgate of the truck then lowered it to the ground hydraulically. At this point, Martie came out and helped him tilt it to one side so he could slide his dolly under the heavy machine. "I was expecting the stork."

"Ms., I am the stork and you got yourself a heavy baby here. Even so, it's pretty quiet, so it won't keep you up nights." They rolled the new machine into her basement. Andre connected the hot and cold water supply hoses, hooked the drain hose over a laundry tub, plugged in the cord then handed Martie the instruction booklet along with a small box of free laundry detergent. As effortlessly as he had brought in the new washer, muscular Andre hoisted the old one aboard his delivery truck and strapped it in place.

"Whatever do you do with old dead machines like ours?"

"We strip them of any usable parts and when we have a truckload, we cart them to the Turtle Creek Landfill. There they get crushed and buried with a lot of other garbage in between layers of dirt and rock."

"Well, she needs to be buried because she's dead. Anyway, thanks, Andre." Just before he drove away, Martie walked to the driver's side and handed him a twenty-dollar bill. "This if for you and your delightful holiday cheer. Thanks again."

"Thank you, Ms.," he said. "Glad to help. Remember, in this business, your dirt is our bread and butter!" After that ridiculous comment, Andre pulled away. Martie walked inside shaking her head. *That man's good humor is infectious.*

2:15 P.M.

At the Latrobe Police Department worked a young woman named Sylvia Keyes, an African-American secretarial eyeful who could make things happen. People phoned Jim or Chief Romeric thinking they were the ones who could cut red tape.

In reality, it wasn't them at all. They would get their information from Sylvia, who knew who to call, what form to fill out, what keys to hit on the computer, what political figure to sway, and where to go for the cheapest prices.

Jim was on his way out of the borough building. As he walked by Sylvia Keyes' desk, she held up her hand and said, "Wait just a minute." Sylvia was on the phone, but quickly ended her conversation. "Hello there, Gumshoe. This time I need some help."

"You don't say! I thought you knew just about everyone and

everything."

"Don't get smart, Jim, I'm serious now."

"Well, how can I help?"

"I know you had your old washer repaired, and I was wondering who fixed it."

"There's a fellow over at Ed Bristol's Appliance Store who is great with machines. You might want to give him a call. His name is Andre."

"— A manly name. Is he cute?"

"Sort of. He's a bit cross-eyed, has a bulbous runny nose, and smells kinda bad, but he sure knows how to fix washing machines."

"Oh, just my kind of man, especially the gooey nose."

"His nose isn't a problem because he just keeps licking the green stuff away."

Sylvia picked up a sheet of paper, balled it up and threw it at him.

"Oh, gross! How can you even think such things? But give me his number. I've got to see this horrid human hunk for myself."

Jim wrote down the number for Ed's Appliance Store and handed it to Sylvia.

"Don't forget, his name is Andre, and remember to hold your nose when you call," Jim laughed as he left. This time, a second wad of paper made a direct hit between his shoulder blades, but he kept on walking.

Although Sylvia needed a repairman, now she was just as interested in seeing this person, Andre, who Jim had caricatured as an ogre. When she dialed the appliance store, a smooth, deep male voice answered, "Hello, Ed's Appliance Store, Andre speaking. How can I help you?" Sylvia was shocked. She didn't know what to expect, but Andre's voice surely sounded decent enough. In fact, it sounded deep, manly—sexy.

"Hello, Andre, I'm Sylvia Keyes. Jim Simmons referred you to me as an excellent repairman."

"A repairman, I am. Excellent, I hope! What seems to be the problem?"

"My washing machine started leaking water onto the floor. It runs okay, but after it's been turned on a while, I see a steady stream of water coming out from under it."

"I have a couple of guesses what its sickness is, but I'd have to examine the patient for a proper diagnosis." Sylvia chuckled.

"Will you be home tomorrow morning?" asked Andre.

"I'll make it a point to be here."

"If my boss okays it, I'll be there about nine o'clock?"

"Great! See you then, Andre."

21 The Black Hunk

December 28, 2002—Saturday
9:05 A.M.

Sylvia was watching for a truck or van to pull up, but instead, a bright red jeep slid to a stop in front of her home. A dark skinned young male climbed out of the driver's seat, took out a toolbox from the rear of the jeep, and started for her front door. When she opened it, she stood there staring. This man was nothing like the character Jim had so vividly described. He was bulky, tall with brown eyes, and seemed to display a permanent grin across his angular face.

"Are you, Andrew—er, I mean Andre?"

"Yes, Ms., that's me." He reached for his wallet. "I have ID I can—"

"Oh, for heaven's sake, I don't need any ID. It's just that Jim described you a bit differently than you are in person. Come in please."

"I assume the patient's in the basement?"

"Yes." Sylvia just stood there as this handsome hunk walked past her.

"Um, maybe you could show me the way?"

"Oh, of course. That's a good idea."

Andre was equally attracted to her, especially her sculptured face. She wore a bright white angora turtleneck that highlighted her dark skin and emphasized her breasts while her designer jeans revealed nice firm buttocks. She was not overly thin but it was obvious she watched her diet. As she passed him, a hint of expensive perfume wafted in the air.

Once in the basement, Andre could see the water leaking from under the washer, running across the basement floor and into a sewer drain.

"Let me get down here and take a look," explained Andre. He took off his heavy brown jacket and Sylvia automatically reached for it.

She became fascinated by its musky, leathery smell and continued holding it close to her face. She did not realize that she kept staring at Andre, but she did notice him glancing at her.

Feeling self conscious, she asked, "Is there something wrong?"

Andre, never one to mince words, answered honestly, "Yes and no."

"What does that mean?"

"Ms. Keyes, yes, your washer needs a new pump. That's what's leaking. And no, nothing is wrong except that I'm having trouble working with you near me."

"Oh, I'm so sorry," she apologized. "I didn't mean to get in the way. I'll go upstairs. I was enjoying your company."

As she turned to go, Andre said, "Oh, don't go. You don't make me nervous about my work; it's just that you are very nice to look at. That's why I can't concentrate."

"Well—thank you for the compliment, Andre, but why do you think I'm staring?"

"You're afraid I'll steal your box of soap powder?" he chuckled. Then they both laughed. Andre said he'd return with a new pump in twenty minutes if Sylvia didn't mind waiting.

"Have you had breakfast yet, Andre?"

"Not yet, but I'll grab something on my way."

"You'll do no such thing. How often do I have a real man in my house for breakfast? Do you like bacon with your eggs?"

"Sure do."

"How about scrambled?"

"Fine with me. Be right back!"

While Andre was gone, Sylvia could not stop thinking about him. She was amazed that he was nothing at all like Jim Simmons had described.

With a huge grin on her face, Sylvia said aloud, "Just wait, just wait till I see that Gumshoe again."

Andre drove to the appliance store, picked up the pump he needed and headed back to Sylvia's place. He couldn't keep his mind off her. *That woman is definitely hot—a nice fine figure—a gorgeous face—and what grace and charm.* Then his imagination took over. *What would she look like stripped to the waist with those painted-on jeans that I could unbutton, or, or naked except for her soft-white angora sweater, calling me, "Andre, Andre, come into my bedro—"*

He almost flew past her street. His jeep tires squealed as he abruptly turned down Sylvia's street, and once again, came to a sliding halt in front of her house. She had the door open, waiting for him. As he entered, he could smell fried bacon, eggs, toast and coffee. The two of them sat and enjoyed breakfast together making small talk and ogling over one another.

Realizing he had been gone a bit too long from the appliance store, without thinking he said, "I need to slide my big pump into your machine and get back—"

When Sylvia grinned at the Freudian implication of his comment, he realized what he'd just said and he started to blush. The two of them giggled together. "Actually," said Sylvia, "that wouldn't be a bad idea, but I need to get to know you first. You know, at least another ten minutes or so."

Of course, her comment cracked up Andre whose face now looked like a lantern.

Still smiling, he walked down to the basement. Twenty-five minutes later, he had replaced the broken pump, thanked Sylvia with a tender kiss to the forehead and headed back to the store knowing he would call her that very evening. Sylvia watched him pull away in his jeep hoping he would.

December 30, 2002—Monday

The weekend came and went without incident except that church attendance at Saint Paul's was even heavier than usual. For the longest time, Father Kerr had presided over Benediction on Sunday nights. Then he began sharing that spot with Father Phillip and Father Walsh. By now, the hysteria that first accompanied the Benediction tears had subsided somewhat, but always, those who sat near the crucifix on a Sunday when the droplets occurred remained awed at the tiny water spot that collected. People still jostled for the pews nearest the front middle aisle. Most came very early and read magazines or books waiting for the ceremony to begin. Ms. Reed helped pass the waiting time for very early arrivals by playing the church's mighty organ. Father Kerr had it overhauled adding some additional trumpet-like pipes, a more powerful air blower to increase its volume, and additional panels to both sides of the console to house the control stops for the new pipes. These pipes were mounted so that they stuck out from the choir loft like trumpets.

As the weeks and months passed, the media's interest

remained high because people of all faiths stayed interested. As awestruck churchgoers continued to flood into Saint Paul's Church, the news media continued their interviews and follow-up stories. There was always a throng of people in the church except for Thursday nights when it was closed at six. Sunday collection baskets could not contain all the donated money. Ushers had to empty their baskets several times when they started to spill over. The coffers at Saint Paul's in particular, and other churches throughout the diocese in general, were overflowing with new moneys. Even if the famous crucifix had not caused a genuine rebirth of religious fervor, it encouraged Catholics to contribute more toward church support.

Due to the inspirational nature of the Oculi mystery, many churches, in addition to Saint Paul's, had returned to the old Latin Mass which somehow seemed more authentic, more like the church of their parents and grandparents, more like the church of the ages.

For centuries, Latin had united Catholics throughout the world. Regardless of the native tongue of a foreign country, travelers realized that church liturgy retained the same Latin tongue, and in many cases, the same Latin hymns that they knew by heart and loved to sing. Thus, they felt at home anywhere Latin was used. It added a definite mystique, an oblique supernatural quality, to church rituals that only the clergy understood. It was they who had the knowledge and power to utter the sacred magical words that laymen could just wonder about.

22   A Corpse's Warning

January 9, 2003—Thursday
7:08 P.M.

A regular maintenance service from Latrobe was busy mopping floors, waxing pews and woodwork, cleaning restrooms, and in general, giving everything within reach a cleaning and polishing. Sister Margaret was busy replacing the myriad number of candles encircling the inside perimeter of the church. Ms. Reed was busy practicing Bach pieces she felt were appropriate for, "a more sophisticated" church going audience. She delighted in both religious and classical pieces, especially Bach's wide variety of toccatas and fugues. The custodian busied himself pulling his Offerings cart from one donations box to another emptying each one's contents.

All was quiet except for the serene classical tones emerging from the organ pipes and the muted sounds from those working in various places. That is, until there was banging and bumping as Father Phillip dragged out the large stepladder from the sacristy steps all by himself. It was the same one used months ago by the police chief when he made his initial X-rays of the suspended crucifix. Ed Bristol working inside the vestibule did not see the priest because the two swinging doors leading into the body of the church were closed.

Weeks ago, Philosophical Father Phillip had resolved to

make his own examination of the Oculi. Now he would do it. To him, anything that exists has *ens* or being. He had difficulty believing in angels, but he accepted Saint Thomas' reasoning that there must be some order of being between God and man. After all, the Bible mentioned orders of angels. To set his mind at rest after devouring volumes pertaining to miracles, Phillip decided to have an up-close look for himself.

The short priest was strong enough to carry and raise the ladder by himself. He scampered up under the cross. He could just reach the heavy elm arms. With him he had a large magnifying glass, a flashlight, and some cotton swabs. Sister Margaret was about to holler at him from a side aisle, but decided instead to walk over to the ladder.

"Father Phillip," Margaret said quietly, "Father Kerr said the bishop forbade anyone to tamper—"

"Oh, don't worry, Sister Margaret. I'm aware of his decree. I have no intention of messing with it. My curiosity has gotten the best of me. I'm just knocking off all this dust." He reached up and touched first one eye, then another. Then he used a fingernail to remove some of the dried residue left under an eye."

"HEY!" shouted the custodian as he swung open one of the vestibule doors with a bang and stomped up the aisle. "What do you think you're doing there, young fella?"

Sister Margaret did her best to assuage Ed Bristol who looked angry, "Oh, Father Phillip is just cleaning off the crucifix, especially those caked on eye deposits."

"For a priest, you're a foolish, young man," squawked Bristol. "Besides, look how you're standing. One slip and you could fall. I'll steady this ladder till you climb down, but stop what you're doing now and get down."

Embarrassed for Father Phillip and by Ed's overreaction,

Margaret started to walk back through a pew toward her previous work area. Father Phillip ignored Bristol's directive because of the curt way it was given. He continued to stretch and scrape with his fingernail.

Everyone heard Ed Bristol yell, "Father, watch out!" But it was too late. Phillip teetered for a moment and then lost his balance. All turned in time to see him plunge downward almost headfirst from his precarious perch. A sickening—*thump*—echoed throughout the church along with a loud yelp as Phillip's right temple struck a pew end on the opposite side of the ladder where Bristol was standing.

Sister Margaret turned in time to see the young priest crumpled on the floor. Instantly, she hurried back toward the ladder. The cleaners hurried over. Hearing the commotion, Mrs. Reed quit playing and turned to look down from the organ loft. Father Phillip appeared unconscious. Blood oozed from the side of his head that struck the pew.

"Go," said Ed Bristol to Margaret. "Get Father Kerr over here at once."

As she ran off toward the sacristy door that led to the rectory, Ed yelled to the cleaning crew, "Quick, one of you call an ambulance. Dial 911. The rest of you wait outside to direct them in here."

With that, the cleaning crew headed toward their van while some used their cell phones. Mrs. Reed started down the steps from the choir loft.

Upon arrival, Father Kerr knelt down and felt Phillip's neck, then his temple for a pulse. He thought he found one, but it was faint. Sister Margaret knelt down on the other side and checked for breathing.

"Father, I don't think he's breathing," she panicked.

"I don't think I found a pulse either," said Kerr in a shocked voice.

Father Walsh stood with his hands folded in prayer. The injured priest looked very bad. His face already wore the pallor of death. Kerr stooped over and pinched shut the fallen priest's nostrils and began breathing into his mouth. Next, he balled up his hand and placed it just at the bottom of Phillip's sternum. He made five quick compressions with his fist, deep into Phillip's chest cavity.

"One, two, three, four, five," he counted aloud.

Sister Margaret saw him readying himself for another breath of air into Phillip's mouth.

"I'll do that, Father—you try for a pulse!"

The two of them continued resuscitation efforts even when they heard an EMS vehicle pull up in front of the church as its siren slowly wailed to a stop. The experienced medical team ran down the aisle and took over. Kerr stayed on his knees but moved out of the way while Margaret stood up crying. Father Walsh's eyes filled with tears as he stood trembling, witnessing the inevitable. Mrs. Reed stood back, aghast in horror. For at least twenty minutes, the Emergency Medical Team tried their best to revive Phillip.

To all present, it became obvious that resuscitation was useless. From his kneeling position at the priest's side, Father Kerr reached down and put one hand along Phillip's cheek. Everyone gasped when they saw Phillip's eyes fall wide open, the pupils staring at nothing. The mouth started to move like a mechanical doll; it uttered, *"Cave, cave—"* (Beware, beware—). Then, while the eyes remained fully open, Phillip's open mouth slid shut forever.

Sister Margaret began weeping embracing Father Walsh. The cleaners and Mrs. Reed stood silently over the dead priest. Father Kerr could not hold back his tears. He made the sign of the cross, *"Benedicat te, omnipotens Deus, Pater, et Filius, et Spiritus Sanctus i nunc, vide creatorem tuum"* (May Almighty God, the Father, and Son, and Holy Spirit bless you. Go now and see your Maker).

Kerr wanted no further explanation. Sister Margaret had already told him what happened on their way from the rectory. More than ever, he was convinced the Evil One was at work right here in this church. He was sickened by his part in the weekly blackmail. Some demonic scheme had been unleashed; it had just claimed another victim.

11:45 P.M.

The priest slept fitfully that night. Horrific Demon images kept bounding into his sleep. He felt himself *falling, falling forward from a very high place over a staircase railing. Steps with sharp metal edges rushed up to his eyes. But his head slammed against a post—no, by God it was a crucifix. Yes! The one hanging right there beside his bed. And money floated down, down, down with him toward the floor; but as it fell, it turned into bright crimson drops of warm blood that ran over his fingers and dripped onto Sister Lucy, lying face down beneath it.*

He tried not to look at the jagged leg bone as he turned the face of her twisted, broken body toward him for a final blessing, but her mouth started to open and shut like a mechanical doll whispering again and again, "Cave—cave—" He closed the eyelids, but it was Phillip's face now. Yes, he had made a mistake. It was Phillip's face. It was Phillip who'd said those words. Yet, it couldn't be. His mouth was shut, and his deep eye sockets—empty in death.

Then the crucifix floated down, down—down to the top of his dresser. "Cave—cave—" *A hooded person was sitting there painting and whispering,* "Cave—cave—" *Anthony! Christ, NO! it was Brother Anthony so, so very artfully painting the corpus—bright red. No, NO! It was red blood. It spilled over the closed dresser drawers until it ran all the way down and dripped to the floor. The hooded figure turned toward him lying in bed. But the hood had no face—only an empty shadow.* "Cave—" *The word echoed in whispers around his bedroom,* "Cave—" He forced himself awake and sat up trembling, sweating, panicky, delirious as if he had a high fever!

January 10, 2003—Friday
3:00 A.M.

It was now very early morning. His mind was racing. Beads of sweat stood out on his forehead. *What can I do? What can I do? I can't go back to sleep, not with—with demons waiting for me. Should I call Father Walsh? He started for his bedroom door then stopped. Should I call the police? Yes, that's it. I'll just call the police and tell them that—tell them that—that, that what? Tell them I had a bad dream? Tell them I might be going crazy? Tell them I need help—an asylum? Good God, what can I do? It's all hopeless—there's no way to get help and I need it—I need help—I must get help to stay sane.*

Never thinking about the hour, he picked up his phone and dialed Jim Simmons. The phone rang and rang but he didn't care. He had to get to the bottom of all this. He had to talk to someone.

A very groggy female voice answered, "Lo?"

"Is that you Martie? Is this Martie?"

"Who is this?" she asked.

"Kerr."

Martie perked up instantly at the sound of his nervous voice. "Are you okay?"

"No, I'm not okay. Well, no, I'm okay but very, very upset. I need to talk with someone, please. I'm sorry about this, but I'm coming over," and he hung up.

Martie was awake by this time sitting on the edge of her bed pulling a robe around her nakedness. As she slid around to put her feet on the floor, she poked Jim several times. Still holding the phone she called, "Jim—Jim—JIM, wake up!"

"Huh, huh, huh, what? Wa ya want, Baby? What'sa matta? I'm not horny now."

"Father Kerr just called and was really upset. He's coming over here to talk."

"It's the middle of the night, Baby. Can't it wait till morning?"

"Jim, something is wrong. Something terrible is wrong with him; he says he's coming over right now."

By this time, Jim was awake. He sat on the edge of the bed pulling on his boxers part way, then he stood up yawning and pulled them up to his waist. "Did he say what the problem is?"

"All he said was, 'I'm coming over. I need to talk to someone.'"

"Gads, look at the time, it must be important."

"Jim, he sounded petrified. I mean he was almost incoherent."

"Maybe he had a wee bit too much of the nippy tonight?"

Martie replied, "Don't tease, Jim, The man sounded terrified. I'll go down and put on some coffee."

205

"Maybe you better put on a tee shirt so your boobs don't flop out. That might make him psychotic."

"Stop joking. He's a wonderful strong priest, but the poor man seemed rattled. She looked over at Jim's shorts. And speaking of things flopping out, I seem to see Richard the Wonderful dangling a bit."

"Hey, you bought these for me. Can I help it if the legs are so short?"

Within minutes, there was a loud knocking at the front door. At the same time, the doorbell rang loudly. Jim opened the door to let in Kerr who, by this time, had calmed down compared to Martie's description of him after their brief phone conversation. In fact, the first thing the pastor did was apologize for waking them at such an early hour.

"So," said Jim, stretching on a clean tee shirt. "What has you so upset at this unholy hour?"

Martie brought in coffee for the three of them then sat on the couch beside Jim folding her long lithe legs under her bathrobe.

Kerr started out telling them about the happenings of the previous evening in church. Once started, his words flowed like an avalanche, coming faster and faster as his graphic recollections of what happened to Father Phillip resembled a scene from some horror film. Martie and Jim gasped when Kerr explained about the young priest falling from the stepladder, hitting his head on the pew, ending up in an unconscious heap on the church floor.

"And, and then, he died!" stammered the priest. "The holy man died while I held him in my very arms."

"Father Phillip is dead?" whispered Martie. "Phillip is dead?" she repeated louder this time.

"Yes."

"How can such terrible things happen? He was just a young man. I can't believe this," said Martie.

Shaking his head, Jim leaned forward, sitting on the very edge of the couch, his eyes trained on Father Kerr who had become more and more upset as he neared the end of his grisly tale. "What on earth happened?" said asked Jim.

"We tried, Jim; the EMS tried but—"

"And you called the police and gave them a report—"

"I didn't give the report, I just couldn't. Sister Margaret told what she saw when she turned around—she was facing away when Phillip he fell. The police asked the cleaning people if any one of them had seen him fall. Some had, but at a great distance. But everyone heard the terrible thump when his head hit the pew."

"Well Ed must've seen the accident. You said he was standing right there by the ladder," said Martie.

"Ed's the one who gave the actual police report," said Kerr. "He was very apologetic because he had just scolded Phillip for daring to climb that dangerous shaky ladder. He said that Father Phillip was picking at residue under the Oculi."

"And, he lost his balance?" asked Jim.

"Ed Bristol said Phillip had to stretch to reach the cross because he is short."

"Tell me he wasn't standing on the tip top."

"No. No. But he was up on his tiptoes, and—and," the priest began to choke up, "and even then he could just reach the crucifix's eyes."

"This just can't be," said Martie. "Two hideous deaths, both since this whole Oculi matter began."

"Martie," he paused. "Jim," he paused. "Listen. Listen to

me." He paused again until the silence became oppressive. "After the EMS team gave up and said Phillip was dead, the man opened his eyes for a brief second, and said, '*Cave—Cave—*'"

"What does that mean?"

"*Cave,*" said Kerr, "means beware! But Phillip died before finishing; I'm sure he was trying to tell me something—I'd swear it was something about that crucifix, that unholy cross."

The three sat in shocked silence. Kerr was the first to speak. "I had a horrible dream. That's why I came over. It was awful. Listen to this. Last to die—was Father Phillip; before him—Sister Lucy; and the first to die, the very first victim, Jim and Martie, I'd swear—was Brother Anthony at Saint Vincent's monastery. I'd stake my life as a priest on that."

Martie let out a gasp. Jim's brow furrowed. Again, there was prolonged silence as the implication behind Father Kerr's words became a reality.

"Look, I have no proof," he said, "but didn't Anthony work on it? Didn't he disappear the very night before I picked up the cross? Now didn't he?"

"Yes, but that's no reason—"

"Where is he? Hunh? Did he vaporize? Did lightning just erase the man? I think Brother Anthony knew something about that cross some strange secret—"

"—And was murdered?"

"Yes!"

"In the monastery?"

"Lucifer—knows—no—bounds, Martie," quipped Kerr.

Once again—a profound silence filled the room until Martie spoke up. "Murder may be a good theory, but no body was ever found."

"Father," said Jim, "I went over there the next day right

after noon and talked to the monks. I searched Anthony's work area. I hunted for a clue, any clue, and I came away convinced that he just decided to leave, period. There wasn't a single shred of evidence to suggest otherwise."

"But," argued Kerr, "weren't you already predisposed to think that murder couldn't happen at Saint Vincent's? I mean, how many murders take place in a monastery or a convent; or a shooting in a church?" The expression on Kerr's face became fearsome. "Anything can happen when Lucifer is loose and he's broken his chains."

"Yes, but we did a police search—"

"Jim, I'm not negating what you did. All I'm saying is that the police did not think Anthony's disappearance was a serious matter because monks do decide to renounce the religious life, and since no clues could be found, the case was dismissed. Everyone was thinking that sooner or later, Anthony would turn up."

"But—he—never—did," said Jim.

"Jeez, my mind's paralyzed with this," replied Martie. "It all seems so wicked, so incredibly evil, yet what you say is possible."

"Father's right," Jim said. "Evil lurks and works in inhumane ways!"

"How did Ed react to Phillip's death?" asked Martie.

"He didn't have much to say except that he was very, very sorry. Sorry he wasn't closer. Sorry he couldn't help break Phillip's fall. But then Ed never says much. He is a private man and very dependable. He works hard. He has been my right hand at Saint Paul's for years. Ed takes care of so many things around the church that I couldn't manage without him. Sometimes, he works too hard which makes him a bit cranky. I've told him so, but Ed is Ed, and he just keeps working, anyway."

"I wouldn't want to be his wife," stated Martie.

"Wife? Ed has no wife. He never married. He sustained some kind of injury in the army on his very first day in combat. He received the Purple Heart, but because of his injury, he wouldn't consider marriage. He's had his share of women though. I think the Vietnam War and his injury warped Ed's personality. He wasn't always so—so bitter."

Several moments passed before Kerr said, "Listen, I've got to go and let you folks sleep. Thanks for hearing me out tonight —er, this morning." He shook his head. "Somehow, I just feel so evil—like, like I'm part of all this."

"Wait just a minute, Father," interrupted Martie. "Why should you feel evil? You're doing your best to figure this out. There's no reason to feel guilty."

"Oh yes, there is," he blurted out without thinking.

"What? What is it? asked Martie. Kerr looked very uncomfortable as if he'd been slammed into a trap.

"Mm, nothing, it's nothing. I'm tired and running at the mouth. But I feel much better now than I did after that horrible dream. I mean, it was terrible. Just telling you two was a real catharsis. And I'm sure you'd both like some more sleep. So, thanks." The priest stood up and quickly walked toward the door.

"Father," said Jim, "if you level with us, we can help. I know you're carrying around some ghastly secrets."

Kerr said nothing more. He left the room and started back to his church.

5:30 P.M.

Since Jim had been up most of the night, he was a bit tired all day. He was one of those physically fit people who worked out at a local gym, but who needed a good night's sleep to function. By the time he got off duty around five o'clock that evening, he just wanted to go home and nap.

To his surprise, Martie wasn't home. She had left a note saying she and Amy, had taken Mildred to the late Saturday afternoon matinee in downtown Latrobe where Spiderman was playing, and then the three planned to stop at Mary Jo's Restaurant for a fast food dinner.

Sounds like fun, Jim thought, *but look out couch, here I come*. Without hesitating, he kicked off his shoes, took off his police uniform, flopped himself down in his shorts and dropped off into a deep sleep within minutes.

The next sounds he heard were the voices of Amy, Mildred and Martie yakking away in the kitchen. He couldn't quite make out what was being said, but he detected a delicious smell wafting in. That brought him to his senses. He sat up, made a loud—*ah-h-h*—as he stretched, then walked into the kitchen.

"What's that delicious smell?" he asked.

Before answering, Martie looked at the legs of his shorts to make sure Wonderful Richard was not dangling. "It's cherry pie. Amy and Mildred made it before we left this afternoon so we could have dessert when we got here."

"Smells wonderful. Is it done?"

Little Mildred said, "Oh, Mr. Jim, it's done, we're just heating it up."

"Can I have a piece, Mildred?" asked Jim. "Pleeeeeeease?"

"Yeah, I think there'll be enough for four."

Jim smiled to himself thinking, I wonder how much this little girl thinks she'll eat.

After he pulled on his trousers, they began to devour their heated, cherry pie topped with a glob of vanilla ice cream. The conversation turned to the awful death of Father Phillip.

"Isn't it strange," said Amy, "that he fell while he was touching the crucifix? Gives me the creeps just thinking about it."

Martie couldn't help herself. "Amy, do you think the priest died because he touched it?"

"Well, no, but maybe God just didn't want him up there."

"Why would an Infinite Creator make him fall? You're talking nonsense. I mean he was a priest, a devoted man, one who'd dedicated himself to serving the Almighty," replied Martie. "What you say is pure craziness!"

"Well," Amy thought for a minute, "could be, but Moses was not allowed to enter the Promised Land because he doubted Yahweh's word. My Bible says he was picked by God himself to lead the chosen people out of Egypt, right?"

"According to your Bible."

"And God punished him just the same."

Bored with this entire conversation, Mildred said, "Can we go home now?" She had eaten a gooey piece of pie and had gotten the filling on both sides of her mouth. When she smiled, her mouth looked like it belonged on a clown.

"Yes," answered her mother, "we can go, but first wipe your mouth, please."

Jim walked over with a paper napkin and handed it to Mildred. "Thanks for my pie, Mildred."

"Oh, you're welcome. Anytime my mother makes pie, you're welcome to it."

"I'll remember that. And you remind her for me."

After they left around seven o'clock, Jim still had not had enough sleep. "Let's shack and sack early tonight," he said. "Why don't you shower first because it takes you a lot longer than me?"

"Why don't we shower together," said Martie, "that would speed things up a bit. I'll even wash off Wonderful Richard for you just as many times as you like.

23 A Blue Pickup Truck

January 14, 2003—Tuesday
10:00 A.M.

The day was frigid. Temperatures hovered around ten degrees mid-afternoon. Earlier that morning, Jim's cruiser had to be coaxed to start because the overnight temperature had dropped to six degrees below zero, not including the wind chill factor. *I think I'll pay Kerr another visit because he'll offer me a nice warm drink. Besides, I want to ask him about church finances.* Sure enough, Kerr offered him a goblet of wine and now the two sat talking in the front parlor.

"Must be the policeman in me, Father. Can you answer a few questions for me?"

"I can try," responded the depressed looking priest.

"Do you and Ed manage all the bookkeeping for the parish?"

"More or less, yes. We try to keep our records up-to-date. Before mid-August when everything was normal around here, bookkeeping was a simple procedure. We had trouble just paying the bills and staying in the black. Most of our income back then came from Sunday collections," said Kerr.

Kerr's mind pictured the thousands he had given to the fake Homeless Relief Fund. "You can see all the improvements I've been able to afford. Our church looks stunning and the school has been reopened. This so-called miracle has brought droves of visitors of every faith who leave very generous donations."

"Does anyone else help with the books?" inquired Jim.

"Dr. Troft set up computer access for us so we could track deposits and withdrawals. He and I used to check the fund together, but he doesn't bother anymore."

"Did he ever tell you why?" Jim asked just to find out if Troft had ever confided his tale of horror to the priest.

"No. But he has resumed ushering on some Sundays; helps count the collections then disappears for the week. He avoids me—I hardly ever see him, and we used to be close friends. Can't imagine what I ever did to him."

"What about Ed Bristol? Does he have access to the church's account?"

"He used to." But Kerr didn't tell Jim that neither Troft nor Ed Bristol could access the account because The Voice had ordered him to change passwords. "Why do you ask?"

"It's just my nature to be curious. Have you ever had your books professionally audited?" Kerr wondered if somehow Jim had found out about the ten-thousand dollar blackmail deductions he withdrew each week. He became uncomfortable, yet at the same time, in his heart he wanted Jim to figure it out.

He answered, "So far, I haven't seen the need for a professional bookkeeper, but when that time comes, I'll hire one. He stood up, put down his empty glass, then continued, "Well, we've both got plenty to do so—"

"Oh, I'm sorry for being so nosy, Father," interrupted Jim when he realized he was being ushered out. "And, you're right. I should get back to my job and I shouldn't have wine this early in the day." Jim recognized that his questions bothered the priest, but still he asked, "So, as far as you know, there is no problem of any kind with the church fund?"

Evading the question, Kerr responded, "Things are as good as they can be. Now, don't you work too hard today." He started walking Jim toward the front entrance just as a new face arrived down the hallway via the side door.

Kerr said, "Oh, I'm glad you came through right now. I'd like you to meet one of Latrobe's best officers."

"Oh, you must be Jim Simmons," said the newly assigned priest extending his hand. "I'm Father McKelvy, and I'm very glad to meet you. Father Kerr has told me about you and Martie."

"You have a good memory," said Jim. "Either that or Father Kerr has said such awful things about us that you couldn't forget our names."

"Nothing of the kind," chuckled McKelvy. "Anyway, I'm taking Phillip's place. May his holy soul rest in piece. He must have done a lot to relieve some of Pastor Kerr's stress." He was looking at Kerr when he finished his comment.

"That he did. He was a great man. I'm glad you're here, but I do miss that philosophical, young fellow. He was on my side."

As Jim drove away from the rectory, he thought, *Kerr has never been that curt. He was trying to get rid of me. I could sense it. Some terrible specters are eating away at him. I've never felt uncomfortable in his presence before, but the man was trying to run me out.*

January 15, 2003—Wednesday
2:30 P.M.

Jim had just pulled over an old blue pickup truck on Latrobe's Main Street not far from the borough building. Both vehicles sat along the curb. The cruiser's lights were still flashing when Jim got out and walked up to the truck's front. The driver was just about to give him a bad time when both recognized one another. The driver was Dr. Troft. "I'm sorry, Jim, I kinda' slid through that light back there, didn't I?"

Jim had been waiting on Oak Street to make a right turn when Dr. Troft's truck passed through the light on Main. Jim never noticed that he slid through a red light, but he had spotted an expired Pennsylvania inspection sticker.

"Doctor, I stopped you because your inspection sticker is out-of-date. You need to get this buggy inspected because you're two months overdue."

Troft peered at the windshield sticker. Sure enough, it expired back in November. Jim wrote out a citation stating that he must get the inspection within forty-eight hours, or be fined, and handed it to him.

"Now, let's see. Should I write out a ticket for sliding through the red light?" he grinned.

Anxiously, Troft took his comment as a serious statement.

"You just said you didn't see me," whimpered Troft. "It's your word against mine."

"You mean you'd lie?" inquired Jim. "A churchgoer would lie?"

"No," said Troft looking dejected. "I wouldn't lie. You can write me up. So, I guess I'll get points, too."

"Doc, I'm kidding with you. That's all. Just playing with you mind."

"That's a relief," said Troft. "A person of my status would hate to get points."

"But I have a few questions to ask you. Mind if I get in?" asked Jim.

"Not at all." Jim walked around and climbed in. Troft was a

bit embarrassed by the flashing cruiser lights behind him, but Jim ignored them.

"Have you had any more threats of any kind? Oh, by the way, I saw your new car last Sunday. It's a beauty."

"Well, you know what happened to the other one. You know I've been ushering at the church once in a while."

"Yep, the pastor told me." Changing the subject, Jim asked, "You know that report I sent you from the scan done by the university folks?"

"Yes."

"In your opinion, was there anything peculiar about those scans?"

"No, except for the nails. I think they're unusual."

"How so?"

"They're unnecessary. The bolts from the back of the corpus are all that's necessary for support."

"Then, why the nails?"

"I don't know. I was just wondering if they were added at the monastery, that's all. They don't serve any purpose."

"And, the eyes?"

"According to the researchers, Jim, the eyes are a bit unusual, too. They appear to be some kind of glass disks bonded in front of hollow metal ellipses. But that's not so unusual."

"Why not?"

"Well, I remember a day when I as a kid. My baby sister dropped one of her most loved dolls. The glue seam between the top of the head and the bottom came apart so you could see inside. The head was empty except for two orbs that formed the eyes. My sister threw the doll down and came crying because what she saw frightened her. I think the Oculi are similar to the doll's eyes."

Jim replied, "Sounds logical to me." Jim felt that to ask Troft any further questions regarding the report was fruitless. The man was intelligent and insightful, and was trying his best to be as forthright as possible, even though he remained anxious and afraid. As Jim opened the passenger, side door and started to exit, Troft reached over and took him by the arm. "Jim, close the door a minute. Will you please?"

"What? Sure."

"Now, you know how squeamish I am, but since you're trying to solve this puzzle, I have a suspicion that may or may not be warranted about another mystery." He hesitated. "I know I'm a pompous ass, which makes me come across as if I'm trying to make myself better than the next person. Know what I mean?"

Jim had to agree, "Well, we all have our peccadilloes."

"Now I'm not blaming anyone, I'm just telling you this as a suspicion that bothers me, see?"

"I see. So shoot," said Jim.

"Well, each Sunday when the ushers take up collections, there is a lot, and I do mean a lot, of money collected. People attending Masses are generous for one reason or another including wealthy tourists."

"Go on."

"Jim, I've seen many twenty and hundred-dollar bills dropped in my collection basket during each Sunday service, and I only collect from the first twenty rows. Even then, my basket goes halfway across a row, then gets passed to the person behind and is returned back through the next row. The ushers on the side aisles do the same to relieve the other half of their cash—uh, offerings."

"So, where is this leading?" asked Jim.

"Well, the collected money gets dumped by each usher into

that large money vault—oops, Offerings repository—that Ed Bristol uses. After the Offertory of the Mass, we wheel it into that storage room on the other side of the sanctuary. We open it, and all the offerings fall out through a bottom door onto a tarpaulin. Then we take up the tarp with the offerings inside and carry it downstairs. By machine, we sort, count, stack, wrap, and then fill out deposit slips so it's ready for the bank the next day."

"Sounds like a good system."

"It might be my imagination, but I've been watching what people put in my collection basket and I figure the other ushers must take in a similar amount. But somewhere along the line, there seems to be a lot less money than there should be when it's all counted."

"You mean the deposit slips are changed in some way?"

"No, that's exactly what I don't mean. The slips reflect exactly what's been counted. It just seems that there should be more when it is counted, that's all."

"But you yourself are right there. Wouldn't you notice someone hiding the money?"

"Jim, it all happens so quickly because as ushers, we try not to get behind. We like to get all the money from one Mass counted and ready for deposit before the next batch comes in," said Troft. "It's an efficient operation, so we're kept very busy."

"I'm glad you told me this," said Jim. "Father Kerr had mentioned that you help with the church finances."

"No, he's wrong. Not any more I don't; not since that horrible night last September. I used to check the fund with my computer to make sure that everything was in order just in case the bishop asked for an audit. Now, all I do is usher and help count. To tell you the truth, I set up the original account and showed both Kerr and Ed how to use it."

"I see."

"Ed used to check the account from Kerr's office, so he knows both the password and correct social security number. I have no doubt both must monitor it now. I explained to Father Kerr that he could do the same with his personal account, but he said, 'One step at a time, Professor.' I'd give you his password, but I'd feel better if he gave it to you along with his social security number."

"Who carries the money to the Latrobe bank each week?"

"Ed goes with Sister Margaret."

"So, back when you did check, was everything okay?"

"Back when Saint Paul's was barely staying out of the red, everything appeared correct. What we put on our deposit slips appeared on the bank statements. I guarantee it all was legitimate. But here's the rub. Now, with all the money being donated at each Sunday Mass, it just seems that there should be more when it's tallied, that's all. Don't get me wrong, what we tally is what Ed deposits or Margaret would notice. Ed carries the money, which is quite heavy, and Sister always deals with the teller."

"Mm, interesting."

"I'm sure it's just a neurotic suspicion. And, Jim, for the Lord's sake, I wouldn't want any of the ushers, especially Ed, to know about our conversation because I think they're all honest people. I don't want to be on anyone's shit list. Know what I mean?"

"Listen, I promise I won't say anything about our conversation, but I do appreciate your information. Thanks a lot for talking with me. I've got to get back on duty. My radio may have been trying to call while I sat here gabbing. By the way, thanks for your thoughts on the scan," He said as he climbed out. Jim thought Troft looked somehow relieved after their short talk.

Troft started his truck, put it in gear and went his way making a mental note to get it inspected within the next two days.

6:00 P.M.

Jim shared Troft's suspicions with Martie. They discussed how they might begin checking right at what could be the source of the problem. "Professor Troft insinuated that the money seems to disappear somehow, right when they count it," explained Jim.

"Well, that makes no sense. If Bristol's taking it, then we need to start with him. And personally, I can't imagine confronting him with mere suspicions," said Martie.

"Well, I promised Troft I wouldn't involve his name in any way. Troft is afraid of Ed," said Jim.

"Oh, come now," Jim, "you know you could take him out."

"You've got to be kidding me, Martie. It would take several people to bring him down. I'd never want to confront that man physically."

Martie sat silently for a moment. Jim watched as a strange frown appeared on her face as if she was in deep thought. "Jim," she said coyly, "maybe the problem isn't with Ed."

"No?"

"Maybe it's his money cart."

"What do you mean?"

"What I mean is maybe we need to peek into that huge Offerings vault he tows around if Troft says money is disappearing right before his eyes! Where else could Ed hide it."

"I hadn't thought of that, Martie. But you're right. That

collection box, or vault as you called it, *is* large enough to hide money, probably a lot of it. Problem is, he keeps it padlocked," said Jim,

"From what Troft told you about the size of each week's collections it's good it is locked."

"Well, it won't hurt to snoop around a bit," added Jim, "You may have something here."

"It might be difficult to do because Ed's always in church. Now, here's another thought. Should we first ask Kerr about any of this?" asked Martie.

"Kerr trusts that man. I think we should check on our own first, rather than involve Kerr or Ed with hearsay."

24 The Ironing Board

January 16, 2003—Thursday
4:00 P.M.

Thursday afternoon when Martie returned home from school, she entered through her garage and laundry room. As she started up the stairs she realized that her dryer was still running. She knew she had emptied the washer into the dryer before leaving for school that morning because she wanted to change the bed linens, something she tried to do as part of each weekly routine.

Opening the dryer she found dry clothes and no heat, yet the clothes were still tumbling. When she looked at the timer dial, its little red dot was almost in the off position, but not quite. Something was amiss so she turned it to the OFF position. As the knob turned in her fingers, there was the distinctive loud, but short, buzz, signaling the cycle was done and the dryer had shut off.

After removing the dried laundry, she turned the knob all the way around and set it so there were only three minutes left in the cycle then took her briefcase and the dried load of sheets and towels upstairs. For a while, she forgot about the dryer as she folded the white bathroom towels, but then remembered she hadn't heard the buzzer. The dryer was still running when she went back downstairs. The little red dot on the dial was stuck just as before.

"Oh, darn," she said aloud to herself, "First it's the washer and now the dryer."

Dialing Bristol's store, she was hoping Ed didn't answer when she heard, "Andre here. How can I help you?"

"Oh hi, Andre, I'm glad you answered. I don't think I'm in the mood for your boss."

Recognizing her voice, Andre chuckled, "Oh, he has his bad days, and then he has his bad days, I guess. At times, Ms. Meyer, I feel sorry for the old geezer. But, he pays me very well so I just MYOB and do what he says."

"Well, anyway, Doctor, remember the last baby you delivered for me. The one that never cries at night?"

"Don't tell me it started crying already."

"No, but the one right next to it just won't go to sleep!"

"Give me a couple of symptoms."

Martie explained how she found her dryer running when she got home. The clothes were dry, but the tumbling cycle was still going.

"Bad resistor," said Andre, "nothing serious. Right behind the control knob is a resistor that slows down the timer during the last five minutes so the clothes tumble until they cool, otherwise deep wrinkles would get kinda baked in."

"Sight unseen diagnosis. Do you have a specialist degree?"

"Nope, I'm just a laborer."

"How soon can you fix it?"

"Hang a minute, be right back."

"Mr. Ed says I'm free to come now. It'll cost you sixty-five dollars."

"For the resistor?"

"The resistor is two bucks, but my professional, medical fee is sixty-three dollars," he teased.

"I'll be waiting for you. Just honk and I'll raise the garage door."

Within a few minutes, Andre arrived, Martie opened her garage door and in he walked wearing his blue coveralls and a heavy leather bomber jacket, and of course, a yellow Steeler baseball cap facing backward. He carried a small metal tool case in one hand and a plastic bag containing the new part in the other.

"We'll have this one purring like a kitten in just a few minutes. Got the new part right here."

Martie found this young twenty-two-year-old not just humorous, but intelligent and ruggedly attractive. She stayed while he worked, watching his muscular body twist and turn as he removed the panel that held the timer, turned it over, then reached inside and pulled out the burnt resistor. Just as quickly, he took the new one out of its plastic bag and installed it.

"You enjoy your work, don't you?"

"Sure do," he answered.

"Do you answer a lot of service calls, or do you usually stay in the store?"

"I used to be in the store a lot, but not any more. I've been on the road almost every day. Already today, I've visited two other places besides here. This morning I was over at the monastery."

"Busy, busy."

"Yes."

"That's interesting," she joked, "maybe they'll turn you into a priest or brother."

He continued assembling the dryer control panel. "Naw, I have one beautiful girlfriend right now, thanks to your husband who introduced us. I'm serious about her," he grinned. "But to answer your question, sometimes I go there to repair their equipment. Besides washers and dryers I work on furnaces, pool equipment, and refrigeration, to name just a few things. Other times, I deliver new machines or pick up old ones to be trashed."

"How did you end up working there for heaven's sake?"

"More or less, I've just taken over Ed's job. He'd been going there for years. Had been doing what I do, but it seems that now he's too busy at Saint Paul's, fooling around collecting all that church money, replacing candles, silly stuff like that. So, because he's too busy, I do the monastery repairs."

"You would think there'd be some monk who can fix their own equipment."

"A Brother Charles used to do it, but he's too busy with his science experiments. Seems like he's always working on some new theory, some new idea. You know, Ms. Meyer, he's a brilliant man when it comes to science. The results of many of his experiments and discoveries have been published in prestigious journals. Sometimes they even publish his theoretical ideas. He's a master thinker. I've tried to read some of his work, but it's hard to understand."

"The brainy sort, hunh?"

Martie's dryer had been repaired, so Andre was done. But their conversation continued. "That he is. You know I'm crazy about science, too. Always have been, and Brother Charles knows that. I love to tinker. You know, find out what makes things tick. I like talking with this brother. Sometimes I think he leaves the laundry repair work for me just so we can talk and share ideas."

"You certainly know a lot about machines," praised Martie.

"Hey, I figure it this way. If someone is smart enough to invent a gadget and put it together, especially some electro-mechanical device then I figure if it breaks down, I should be able to take it apart, then use my wits to fix it."

"You sound like college material to me. Ever think about it?"

Andre paused, thinking. "One of these days, maybe. Mr. Ed pays me a good salary. Lately, he's given me several raises. Sometimes I wonder where he gets all his money, but why question a good thing."

"Can't blame you. Why don't you ask this Brother Charles to show you some of his work—in your spare time, of course," she joked.

"Spare time? I wish I had more. But when he knows I'm coming over, he makes a point of coming down to see me and talk. Can't be just 'cause I'm black," howled Andre. Martie was thinking how much she enjoyed watching his well defined, virile body at work. "He likes to talk with me about his projects. He said he was working on some kind of pinpoint refrigeration that could kill cancer cells instead of the usual radiation."

"No kidding. Wouldn't that be a breakthrough? Why don't you work with him? You'd learn a lot just watching. I can picture you in a lab, experimenting with all kinds of things—your own new ideas."

"Like inventing better washers and dryers, or an improved ironing board, maybe even a better mousetrap," grinned Andre.

"Look, I'm serious. As a school teacher, I think I can recognize potential, and you have it."

Humbled, Andre replied, "Thanks. Thank you very much for the compliment. Now to answer your question from before, Brother Charles does most of his work away from Saint

Vincent's. I know he lives there, but he says he uses a cabin in the mountains for his experiments. I'd love to see his lab or as he calls it, his retreat."

"Sounds like he wants to keep his work a secret."

"Maybe." said Andre. Changing the subject, he said, "Hey, I've got a question for you. It's kinda personal. Are you and Mr. Simmons married?"

"Well, yes but not officially. We live together as husband and wife. We love one another trust each other."

"Kids?"

"Not yet. Maybe someday—" Martie's voice sounded a bit disappointed.

"I was just wondering about that because you seem to like children or you wouldn't be teaching. You remind me a bit of my own mother. She has the personality of a saint and did a good job raising us kids. I'd think you and the Mr. would make great parents."

Martie replied glumly, "It's not that we haven't tried. We'd like to have a family, Andre, but no luck so far and we've been living together for several years now."

"You never know, one of these days, hot damn, it'll happen."

"We've both been tested and the doctor says, now this is very personal between you and me—"

"Gotcha."

"Jim's sperm count is very low for some reason. Hard to believe for a strong, strapping fellow like him; so my chances of conceiving are not so good."

"Ms. Meyer, mind if I tell you something?" asked Andre.

"Go ahead." Martie hadn't the faintest idea what this bright, young man was going to say.

"You need the ironing board—yep," he grinned.

"What?" asked Martie trying to make sense of this disconnected suggestion.

"You need the ironing board after you make love." She was beginning to wonder if this fellow was so intelligent after all.

"What in highest Heaven or in deepest Hell could an ironing board have to do with conception?" giggled Martie at Andre's suggestion.

"My older sister, mind you, had trouble conceiving until my Mama told her about the ironing board," he said with the silliest of grins on his face. "I'm serious, now," he continued, grinning even more. "I know this sounds absurd, but you place a closed ironing board at the side of your bed so that it slants down to the floor." Martie continued grinning back at Andre as if he was joking. She could feel a fit of laughter rising inside but he went on. "As soon as you know Mr. Jim's ah, ah, well, um, you know, as soon as he has blasted his wild deposit so to speak, you slide over onto the ironing board with your head toward the floor."

Martie was having trouble stifling a fit of laughter. She held her hand over her mouth while her insides shook. "I know you aren't taking any of this seriously, Ms. Meyer, but my Mama says this will improve your chances of getting pregnant." Martie couldn't contain herself any longer and burst out laughing uncontrollably. Andre did the same, but he laughed because Martie was laughing.

As she calmed down and realized the young man was serious, once again she put her hand over her mouth, and said, "Andre, I'm sorry for laughing, but how could that help?"

"Well, lying in that position, it's easier for those little fellers to swim downhill."

Martie held her sides and doubled over; it took several

231

moments before she could say, "Andre, I have to admit I've never heard that in my entire life. I guess in a way it makes sense, and I do apologize for laughing, but you must admit, it sounds silly; you know, sliding naked onto an ironing board after making love." She continued chuckling to herself.

"Well, my sister had not become pregnant after two years of marriage until Mama told her about the ironing board. Then— *whamo*—just like that, she had two children within three years."

Martie still held her sides. "Well, well thank you for your insemination advice and for fixing my dryer. I'll be sure to tell Jim about the ironing board."

"I know he'll laugh just like you did, but it can't hurt to try, now can it?"

"Nope."

"Hey, I gotta' go. Mr. Ed will think I made the wrong diagnosis regarding your machine."

Martie paid him his sixty-five dollars then tipped him an extra ten spot. She couldn't help thinking how great the world would be if there were more Andres.

7:00 P.M.

That evening while relaxing after dinner, Martie told Jim about her day. She explained how Andre had come from Bristol's store to replace a transistor. "At least I think he said it was a transistor," said Martie. "Transistor, resistor, I wouldn't know the difference if I saw one, but that young man knows what he's doing."

"Did it take him long?" asked Jim.

"Ten, maybe fifteen minutes, but we got to talking about a

lot of different things. You know, he's a very intelligent young man who would like to go to college. He is knowledgeable about all kinds of machines, and he says he loves science."

"He's a wit. He loves to laugh and make jokes. I remember reading somewhere that a person's sense of humor is a good indicator of head smarts," said Jim.

"That's true. When the psychologist at my school tests a student for the gifted program, she looks for an IQ score of one-hundred-thirty and above. Then she passes around a form on which teachers rate that student for creativity, sense of humor, originality and so on. But speaking of a sense of humor, Jim, Andre had my sides splitting today because of a remark he made. I mean, I was laughing out of control."

"What was so funny?"

"He asked if you and I were married. I told him not officially but that we considered ourselves as husband and wife." She started to grin to herself.

"And?"

"Then he wanted to know if we had any children." By this time, she started to chuckle.

"I told him no, but not because we hadn't tried."

She started to giggle just thinking of what she was about to say. "Then he said we need to use the ironing board."

Martie broke out laughing which made Jim start to laugh with her.

"An ironing board?" Jim could barely repeat what Martie said.

"Yes, an ironing board. After we make love," laughed Martie, "I'm supposed to slide over and lie head downward on a closed ironing board propped up against the side of the bed." She had to pause because she was laughing so hard, "Because—because, get this, it's easier for the little fellas to swim downhill." With that comment, the two of them roared. Each time Martie began to stop, she'd hear Jim giggling and start all over again.

"That young man's really funny," said Jim. "I'm trying to picture you lying naked, head downward on an ironing board."

"Maybe you should straddle it, and we could make love on the ironing board," said Martie and once again, the two of them were bellowing.

"Oh, was that funny," said Jim, regaining his composure.

"I'd like to see Andre get a college degree," said Martie. "He deserves the chance. He said he does repairs on the washers and dryers over at Saint Vincent's Monastery, and that a Brother Charles talks to him a lot about science. He said this Charles is a brilliant thinker and loves to discuss his scientific work. This man used to repair monastery equipment himself, but is just too busy now. He leaves the repairs for Andre each week, but he always comes to see him when he's there."

"That's interesting," commented Jim,

"But this is odd. When I asked Andre if he'd ever seen any of Charles' scientific work, the brother told him he did his experimenting in a retreat cabin up in the mountains."

"Why?"

"Haven't the foggiest. But doesn't that sound a bit strange?"

"I'll say," answered Jim, "but a lot of scientists are loners who work in solitude. But you're right. You'd think the monastery would be the perfect place for a recluse."

† † †

During the next two days, Jim traveled to four schools discussing general safety with elementary youngsters; saying no to drugs in two middle schools; and driving safety tips in a senior high school. Some of these schools were in areas outside the immediate Latrobe vicinity. Jim liked the idea of planting in young minds the idea that police are to help prevent crime, not just track down evildoers. His reputation as a good speaker brought him lots of speaking engagements.

25 Offerings Cart

January 20, 2003—Monday
8:30 P.M.

After two very busy weeks, Jim and Martie picked Monday night to inspect Bristol's cart.

"Do you think he's in church now?" asked Martie.

"Let's find out. Got his store number?"

Martie pulled out a card from her wallet that Andre had given her. "Here it is," she said. Jim punched in the digits.

After four rings, Andre's voice answered, "Ed Bristol's Appliance Store, Andre speaking?"

"Hi, Andre, Jim Simmons here, how are you today?"

"Just great. You?"

"Fine, but I was wondering if Ed was there in the store."

"Sure, just a minute, I'll get him for you," said Andre. Within seconds, "Ed Bristol here."

"Hi, Ed, this is Jim Simmons."

"Yes?"

"Got a minute?"

"Sure, a minute—or two."

"Listen, our hot water tank doesn't make water as hot as it used to even though it's turned up to 'Hot.' We were thinking about having a new one installed. Do you carry them?"

"No," answered Bristol, "But I can get you one from my

supplier in Johnstown and have Andre install it. I don't bother with them anymore, but since it's you folks, I wouldn't mind. Do you drain off a little water every week or so by turning that little valve on the bottom?"

"Um, don't think we *ever* have," responded Jim.

"Then you've caused your own problem."

"How so?"

"Well, the purpose of that valve is to draw off the sludge that collects on the bottom of the tank. If you don't drain it on a regular basis, sooner or later the sludge hardens and cakes there on the bottom. Then the heat doesn't penetrate well. Once it's hardened, there's damn little you can do except replace the tank. It will get a hell of a lot worse as time goes by."

"Well, thanks for the info. If you have any brochures, I'll ride over and have a look."

"Can't see you tonight," he said. "I need the evening to catch up on customer bills. I'll have to get Andre involved with bookkeeping. It will save me a lot of time. He's a smart boy. But when you're ready for a new tank, give me a call and we'll take good care of you."

"Thanks!" Both hung up. "Let's go," said Jim. "Ed said he'd be taking care of store business this evening. Couldn't have planned any better."

When they got to the church, people were milling around inside taking pictures. By now, the building was resplendent with its bright ivory walls that contrasted with the blue and gold-leaf painted wood trim of its eight soaring Gothic arches.

Entering through the main doors, Jim and Martie walked through the vestibule then up the right side aisle and into the utility room. There sat Ed Bristol's invention: a large rectangular metal box, bolted with angle iron to a heavy wooden cart with metal wheels, the type used to haul huge, heavy warehouse items. The box was three feet long, two feet wide, and thirty inches in height. After a furtive examination of its exterior, it looked harmless.

"It's sound enough," said Martie. "Reminds me of something Ed Bristol would make. Looks like all the seams are welded."

"It's quite clever. Look at the way he made the cash slot," said Jim, attempting to reach his hand inside. "There is a baffle in here slanted to the right to keep any wandering hands from reaching in more than a few inches." He shined his light inside the opening but could not see down and around the end of the baffle. "And it's much too heavy to be carried off."

"Clever man," said Martie. "I don't see a door. How does he empty it?"

"According to Dr. Troft, there is a keyed door in the bottom." Both stooped down to reach up underneath. The opening felt square, about twelve inches on all sides. "The professor told me they roll the cart over a tarpaulin, open the door with Ed Bristol's key and all the money falls out. After the cart is pulled away, the ushers pull up the four corners, sack-like, and then carry it downstairs."

Martie started to giggle. "I can just see Dr. Troft, or one of the ushers, slinging the money sack over his shoulder like the boogie man stealing little kids."

"I wish we could see inside," said Jim,

"Why?"

"It may not be as innocent as it looks, but I'm probably just being neurotic."

"Can you open it?" asked Martie. "Don't police have skeleton keys for different kinds of locks?"

"Not anymore. Today's locks and tumblers have gotten rather sophisticated. Even a veteran locksmith has to drill out the tumblers to open a good lock these days, but I do have something in my car that might be helpful."

He was gone just a few minutes during which time, Martie went out and sat piously in a pew. He returned with what looked like an oversized dentist's mirror. It was about two inches in diameter with a handle that could be extended like an auto antenna.

"Now, you hold the flashlight, and I'll slide the mirror down past the edge of the baffle. If there's a second one, we're screwed," said Jim. Martie held the light so its beam followed the incline of the baffle right to its edge.

Jim slid the mirror in and out several times before he said, "Just keep the light right there; we're in luck, no second baffle. I can see down inside." He kept readjusting the mirror so the flashlight beam reflected on the inside walls.

"There is something peculiar here," said Jim, "There is a wooden wall running down the inside of this thing separating the entire case into two separate compartments—but wait, let me see over here." He took out the mirror and twisted it just a bit then looked again and again at various angles. "Part way down the middle wall, there appears to be a door that must open into the second compartment. Here, Martie, you take a look."

Now Jim held the flashlight while Martie twisted and turned the mirror during her examination. "I see it. Did you notice that little silver motor in there? It looks like it's connected to one of the door hinges."

"Let me see," said Jim, He re-inspected the inside of the box. "Now I see it. You are a keen observer. That motor must open and close that door."

"I'll bet Bristol has some kind of remote that allows him to open the door allowing money to slide down into the other side of the box. Why else would the motor be there?"

"So, when the door on the bottom is opened, it only appears that everything falls out."

"But not Ed Bristol's secret stash," interrupted Martie. "But why doesn't that money fall out, also?"

Jim answered, "If whoever made this contraption was clever enough to make one radio-controlled door, I'll bet there is another one near the bottom of the second compartment that Ed Bristol leaves closed when the ushers empty the offerings. The cart is too low to the floor to see up inside and much too heavy to lift or even turn on its side. Besides, the ushers would never suspect foul play. Even if you stuck your hand up there with the bottom door open, you couldn't reach up high enough to touch the second trap door, so you'd assume the cart was empty."

"I'll wager that Ed Bristol keeps his radio transmitter in his pocket and opens and closes the two doors when no one is around. I'll also bet that on any given Sunday, the money skimmed is quite good."

"Know what bothers me the most?" asked Martie. "I don't think Ed is capable of building such a contraption by himself. He may have welded the outside box together, cut the hole in the heavy cart and bolted down the box, but the motorized guts, not a chance—Andre, maybe."

"Nah, he's too honest to get caught up in something so shady."

"One thing we know for sure," said Martie, "Dr. Troft's suspicions were correct."

Jim added, "Troft admitted the bank statement agreed with the amounts tallied on the deposit slip. But Bristol siphons off the money before it gets counted, god alone knows how much has been pilfered by this time," said Jim.

January 31, 2003—Friday
10:30 P.M.

After finishing at Ed's Appliance Store, Andre picked up Sylvia. Both were now in Saint Paul's Church staring at the miracle cross.

"So this is what's causing all the fuss in this city," said Andre as they stood under the crucifix.

"What'ya mean in this city. This crucifix has become a national phenomena."

"Somehow, I expected it to look different, more mysterious."

"Looks like a normal cross to me," replied Sylvia. "Does it really cry?"

"That's what witnesses have said, Syl. As of yet, no explanation has been found."

"Well, if I saw it happen, I guess I might believe it, too." They walked around the church looking at the myriad of burning candles. "It's beautiful here in a way. Very peaceful."

Leaving the church, they drove over to Ye Olde Pour House where Sylvia had a Merlot and Andre had his usual dark beer. The pub was always crowded on Friday night, so they reacted quickly when a booth became available where they had been standing. They gabbed for quite a while. Even talked about the crucifix they had seen earlier. When Andre noticed that Sylvia finished her wine, he looked around for the waitress. "I'll get us a refill."

She leaned forward over the table and said, "Know what? I've got beer and wine at my place, along with other goodies."

"What kind of goodies?"

"Goodies like chips."

"That's it?"

"And pretzels."

"And?"

"Popcorn if you'd like some."

"Anything else?"

"And a nice, warm shower."

"All those things sound fine, but what about you?"

"I think I'd like the chips!" Sylvia teased.

"That's not what I mean."

"You mean the warm shower?"

"No. I—Andre—want—you—Sylvia."

A huge grin came over her face. Andre put enough money on the table to pay the tab then they both left. They sat outside in the parking lot kissing and fondling one another until Sylvia said, "Baby, I can't take much more of this, let's go to my apartment." And restarted his jeep and drove away. While Andre drove, Sylvia reached over and played with his curly hair for a few minutes, then slid her finger around his earlobes.

"Syl, I can't drive. You're distracting me too much."

"That's okay. There isn't much traffic to worry about. You can do it." Andre reached up, took her hand and held it. Within a few minutes the two entered Sylvia's apartment.

Andre asked, "Have you ever played shower curtain?"

"What?

"You heard me—shower curtain."

"No, but if it's sexy, I'll play."

"Let's shower first, then I'll explain my rules for the game."

"Ewie, I hope it's exciting because I'd play any game with you."

When they finished in the bathroom, Andre unhooked the shower curtain and laid it across Sylvia's queen-sized bed. Both wore only towels.

"You first," said Andre. "Just lie face down and relax." Then he poured a thin stream of baby oil on her back from neck to her towel and methodically massaged it over every part of her except her hair. "Now, lie on your back," he commanded. He continued with his oil treatment starting at her toes and working his way up to her chin. Since he had been straddling her, he, too, already had some oil on parts of his body. "Now, it's your turn. But you're not allowed to have the bottle. You have to cover me with the oil I put on you."

"Oh, do I like this game!" she said. Andre laid back and Sylvia began sliding her oil covered body around him, twisting and turning in every way she could, to cover him with oil. Before long, the two were grappling at each other like a pair of greased wrestlers. "I think it's time for me to ride, pony boy!"

February 1, 2003—Saturday
5:00 P.M.

Weary Father Kerr had prepared to leave his confessional when he heard footsteps coming down the aisle. The person entered and said nothing.

"I'm listening," he said, "Go ahead please." There was a long pause. The priest anticipated what was coming.

Then, the dreaded voice said, "You've done a good job, Father Kerr. I just wanted you to know that. Please keep delivering the money and everything will be okay—no one will get hurt. Remember, don't mention our plan to anyone." Father Kerr remained silent.

"Did you hear me?" The Voice asked.

"Yes." This time there was no request for absolution. The Voice left the confessional. Soon afterward, Father Kerr returned to the rectory.

February 3, 2003—Monday
7:30 P.M.

"How much do you suppose he steals?" asked Martie.

"I've been running that question through my mind trying to guesstimate an amount. Kerr tells me that a lot of people now come to services here that used to attend their home parishes."

"I mean, make a rough guess. How much would the collection be for just one Sunday Mass?"

"Let's just say six-hundred people attend each service. Some have mucho-moola, some a lot less. But if the average person drops in two dollars, and I'm sure that is low, then twelve-hundred dollars would be collected per Mass. And, since there are five Sunday Masses, that would make six-thousand dollars on any given Sunday."

Martie said, "I have a feeling that's a very low figure, don't you?"

"Well, just for fun, let's raise the stakes to five dollars per person then three-thousand people times five dollars is fifteen-thousand dollars per Sunday, and I still think that might be a low estimate."

Martie added, "When I think of all the money collected from those perpetually-burning candles, we're talking about big bucks. You said imagine 600 people per Mass. I'll bet Dr. Troft squeezed in a lot more people than that."

26 Two Names in One Person

February 4, 2003—Tuesday
9:05 A.M.

In the Latrobe City Hall Building, Jim walked down the hall to the police department area, and straight up to Ms. Keyes' desk.

"Hi, Sylvia. You always have such a bright smile in the morning."

"Morning, handsome," said Sylvia. "It's that cross eyed monster with the runny nose that makes me so happy."

"Oh, you mean, Andre?"

"Who else? I'll never forget how surprised I was when that hunk arrived instead of the geeky creature you described. Andre turns me on and on and on."

"Is it his crossed eyes or his runny nose?"

"Oh, it's everything about him: his face, his hands, his hard body, even his smell."

"I told you he smelled!"

"Jim," she replied. "I mean he and I've been seeing each other a lot lately. He is one terrific man. I know you keep jagging me, but thanks for the tip."

"Shucks, that means I've got competition, right?"

"Gumshoe, there is no competition; Andre wins thumbs down. No insult intended, of course."

"None taken. Anyway, I've a favor to ask. Do you know anyone over at Latrobe City Bank?"

"Are you planning an inside job? Policeman's pay not enough for you?"

"If you'll plan with me!" said Jim. "No, I have a simple request. I'd like to know whose name or names are on the signature card for Saint Paul's Church Fund. How'd I do? Does that make sense?"

"Sure does," answered Sylvia. She turned to her computer console, punched a few keys and said, "Ah, here it is." She had found the bank's phone number and with ease, punched in the digits on her phone. She then clicked another button to turn on the speakerphone.

Jim could hear the phone ringing at the bank until a cheerful voice answered, "It's a great day at Latrobe City Bank. How may I help you?"

"Beth, this is Sylvia over at the Police Bureau."

"Oh, hi, Syl, how are you?"

"Just fine and how's that big, black, nasty stud of yours?— The one that won't scratch its fleas for fear of hurting them."

"You mean Bob? Well, he's okay. Still makes me feel sad to leave him in the morning, but what a welcome I get at five-thirty every day."

"On the sly, can you check something for me since I know you're not supposed to give out account information over the phone?"

"Let's have it."

"Can you look to see whose name or names are on the signature card for Saint Paul's Church Fund?"

"Hang a sec, will you?" It was obvious that Beth had gone searching. Jim just shook his head at Sylvia's efficiency and her

248

connections.

Covering her phone, Sylvia said, "Beth's Bob is a delight. Loves ice cream and of all things, he likes rum—"

That quickly, Jim heard Beth's voice over the speakerphone, "The fund has two names listed on its signature card: Paul Kerr and Ed Bristol. Did I answer your question?"

"Yes," replied Sylvia, "How about lunch sometime?"

"Hey, how about today?" inquired Beth.

"Tell you what; I'll meet you at Ye Olde Pour House at 11:30."

"Okay. Bye, Syl."

"You've helped," said Jim. "You get a nice gift for that." He handed her a single stick of gum and walked away.

10:05 AM

Martie and Jim had loose puzzle pieces, some of which were beginning to fit together, but there was no sense making accusations or assumptions until they had undeniable proof. As he drove down Main Street past Ed Bristol's Appliance Store, Jim thought of Andre working inside. He grinned, thinking of Andre's "ironing board" comment.

Then his mind wandered to something else Martie had said about a Brother Charles taking a particular interest in Andre because they both loved to talk about scientific ideas. He drove around the block again, and then parked in front of Bristol's store beside a yellow line and a sign on a telephone pole which said "No Parking. Loading Zone." He left his blinkers on and walked inside to see Andre. He hadn't even considered what he'd say if Ed Bristol was there.

"Hi, Andre, your boss around?"

"No, sir, he's over at the church. Speaking of church, which you weren't, are you going to write yourself a ticket? I mean, aren't you parked in a Tow Away Zone? Shall I call the police?" he giggled. "I am offended by your openly flagrant disobedience toward a civil statute of Latrobe, Pennsylvania, USA," and he grinned all the more.

"Sorry, Judge, let me off easy, I'd like to ask you a question or two."

"Shoot—well, not literally he said glancing at Jim's holster."

"Martie mentioned you repair the machines at Saint Vincent's."

"I do now. Mr. Bristol used to make the repairs, then a Brother Charles, and now it's my job."

"So this Charles and Ed Bristol are good friends?"

"Yes, Mr. Ed still goes over to visit him once in a while," said Andre.

"To repair laundry equipment?"

"No. Sometimes he just says 'I'll be back, I'm going over to the monastery,' and then he leaves. Doesn't take tools or any new parts or anything."

"How do you know he sees Brother Charles?"

"I just assumed he did. Several times while I was there working, Mr. Bristol came in, and the two of them walked off talking while I was working."

"Did you and Ed drive there together?" questioned Jim.

"The very first time, we went over together so Mr. Ed could introduce me to Brother Charles. That's when this brother quit making repairs and I started. Now, I drive our truck over there myself."

"This Brother Charles is quite a scientist, Martie tells me."

"Well, he always comes over when I'm working and watches

me and what I'm doing. Sometimes his staring makes me nervous, so I start talking to him. Once I discovered his interest in science, we always have plenty to talk about."

"I'm curious, Andre, why did he make you feel nervous?" asked Jim.

"Well, you know when you're in a room and no one is talking, you start to feel uncomfortable, like, like you should say something? The silence and his staring just made me feel uneasy."

"Martie says he does a lot of his experimenting in a mountain lab of some kind."

"Brother Charles says he likes the solitude of his retreat cabin where he can think and do his experiments without interruptions for prayer and other obligations."

Jim pried further. "Does he ever mention what he's working on?"

"One time he mentioned something about a low temperature device he was inventing; had something to do with cancer cells." Then Andre chuckled, "maybe just a new type refrigerator. I know he does a lot of theoretical writing there."

"Oh?"

"I found one of his published articles in a science journal one evening at the monastery library. Something titled 'Physics and Being' if I'm remembering right."

"Sounds deep."

"Some of it I understood, but a lot of it was umbrella."

"Umbrella?"

"Over my head," laughed Andre.

Jim thanked him and promised Andre he'd issue a certain Jim Simmons a citation for breaching the law.

"Just don't become a repeat offender," laughed Andre.

Jim left the store and drove away.

1:00 P.M.

Jim recalled his conversation with Brant Hardy at the Federal Building in Pittsburgh where he learned about Ed Bristol's personality during his army stint. Brant had mentioned that their buddy, a man named Schaler, was very bright. Brant said the man wanted to become some kind of scientist but was drafted into the Vietnam War. He dialed his friend Henry Collins at the Federal Building and after a few moments of comical verbal exchange, Jim asked Henry to connect him with Brant Hardy.

"Hardy, here."

"Brant, this is Jim Simmons, I talked with you in person back in December about an Ed Bristol. Do you remember that?"

"Yes."

"I was wondering if your other buddy you mentioned, Schaler, ever followed a career in science."

"Last I heard, and that was about ten years ago, he was still teaching at MIT. He held several degrees, I believe. I know because some of his research has been published," said Brant.

"I wanted to look up some of it, but didn't have a last name. Can you help me with that?" asked Jim.

"Schaler. Schaler is his last name, Arthur Schaler. Does that help?" asked Hardy.

"Yes, thanks for the information," answered Jim,

"I'm more curious than ever about why you're checking out those two characters, but I don't suppose you can tell me."

"Not right now," replied Jim. "But when I get this case all figured out, I'll let you know. It may be nothing at all, but I wouldn't want to spread rumors that would damage Schaler or his wife and family."

Brant laughed for a moment, "Schaler's gay. He has no wife or kids, none that I ever knew of."

"Everywhere I find surprises today. Well, thanks for your help, and I will be in touch."

8:00 P.M.

On their way to Saint Vincent's Monastery library, Martie and Jim decided that she would check out research done by Brother Charles while he looked up published articles written by Arthur Schaler. At the library, each could use a separate computer with a fast cable connection their home computer did not have. Martie searched using the name Brother Charles.

There were countless matches for those two words. So she searched on brother Charles Saint Vincent Monastery. Now she came up with a few hits that might be appropriate. She showed them to Jim. The first was a volume titled: *Prime Matter, the Ultimate Nuclear Particle.* The next was also a book: *God, Being, and Physics.* The third and fourth were both articles published in scientific journals: "A Low-Temperature Device for Wart Removal," and "Radiation Versus Freezing to Control Cancerous Growths."

Jim had a lot less difficulty. When he typed in Arthur Schaler physics, the search found a few hits that instantly seemed related. Since Martie had already shown him what she found, he scanned his list. Item fourteen struck him. It was an article titled: "Destroying Tumors: Freezing Instead of Radiation." Item thirty-two was another article that seemed philosophical: "Atomic Properties as Accidents of Matter." Two items further, there was a book: *Mind: Electrochemical Personalities.*

"Odd," said Martie, "that both people seem interested in

similar subjects. E. Charles and A. Schaler both seem interested in freezing techniques."

"Just coincidence; the names are different."

"I wonder if they know one another or have ever worked together?" asked Martie. It had gotten late. She had been doodling on her notepad writing down the two names randomly. While he watched, Jim noticed a change in concentration come over her as she stared at her notepad.

"What?" he asked. She didn't answer.

"Whaaa—t?" he asked a bit louder looking over at her pad.

"Jim, look at this. It might be mere coincidence but look." She printed the name E. Charles above A. Schaler:

E. Charles
A. Schaler

Then she drew lines from the letters of the top name to the letters of the bottom name.

"Well, I'll be damned," remarked Jim. Then he continued to look through his hit list to find an increasing number of similar items. "You don't suppose they're the same person, do you?" he asked, as if he already believed it.

"Guess what, Jim, if they are the same person, the brilliant Schaler that Ed Bristol served with in Vietnam is living as Brother Charles at Saint Vincent's Monastery as we speak."

"Preposterous. Just can't be. It's got to be sheer coincidence." Martie added, "If Schaler is the brain he's supposed to be, then he and clever Ed Bristol put together one neat bilking scheme. Remember Ed's reaction the day after Christmas when you mentioned Schaler's name?"

"Shit, you're right. I can't believe this. If what you say is true, then this is better than robbing a Brinks truck or a bank.

A robbery is a one time risky deal. Their scheme could go on indefinitely."

10:00 P.M.

Just for enjoyment on a beautiful starlit night, after they left the Monastery, they turned right on 981 heading towards Route 30. From there, they went east for a few miles and then turned left on a back road that would lead them back into Latrobe. Along the way they discussed the bits and pieces of information they now possessed. Some of the pieces seemed to fit, but the most intriguing one of all was the actual cross itself. Martie was the first to mention it.

"Jim, I know that coming from me this will sound crazy, but suppose there is something supernatural going on here. That could mean Ed Bristol and his friend are capitalizing on a good thing. You know, the money I mean. He doesn't want anything to interfere with the money he steals. He could care less about religion or divine intervention."

"Or diabolical possession!"

"Frightening thought!"

"Interesting comment from you. I hate to admit this, but since you've confessed, I admit that I've had similar thoughts about the miracle," said Jim.

"As weird as it seems, maybe something other-worldly killed Sister Lucy and Father Phillip."

"And Brother Anthony?"

"Maybe all three deaths, or two if Anthony is still alive although I doubt that. But we may be reading more into these happenings than what is logically warranted." There was a long silence between them.

"Martie, one day back before Christmas, I think it was

December 17th, I stopped at the rectory. I don't remember what I asked Kerr, but he replied, 'I hope you catch that murdering monster,' Martie. I had never suggested that the nun's death was anything but an accident so I asked him if he knew something he wasn't telling us. He clamped shut."

"If something supernatural is going on, is it inspired by God or Lucifer?"

"Geez, Jim, what a frightening thing to talk about."

"So, what if the place is possessed, Martie? Think about it. We have three deaths, two near misses, and a crying crucifix. Seems to make more sense that fiendish evil is involved, rather than anything good. And I think Kerr knows that, but just can't tell us."

Martie said joking, "Maybe the church should be exorcised. I just get this creepy feeling of dread when I go in there."

At that exact instant, Martie's automobile engine quit. It didn't cough or sputter. It stopped—dead! She steered to the side of the road with a spooked look on her face. Both sat in silence staring at one another. Martie turned and looked behind to make sure no one or no thing was hiding in the back seat. "Jim, I'm scared," she whispered. "What happened? Should we not have been talking about evil, Satan, devils?"

"Coincidence," replied Jim. But even he thought, *Spooky that it happened at this precise moment.* "Give it a minute then try again."

Martie waited then tried several times with no luck. Both of them checked the fuel gauge, but it read at least a half tank.

"Jim, I'm not kidding. I'm afraid. Why did this happen just when we were discussing the Evil One?" *Very creepy very, very odd,* Jim thought. *I'm nervous, too!*

To cover his feelings, Jim said, "I thought you didn't believe in the supernatural?"

"Well, I didn't—but, but what just happened? Can you explain it?"

"I haven't the slightest idea, but I'm sure something just broke down. At least, I hope that's what happened."

He turned and looked in the back seat, remembering what Troft had told him about his automobile experience. Then he got out walked to the front and lifted the hood. *Everything seems okay: no smoke, no bad smells, no hissing or leaking sounds. But I'd need a flashlight to check further.*

He asked Martie to try several more times while the hood was up, but all he heard was a clicking sound. "I think your battery is bad, maybe the alternator. Sometimes the terminals get so corroded there isn't enough amperage to keep the car running. I can check it out tomorrow or we can have it towed to a garage."

"And just how will we get home?"

"We'll walk. It's not that far, and it's a beautiful night."

Martie agreed to the short jaunt, but she was very apprehensive. For fifty yards or more, they walked inhaling the cold crisp night air. But suddenly, they noticed the lights of an auto approaching from their rear, but there was no sound— just bright lights. Both turned at the same time. No car was approaching—the light was coming from Martie's abandoned automobile.

"Uh, Jim, what's going on back there? Someone must be inside. Let's get out of here. I'm more than scared, now."

"Did you lock it when we left?"

"No, I figured it wouldn't start, no one could steal it." Jim started back toward Martie's car, but she grabbed his arm.

"I'm not going back there," she declared, "you're not going

back there, Jim, let's just call the police!"

"Martie, I *am* the police, and I'm going to find out what the hell's going on."

"Oh, please, Jim, don't pull this macho crap with me. Can't we just get out of here? What if you get shot? You'd be the perfect target—good, Lord—we're both perfect targets—right now," whispered Martie.

Without hesitation, she yanked Jim into the bramble-like shadows along the roadside. "Jim, you are not going back there. Do you hear me? I want you alive and in one piece. You are no match for the Devil. I love you too much to see you resting in Hell's casket."

"Martie, you're making too much of this. Did you turn off the headlights before we left?"

"Headlights, schmed lights, I don't remember what I did and I don't care. But I do know that we're safer here than back there." The headlight beam flickered for a moment, and then went out. "Jim, someone is in that car and they're toying with us."

But in the immediate darkness, Jim had already slipped away into the brush along their side of the road.

"Stay put, Martie, I'll be right back." He whispered. But Martie was holding on to the back of his jacket almost tripping over him.

"Why are you doing this? I mean why? Jim, this makes no sense at all."

"Sh-h-h," he whispered. Ever so quietly, they made their way back to Martie's car by making a large semi-circle through the dried brush and snow covered brambles. When the car was ten feet away, both stopped and listened.

No sounds.

None at all, except for an occasional click of some contracting motor part as it cooled. Convinced he hadn't been seen, Jim stooped low, and crept up to the car's rear bumper. He moved along the side until he could raise his head to peer into a back rear window. The vehicle looked empty. He carefully moved along the side and stared directly inside. No one. He pulled the door open and felt for the headlight switch. Sure enough, it was in the full, on position.

"Martie, it's safe. I know what happened. Keep your eyes on the headlights."

He walked around the open door, lifted the hood and jiggled the cables leading to the battery terminals.

Thick sparks appeared as the electrical current arced its way through the loose anode connector. The headlights came on, but then went out as sparks danced around the battery terminal. "This wire is so loose, Martie, it barely makes contact. That's why your car stopped."

"You mean that's it?

"Yep."

"No Devil, no demons?" Martie's heart was still racing.

"Nope, just one very loose terminal. But the bolt that connects this wire to its terminal is missing."

"Are you sure it's okay?"

"Certain," said Jim. "Let's just leave it sit here. Tomorrow I'll drive out and fix the damn thing in the daylight."

"That scared me," said Martie. "Let's get out of here fast!"

"Baby, I was scared, too. Don't think I wasn't!"

Before starting off, Martie locked her automobile. Since there were few lights of any kind, the stars appeared brilliant. "Beautiful night," she said.

"I'll say."

Within thirty minutes, they were heading down Greensburg Avenue right into Latrobe.

"That cold February air wasn't exactly refreshing," said Martie. "I'm frozen."

At Elm, they made a left and were soon inside the warmth of their home.

"You know," said Jim, "ever since we started walking, this thought keeps popping into my head."

"If it has to do with the supernatural, or demons, let's skip it for tonight because when that engine died, it frightened me—all that talk about Satan, exorcism, fiendish devils. Yuk!"

"Actually, it's a couple of thoughts, and it does involve the mystery. Want to hear?"

Martie asked, "Will it give me nightmares?"

"Hope not. Suppose for a moment that Ed Bristol and Charles are in cahoots together. I remember old Father Martin telling me something about the laundry room the day after Anthony disappeared."

"Go ahead. Two disconnected thoughts so far."

"Suppose there is some, some thing, some gadget, some whatever that makes the tears appear."

"Now, I have three disconnected facts, but go on. I can handle four, I think."

Jim continued, "Suppose that after Anthony had finished restoring the crucifix seven years ago, someone went into his workshop to alter it."

"Now we have two disconnected thoughts, and two that tie together a bit," teased Martie.

"I'm trying," said Jim as he went on. "I'm trying so give me credit. Now suppose that a person was in the act of altering the cross when Anthony bumbled in, so to speak, or was about to."

"I'm still with you."

"What if Charles was altering the crucifix while Ed Bristol stood guard at the bottom of the steps when Anthony arrived?"

"Okay."

"Ed Bristol kills Anthony, and then carries him into the laundry room."

"But Jim, there would've been noise, a yell, a scuffle of some kind," entertained Martie.

"Ed Bristol is a huge man, agreed?"

"For sure."

"I think he could kill a rhino with his bare hands! There probably wasn't much of a scuffle."

"My goodness, Jim, how can you imagine such terrible things?" asked Martie.

"Shall I stop, Baby?" asked Jim,

"Well, I don't know, this is upsetting me after what just happened back there, but you might as well finish."

Jim went on. "Old Father Martin told me that the very next day after Anthony's disappearing act, his dryer was out of order. The tumbler had been removed and was sitting on top of it. Father Martin said there was an Out of Order sign on the dryer's front."

"Oh, my God," inhaled Marty raising the back of her hand to her open mouth. "Jim, I think I know where you're going with this, and it's pure fiction, don't be ridiculous. If the body was inside, anyone could've opened the door and seen it."

"Are you ready for this?"

By now, Jim's enthusiasm was hypnotic.

"Martie, Old Father Martin said he—could—not—open—that—door."

"Really? Jim. It was wedged or bolted shut so the monks

261

wouldn't try using it and find the corpse. Is that what you're thinking?" asked Martie wanting to put a quick end to Jim's gruesome tale.

"I'm almost finished," promised Jim, "Father Martin claims that the very next day a new dryer appeared."

First Martie began to tremble, and then her face screwed up until she began to cry. Tears ran down her cheeks even after Jim walked over and held her in his arms. "I'm sorry, I'm so sorry, Baby. I didn't know you were that upset." He pressed her to his chest. "You're right, all of it is hypothetical. Good grief, I'm sorry—I didn't mean to hurt—to upset you." Then he stood holding her, rocking gently from one side to the other. A few minutes passed before Jim could feel her shaking stop. She stopped crying. "Jeez, I'm sorry," he apologized again.

"Jim, don't apologize, it's just that—" Jim knew fresh tears were forming in her eyes and that her voice was about to break. "It's just that Andre told me they take all the old, broken washers and dryers out to Turtle Creek Landfill." She began to sniffle. "Oh, please, Heaven, don't let that poor holy man be buried down there."

27 The Landfill at Turtle Creek

February 7, 2003—Friday
2:35 P.M.

"Sylvia," said Jim, after dialing her desk at the Borough Building. "Want some more gum?"

"I'm impressed, big spender, can you gift wrap it this time?"

"All depends. Can you get me some information?"

"Like legit or what? One type costs a stick more than the other!"

"There used to be a landfill operation in Turtle, Creek, not too far from Wilmerding."

"Wilmerding?" She started to giggle.

"What's so funny?"

"Wilmerding reminds me of, of—oh, forget it. It's just a comical name, maybe just a bit suggestive, to me at least."

"Can you find out if that landfill operation still exists and whether they keep records of who dumps there?"

"I'll give it a try," she said, and then he heard Sylvia giggling at the word "Wilmerding" as she clicked off.

Immediately afterward, Jim was called to a vehicular accident involving entrapment where rescuers had to use the Jaws of Life to cut apart an auto that had gone out of control and flipped on its roof, then back over on its wheels. The driver was a seventy-six-year-old man who remained conscious during the entire rescue operation and had received minor injuries. He did not go into shock. But it became clear he missed his turn because he was DUI.

One of his rescuers remarked, "If acetylene torches had been used to free him, the flame would've ignited his breath and the entire rescue crew would need landing clearance at the Latrobe County Airport." After tow trucks cleared the accident from the roadway and traffic restored to normal, Jim drove back to the Police Bureau thinking about all the accidents caused by DUIs. He also remembered to call Sylvia.

"Hi, Syl, got delayed a bit, sorry!"

"No problem, Gumshoe. Turtle Creek Landfill still operates but not for long, another six months at best. The dump is almost full. Apparently its owners are hoping to parcel out the land and sell it once the dump settles. And, yes, they do keep a log of dumpers, dates dumped, time, and type of vehicle.

"The owner said the log did not contain what type of material was dumped but added that only 'acceptable' fill was permitted. When I asked him what that meant, he said no tires, no chemicals, no medical supplies, no large vehicles like junked cars or anything."

"Gee, thanks, Sylvia. I can't give you your prize because I'm here and you're there."

"Oh, you really are an intelligent Gumshoe."

February 10, 2003—Monday
10:00 A.M.

Chief Romeric gave Jim permission to drive to the Turtle Creek Landfill, a drive of thirty-seven miles west on Route 30 heading toward Pittsburgh. Route 30 skirted around

Greensburg, then Jeanette and Irwin, until it intersected with Route 48 in East McKeesport. Turning right, he followed Route 48 down into Wilmerding and then Turtle Creek itself. Just after driving under the Tri-Borough Expressway, there was a small, unobtrusive sign that said "Landfill" with an arrow pointing to the right up a long, but not steep grade. At first the road was paved with asphalt but changed to gravel as he approached the fenced-in landfill area. He parked his cruiser just outside two very wide gates in a high, cyclone fence that surrounded the entrance. The gates stood open, but a huge red STOP sign hung on each one. A battered old mobile trailer served as an office.

Although there was a light in one of the dust covered windows of the mobile trailer, it appeared empty. Jim climbed the four wooden steps up to the trailer and pulled the door open. To his surprise, the trailer was warm and neat inside.

A gentleman dressed in work clothes got up from behind a desk and greeted him. "Hello, Officer, a mite cold today."

"Agreed," responded Jim, "Kind of a lonely job up here all by yourself."

"You get used to it. I keep my radio playing and I read lots of books. Every two hours, we switch jobs. Leslie mans the office while I work the dump."

"Leslie?"

"She drives the MS around to smash down things that are dumped." Jim looked a bit puzzled. "MS is our Monster Smasher. It weighs about thirty-five tons and has large, spiked, metal wheels. Everything dumped here gets smashed flat. Then the MS pushes it over the edge. When junk from torn up streets and highways or demolished buildings comes in, it gets pushed over to cover the other stuff. By the way, I'm Chris Boyd."

"Nice meeting you, Chris; I'm Jim." He paused a moment

then asked, "So, Leslie spends half her day outside?"

"Well, like I said, she rides the MS for two hours, then we switch places and I take a two hour shift. It breaks up the monotony of the day for both of us. The MS is closed in, quiet, and heated. It's not a dirty job at all. It has a wonderful radio. But anyway, what brings a police officer to my door?"

"I'm from the Latrobe Police Department and would like to look at your logbook for 1995 if possible."

"That's going back a few years but let me take a look."

The gentleman turned and walked toward the back of the trailer. Along both trailer walls were shelves containing rows of logbooks.

"I've tried to keep these in order, although I don't know why. Very few people ask to look at them. A busy year '95 was. Back then, we used to accept raw garbage from several municipalities. The smell was pretty foul even though we tried to cover a layer of refuse with another layer of dirt or rock like I said before."

He pulled out a log and brought it over to his desk. Jim stood behind his chair so he could see the book. Sure enough, just like Sylvia had said, he saw five columns: *Name, Date, Time, Vehicle Type, Paid.* Although Sylvia had not mentioned the Paid column, it listed how much it cost, to dump a particular load.

"This book runs from January through June."

"I need the log for August 21st. I believe that was a Tuesday, no wait, it was a Monday." Chris returned that logbook to its shelf and retrieved another.

He began flipping pages until he came to August 21st then stood up and said, "Here, you sit and take a look since you know what you're looking for."

Jim's heart began to race. He ran his forefinger down the list of names until it stopped beside a line that had been starred: |

8/21/95 | Bristol | 9:30 a.m. | Pick Up | $45 |. He reread the line again and again in disbelief. Seeing no copier in the office, Jim copied out on his notepad the information from the logbook exactly as it appeared. Then he asked Chris, "Were you working here then?"

"I've been working here since 1986, so has Leslie." He walked over to the logbook and pointed to a small letter on the very left of the entry line. He stooped down for a closer look. That "C" means I was working the office and Leslie was driving the MS."

"Mind if I talk to her?"

"No, but be careful where you drive. There's a lot of debris out there that can cut up a tire." After thinking for a moment, he added, "Wait, I'll radio her in, we're due to switch at eleven. Then the two of you can talk a bit."

Chris returned to his desk and pushed down a button on his short wave radio. "Leslie? Leslie?"

A female voice responded with the sound of the MS in the background. "A gentleman is here to see you, how about coming in?"

"Is it my husband," asked Leslie?

"No."

"Then I'll consider it."

"He's wearing a uniform."

"He is? I'm coming in for sure," Leslie laughed.

Jim watched out the window for a glimpse of the MS as it arrived. Long before he saw it, he heard its enormous diesel engine. Just before it came over a mound in the dump, he could see puffs of smoky diesel exhaust coming from its upward extended exhaust pipe. He could see the entire machine as it drew closer and knew why they called it the Monster Smasher.

Jim was certain the ground thumped when the MS drove

along the fence beside the office and parked near his cruiser. Leslie climbed down, leaving the engine idling. The bottom of its glassed-in cab stood about eight feet from the ground. The giant crusher had four wheels about four feet in diameter.

The surface of each consisted of a series of large metal spikes, which Jim guessed were eight-inches long; long enough to puncture and compress anything they rolled over. The crusher had no steering wheel. Instead, its two ends pivoted hydraulically in the center, allowing it to make fast, sharp turns. The cab sat above one set of wheels, the huge diesel engine above the others. *Wow!* thought Jim, *it's amazing that this enormous machine can even move under its own weight. Why the damn thing dwarfs my whole police car. I wonder how flat and how far down in the ground it could push my entire cruiser on just one pass.*

When Leslie entered, Chris introduced the two.

"Hey, I'll talk to anyone in a uniform," smiled Leslie.

She was a pert little woman about thirty-six years old, wearing the same type of male uniform Chris wore. It looked like the standard fare provided by the landfill company, but on her it was attractive. Her hair would have sprayed over her shoulders had it not been pony-tailed by a bright yellow scarf.

She was cheerful and seemed more than willing to gab with Jim, "Leslie, do you remember a man named Ed Bristol who used to dump old washers and dryers here?"

"Still does. He comes a few times a year, but yes, I know him. Large fellow," replied Leslie.

"What happens to the loads he dumps?"

"Since most of his items are old appliances, which of course are hollow, they get smashed like everything else and buried or pushed over the edge, then dirt, rock, what have you, gets pushed over top. That's how we expand the dump."

A look of disappointment crossed Jims face. He thought *a dryer containing a dead body would smash and break apart exposing its contents. Severed body parts might even be seen. So-o-o-o, this is a wild goose chase. Ed Bristol wouldn't chance that happening.*

"Did you ever notice anything odd about him, or the loads he dumped?" asked Jim,

"I talked to the man only twice. Once, when he first came, I explained the routine of dumping in the center so I could first crush his junk before pushing it over the edge. After that, he'd just wave to me, dump and leave. The only other time I talked with him, we had a bit of a confrontation."

"Oh?"

"It was the time he backed his truck right to the very edge as if he was going to push off his load without me first crushing it. His truck was so overloaded that he had old machines sitting on his tailgate. They had been tied on so they couldn't fall off before he got here."

"That's interesting," said Jim, "So what happened?"

"I saw what he was about to do and drove over there blowing my horn."

Jim could imagine the MS having a monster horn to match its incredible size.

"He had already untied the load when I got there, but he stopped and faced me. I opened the door, stepped out on a wheel and yelled 'Hey, you know the routine. Move that shit over where I'm working. You can't dump like that. Besides, that side of the dump is closed, you dolt. He got pissed, but wasn't about to have me nudge his new truck with my MS, which I'd have done—um, by accident of course, officer."

"Of course. So he obeyed your order?"

Leslie chuckled a bit and said, "He got in his new truck, angry and a little flustered, and must have put it in reverse because at first it lurched backward about six to ten inches. Then it shot forward so quickly that two machines sitting on the tailgate tumbled off and rolled end over end all the way to the bottom of the dump."

"Were they ever brought back up?"

"I was pissed because in all the years I've worked here, very few large items went uncrushed on my duty. Uncrushed items leave large air pockets. So when they deteriorate and rust away, the dirt above them collapses causing sink holes, and no one wants to buy that kind of property to build on."

"So," asked Jim, "what did you do?"

"I pulled so close to his new truck while he was dumping his load where he was supposed to, that it scared him. As big as he was, he got out and apologized. I said, 'I ought to make you crawl down there and haul that junk back up here. You hear me?' He didn't answer. Instead, he pulled out his wallet and offered me a couple hundred dollars. Imagine that! I told him to keep his damn money. The next day when several truckloads of rock and dirt came in, I had it dumped over the edge to cover his two uncrushed machines. One looked like a washer, I think the other was a dryer. I mean, this is a landfill and the owners don't want it looking like a junkyard to the neighbors who live nearby."

She walked over to the logbook that Chris had placed on the counter then answered, "See here," she pointed to a line in the book, "I put a star beside his name as a reminder. I had every intention of having the owners prohibit him from dumping after that."

"Did you?"

"No, officer, I came off duty, looked at the star and thought, the hell with it, just some laundry equipment, no big thing."

Jim felt he had struck pay dirt. "Leslie, this is very important, how far down would you guess that dryer is buried?"

"At most, I'd say six to eight feet in from the side, if that. Remember that section had been closed. I covered the machines just enough to keep the public from seeing them."

"Man, I don't know how to thank the two of you; you've been very, very helpful."

Chris asked, "Why are you so interested in an old dryer. Had it been stolen or something or was it filled with drugs?"

"We're working on that," Jim answered tactfully, trying to mislead but not telling a lie. "At least, we now know where it is."

"Imagine that," replied Leslie. "A dryer full of drugs just rotting away."

Jim thanked her again, then asked that they not mention his visit if Mr. Ed Bristol should arrive. He told them that in due time, the full story would come out.

Jim drove back to Latrobe thinking that so many of the puzzle pieces seemed to fit, but still, the only proof he and Martie had of deliberate wrongdoing was Ed Bristol's collection cart. *I wonder how much convincing it would take to get Romeric to unearth that buried dryer. He might just act on the information we already have except that the dang landfill is out of Latrobe's jurisdiction.*

28 Ye Olde Pour House

**February 22, 2003—Saturday
5:15 P.M.**

Andre was setting up new display models when Brother Charles entered.

"Hello there, Brother," said Andre with a smile. "Nice to see you."

Brother Charles walked back to where Andre was working. He stood and watched him for several minutes before saying a word.

"I see you're setting up some display machines," he said. "Takes a lot of brawn to move them all by yourself."

"Nah, I'm used to it by now," replied Andre, "these machines are light compared to the weights I lift."

"Is that so," said Charles. "Do you lift at a gym or spa?"

"Naw, mostly at home. I used to go down to the Y but that took too much time. So I bought myself some weights. How about you, you look like you work out?"

"We have a gymnasium at the monastery and a small swimming pool. It isn't much, but I try to exercise enough to keep my body, especially my ticker, in good shape."

"Same here. Well defined muscles seem to attract the kind of person I like." Andre went on with his work while Brother Charles stared at him. Andre began to feel uncomfortable. Once again, he asked Charles about his latest project at the monastery, and they chitchatted while Andre worked.

When Ed Bristol did not show, and the small talk wore thin, Andre said, "Do you want something, Brother? Maybe I can help? Mr. Ed said he'd be right back, but he obviously got delayed. Why don't you have a seat over there." He pointed to a chair up near the store's front entrance at a distance from Andre's work area in the rear.

"Okay," said Charles. "Hope I wasn't bothering you. You're a good-looking fellow. Bet you'd look great in a striped Speedo."

The Brother moved to the front, but sat so he could continue watching Andre. Now, Andre noticed the staring. About seven minutes later, Ed Bristol arrived.

"What the Hell are you doing? You know you're not to come here?" said Ed.

"Is everything still okay?" asked Charles.

"Of course. Why wouldn't it. Payments are being made."

"And the account?"

"It's growing steadily."

"Great," replied Charles. "And the password?"

"It's what it's supposed to be."

"Couldn't be better!" Then he yelled to the back of the store, "See you around, Andre. Let's work out at the monastery sometime soon."

When Andre didn't answer, Charles walked out of the building.

"And don't come here again!" asserted Bristol, peeved. Andre made himself look busy working in the back of the store. He had deliberately pretended not to hear their conversation, but heard every word.

"Andre," Bristol called. Andre still pretended not to hear.

"ANDRE," he bellowed.

This time Andre responded, "Oh! Hello, Mr. Bristol."

"Any repair calls, yet?"

"None," answered Andre and he went on with his work.

8:45 P.M.

Jim and Martie entered the appliance store hoping to talk with Andre. If Ed was there, they would pretend they had stopped by for information about their "failing" water heater when, in fact, their heater was doing just fine. A tiny bell attached to the front door jingled as they entered and were greeted by Andre's voice.

"Hello, folks, this is a switch seeing both of you together for a change. One would think you were a married couple or something," Andre chided. "What can I do for you folks this evening?"

"We came to buy a new ironing board."

Andre put his hand to his mouth and burst out laughing. His dark skin started turning deep red.

"Well, my mama told my sister about that and she has two children now."

"Do you have an ironing board that would hold the two of us?"

For once, Andre could not respond for laughing so hard.

"Well, anyway," said Jim, "are you alone?"

"No, no, I'm not; there are two people standing here with me," and he started to laugh even harder. "Let me get serious now, I think Mr. Bristol has gone for the evening."

Rather than take any chances, Jim asked, "Could you meet us at Ye Olde Pour House for a drink after you close up?"

"At the Pour House?"

"Yes, we have a favor to ask."

"Anything to do with ironing boards?"

"No."

"In either case, I'd love to," replied Andre. "I was just getting ready to close up when you walked in. I'll be over in a few minutes."

Martie and Jim crossed Main Street and went into Ye Old Pour House. There they took a booth, ordered drinks and waited. Martie had her usual wine, and Jim had his rum and Coke in a very small glass so the rum didn't get "drowned" as he always said. Soon Andre walked in and spotted them. On his way past the bar, he asked for a dark beer then walked back and took a seat opposite them in the booth.

"S-s-up?"

"We need your help, if you want to give it."

"Oh?"

"This is a delicate police matter, and a lot is guesswork. It may shock you a bit, but we need some information you might be able to get."

Andre, puzzled, said, "Lay it on me. Sounds mysterious— intriguing."

Martie said, "Okay, I'll be brutally honest. Some of the funds at Saint Paul's are being, um, for want of a better term, misappropriated."

"Stolen?" asked Andre.

"Yes," said Jim.

"And you have proof?"

"We think so."

"So why do you need me?"

"Because you know the two people we think are involved."

"I do?" questioned Andre.

Martie responded, "You work for one of them!"

"Mr. Bristol?"

This time Jim replied, "Seems that way, Andre."

"Naw. You're jangling my wires now."

"I'm dead serious," Jim continued. A short period of silence followed while Andre internalized the accusations.

"So that's why he spends so much time at the church. Man, this is hard to swallow."

"But, we think it's true—actually we're certain. And in addition to that information, we think he is somehow connected with the cross in the church."

"You think the crucifix is a fake?"

"Not sure about that." Jim continued, "But here is the delicate part. We think your boss and Brother Charles are involved in this money scheme together."

Andre's jaw dropped open. "Holy shit!" he exclaimed. "I mean ho-o-o-l-l-ly shit!" he said even louder. "Wait, wait just a minute, you two are always joking with me."

"Not joking," responded Martie.

"Not teasing at all?"

"Andre, this is serious, and these are serious allegations," said Jim. "But we need proof, real proof. We have some pieces of information that are beginning to fit together, but like Chief Romeric says, 'You need real proof before you make any kind of accusations.'"

"Man," said Andre. "Ed Bristol and Charles both? Holy Hell," he said, shaking his head. "But you know I wouldn't put it past either one of them."

"We keep trying to fit the puzzle together, but we need a few critical missing pieces."

Suddenly Andre leaned forward across the booth's table as if he'd leaned back on a tack. "Hey, listen to this. Brother Charles came to the store today and Ed Bristol read him the riot act just for coming. I overheard them talking about payments being made. Charles seemed pleased and then left."

"Payments? Is—that—so," said Jim. "Even that bit of information is extremely helpful."

Martie added, "What we'd like most of all Andre—notice how this teacher has turned detective—what we need most of all is the location of Charles' mountain retreat lab. Do you think you can get that information?" Martie inquired.

"I don't know; I know Mr. Bristol would never tell me plus I'd never ask. I might be able to trick Brother Charles without causing suspicion. I'd sure hate to get fired because like I've told you Martie, Mr. Ed pays me a good salary."

"If you could do that," said Martie, "and we can sneak up there; we might find some of the missing puzzle pieces."

Andre sat back looking concerned. "Now here's the rub. If your suspicions are wrong, then I'll keep my job. If your suspicions are wrong and Mr. Ed finds out that I've been snooping around, I won't have a job, but I might have two even black eyes. And last of all, if your suspicions are correct, and Mr. Ed gets arrested, then I'm out of work. It seems two to one that I might lose and that worries me."

Andre's truthful statement was followed by a long pause as all three sat saying nothing, just looking at their drinks. Then Andre's very serious face broke into a grin.

"Of course, the two of you would help me find a job, right? Maybe make me a police officer? Or maybe I could collect parking tickets?" Then very sheepishly, he said, "I think I know a way of getting Brother Charles to cooperate without making him suspicious."

"It's critical," said Jim, "that neither Charles nor Ed get curious."

Once Andre committed himself, the three of them sat and chatted over anything and everything. Silliness returned to the conversation. They ordered more drinks and, of course, Andre's wonderful sense of humor eased the tension. Around ten-thirty, they all departed for home.

February 24, 2003—Monday
9:15 A.M.

Before Andre came in for the day, Ed talked with Brother Charles at Saint Vincent's about a broken furnace in one of the monastery's many buildings. He always responded to the monastery calls because the arch abbey paid big bucks for repairs and they paid immediately. This time, the heating system for the library had shut down, and since it was a favorite haunt for many of the monks, the abbot wanted it repaired as soon as possible. Andre had a way with machines, which Ed Bristol lacked. Ed would never have attempted to work on a furnace, but he knew Andre had a logical mind and would find the problem and fix it. To Bristol, Andre was a mechanical genius, so he paid him well. He knew he was fortunate.

Just then, Andre walked in. Ed handed him the phone, then walked to the rear of his store. Andre asked the make and model number of the broken furnace so he could locate its schematic online using the store's computer. Andre could not always find a schematic on equipment, so having this information at his fingertips beforehand would save some time.

"Andre," said the brother, "In addition to the library heating system, I've got a refrigerator that freezes everything. I'm guessing the latter needs a new thermostat. Can you come over?"

"Have you checked this out with Mr. Bristol?" asked Andre.

"Yes."

"Then, I'll be over around two-thirty." He lowered his voice almost to a whisper. "By the way, I missed my workout last night. Remember when you told me the monks had a gym and pool?"

"Yes, yes. Why?" asked Charles.

"Do you think they'd mind if I used their gym today? Not for long, mind you, just enough to harden up a bit. We can spot one another it that's okay with you."

Delighted, Charles answered, "Hey, that would be great. I might even go down and check out the broken machinery myself just so we'll have even more sensual sweat time."

"Now, I won't be able to stay long, just enough to pump up a bit and shower off. See you then," said Andre.

2:45 P.M.

When he arrived at the library, Charles had already put a new belt on the blower which fixed the furnace instantly. In addition, he had defrosted the large refrigerator so Andre had an easy time replacing its defective thermostat. Fortunately, Bristol had a usable replacement in stock. Within thirty minutes, Andre plugged in the refrigerator. Rather than wait to see if it shut off, Charles and Andre headed for the gymnasium.

"I'll check it when we're finished here," said Andre. "No sense waiting for that huge thing to get cold."

When they reached the locker room, Andre quickly stripped to the waist then tugged on the tightest ribbed yellow A-shirt he'd brought from home that clearly enhanced his muscular physique. The shirt was frayed at the bottom so it barely reached his navel. He watched Brother Charles giving him that same discomforting stare he'd given him so often in the past, only now Andre knew why.

Instead of dropping his shorts, Andre first wrapped a white towel around his waist then slid off his shorts and pulled on a jockstrap and workout sweat shorts without exposing himself frontally. Brother Charles kept moving around. Andre thought, *the brother seems disappointed.*

The workout went well. Both men did warm ups, stretching exercises, then lifted heavier and heavier weights for the better part of forty-five minutes. They spotted each other doing bench presses. Andre deliberately stood above Charles with his pelvis as close to the man's head as he struggled to lift the heavy weights.

As it got later, Andre said, "Hey, this has been great, brother. Let's do it again real soon. It's great having another jock for a spotter instead of working out all alone. But, listen, I've got to get back to the store."

"Suits me fine," said Charles.

The shower area had no stalls; it was one common room with eight separate shower nozzles and water controls mounted to the walls under them. Andre stripped, picked up his white towel letting it dangle loosely in front and deliberately waited so Charles could fall in behind. He stood in the warm water, lathered up several times and rinsed, always keeping his back toward the brother who walked from one nozzle to another trying to catch a frontal glimpse. Andre watched Charles' lascivious eyes.

"I've tried to read some of your articles," said Andre over the sound of the splashing water. "Could you take me to your retreat lab sometime to see your work?"

"My lab? You're that interested?"

"Sure am. I love science and working with machines. We

could work out here at the monastery and then drive up. If you have weights up there, we could do some serious lifting—harden up until our muscles burn so bad they feel like they'll pop."

"I have a few free weights. That's about it."

"The most important thing is that I'd love to see what you're working on, especially your freezing technique to stop cancer. That's got me all excited. Is your lab far?" Andre finished showering, grabbed his towel and headed out to the main locker room.

Following behind, Charles answered, "About eighteen miles. It's very isolated, but not hard to find once you've been there. It's about nine miles or so from Route 30. Hell, we could exercise naked there like the ancient Greeks and not be seen."

"Hey, don't laugh. I do that at home when it's warm enough." Charles' eyes widened at that comment.

"No reason why we can't turn up the thermostat. The place is small and well insulated."

"Great idea," said Andre. Exercising in the nude feels great—animalistic—ain't anything wrong with a nude body. Besides, the sweat evaporates more quickly."

"Sounds great to me."

Andre was sure the brother had misunderstood his intentions by now so he continued leading him. "I don't know if we should leave here together. The monks won't get suspicious if we drive up separately. I can meet you at your lab or along the way. No one will be the wiser but you'll have to write down the directions."

"Are you free any day this week?"

"This coming Saturday," said Andre. "Now, if I have to work, we'll set up another day, but I'd still come over here for a short workout like today. You'll have to call and request my services from Mr. Bristol."

By this time, Andre was dressed and just about ready to leave. He had balled up his thin A-shirt and discretely shoved it down into the front of his shorts. Shirtless, he turned to face Charles tugging at the zipper on his jeans as if there was just too much Andre to stuff inside.

"Do you want me to help with that zipper?" said Charles grinning. "They can be tricky at times."

"Naw," said Andre, "It's stuck. I'll fix it later. But since I've got to run, would you check that refrigerator thermostat for me?"

"Sure will. But wait." Brother Charles took a few minutes to scratch some very simple directions on a notepad, ripped off the sheet and handed it to Andre who was still tugging at the bulge in his jeans.

"I like the idea of driving up separately and meeting you there because it's not that far."

"Fine by me," said Andre.

"I'll be waiting for you. Got lots to show you! No need to bring gym clothes. I have some towels up there and I'll turn up the heat."

With that upsetting comment, Andre left the locker room, hurried over to the parking lot near the laundry area, hopped aboard Bristol's truck and sped back to the appliance store.

29 The Bulldozer

A large semi arrived at the Turtle Creek Landfill and parked outside the office trailer. The back of the semi was a long, reinforced, open trailer with a medium-sized bulldozer chained to its bed. Following behind in a police cruiser was Chief Romeric and Jim Simmons. After Romeric parked, both men got out and walked with the truck driver to the office door.

Chris Boyd welcomed them. "Come inside," he said. "It's a bit warmer in here."

Warm? thought Jim. *It's like Hades. He unbuttoned his coat.*

Leslie joined the group. After a few minutes of introductions and small talk, she said, "Hello, gentleman. Well, I'll lead you to the place where Bristol's old washer and dryer went end over end. I'll take the MS and you two can follow."

"MS?" inquired Romeric.

"Monster Smasher. That's what we call that thing sitting out there." Leslie pointed toward the huge machine idling in the distance.

Chief Romeric and Jim both stared at it. "Its nickname fits its description," said the chief.

"I'd like to know more about this mysterious dryer. Don't suppose you'd care to share?" When the two officers remained mute, she said, "I hope that bulldozer has tractor tread cleats. The side of the dump is steep. It might slide *down* there, but I doubt it'd get back *up* without them."

The semi driver, who was also the bulldozer operator, spoke up. "It'll take me just a moment or two to get it started and unloaded. Then I'll follow you." He left the office without further comment. Jim walked out with him but the others stayed inside where it was warm. First the dozer operator removed several large chains that had been pulled down and over the machine from one side to the other.

At the back of the trailer, and with some effort, he pivoted a heavy triangular ramp from its stored position up and over the right-rear wheels, so that it fell to the ground behind the trailer. He did the same thing on the left side. Next, he started the powerful diesel engine, put the bulldozer in gear and drove it toward the back of the trailer until it tipped down the reinforced ramps. Afterward, he drove it around to the dump entrance and signaled "ready" to those watching from inside the office window.

Wearing a light jacket, Leslie came out of the office. She walked some twenty yards then climbed the eight ladder-like steps up into the cab of the MS and led the way. As large and heavy as the bulldozer was, it was a dwarf compared to the MS. Jim and Chief Romeric followed in their police car trying to avoid anything that might puncture a tire. The dumpsite was so huge that both Jim and the chief began to think this could be an impossible task.

The vehicular threesome could travel as fast as the bulldozer could run at top speed. Leslie drove the MS on ahead, but they could see her veering to the right about two-hundred yards ahead of them. She stopped the MS precariously close to the dump's edge and got out. "See that creek down there? That's Turtle Run. It empties into Turtle Creek about a mile or so from here. See how the water meanders like a large inchworm that has lifted its middle in the air? Well, I remember looking down there and seeing that when Ed dumped. The dump isn't supposed to get any closer than twenty yards to that rill. The area right down there, as you can see, juts out a bit more than the rest. You can see there isn't any twenty-yard clearance right there. But that's approximately where the two tumbling laundry machines came to rest.

"The next morning, I had two large piles of clean fill dumped where we're standing then I shoved them over with MS. The dryer has to be somewhere under that fill down there."

"This may not be so hopeless after all," said Jim.

Without hesitation, the bulldozer driver aimed his vehicle for an area about fifty yards beyond where he'd be digging. Then, he went straight over the side. The bulldozer slanted downward at a precipitous angle as if at any moment the machine might start to roll end over end. The veteran operator kept the powerful machine's scoop very low, almost against the side of the dump to keep that from happening. Several times he lowered it to dig into the ground when the rear of the bulldozer lifted upward. At the very bottom, he turned, and at Leslie's hand signal, he began digging into the hillside.

The digging went slowly. The operator wanted to make certain he dug in far enough to remove eight to ten feet of hillside. Rather than turn and deposit the dirt behind the bulldozer, the operator dug in, lifted a load, backed out, and then dumped it to his right. As he continued digging to his left, he'd fill in what had just been removed. This would leave only one small pile, the very first, that would have to be carried back to the other end of the dig to fill in the last empty space.

It had not been hard at all to get permission to dig at the landfill. Jim had invited Chief Romeric to have dinner at their place the previous night, Monday. After dinner, the two outlined their suspicions thus far to the Chief. The very next morning he asked Sylvia Keyes to cut all the red tape to get the Turtle Creek police chief and the landfill company to agree to an excavation. He knew they could not dig miles and miles of landfill, but Sylvia had found out from phoning Leslie that the digging would be in a small area, fifty to sixty yards wide.

By noon, Sylvia called Jim, "Gumshoe, your bulldozer is on its way. You better get down there. Driver says he'll be there by two o'clock."

"What?" asked Jim.

"Romeric wanted the dump dug up and asked me to cut all the red stuff and get it going ASAP. They'll be there before you if you don't get started."

"I don't know how you did it, but I owe you one," said Jim, "gift wrapped." He had then located the chief and the two of them started for Turtle Creek.

"Absolutely remarkable woman," said Chief Romeric as he drove towards the dump. "Imagine being her adversary in court?"

"I can't."

"Why she'd run the show right from the start. Things would go her way or else," said Romeric.

"When she graduates at the end of this summer, she'll be sorely missed."

"Listen, Sylvia would be a number one candidate to purchase after she graduates to make sure she stays with us as Chief City Prosecutor or something like that."

"By all means, do it," said Jim.

6:00 P.M.

There was a knock on their front door and Jim answered.

"Hope I'm not interrupting anything," Andre said.

"Why yes, yes you are. We're having a gourmet dinner I prepared, but since you're already here, rudely unannounced I might add, you might as well eat," teased Jim.

"Naw, I just stopped—"

"Hey, do you like dogs? Hot doggies?" asked Jim.

"Doesn't everyone?"

"Well, our gourmet dinner consists of gourmet hot dogs wrapped in American cheese in a real bakery bun. Now, tell me sir, can you turn that offer down?"

"Let me at 'em." said Andre, and he walked out to the dining room.

"Here you are, Ms. Meyer. Directions to the cabin retreat in Charles' own handwriting."

Jim's jaw dropped open, "Okay, genius, what part of your brain did you use to get this information?"

"It wasn't my brain at all."

"No?"

"It was mainly the manly part below my navel," laughed Andre.

"What?"

"The peculiar anatomy below my belt."

"Wait." asked Martie, preparing her mind for what she knew would be a crazy story. "Just what does that mean?"

Andre began to dramatize so suggestively how he took his shower with Charles watching, that the three of them could not eat for laughing. When he finished he said, "You see what you're having here for din-din tonight?"

"Yes," said Jim and Martie, almost in unison.

"Well, black-skinned fleshy hot dogs mean an awful lot to that brother."

30 Dark Night of the Soul

February 26, 2003—Wednesday
6:30 P.M.

"Hello, Martie. This is Dr. Troft."

"Really, I haven't talked to you in ages. Seems like you up and disappeared."

Martie knew Troft had withdrawn his help, but Jim had never told her why.

In a rather anxious voice, Troft replied, "I've been too busy at the university to offer much assistance. Sometimes my time is not my own. You know how that is."

Martie sensed he was lying through his teeth but dropped the matter.

"So, how can I help you?" she asked.

"Well, today, my curiosity got the best of me—it was my conscience. I decided after all these months to have a peek at Saint Paul's Church Fund. But my laptop kept telling me I was using an incorrect password. At first, I thought there was a problem at the bank, so I waited until this evening, but I still could not get into the account."

"Jim told me you set up the account and monitored it. Is this problem something that just happened?

Embarrassed, Troft responded, "I don't know because I, I haven't checked for weeks, truthfully—months, not since

291

September. But Kerr has obviously changed his password."

"That's understandable. In fact, it's advisable, isn't it?"

"Yes, but Kerr never wanted to change it. He claimed it was too much hassle. I just wondered if everything was okay." stated Troft.

"Have you asked him about it?"

"Me? Hell no, I'm too embarrassed to ask. After all, it's his business, his church. But I'm just a bit worried. That's all."

"Well, I'll pass the info along to Jim and see what he thinks. Thanks for calling." Martie relayed Troft's message to Jim.

"That's odd," said Jim. He knew Ed's name was on the signature card at the bank, but Troft being locked out of the account was a surprise.

"Maybe he just doesn't want Troft snooping around now that so much money is involved," said Martie. "After all, Troft did let him down."

"But that isn't like him. If he's changed it, there must be a damn good reason. Kerr wouldn't do anything just for spite."

"Should we call?" asked Martie?

"I hate to sound like I'm prying into his business. What do you think?"

"I think one of us should call and explain that we were concerned because Troft noticed the password change. We just want to know if everything's okay," suggested Martie.

Jim's instincts took over. He dialed the rectory, but Mrs. Pierce's voice grew sad when he asked for Father Kerr.

After a momentary pause, Mrs. Pierce finally told him, "Jim, his spirit's hit rock bottom. He is very blue. Hardly speaks to anyone. We're all very worried about him. Says he feels nauseous and doesn't want to eat. I'd swear he's lost at least twenty pounds. Hardly comes out of his room."

"Has he gone for a checkup?" asked Jim,

"No! We've all tried to make him go, but he refuses. He just seems depressed. He looks like a sick man. His spirit is gone—empty. Something is troubling him deeply."

"Can I talk to him?" asked Jim,

"Just a minute," said Pierce. "I'll see if he'll come to the phone."

Several minutes passed before a very quiet, dejected voice said, "Reverend Kerr here." The voice was flat, without a hint of cheer.

"How are you, Rev.? I heard you were not feeling well?" said Jim.

"Oh, it'll pass."

"Ever feel this down before?"

"No, why do you ask?"

"How about I drive by and we go see your doctor?" said Jim, growing more concerned as they talked.

"No. Just a bit of an upset stomach."

"Tell you what, let's let your doctor decide." *Boy, that man is stubborn,* thought Jim.

"Good grief, I don't know what all the fuss is about, I'm okay, I'm okay; I just want to be left alone right now," he said peevishly. "Now, *is* there anything I can do for you?"

Jim hated to bring up a worrisome topic, but he needed to know. "Dr. Troft said the password to Saint Paul's Church account has been changed. You're aware of that, right?" There was a rather long pause.

"Yes—Yes I am," he sighed.

"Is everything okay with the fund?"

Kerr answered vaguely, "You know, I've never been too concerned about money. So I don't worry about it."

"I know that, Father," said Jim, "but do you feel dejected because there is some kind of financial problem?"

Kerr wished he could just confide in Jim about the dreaded voice, the murders, the blackmail checks. Instead, he answered, "Listen, I'll feel better in a few days. There is plenty of money in the fund, so why worry about it?"

Jim reassured him, "You've always used church money wisely, so I know it's in good hands. I just wanted to make sure you were aware of the password change."

"I'm aware of it," he said. "Tell Martie I said 'Hello!'"

"I will, and the second you feel ready for a checkup, give me a call. I'll be there in a few minutes, even if it's the middle of the night."

"Thanks, Jim," muttered the priest and he hung up.

"Boy, he is down, Martie. Maybe he needs a good psychologist or psychiatrist. Mrs. Pierce was right. His spirit is empty!"

"Jim," said Martie, "I think you need a distraction of some kind. Your mind is too preoccupied with worry tonight."

"Sorry, hope I'm not acting distant."

"I know how to get you to relax—"

"And, you're so good at it I think you should start right now."

"Let's go in by the fireplace."

"Should I get the ironing board and prop one end of it up on the couch?"

February 27, 2003—Thursday
9:00 A.M.

"Good morning, Sylvia," said Jim as he walked up to her desk.

"Good morning, Gumshoe. I know you want something, otherwise you'd have kept on going."

"That's not true; I always stop to look at—uh-h talk to you."

"So, what's on your mind—if that's possible?"

"Now, now, Ms. Keyes, I have another favor to ask, and my mind is smart enough to know you can get the info faster and easier than I can."

"Depends on how many sticks you give me this time."

"Name your price."

"Three and a half sticks, but it has to be Juicy Fruit."

"Damn," said Jim, "all I have is Bazooka."

Keyes just sat there grinning. It was obvious there was a genuine friendship between these two people.

She extended her hand. "I'll take it," she said.

"Okay, here's what I need."

"Uh, uh, uh. Gum first." Jim reached in his pocket, pulled out three pieces of gum and put them in her outstretched fingers. Sylvia continued. "You were saying—"

"I need a bank statement from Latrobe City Bank for Saint Paul's Church Fund."

"How far back?"

"How about since last August. Can it be faxed here?"

"I'll try to arrange that, but it could cost you even more, Gumshoe."

"Tell you what. If you get that faxed here sometime today, I'll buy you a whole pack. One—whole—pack."

"Promise?"

"If I break my promise, you can have one of my wet soul kisses."

Pushing back in her chair while glancing up to the ceiling and rolling her eyes until only the whites showed, Sylvia replied, "Oh, please someone—everyone, don't let this man break his promise."

With that, Jim smirked and walked down the hall. Exiting a side door, he crossed to a drugstore where he bought one pack of Juicy Fruit gum. He knew Sylvia well. She would get the information.

Two hours later, Jim returned to the station after assisting in the arrest of a woman whose house the police had been watching for several weeks. Neighbors had reported a variety of shady characters coming and going from this home, especially during the wee hours of the morning. An undercover policewoman had gone to the house pretending to find out where to purchase drugs. She had entered with several hundred dollars rolled up in her fist.

Hesitating for a moment after seeing the money, the woman had sold the agent several different drugs. As soon as the officer had the drugs in hand, she took out her beeper and signaled Jim to come in. Jim stood back as the policewoman read the suspect her rights, and then they made the arrest.

When he was finished with his part of the drug bust, he walked back up the hall and plopped the whole package of gum on Sylvia Keyes' desk. She was busy typing while holding a phone to her one ear. Without making eye contact, she took the gum, opened her top desk drawer, pulled out several faxed sheets and handed them to Jim. All of this, she did without losing her place in her animated phone conversation, and while continuing to type with her right hand. Jim watched her in awe. *Computers have a lot to learn from this gal.*

Jim glanced down at the church's bank statement and there they were—withdrawal entries of ten-thousand dollars each week beginning in early December. Now he knew why the pastor did not want to answer questions about Saint Paul's finances.

2:30 P.M.

Jim drove to Johnstown, Pennsylvania to attend a Police Association Conference. The sessions he registered for this afternoon and evening dealt with the latest scanning devices, the validity of lie detection tests, and the use of chemical sprays for disarming threatening people. Tomorrow, he was scheduled for physical training classes in judo, karate, and self-defense in general, to learn new skills and to improve those he already had.

March 1, 2003–Saturday
10:30 A.M.

Mr. Ed Bristol did not ask Andre to work today. Since Andre had committed himself to meet Brother Charles at the monastery so the two of them could walk to the gym for a workout together, Andre stuffed his workout gear into his gym bag along with his cell phone, and drove to Saint Vincent's Monastery. Charles was already standing by the laundry room door when Andre entered the building and came down the stairs.

"Good morning, young man," said Charles.

"Oh, hello, Brother," said Andre. "I brought my gym bag and I'm ready. Had a good hearty breakfast, but now I need a hard workout, maybe even a nice rubdown afterward."

"Great, let's exercise here first then go to the cabin." The two men, along with several other monks, worked out using machines instead of free weights. Andre was amazed at the number of older monks who were working out on rowing machines, treadmills, bicycles and the like, some still wearing their monk's garb. He could hear the shouts of others that were enjoying themselves in the pool or taking turns swimming laps.

Andre had no problem showering or changing today because other monks were present. Nevertheless, he could see Charles' reflection in the sink mirror, watching him while he stood shaving with his towel wrapped very low around his waist as if ready to fall off.

Andre dressed first. "Why don't I meet you two miles east on Route 30. There is no reason to drive separately, is there? Besides, I lost your directions. I'll pull over then we can ride up in your truck or my jeep. You can't miss my jeep. I'll be parked along the side of the road. I'll have my emergency flashers on."

"See you soon!" Andre called out to Brother Charles, after he finished dressing. Without another word, he took off in a hurry.

The brother dressed, put on his robe, and hurried to his truck. He pulled out heading east along Route 30 and turned on his radio. Brother Charles had become a monk eight years ago and still maintained the truck he owned when he joined the monastery. He smiled to himself when he thought of the clever scheme he and Ed had dreamed up that was making both of them wealthy men.

Charles went through all the motions of being a monk if and when he cared to. The monastery never questioned his motives because published articles brought the place a certain public notoriety and recognition in academic circles along with a nice amount of money. For the most part, he was free to study and do his research. He had always been a gay loner in the sense that he was not seeking a permanent soul mate. He enjoyed exploring sex with any young male that piqued his fancy. He had been uncertain about staying in the monastery as his private bankroll accumulated.

But he knew there were expensive research devices needed to complete some of his more theoretical work, and his newfound wealth would allow him to purchase them. The monastery and the mountain lab were perfect for experimentation. The abbot and the monks assumed Charles had made his fortune before he entered the monastery and was now sharing it with his monastic community. The monks had never seen his darker side. When he was there, he attended services and appeared to take part.

As he crested a hill, he was shaken from his reverie by the flashing lights of a police car up ahead that had pulled over some unfortunate driver. As he drew closer, to his amazement, he recognized the blinking lights as those of Andre's bright-red jeep. He didn't know whether to interfere, or just keep going.

There appeared to be a rather heated exchange going on between the officer and Andre. Brother stopped along the berm about one-hundred yards behind the two stopped vehicles. The officer was a woman—no physical match for Andre who appeared to be belligerent and angry. The argument continued. Andre opened his door as if to get out, but the quick-thinking officer whipped out a can of Mace from her belt, and sprayed him at close range.

Then she took control. Andre was holding his eyes and shouting obscenities as she took him by the arm, marched him over to her police car, opened the back door, pushed him inside and slammed the door shut. She returned to his jeep, reached in to take the keys then walked around making sure both doors were locked. She drove off with no siren but with lights blinking and at the first possible place, she U-turned and started back toward Latrobe. As they passed on the far side of the road, Brother Charles could see Andre rubbing his eyes, caged in the rear seat.

The brother was aghast at what had occurred. He could not believe that this, this woman, this policewoman, had subdued muscular Andre. He cursed her for ruining their afternoon of sexual exploitation. He had been physically attracted to Andre, but now he'd have to work out another arrangement. He wondered if Andre would be detained or have to face a hearing of some kind. In truth, Charles had witnessed the incident and did see Andre angrily getting out of his jeep although he never laid hands on the officer. If need be, Charles would serve as an eye witness to the entire embarrassing disagreement.

He considered driving to the Latrobe Police Department, but then changed his mind deciding not to get involved with *any* kind of woman, especially a policewoman. So, he drove directly to the monastery.

"You are one terrific actress," said Andre to the smiling police officer. "I can't imagine what was going through Brother Charles' cranium when he saw my jeep pulled over with you standing by the door."

"I enjoyed it! It's fun to entertain people. I think the two of us did one hell of a good job."

"Jim Simmons told me where to pull over and to expect an officer, but when you showed up, the irony of the entire situation made me burst a gut inside. Well, it will give the good brother something to meditate about—being overpowered by a woman. Tell you what, though."

"What's that?"

"I can't wait to shower off whatever you sprayed on me. You must have used the entire can. Shit, that surprised me. What a neat idea."

"It's nothing but wasp spray. But I remembered it was in my glove compartment so I grabbed it before getting out and stuck the can under my belt." Once again, Andre laughed.

"Bug spray. Foiled by bug spray!"

"Now that you've mentioned it, I can smell you up here. You

stink. I hope you don't have asthma or breathing problems."

"Naw, I'm okay." The officer had pulled into and partially behind, a fast food restaurant near the junction of Route 30 and Route 981. They watched Charles turn right on 981 and stayed just long enough to see if his course was set for the monastery or the police station. As Andre predicted, Charles turned left toward the monastery. The policewoman pulled out and started back toward Andre's parked jeep.

"Thanks for everything," he said. "You were terrific."

"Sorry if I spoiled your sexual interlude."

"Bug off," laughed Andre. "Just bug off."

4:45 P.M.

The heinous voice returned once more to Kerr's confessional. The priest sat and listened.

"You've done very well, Father Kerr, but we still need more money, so please keep sending it. Your parish is filthy rich now; you can afford it. Keep opening your mail for the new address every Monday. We don't want anyone to get suspicious now, do we. Since I haven't killed anyone since my last confession, will you bless me now, Father?"

Silence.

"I asked for your blessing, give it to me."

Just as he had done several weeks ago, Kerr put both hands where The Voice's hated devil head would be, and said, *"In saecula saeculorum i ad ignes inferni"* (Burn in Hell for all eternity).

"Thank you, Father," said The Voice. "I feel much better now."

Kerr did not get sick this time. Nothing could shock him now. He was involved in abetting the sin of blackmail each week. More than that, he considered his evil deeds as stealing from God himself. Yet he could say nothing to anyone; he could do nothing. He had to go on with his daily life acting as if these horrific confessions had never occurred.

When there were no more penitents, he left his confessional, but instead of walking to the front, he went down the side aisle. When he reached the last pew, he turned and walked through it, the same pew in which McCarthy had fallen asleep. Just before reaching the center aisle, he sat down. All around him he could see the flickering, vigil wicks. If he wasn't so dejected, it might all appear beautiful. His mind was numb. *I've given my life to God. I've never lost my zeal to help others lead more Christ-like lives—not until now. Now, I feel damned for being alive.*

He mulled over the awful events of recent weeks. He looked toward the altar; a place where he had presided over so many, many ceremonies during the past years. He had spent a good part of his life in this church, but how could he continue? He stared at the suspended Oculi crucifix and thought of long-gone Brother Anthony who so artfully refinished it. He sat for a long time, a very long time. His mind grew very quiet as if he was going to sleep. He was exhausted, but no matter, he didn't care anymore.

He sat in silence, utter quiet, staring past the Oculi cross, staring, staring at nothingness. Staring—the church, the silence, the flickering candles. It all started to calm him; the priest became hypnotically silent, almost peaceful.

From the deepest recesses of his very soul, a concept started to form. At first, he blinked his eyes a few times then shook his head trying to understand, trying to make sense of the images bombarding his brain. He began to concentrate more on his thought process than what was physically around him. It was as if he could see his own mind fighting itself until a terrible, frightening idea began to form. At first, it was just a vague notion. But it became increasingly sordid as he forced the jagged puzzle pieces together.

He began to wonder, to question, to wonder, to re-question. Time seemed to pass very slowly until the astonished man had his horrible morbid answer. *Unconscionable! Unthinkable!* He through, *but I think I have my answer. Now I can plan what to do.* He closed his eyes to concentrate, and then a strange, exceptionally sad look crossed his face. First, he sat up a bit, then he sat up straight, then he stood up, squared his shoulders, and stepped sideways into the center aisle. He walked briskly to the front of the church stopping under the Oculi crucifix, but he never looked at it. He knew what to do.

6:30 P.M.

Instead of driving, Kerr walked over to Martie's house; Jim was there, too. The priest's distraught appearance looked terrible. He looked gaunt from weight loss as if suffering some fatal disease. His face remained unshaven. Neither Martie nor Jim mentioned his appearance.

"Good to see you, Father," said Martie. "Come in."

"I can only stay for a few moments," he said.

"How about a short drink?" asked Jim.

"Why not," answered the priest. "Why not make it a hefty double." Both Jim and Martie were thrilled that the priest wanted a drink. They felt the alcohol might lift his spirits a bit; maybe get him talking.

"We're glad you stopped in."

"I came for a reason, you know!"

"Oh?"

"Jim?" said Kerr. "Martie?" Neither responded at the odd way he said their names as if an important question or statement was about to follow.

"I know you two well enough that I think you should level with me."

"About?"

"Jim, remember when you thought I was hiding information from you?" Father Kerr was fishing of course.

"I do."

"I think you and Martie know a lot more than you're telling me about what's going on around my church. Maybe you're afraid of hurting my feelings, or telling me things I don't want to hear, or losing my friendship, but one of the reasons I'm so down is that I feel helpless—abandoned. Jesus cried, 'My God, why hast Thou forsaken me?' That's how I feel right now."

Martie looked at the priest, cleared her throat, then announced, "Father Kerr, we are starting to put pieces together, and the picture is not good. It involves someone you've trusted since childhood and a brother from Saint Vincent's."

"You know what? At this point," said Kerr, "I'm ready for anything, so let's hear it; all of it."

The priest's face was void of expression; he appeared lifeless, expecting the worst possible scenario.

For the next thirty minutes, Martie and Jim took turns sharing with Father Kerr their damning suspicions regarding Charles, Ed Bristol and their money scheme. The holy man sat there entranced by their accusations of Ed, a man he had known longer than either Martie or Jim had been alive, a man he had trusted implicitly. They told him about the money cart; the digging going on over at Turtle Creek Landfill to find a dryer which might contain Brother Anthony's remains.

The priest never touched his drink once they began disclosing. He sat without moving. What Jim and Martie thought would have devastated this man who appeared sickly seemed to be revitalizing him with each word. Jim and Martie did all the talking while Kerr sat, the ice cubes melting in his scotch. When they began, his face looked shocked, but slowly, ever so slowly, the faintest grin began to form. When they had finished talking, Jim and Martie sat waiting for him to make some response; yet he said nothing.

"Sorry to lay all of this on you," said Martie, "but you asked for it and there it is."

Jim spoke up next, "We should know about the dryer tomorrow if the bulldozer operator will work on Sunday. He is about two-thirds of the way through the area where the MS operator saw the dryer come to rest."

There was a long pause. The pastor picked up his drink and downed half the glass in one large gulp. "MS means?"

"MS are the initials they've given their Monster Smasher. They use it to crush everything before burying it. The dryer got dumped over the side of the landfill by Ed Bristol and rolled down to the bottom before Leslie could get to it. It never got crushed." Again, there was a long pause while Kerr finished his drink with a second gulp. The priest seemed utterly relieved.

He took in a deep breath then let it out saying, "Thank you. Thank you. Thank you both so much for the information. You can't begin to imagine what you've just done for me. My dark night of the soul is passing. Soon it will be over."

"Uh, what will be over?" Martie asked.

"It's not important," said Kerr obtusely, deliberately ignoring her inquiry. "Now let me add this to your puzzle. When I entered the church after Phillip fell, I'm sure the man was dead. It was obvious. Sister Margaret and I tried CPR until the EMS team took over."

"Yes, you told us Phillip said, *'Cave.'*"

Jim added, "You said it means 'Beware,' right?"

"Yes! I was there. So was Sister Margaret, the cleaners, Mrs. Reed and Ed—my trusted friend, Ed Bristol. After what you just told me, the puzzle pieces do seem to fit." Warmed inside from the scotch, Father Kerr appeared cheered by all the information dumped on him. The fact that they were homing in on the killer was great news. "Thank you," he said as he stood to leave. Jim walked outside with him while Martie stood in the doorway, puzzled by his abrupt departure.

As Kerr turned to go down Elm Street, Jim asked, "Father, I have one more question. I promise it will be the last."

"Ask and you might receive."

"Where is all that money going you are withdrawing week after week?"

Silence, utter silence.

"Did you hear my question, Father?" Jim asked.

"Yes, I heard every single last word of it."

"Well?" Father Kerr remained continued walking in silence. *I thought they'd never ask!* The smile on his face grew broader but Jim and Martie could not see it; now he knew they had discovered the weekly withdrawals, and it comforted his soul.

After Jim came in and closed the door, Martie said, "Jim, that's odd. He seemed like he wanted help, yet wouldn't answer you after all the disclosing we did."

"Oh—but—he—did, Martie. In the only way a true priest could."

31 Squished Bug

March 3, 2003—Monday
9:00 A.M.

Ed Bristol began his day like every other day. He opened his store as usual at nine o'clock then went over some of his financial affairs. Although he had some inventory stored in the basement and on the second floor of his store, there were those occasions when a customer purchased an appliance but refused to take the floor model, even though it was brand new.

On those occasions, he'd pretend he had the machine in stock and would offer delivery on a date after an identical machine had been carted to his store from one of his suppliers. This was one of those days and the Pittsburgh supplier promised to deliver around ten-thirty in the morning.

When Andre arrived at ten, Ed Bristol explained about the expected delivery and then left for Saint Paul's. He let himself in the side door of the rectory like he always did, but he noticed an unmistakable change in Father Kerr's demeanor.

"Good morning," Ed said as he came in and removed his coat.

Often, Ed would have a cup of coffee while sitting and chatting a bit with Mrs. Pierce and the pastor before starting any chores.

"Great day today," said Kerr, "I'm feeling a lot better."

"He's got his old spirit back," said Mrs. Pierce.

Looking at the bright smile on Kerr's face, Ed said, "I can see that. Are you sure you're all right, Father?"

"Of course," he said. "My troubles are coming to an end."

Baited, Ed asked, "What kind of troubles, Paul?"

"Ed, my conscience has been bothering me a lot these past weeks—months perhaps."

"Oh, come now, Father," said Mrs. Pierce. "What could the likes of you be worried about?"

"Yeah," said Ed. "Why should you be upset about anything?"

"Well, I've been doing some thinking," said Kerr. "Martie and Jim and I had a conversation last night and they told me about some of their suspicions."

"Oh, like what?" asked Ed beginning to perspire.

"Well, remember Brother Anthony who disappeared a while back?"

"I remember that story well," said Mrs. Pierce. "I could never understand how he could just walk out like that."

Ed insinuated crudely, "Mrs. Pierce, if you were considered a holy brother for many years, wouldn't you be a bit ashamed to quit? Like you were walking out on God or something?"

That one comment by Ed set Kerr afire. He couldn't imagine it being uttered by the person who may well have been Anthony's brutal killer. He lost his cheerful personality, and it became obvious. He couldn't help himself.

"That man is with his Maker. Believe you me, his killer will burn and burn and I do mean burn till he is no more!"

"Father!" exclaimed Mrs. Pierce. "Stop it. Stop that foolish talk. Some people suspected murder, but nobody was ever found. How can you even suggest such a terrible thing? That is not a good way to start your day."

But Kerr would not let it rest. "According to Jim, the police think he was killed, but you're right. They never found a dead body, but I think they will."

"Or any trace of him," added Bristol. Mrs. Pierce could see the anger increasing in Father Kerr's face. She felt herself becoming alarmed.

"Well, enough of that kind of talk. Now, go on you two, out, out of my kitchen. I've got things to do," she said, trying to act her jovial self. Ed got up and went over to the church.

After he left, Mrs. Pierce said, "Shame on you, Father. I've never heard you talk like that, ever. Why I'm embarrassed for you!"

"It needed to be said, Mrs. Pierce. Believe me, it had to be said."

Father Kerr sat for a moment to calm down and then said, "Remember me telling you about Father Phillip's words when he died?"

Pierce was almost afraid to respond. She said meekly, "Yes, I remember, you said they were Latin words. I never knew what they meant."

"I think he tried to say, *'Cave hominem.'*"

"I remember you telling me something like that," said Mrs. Pierce still peeved at the pastor.

"The Latin he was trying to say means beware of the man, or better still, beware of that man."

"Poor fellow," added Pierce without any understanding. "He must not have been in his right mind."

11:30 A.M.

Kerr left the kitchen and went about his day's work. Much

later in the afternoon, he stopped to visit the latchkey students. Sister Margaret was in the back of the room and didn't see him enter. Martie was down on her hands and knees near the door, crawling forward. The pastor entered looking straight ahead for a teacher. He didn't see Martie—not until he fell sideways over her, landing awkwardly on the carpeted floor after his hand and arm slid along the chalk ledge.

Martie had crawled from the back of the room to the front along with two other students. Looking up and seeing the priest, the young children, in perfect unison, sang out as loud as bearable, "Good—AFTERNOON—Father—Kerr!"

"Oh, I'm sorry, Father, are you okay?" asked Martie getting to her feet. The two third graders stood up and helped the priest.

"I'm fine," he said, dusting the chalk off his sleeve and the side of his cassock. "Just a bit curious."

He pointed to little Emily while Martie rearranged her own clothing a bit.

"Can you tell me what you were doing on the floor?"

Emily said, "First, we were looking for a bug that Ms. Martie stepped on. Then we were learning how to measure the room with a ruler."

"Can you tell me how long the room is?"

"No, 'cause we didn't finish yet, but we found the dead bug."

"Well, that's quite an accomplishment," said Kerr grinning.

"I don't think it was said one little tot. Yuck, it was all squished. Ms. Martie picked it up with a paper towel and threw it in there." She pointed to a waste can.

Martie spoke up at this point, "We were crawling across the room laying down a ruler, marking the floor, then laying down the ruler, marking the floor—"

"I understand. And I interrupted your measuring. I'm so sorry, but I am glad I stopped in to see how well all of you are doing."

He looked out over the entire group of twelve students of all different ages. Martie was glad to see him smile.

Emily spoke again. "The room is fifteen rulers long up to that chalk mark there." She pointed to the last white mark on the carpet. "That other mark over there is from the squished bug."

"Well, I've learned a lot today about rulers and bugs," said the priest cheerfully as he started for the door.

Once again in singsong unison, the small children in the group chanted, "GOODBYE—Father—Kerr."

32 Ghastly Recall

March 4, 2003—Tuesday
3:15 P.M.

To a casual observer, it would not appear unusual that Brother Charles was sitting in Saint Vincent's basilica lost in thought. Other monks or lay people seeing him in his stall would assume he was praying or meditating according to the monastery's tradition of *Ora et labora,* or vice versa.

He was meditating but not on any religious subject. Rather, he was reminiscing about how he and Ed had worked out their money scheme. He liked obsessing about it and did nothing to stop the flood of pleasant memories that careened through his mind.

He remembered how he and Ed Bristol had served in Vietnam, and some of the horrible things they had seen and suffered together. He remembered how they had vowed to remain friends upon returning to the states, but that closeness had lasted just a few years.

He had attended the University of Pittsburgh and was offered a job teaching at MIT doing research as a full professor. He endured the teaching part of his tenure, but loved doing special research projects in chemistry and physics or a combination of both. He enjoyed the notoriety and prestige given him from fellow scholars when his research or his philosophical treatises were published.

313

Then too, he enjoyed the opportunities for sexual companionship that campus life provided. Most of his older gay contacts chose to remain closeted, but the younger generation of males had become more vocal about their rights and status at the university and in their communities at large. These young men were highly knowledgeable regarding sexually transmitted diseases and remained very cautious regarding casual sexual contacts.

Charles was always distraught over the salaries professors earned. It disgusted him that movie stars and athletes earned monumental salaries for something as unimportant as entertaining the public, while researchers and scientists had to beg for grants and awards to advance important scientific theories and philosophical issues.

For the better part of twelve years, he had lost contact with Ed except for the once-a-year Christmas and birthday cards on which each would scribble a few words just to keep in touch. However, about nine years ago, he had written a short note on a Christmas card telling Ed how bored he had become with university life and that he had dreamed up a gimmick that could help both of them get rich provided they work as a team. He knew Ed owned an appliance store, but more importantly, that he was the trusted caretaker of Saint Paul's Church, the perfect milieu to pull off their deceit.

The brother had made several visits to Latrobe to discuss his idea. He resigned from MIT and moved to Latrobe where the two of them could continue with their long range plans. By this time, he had stashed away a sizable amount of money and could afford the move.

When he learned of the nearby Saint Vincent's monastery, he concocted the devious plan of becoming a monk, not because of any religious fervor, but because it was the perfect location to get free room and board, and to pursue quiet research while perfecting his invention. Besides, he liked philosophy and science, particularly that dichotomous realm where the two intermingled. With his prestigious background, Saint Vincent's welcomed him. He would have no overhead and there was always the possibility of gay activity in Latrobe.

As he sat with his eyes closed, Charles' memories shifted to the suspended cross he had altered while Ed stood guard outside Anthony's workroom. Living as a brother, he had learned the routines and habits of the monks and was certain no one would enter Anthony's work area during mealtime or during the Angelus prayer, which followed afterward.

He would have plenty of time to make his meticulous alterations. Even so, Ed Bristol was to stand guard to prevent anyone from entering. What Ed would do if someone tried, Charles never questioned, but as luck would have it, although the careful alterations to the crucifix were right on schedule, Brother Anthony wasn't.

First, Brother Charles had to remove the plaster corpus from the wooden cross. Then he picked out the original glass eyes and drilled two deeper holes so his tiny eye capped cylinders would slide into place. These contained a special Freon-like gas that he had perfected which was far more efficient that the gas normally used in air conditioners.

Next, he drilled holes through the hands so long thin nails could eventually pass through and into the crosses heavy wood. Using a small but powerful drill with a thin, round cutting disk in its chuck, Charles quickly cut a tiny channel down the backside of each arm from behind the head/neck area to the rear of each hand. The groove needed to be just wide enough, one-eighth inch at most, so that one thin wire could be buried. It was a clever idea, but then Charles considered himself a brilliant man.

The wiring was basic. He twisted together a wire from each orb connecting the two in a series circuit. Those connected wires were pushed into the channel he had cut behind the head/neck area of the corpus. The other wire from each orb he buried in the channel running up behind each arm.

He cut the ends of each wire so that one-half inch could be turned into the hole a nail would come through. He carefully smoothed plaster of Paris that set in less than eight minutes, over any tiny grooves hiding the buried wiring. There was no angle where the groves could be seen in the small space between the back of the corpus and the wooden cross unless it was taken down. He and Ed were convinced, even then, that Bishop Mallory would not let the cross be taken down.

He remounted the corpus to the wood via the original bolts extending from the back of the figure. But in addition, through each hand he inserted long galvanized nails so that as they passed through the hand holes, they contacted his buried wire ends. And then when he pushed them further into the cross arms of the crucifix, he made certain they contacted the hooks that would touch the chain links from which the cross was suspended.

Brother Charles remembered watching his time carefully. He had calculated that the entire operation would take about two and one-half hours including cleanup time. Knowing the use of the cutting disc would make plaster dust, Charles worked in the hood area where Anthony spray painted his statuary. With his work completed, he wiped clean the entire crucifix. The only fingerprints on the cross would be Anthony's because

Brother Charles wore latex gloves.

Looking up now at the suspended crucifix, the brother felt pleased with himself. He recalled that even when the cross was scanned with the police scanner and the more powerful one brought out by the researchers from Carnegie Mellon, his additional wires simply appeared as part of the supportive wires over which the original corpus had been formed.

He remembered well that when Brother Mark asked him to substitute at the card game seven years ago, he had expected Anthony to return. It wasn't until the card players questioned Anthony's whereabouts and started searching that Brother Charles deduced Ed Bristol intercepted him. Charles never asked Ed outright if he had killed Anthony because he heard no commotion while he was working, yet he was almost certain what the answer might be.

If Anthony had found out, he would've spoiled their seven-year plan. It was Ed's ingenuity to wait seven long years before starting the miracle tears. By that time, there would be no suspicion that the crucifix had been changed in any way because it had been hanging and collecting dust for so many years.

Ed would test it on any Thursday night after the church had been locked and the cleaners had gone. To perform the test, he had instructed Ed to push and re-push the remote radio control in his pocket then wait for a few tiny teardrops to form and fall.

Of course, he would never forget how he and Ed had built the money cart. That was Ed's design except for radio control of the moving panels inside. For the past seven years, they had benefited from church collections. They provided enough cash to build the mountain retreat cabin and supply it with expensive equipment so Charles could continue his research while they waited for the years to pass by. Charles couldn't help grinning at the cleverness of the entire plan. He was proud of himself, proud of his ongoing research, but most of all, proud of his miracle!

5:15 P.M.

Ed Bristol was not paying attention when he walked through the rectory and overheard Mrs. Pierce talking to Pastor Kerr. It was Thursday. Ed had come from his store to lock the church so both the cleaning and candle replacement crews could get started.

"And—and I heard it on the news just a few minutes ago," said Mrs. Pierce to Kerr. Her voice could not hide her excitement.

"You must be kidding," said Kerr as he walked into the parlor room across from his office and clicked the TV remote. "Maybe we can catch what's left of the five o'clock news." As the TV warmed up and the monitor brightened, they could tell the news was just about over.

Having seen them scurrying from the kitchen into the front parlor, Ed said a bit loudly as they both passed him, "I'm going over to the church. See you in a bit."

Then he thought he heard the name, Anthony, spoken on the television set. He returned to the parlor where Pastor Kerr and Mrs. Pierce now stood shaking their heads.

"Did I hear Brother Anthony's name?" Ed inquired.

The news summary was over and an advertisement had begun.

"Ed, they're digging for him. Can you believe it; after all these years? They think they know where he's buried," said Mrs. Pierce. "And to think we were just talking about him this morning."

"Who?"

"Brother Anthony," answered Mrs. Pierce blessing herself.

"God rest his holy soul."

"Is that true?" asked Bristol.

"Seems that way," answered the priest curtly, making no eye contact.

"Where on earth are they digging?"

"Oh my, Ed! Of all the forsaken places—you won't believe this—in the Turtle Creek Landfill," said Mrs. Pierce, "in that filthy landfill."

"You've got to be kidding me."

"No, they just showed pictures of a bulldozer moving tons and tons of dirt," she added.

"They can't dig up the whole dump; that landfill covers over a square mile, maybe two, maybe more."

Father Kerr interjected, "Well, they seem to have an area localized. If he's there, they'll find him."

"But Paul," Ed went on, "he'd be, you know, dissolved, rotted away by now, wouldn't he?"

The priest replied, "All I know is what the news said, but I do know that bones last a long, long time. When they find him, they'll check dental records. Those records never lie."

"Sounds gruesome to me."

"It sure does," said Mrs. Pierce, holding her arms and shuddering.

"God—always—has—his—way," predicted Kerr. "One can't hide from The—Hound—of Heaven—forever."

5:35 P.M.

Ed tried to remain calm on his way from the rectory to the church, but now it was his turn to recall memories, but not pleasant ones. His mind began racing out of control.

He started talking to himself. "That priest—that damned

Paul Kerr squealed on me. He broke the seal of the confessional after all. That has to be it."

But then he stood absolutely still. His memory bank searched for more information. He remembered he had never mentioned Anthony to Paul. "No, it couldn't be him because he just wouldn't know the details."

He started walking again. Ed never said good-bye to either Kerr or Mrs. Pierce. He went directly to his truck and started for his store. Once again he began talking to himself. "How did those bastards figure it out?"

He recalled how well he and Charles had planned and had waited out seven years.

Speaking even louder, he continued, "Those damned, impudent, freaking police, how could they know? Was it Jim who figured it out all out by himself, or maybe his bitch, Martie?"

Bristol began to drive ever slower, trying to remember.

"It was all so—so secret—so very private—so very long ago!" he shouted.

As he drove, he kept mumbling to no one. Deep terrible thoughts started crashing through his brain.

His talking became louder. "Phillip—damn Phillip—why did he have to climb that fuckin' ladder? I told him to be careful, didn't I? 'Be careful,' I yelled. *'Be careful!'* But he wouldn't come down. So, I jiggled his ladder a bit, but just a tiny bit to make him stop. But no, Phillip, you had to fall and hit your damned skull you stupid fool; but that didn't kill you, did it? Oh, no, Phillip, I had to do that after sending Margaret and the cleaners away," he shouted.

By now, he was driving so slowly that cars behind him started to honk. Ed never noticed. His face was purple with rage. Salty beads of sweat ran down his forehead into his eyes making them burn. Again and again he wiped them away.

Then he recalled how Phillip started to regain consciousness while those around him dashed for help.

"Mrs. Reed couldn't see me. She was in the stair tower, Phillip."

Cars behind Ed continued their loud honking.

"It had been so easy to lift you just high enough to slide my arms under your armpits and then snap your thick neck."

Ed made a turn at the corner. The loud honking stopped as traffic behind him went its way. He continued scolding the young priest. "Why would the church ordain you, Phillip, hunh? You? You had some nerve, Phillip, coming to this city, to my church, fucking up my thought out plan."

A hateful frown crossed Bristol's face.

"You were so virile looking, Phillip, like me when I was young—still a young boy," he yelled, "but you vowed never to use your sexuality. But I'd lost mine, lost it to the enemy."

"Damn!" he shouted, as if the little GI was present. "I'd have lost my life, too, except for you running beside me and stepping on that land mine. You poor thing! You poor brave man!—I can still feel you. I had to wipe you off my face and out of my eyes. But you know what? I got even. I went back. I killed and I killed for you."

Ed smiled as he remembered killing for sport, for the fun of it. He had grown to enjoy it.

"I remember stepping off the chopper skid and those murderous shells—*ping-zing, ping-zing*—why I hear them now!"

Horror overwhelmed the man. "I hear you," he shouted. "I hear you, Anthony, coming down those stairs. I hear you. So scared, yes, I remember how you obeyed me in the dark; you

321

put your hands on your hips—as if that would save you. It is too late, don't you see? Ha, hah! Much too late," laughed Bristol.

"Why, you'd have killed my seven year plan. Yes, I remember you, ANTHONY!" Bristol shouted. "I remember you. You've haunted me for years, just like my enemy." He clenched the steering wheel as if to recall the feeling in his powerful hands. "But you weren't supposed to come down there, you dumb ass," he yelled to the inside of his truck.

His voice began to shriek the unearthly falsetto he used in the confessional. "That second dryer was a perfect coffin for you, Anthony. Hah! Why even an asshole could pry open the top of that cheap model with a screwdriver. Hah! I took out the two hex-head screws on the inside and lifted off the front so the tub would slide out. It was so easy, much too easy, too much fun, because it made the perfect casket, ANTHONY." He laughed hideously. "Wasn't I clever to bring my tools just in case. Ha-hah! I drilled just three small holes, ANTHONY," he shouted.

"One on each side of the top, and one right through the damned door latch. Oh, but you didn't know it, ANTHONY; you were *dead*," he shrieked. "Now no one could pop it open. No one! No one could look inside the little door and see your staring eyes, Anthony, no one! It was a perfect plan and we drove to the landfill the next morning; you and me together, didn't we, hunh, ANTHONY."

"But how in the hell did they figure it all out, Hunh? Well, damn them all to Hell with the rest of my demons," he shrieked. "Damn them all to Hell! I'll take no chances. I know what I have to do."

By now, Ed had parked behind his store and walked inside. He was still ranting to himself when he took out his cell phone and dialed.

"Brother Charles here, can I help—"

"Burn the evidence, damn it. Go burn your lab this evening."

"Why?"

"Do it you stupid idiot. Do it now," he roared. "You hear? Those bastards are digging at Turtle Creek as we speak."

"Why don't I just ditch the equipment?"

"Torch the whole place, asshole!" shrieked Ed. "It's mine, isn't it?"

33 The Raging Inferno

5:35 P.M.

Andre couldn't help overhearing Ed Bristol's brief, shouted phone conversation with Brother Charles. "Be right back, Mr. Bristol. I'm going over for a candy bar." When Ed did not answer, Andre walked out the front door and across the street.

He phoned police headquarters and explained to Romeric, "Chief, I need to talk to Jim Simmons right away."

"Let me have him call you back. Give me your number."

"I'm calling from a booth. I'll wait here until he calls."

"Sounds like an emergency."

"I think it is."

"I'll rouse him and have him call. It should take just a minute or so." Andre remained in the phone booth; within a short time the phone rang.

"Andre, I was in the shower. What's the matter? Chief sounded urgent."

"Sorry to bother you after such a busy day, but Mr. Bristol was just here."

"And?"

"He just called Charles on the phone and I overheard him say, 'Get up there this evening and burn the evidence. Torch the lab.'"

"No way!"

"Would I kid you?"

"Okay, Andre, I'm going up there right now."

"Don't think you're going alone."

"What?"

"You're not going without me."

"I'll be okay, Andre. I can handle this."

"Oh, no, I'm going with you just in case. In fact, I think we should take my jeep just in case we need four-wheel drive."

"Well—um, I guess you've got a point there. If you wouldn't mind—that's a great idea. Do you mind picking me up at home? Martie is over at the school. I think she stuck your directions to the kitchen bulletin board. I'll pull on some sweats and meet you outside."

Andre replied, "I'll be right over."

Jim was already standing outside by the curb when Andre's red jeep with its white winter hardtop came to a screeching stop in front of his house. Jim climbed up and in. Before he had the door shut, Andre took off like a deer, throwing Jim back into his seat.

"Oops, sorry."

"Hey Andre, if you're going to drive, I'd like to get there with soul and body still attached," he teased.

He unfolded the notepaper Brother Charles had written out.

"According to these directions, the place can't be too far. For sure, we want to arrive and leave before Charles gets there. Who knows what we might find."

"Do you think he's a real monk?" asked Andre.

"If he's involved in a scheme like this, I wouldn't call him a good monk. I wouldn't be the least bit surprised if we check his past history and find that he became a monk about eight years ago."

"If they've messed with the cross, why did they wait seven years to start all of this?" inquired Andre.

"Because, every time someone suggests that the cross has been tampered with, the answer has been 'no, it's been hanging for years.' As crazy as it seems, I think the seven years threw everyone off, including Father McCarthy and the rest of us. I think that's the main reason the Greensburg bishop wouldn't let the crucifix be taken down and examined by scientists; the seven years is what turned a magic trick of some kind into a miracle."

"Maybe you're right, Jim, but keep your eye on those directions. Let me know when to turn," Andre reminded him.

"It says: 'Drive east on Route 30 about eight miles. After you cross over a small bridge you'll see a gas station on your right and a high electric tower on your left. After you pass the gas station, turn right. It's an unmarked gravel road.' Funny thing is, I've lived in this area all my life. You'd think I'd know all the side roads."

"Up ahead in the distance, Jim, I see power lines running down from my left." As they crested a hill several miles later, they could see the power lines atop metal towers across from a gasoline station coming up on their right. They crossed a bridge, which one would hardly notice because there was no noticeable bump on either end of it.

Andre made a sharp right turn onto a narrow gravel road just wide enough for one vehicle. It would be difficult for two to pass. Whatever berm there was on either side of the road was covered with last year's dried bushes and brush and the remains of melting snow.

"Then it says to continue down this road about five and a half miles until—" Andre slid his jeep to a stop. Jim wondered why until he watched Andre reach up to the speedometer and set the odometer to zero then he drove on. "Now you know Andre, I wouldn't have thought to do that."

"Aren't you glad I came along?"

The road started to climb very steeply, twisting and turning like a snake slithering over a rock pile. As they climbed, the road surface was strewn with rocks. Andre yanked the jeep into four-wheel drive. "My cruiser would never have gotten up here."

"Aren't you glad I came along?" teased Andre again.

Just as the odometer read five miles, Andre said, "Now what should I be looking for?"

"It says here, there will be a thick stand of pines on your left, then watch for a break in the trees."

He decelerated his jeep to a crawl. Sure enough, there was an opening in the trees where two old, rotting posts stood connected by a rusty chain draped tightly from one to the other. It appeared the posts had been there many years. Old tire tracks made it obvious that vehicles, presumably those of Charles and/ or Ed Bristol, had gone around the right post regularly. Andre made a left turn, skirted the right post, and drove on. "Your note says the cabin is at the end of this road," said Jim.

On both sides stood very tall trees whose outreaching branches intermingled over the road's center, giving the impression the jeep was rolling through a straight, dark tunnel.

"These trees must have been planted as some con-servationist's project because they're as straight as soldiers standing in file."

It was nearing dusk now. Cloud coverage was heavy, making it a dark day and an even gloomier evening. The roadway under the pines was muddy—swamp-like in places. After one mile, the road once again climbed higher and twisted first one way, and then the other. The pines became less and less dense while the road was almost impassable even for Andre's jeep. Several times, the wheels spun but he just kept his foot on the accelerator.

"Once you commit, you've got to keep going," said Andre who handled his vehicle with real savvy.

"I'd love to own one of these. It looks like you're having fun."

At length there was mostly brush along the roadside with oaks, elms and birches scattered here and there. They drove on until they rounded a sharp bend around a huge glacial rock. A quarter-mile ahead sat the retreat cabin in a large clearing. One huge oak tree sat in front of and to the left of the cabin.

"Whoa! Would you look at that."

"Doesn't look like any cabin to me," announced Jim as they drew closer. "It looks like a regular home."

"How in the hell did they ever get materials and supplies back in here?" When they neared the front, Andre turned sharply left and parked parallel to the cabin's small front stoop. His front bumper was inches from the towering oak.

6:15 P.M.

"Let's not delay because we want to be in and out before Charles gets here," said Jim. "There's no telling what that man may do." Andre picked up a rock about half the size of a house brick and broke one of the front windows to the left of the door. After knocking away any glass shards from the window frame, he crawled inside and opened the door for Jim. Flipping on lights, they looked around the room.

"This is no wooden shack," said Andre.

The room was large, about twenty by fifteen feet. The area along the left wall was obviously the kitchen. Lining it were cabinets, a sink, a refrigerator and stove. In the center of the room, sat a table and two mismatched chairs. The other side of the room contained a sofa, two easy chairs, and two short end tables with rustic looking lamps on top. In the corner was a narrow spiral staircase that led to a small loft.

Along the back wall, opposite the main entrance, was an open door that led to a bathroom and another closed door. Without hesitation, Jim walked over and opened that door. It was dark inside—not a single window. After flipping on the light switch, both men could see that the room was filled with a wide variety of scientific equipment. Shelves extending the entire length along the right side of the room, contained bottles of acids, test tubes, flasks, burners, ring stands, and a variety of chemicals in Erlenmeyer flasks, each one labeled. On the left side of the room, there sat electrical equipment: transformers, open boxes containing capacitors, resistors, LED's, transistors, etc. Running down the center of the room was a long worktable which held meters, an oscilloscope, scanners and other rather sophisticated, expensive looking equipment which neither Jim nor Andre could identify. Then, too, the table held a peculiar experimental apparatus hooked together—some experiment the brother had been working on.

The two snooped around not knowing what to look for. The center table held any number of experimental apparatuses in what looked like various stages of testing. There were ring stands with wires and coils attached. On some were suspended, rounded, spherical orbs. Power units for both AC and DC voltage sat disconnected amid an array of batteries of different voltages.

Andre said, "Jim, look over here. What do you think this is?"

Jim looked, but was puzzled. There sat a metal ring stand and about twelve inches up from its base, a screw clamp held a large, round ring about six inches in diameter. Attached to each side of the ring was a cylinder. A flat surface closed off the cylinder end facing them. Around that end the two men saw a tightly wrapped coil of wire.

"This wire is as fine as human hair," said Jim. "It must be wrapped around this cylinder a bazillion times."

"And look," added Andre, "one wire from each cylinder is twisted together to connect the two."

"I see that," said Jim. "But isn't there a second thin wire dangling from the outside of each coil?"

"Yep." Andre followed the two wires down to the table letting it slide through his fingers. "Look, this is weird; each end is soldered to an alligator clip. It looks like this is part of a very simple circuit of some kind. See this clip here?"

"Yes."

"Well, if this clip was touched to a power source, the electricity would flow up to here," he said pointing. "It would go around and around this left coil, and then cross over and go around and around the right coil. Then it would come back down through this wire," he pointed again, "to this other alligator clip."

"So, what does this contraption do?" asked Jim.

When Andre turned the ring stand around until it was facing them. Jim was speechless. He gasped several times and pointed. Andre just stared at the macabre apparatus.

Two half-spheres closed the front of the two cylinders—they looked exactly like eyeballs taken from inside a dolls head, only much larger.

"Holy hell!" said Jim, "is this a prototype of the crucifix's eyes at Saint Paul's Church?"

Behind, and to one side, was a row of nine-volt batteries standing one behind the other like dominoes. Two bare wires had been soldered across the tops of all the batteries so that they were all connected in parallel: one wire was soldered to all the positive terminals, another to all the negatives.

Andre just could not help himself. The man was curious by nature. He never gave it a second thought. While Jim stood beside him, Andre connected one alligator clip to the positive anode of the ganged nine volt batteries and the second clip to the negative terminal.

Nothing happened. Andre knew about coils and wires from working with a variety of appliances including refrigerators and air conditioners. He touched the coiled wire around the end of one of the half-spheres, and said, "The back of this orb is getting hot."

Jim reached up and pinched the other coil between his thumb and first finger. "So is this one."

They waited. Nothing happened. Then Andre noticed that the glass front of one of the orbs was clouding up. He touched it with his finger. Andre did the same to the other orb. "But feel how cold it is in front," he said.

"You're right, it is cold, and if I'm not mistaken," said Jim, "it looks cloudy." Amazed, both stood back watching, waiting. Both orbs misted over but that's all that happened. Within a short time, the water vapor began to evaporate. "How can that be?"

But Andre's mind was analyzing, thinking, wondering, re-analyzing, trying to make sense of what he'd just seen because once the water vapor had formed, the process stopped and the vapor started to dry up.

"Andre, talk to me. I can't read your thoughts. Can you explain that? You know a lot about mechanical things?" Still, Andre said nothing. He stood there staring at the entire apparatus.

"Do you suppose there's water in each sphere?" asked Jim.

"No. NO! That's the beauty of it all."

"But then where does it com—"

In a flash of insight, Andre grabbed Jim by the arm and spurted out, "I know where it came from. I—know—where—it—

came—from."

"But it's already stopped," said Jim.

"The vapor mist formed on the glassy eye-front because it got very cold, very fast. The air all around us always has some water in it—you know, relative humidity."

"Yes, but—"

"When the front of the eye got cold, vapor from the air we are breathing in this room condensed on the cold spot just like water forms on the outside of a glass filled with ice cubes and water."

"So what good is that?" muttered Jim not so sure about Andre's explanation.

"Let me try something. If I unclip the battery connection, then the front surface of the eye will return to room temperature rather quickly, because it is so small. But, before that vapor evaporates, if I reconnect the wire, the glassy front gets cold once again, and more water forms until it eventually falls to the table as a droplet."

"You're sure about that?" said Jim.

"Well, let's see. So now, let me disconnect this wire."

He undid one of the alligator clips breaking the circuit. Neither Andre nor Jim spoke. *This man has real smarts. Martie is right about him,* thought Jim as he stood waiting.

After but a moment, when Andre reconnected the alligator clip, the same process began again: first the heat in the tiny coils, then the very cold feeling in the front of each eye, then a tiny bit more water vapor. After repeating this procedure many times, the water vapor began congealing into one, tiny droplet. After many more on-off cycles, it fell to the tabletop.

Andre said, "You know how a cold glass with ice cubes inside gets wet on the outside, even though no water spilled over the top."

"I know what you mean, that's why I always put cold drinks on coasters so they won't put water rings on our furniture."

"Well," Andre went on, "refrigerators and air conditioners use a compressor to condense a gas like Freon into a very small space. Then it is allowed to expand through a tiny orifice into a larger space. When that happens, the larger space gets very cold, very fast. That process keeps refrigerated foods cold and your entire house cool in the summer time."

Andre is brilliant! thought Jim. *Here is a mind that reasons in a realm where I could never go.*

"But don't you need a compressor, Andre. A compressor couldn't be that small."

"Well ... let me just think a minute," said Andre taking off his backward baseball cap and scratching his head.

He thought for several more seconds and then cocked his cap sideways.

"Okay, here's my theory, which I'm making up as I go along, of course," he grinned.

"Nevertheless, you're doing unthinkably well," Jim smiled back.

"Heat makes molecules move apart, right?"

"Yes. That much I remember from my science classes."

"The rear of each orb has a heating coil, right?"

"Right, I felt it with my fingers and I can see it right there," Jim pointed.

"Now, imagine each orb has not one, but two compartments that are connected by a microscopic hole."

"But, Andre, the CAT scans done by the Carnegie Mellon crew suggested the orbs were hollow, but never mentioned two chambers."

"For sure they are hollow, but if one chamber is behind the

other, the scan might not've picked up the subtle difference."

"You may be one-hundred percent correct."

"So let's just suppose for the fun of it there are two. The rest is simple. When the coils heat up, the gas inside them expands very rapidly. The molecules push through a microscopic hole, cooling the front chamber very fast. The water in the atmosphere does the rest. It's that elementary. When the coil cools down, the gas molecules move closer together and flow back through the hole until equilibrium is reached."

"If you're right, Andre, then the miracle of Saint Paul's is sheer gimmickry."

"Sorry, Jim, I wish that were true, but it can't be. You told me, and so did Martie, that the scans showed not one single piece of evidence to indicate batteries or dry cells of any kind. They are metallic. The carbon center would've shown up on both your police scan and the university's.'

"These cylinder-like orbs are clever if they work as I imagine they do, but the Oculi must use yet another very clever principle. Brother Charles is indeed a brilliant man. What an inventive mind he must have."

Jim thought to himself, *Andre, you should give yourself the same credit.*

7:00 P.M.

"What was that?" Andre quipped, "Someone just drove up."

"Shit!" exclaimed Jim, as he glanced across the outer room through the front window Andre had broken. "It must be Charles. Andre, hide in the backroom. He won't know you're here."

"Jim, it's my red jeep out there. He'd recognize it anywhere. He'll know it's me. You get in the backroom and let me try to appease him." There wasn't time to argue, or any reason to. Jim bolted into the lab area and pushed the door until it was almost shut then doused the lights. He couldn't see, but he could hear what was going on.

Brother Charles was pissed. He roared up in his large, powerful black pickup, threw the gearshift lever into park and jumped out leaving the truck idling and the door wide open, blocking Andre's jeep from backing out. As he bounded up onto the stoop leading into the cottage, he took a pistol from his jacket and kicked in the partially open door.

When Andre saw the gun, he knew he was in deep trouble. Without it, Andre knew he could have given him one good fight. There was no chance to hide anywhere.

"So, you found the place on your own, did you?" shouted Charles angrily, standing just outside the open door.

Andre stood his ground inside the cabin.

"Yes, you gave me good directions on Saturday. But I got all screwed up with the police along the highway and everything, so I thought I'd take a ride up here and see the lab for myself."

"You lie! Liar! You know it's damp and muddy outside, and if I'm not mistaken, there are two sets of footprints on the front stoop. One set comes in the door and one set leads to that broken window over there where you came in."

"It's Martie, isn't it? Bitch! She's back there. I know you've got the hots for her, she's your type. You're not gay. You two came here to screw. She wanted some of that muscular body just like I did. And I'll bet you two got an eyeful examining my workroom back there, didn't you and that's too damn bad."

As calmly as he could, Andre spoke out. "It looks like you have a several neat projects going on, Brother. Which one do you mean?"

"The one I worked on for so long? Did you two see it? Do

you know how it works? Do you? Well, say something big black man, say something because you can't leave here, nor can that white-trash bitch since you know about my experiment. This has been planned far too long—far too many years for you to end it. You fool."

"You're the fool Charles, parading around like a monk in that brown robe. You could never be any monk—a monkey perhaps! You're a disgusting dunghill with too many brains, some of which don't function right. You and Ed Bristol, getting rich stealing from a church."

"Who said anything about Ed Bristol. You'd have to ask him if he's involved. But now, you'll never get the chance. He'll be in the clear."

Andre didn't answer.

"Come out, Martie, dearest," shouted Charles.

"Leave her out of it you maggot-faced coward."

"So-o-o, she is back there!"

"Don't you touch her," commanded Andre. "Put down that pistol, and I'll show you what this black man can do to your unholy, white, ape face."

Charles became wrathful as Andre continued hurling insults. "I know you're back there, woman. Come out NOW!"

Damn! thought Jim. *Why didn't I bring my revolver or at least a can of Mace?*

The door to the lab creaked open, and Jim did as Charles had commanded.

"Well—look—what—we—have—here! One big, unarmed police officer. Looks like I caught me two big fish. And all along, I thought he had the hots for your wife, you assholes."

Jim said nothing but walked across the room with his hands up. *Speaking of asshole,* he thought, *I certainly don't want to intimidate this demented man to pull that trigger. He may be brilliant, but he's acting psychotic now.*

"Stop right there, flatfoot. Have you ever seen a black man die before? You will now, and you'll have a front row seat. Maybe I'll just shoot him in the leg first and, once he starts screaming and rolling around, it will be your turn for punishment."

Holy shit! This crazy idiot is going to kill him and me, too. Jim had crept just a bit closer. He stood in front of Andre, but to his right. The partially-opened door was inches away from his left foot.

"Any last words?" asked Charles.

He cocked his gun and began raising it toward Andre's head.

"NO!" bellowed Jim as he kicked the front door hard to his left, then slammed his entire weight against it. But a bullet blast had already struck Andre's head and he went down hard.

"You've killed him, you unholy, murdering, demonic bastard!"

The door slammed hard against Charles' wrist. A loud cracking noise came from his injured hand, trapped inside. The bone had broken. The Brother howled in pain, pushing in against Jim's weight just enough to pull his arm out, letting the door slam shut, but he didn't drop the gun.

He stood outside on the stoop, cursing and swearing and holding his agonizing wrist. Jim clicked the lock, turned off the light switch, and then dropped down very low to Andre's body. The man lay groaning with his hand raised to his temple.

In the darkness, Jim followed Andre's hand until his fingers felt the wound. He was bleeding from a gash in the flesh, right at his left temple. The wound felt more like a tear than a bullet hole.

"Jesus Christ, Andre! No! Don't die on me now. Please,

Man, please!"

In the next instant, he heard the front door window shatter, but not all of the glass broke free. A wild shot rang out but missed because Jim was crouched so low and it was dark inside. With his pistol barrel, Charles started to knock the rest of the glass out of the small window.

Jim knew he had seconds to act since Charles was just about to reach in and unlock the door rather than chance climbing through the window Andre had smashed. He crawled low across the outer room and into the lab where he remembered seeing a bottle of acid.

Picking up what he hoped was the right one, Jim felt his way across the outer room then stood upright, flattened against the wall beside the locked door. He pulled the stopper and waited, his heart pounding against his ribs. Fumes from the open nitric acid wafted up his nostrils, forcing him to turn his head.

With the gun outside in his injured hand, Charles reached inside the broken door window to release the lock.

Damn, why didn't he stick his hand inside with the gun so I could've twisted it free?

Jim could barely see the demonic hand come in and turn down toward the knob on the lock. He was certain the Brother would start shooting in all directions the instant the door opened. He upended the nitric acid dumping much of the bottle's contents on the fumbling wrist and hand. At once, the outer layers of flesh began to shrivel and dissolve as bubbles formed along with a wisp of dark brown heavy smoke. A putrid odor arose from the shriveling tissue.

If ever a human screamed like a howling coyote, it had to be Charles when he let out a terrifying, pitiful outcry as the acid ate through his skin. He jumped off the stoop, ran across the muddy area in front of the cabin, past his idling truck, and rolled himself down into the damp brush and began tearing up clumps of dirt and roots, trying to wipe away the acid that was dissolving his flesh.

Jim could hear him, half crying, half screaming in the distance, but he knew he'd be back for the kill. *I've got to act fast because he still has that damn gun. I've got to sneak out now and jump the unholy bastard*—but just then Andre gave out a moan and began to speak.

"Jim? Jim, are you—"

"My God," he said kneeling beside Andre, feeling his head a second time. "Andre, I thought you were—gone. Your head is bleeding. I've got blood all over my fingers."

The bullet had made a neat, four-inch wound as it furrowed along Andre's skull. *I know scalp wounds bleed a lot. But I don't know if any part of the shell went through his skull bone. The gash feels rather deep; if we could just get out of here and get medical help.*

"Andre! Andre! Listen to me. Get up! We've got to get out. Now! He'll be back to kill us. He still has his gun!"

Andre said nothing, but he had heard and somehow understood; Jim rolled him onto his stomach. He pulled one knee up under himself, then the other, and with Jim's help, he staggered to his feet. Jim opened the cabin door.

Charles' idling pickup sat facing the cabin. It hid their movements. The suffering thing was at the rear of the SUV kneeling near the bumper. His side was toward them. He continued wiping at his acid-eaten hand with globs of muddy earth. They could hear him whimpering and talking to himself like a madman, insane with pain.

Leaning on Jim, Andre stooped low and crept across the

narrow four-foot porch, then rolled off into the mud in front of Charles' truck just as the injured man stood up and faced their direction. He hadn't seen them. Jim knew he couldn't get himself and Andre up into Charles' truck. Instead, he crawled along the passenger side of Andre's jeep dragging Andre along. The two disappeared around the front of it by the large oak tree.

They were now hidden by the jeep's right fender and radiator. Charles' idling truck engine helped cover any noise they had made. Andre began to focus on what was happening, but he was losing blood rapidly and going into shock. He tried to raise himself from a lying position while Jim crouched low. Jim kept looking for the best vantage point where he could avoid Charles' gun yet take the brother down by a sudden rush from behind.

Although both hands agonized with pain, Charles recovered enough to finish his evil scheme. From the back of his truck, he lifted a gallon container of gasoline. The pain in his cracked wrist must have subsided somewhat because that hand held the gun firmly. He managed to pick up the can and hold it against his body with his raw, scorched hand.

"Now, you two will DIE!" he shouted. "You've met your match you two heaps of filth. Now, you'll feel what it's like to fry alive and die."

He opened the container and splashed the gasoline all over the front door stoop and each of the two windows. Stepping back from the porch, he took a full book of matches, lit one, then lit the entire book and tossed it onto the gasoline. A loud— WHUMP—followed as the fuel ignited, turning the entire front of the cabin into an inferno.

It was pitiful for Jim to watch. The injured, whimpering, hooded figure, still clutching his revolver, returned to the back of his truck and managed to carry back a second container

341

of gasoline. He was very careful not to get close to what was already ablaze.

Leaving Andre's side, Jim crawled around to the far side of the jeep hoping to jump the crazed gunman when he returned. But when Andre saw Charles walking toward the rear of the burning building, as weak as he was, he crawled the length of his jeep, and then a few feet more, until he reached the truck—its driver's door still fully open. With a massive surge, he raised in a stooped position and flopped inside across the front seat.

Charles upturned the gasoline can and propped it against the rear of the lab on top of a pile of logs, then stepped back to toss another lit pack of matches. Now the rear of the building was ablaze. Both men heard the second—*WHUMP*—and knew what had happened.

Charles stopped along the far side of his truck and stood facing it. He still held his revolver, Jim could not jump him. The brother could not see Andre prostrate on the seat, his feet hanging out the door. The brother stood waiting—waiting, listening—listening.

Something was wrong. There were no cries of pain—no agonizing screams. Andre was dead, but surely Jim could not burn to death without howling in pain or trying to run out the door. He wanted to hear the tortured shrieks. Something was definitely amiss. He aimed his pistol up at the second floor window, shot out the glass and yelled, "Jim, I know you're up there. You're going to cook, man. Cook until well done." He continued standing, thinking—thinking—thinking.

As Charles stared intently through the flames that had now filled the entire kitchen and were licking at the first floor ceiling, it dawned on him that the front door had been open when he poured the gasoline on the stoop. He realized that Jim might have run out the door when he went for the first can of gasoline. Ah-hah, Jim, I know where you are, you stupid fool. You're hiding around the front of that damned jeep.

Andre lay prone on Charles' truck seat. He was lightheaded, having trouble focusing; black spots came and went in front of his eyes. He knew he was going out.

Then he heard Charles say, "You wouldn't be hiding inside that jeep, would you, Jim?"

The brother shot at the heavy, fiberglass winter-top. The bullet went in through the side at an angle and out through the driver's side window. The safety glass exploded into thousands of small, harmless pieces. Then the hapless brother crossed in front of the truck intent on making certain Jim wasn't hiding in, or under, the jeep or on its far side.

From his prone position, Andre shoved his hand down on the gas pedal. The huge four-by-four roared forward as all its wheels spun at one time. As it moved, the driver's door slammed against Andre.

Charles turned, but the front of the truck caught him head on in the gut so that his arm with the gun, was resting over the hood aimed at the windshield; the rest of his body was folded around the pickup's front grill much like a ragged doll swept off its feet. Charles fired with no accuracy missing the windshield, but it was far too late. The huge vehicle plowed all the way in through the burning stoop, stopping only when it was halfway through the kitchen. Part of the heavy second floor collapsed onto the roof and bed of the pickup.

Jim was incredulous. He left the far side of the jeep and ran over toward the back of the truck.

"Andre, ANDRE," Jim shouted as loud as he could, "PUT IT IN REVERSE!"

He could get no closer than the tailgate because of the intense heat. The truck's front tires were already on fire. Jim stared morbidly, his eyes drawn to the writhing, naked, flaming figure of Brother Charles. Andre, lay quiet. He could see the burning debris on the windshield. He could feel the heat of the conflagration; hear the crackling flames outside the truck. He could feel his own pants legs overheating. It was just a matter of time before they caught fire. He pulled his feet up as far as he could and shoved himself across the seat. He heard Jim yelling at him.

"Reverse, Andre, reverse. Please do it, Andre. DO IT NOW!"

He thought he understood what Jim meant. He raised his left hand and shoved the gearshift lever all the way to the top and pushed down on the accelerator. The huge engine roared. Nothing happened.

"Andre," he could hear Jim yelling, "put it in reverse— REVERSE."

Andre tried to think. There was a "P" beside the shift lever that looked a lot like the "R" below it. He couldn't reason correctly. The heat inside the truck was rising rapidly. He could hear the burning, crackling wood and see the red-hot coals that had fallen down onto and over the hood and against the windshield.

The air was stifling. Finally, he moved the lever just one click to stand beside the "R" and pushed on the accelerator. The engine roared, but this time all four wheels spun backward at the same time. The pickup careened out of the burning building narrowly missing Jim.

The second floor that had been resting on the truck, collapsed engulfing what was left of Brother Charles. The truck reversed in a slight arc, and because Andre's hand slid off the accelerator when the truck lurched backward, the vehicle rolled to a stop by itself with its two front tires afire giving off thick acrid smoke.

Jim ran to the cab door. Ignoring burning debris on the hood and in the bed of the pickup, he blistered his fingers opening the door and shoving against Andre so he wouldn't topple out. He pushed and shoved until the semi-conscious man was far enough over on the passenger side that Jim could get in and drive the truck as close to Andre's jeep as possible.

A barely audible Andre said, "Officer—mind driving?"

Jim could only smile at his courageous remark.

This man is unbelievable, just like Pastor Kerr, thought Jim.

"No, I'll drive, Party Pooper."

He backed the truck alongside the jeep so he could slide the injured man from the passenger side of the truck into the passenger side of the jeep. With Andre locked in, Jim climbed behind the wheel, started the engine, put the jeep in reverse and backed away from the oak tree, then barreled down the dirt road away from the burning lab building.

Just before they disappeared around the huge bolder they had passed coming in, the gasoline tank on the truck ignited. There was a brilliant flash followed by an explosive roar, which sent truck parts flying in all directions.

"We missed the grand finale, Andre," Jim teased, but Andre was propped against the passenger door, his eyes closed. Oh shit! Don't leave me, Andre! You can't check out now. Not after all this. When the conflagration was no longer in sight, Jim stopped. He took his jacket off and pulled his sweatshirt up over his head, revealing only a tank top underneath.

"Gee," teased the semi-conscious Andre, "Charles wanted me, but I didn't think you'd be the one to take advan—" he didn't have the strength to finish his outrageous remark.

Jim folded his sweatshirt to make a bandage, which he tied tightly around Andre's head covering the wound. Then with some difficulty, he reached across him and pulled the lever to tilt back the passenger seat into a more restful position. He draped his jacket over the injured man, then mashed the gas pedal and headed for the highway.

34   The Emergency Room

7:45 P.M.

As they careened along the roadway, Andre slipped in and out of consciousness. Jim knew he needed serious medical attention. Steering with his left hand, he reached over and searched through his jacket pockets with his right hand until he located his cell phone. Once more, he stopped the jeep long enough to punch in Romeric's number, then drove on. He tried to remain as calm as possible while explaining their emergency.

"Andre has one serious bullet wound to the side of his head. He's bleeding and needs emergency medical attention."

"What on earth happened? Where are you? Are you okay? What's this all about?" Romeric asked.

"It's a long story, Chief. I'll tell it when I see you. Right now, we need to get Andre to an emergency facility as soon as possible. I don't want him to die on me."

"Where in hell are you?"

"In a few minutes, we'll be turning west on Route 30. Then we'll be about twelve miles from Latrobe. Can you have an emergency vehicle intercept us? The driver's side window was shot out and it's ice cold in here."

"Good grief, just a second," said Romeric. Jim could hear him talking on his radio. "Sylvia, I need an emergency crew to meet a vehicle coming toward Latrobe on Route 30. A passenger has a bullet wound to the head and is unconscious. Tell the crew that the oncoming vehicle will have it's flashers on and will be flicking its high beams on and off. It's a bright-red jeep." Then he returned to his conversation with Jim.

"Did you hear that, Jim? Use your flashers and intermittent high beams."

"I heard, and I hope they meet us soon, very soon. I'd sure hate to lose this man!"

"Jim, I just don't understand, but it must be bad. How in the hell did Andre get shot?" he asked.

"Too much to explain now. Brother Charles is dead and the lab burned to the ground."

"WHAT?"

"It was atrocious, Chief."

"Holy shit! How can one off-duty officer and one repairman get themselves into this much trouble? He could have shot both of you!"

Then the phone signal began to fade as Route 30 dropped down into a deep valley.

"I'll see you so—" said Jim as his cell phone beeped twice and shut off with the message, "No Signal!" across its small screen.

They had driven about seven miles west when Jim saw the blinking red and white emergency lights of an EMS vehicle coming toward them with its siren wailing. He switched on the flashers then clicked the high beams on-off-on-off to make sure the EMS spotted him. He pulled over onto the highway berm, opened his door and stood outside waiting to see where the EMS vehicle would make its turn.

When it reached the crest of a hill where Route 30 intersected another rural road, the vehicle made a wide U-turn, and within minutes, it pulled up behind the jeep. The crew rushed up to the passenger side door with a stretcher. They opened it while they pushed the unconscious Andre back into a sitting position. When their stretcher was in place, they pulled his feet out first, then gently but efficiently, slid his entire body onto it. One of the crew checked for breathing.

"He's go!" the woman said, "but not by much—shock!"

They hurried him to the back of their vehicle and slid him inside. Within seconds, an IV drip had been inserted into his arm, a heart monitor placed on his chest, a blood pressure cuff added over his left bicep, all of which were connected to a TV monitor. When the crew felt Andre had been stabilized, they removed Jim's blood-drenched, shirt bandage, and redressed the wound with halos of sterile gauze.

"That's a nasty one," said the woman who had checked for breathing. "Looks like the bullet slid across the skull bone, taking some along with it. We're heading for Latrobe General. See you there in the emergency area." With that terse directive, the EMS crew pulled both rear doors shut and roared away.

Jim sat in Andre's jeep staring straight ahead. He began to shake uncontrollably as he thought of the events that had occurred during the past hour. An overwhelming feeling of wanting to close his eyes and sleep overtook him, but he refused to give into shock.

I can't lose it now. I just can't. That man needs me.

He jumped down from the jeep and walked back and forth along the highway taking deep, deep breaths of the cold, night air and then slowly blowing them out.

Breathe in—and blow out, in—then out. His composure began to return. *Breathe in—and blow out.*

When Jim felt capable of driving, he climbed back into the jeep and started for Latrobe General. The bitter air blowing in through the wide-open side window helped him keep alert.

Instead of concentrating on the horrors of the evening, he busied himself by thinking of all the crazy, comical remarks Andre might say when he got to the hospital.

That man keeps me in the best of moods. I'll never forget his Mama's ironing board theory. What a comedian! She must have been a real character.

As he neared the hospital, Jim's cell phone beeped. It was Martie.

"Jim, please be okay. Romeric called me and explained the little bit he knew about Andre."

"Baby, I'm a few blocks from the hospital, so I'll soon find out. Gee, you don't know how much I'm missing you right now, Martie; I love you. So much has happened, and he's just got to be—" Jim could not finish his sentence.

"You were right in every way about that man. And the worst of it is he wouldn't let me go up there alone. He insisted on coming along. If he hadn't been there, Heaven alone knows what might've happened to me."

"I'll be there very shortly. They've quit digging for today, and so far there are no signs of a dryer, let alone a body. Baby, I'll see you in just a few minutes."

10:45 P.M.

When Martie arrived at Latrobe General Hospital, she found Jim indeed shaken after what he and Andre had just lived through.

"Just hold me, Martie, just hold me for a while, then I'll tell you about it."

Martie put her arms around him and he pulled her against his chest. The two stood there embracing in the emergency waiting room. She reached up and stroked his hair trying to calm and reassure him.

"A doctor came in to talk with me just before you arrived, Martie. He said a small piece of the bullet veered off and had lodged in Andre's skull. They were uncertain how far it had penetrated. They've taken him to the operating room to remove it. I don't know how to reach his family. I know he has an apartment here in Latrobe, but I don't know where. Martie, it was a hellish nightmare. He had such a terrible gash and there was so much blood, and, and, I can't believe this happened to him."

"Did they give you his wallet and belongings?"

"His bloody clothes are there in that plastic bag the nurse gave me. His wallet and other personal items are here in his gym bag. I tried to phone his apartment hoping he was living with someone, but there was no answer."

Martie reached out for the bag and Jim handed it over.

"I'll be back in a few minutes. I'll call the borough building and they'll track down Andre's family. Ms. Keyes—*Ms. Keyes! Oh, shit!* Shit, Oh, Sylvia—Sylvia Keyes and Andre!" Jim shouted as it dawned on him.

"Sylvia Keyes and Andre are in love. Those two may be living together. She's working the late shift tonight. Sylvia! Why—she's the one who sent the EMS crew. How in Hell could I be so thoughtless? Oh shit! I've got to call her right now."

As Jim had expected, Sylvia Keyes was nothing less than hysterical when she heard the news.

"Jim! Jim, tell me! Please! Is he the person I sent the EMS team to intercept?"

"I'm so sorry, Sylvia, I didn't think to tell you because I was so up—"

"Oh, Sweet Jesus, is he alive? Tell me, is he alive, Jim? Is he all right? What happened?" Then she began to cry. "Oh, how could this happen to that man?"

"Sylvia, he's going to be all right. He *is* going to be okay. The doctor's have reassured us he'll be fine. I'm coming to get you."

"Oh, I'm shaking. I need to sit down."

"Syl, Honey, Andre's a tough man. He'll be fine. I'll be there in just a few minutes."

"No, no! That will take too long, I'll be right over. I'm coming now. I'll be right there! Tell him I'll be there, please? Please tell him I love him and I'll be th—" *Click*.

Jim explained to Martie how upset Sylvia was on the phone. He was glad he'd called, but felt sickened that he had omitted telling her what had happened when he'd radioed earlier for an ambulance.

Within seventeen minutes, Sylvia arrived, parked outside the emergency room door in spite of the No Parking signs and dashed inside. Seeing her coming through the door, both Martie and Jim intercepted her.

"How is he? Please tell me he's all right? Can I see him? Can I talk to his doctor? Where is—"

Jim put his arms around her and could feel her sobbing. "Sylvia, I think he's going to be fine. That's what the doctor says. We're just waiting for his report."

Then the three of them pulled chairs around so they could sit facing one another. Jim started to explain how Andre had gotten involved with the whole affair. Sylvia got up and paced around and around while Jim talked. She agonized as he and Martie took turns revealing first one part of the story and then another. At last Sylvia sat down, awestruck, shaking her head in complete disbelief. Martie reached over and held her.

Then Martie looked at Jim and said, "Can you tell us what happened to the two of you up there or do you want to wait for a while?"

"It was so awful," he began. Then bit by bit, he told Sylvia and Martie the entire story. He ended by explaining how the injured Andre crawled over and up into Charles' truck, then rammed him into the burning building. He excluded the gory details since they served no useful purpose.

"I was so afraid he wouldn't get the damn pickup truck in reverse before it caught fire and blew up. I kept hollering, 'put it in reverse, in reverse.' I even tried to pull on it. Sylvia, Martie, it was so hot I couldn't stand near the tailgate, and yet, he was inside the cab. I—I just don't know how he did it."

The two sat there and listened for the better part of twenty minutes for Jim to end his bizarre tale.

"What a guy, Sylvia! What a courageous man he is."

The door to the waiting room opened and Andre's surgeon walked in still dressed in cap, gown but with gloves removed. He looked around, and Sylvia jumped up immediately.

In an instant, she asked, "How, how is he? Is he okay?"

"He's doing quite well considering the extent of the wound. A tiny piece of lead from the bullet was lodged in his skull bone but never went through. Had it done so—"

"—Oh, please, spare me. Please don't tell me about that," gasped Sylvia.

"He's very lucky," said the surgeon. "He has one hard head."

"Oh, thank the Lord Jesus for some things."

"Now, he's rather weak so we'll want to observe him for a few days. The stitches in his head will dissolve and his hair will cover the scar. He'll be fine. The nurse will be out to tell you what room he'll be in so you can visit him. Just don't stay too long because he needs to rest." Martie put her arms around the doctor and gave him a huge hug.

"Thanks for everything doctor—um—"

"McDonald, Ted McDonald. I'll be checking up on him tomorrow morning, maybe see you folks then," and as he turned to leave, Sylvia's eyes filled with tears.

"Thank you, Doctor, he means so much to me."

She threw her arms around him and would not let go for a long time. McDonald simply patted her back. When the surgeon left the room, Sylvia took out her cell phone and called Andre's folks. Sylvia was half crying. She related to Andre's mother about his injury and that they had just spoken to his surgeon who said Andre would be fine.

Jim listened to Sylvia as she skillfully calmed whomever she was talking to and fielded what must have been a flood of questions. They could hear Sylvia reassuring that "Andre was fine, just a little groggy," that "he had done a very brave thing," that "he'd be in the hospital for observation for a few days," and that "the doctor said he expected a full recovery."

Sylvia said, "She'd have Andre call as soon as possible," and "yes, she'll call back with the number for the phone in Andre's room." Whoever was on the line needed a lot of reassurance so Sylvia continued to talk.

When her phone conversation finally ended, Sylvia walked over and said, "That was his mom. She was very upset, but she is one wonderful woman. It's no wonder Andre has such a remarkable personality."

"Oh, I can't imagine getting a phone call like that," said Martie.

"I think she calmed down near the end of our conversation.

She was worried about him being shot. She wanted to know if he had been in trouble with the police. I just couldn't explain the whole story to her because what you told me is unbelievable.

"His mother thought that maybe he'd gotten in with the wrong crowd and was stealing or doing drugs. I think she thought a police bullet hit him. When I explained that some deranged person shot him, she wanted to know how he ever got involved with someone like that. She kept saying he's always been such a good boy, a hard working man just like his father was. I just couldn't tell her the entire story. So I told her I'd call her back when I had Andre's room number."

A nurse informed them that Andre was in room 317. They could go up and see him. The doctor had ordered sedatives to keep him quiet for the first few hours. She told them about visiting hours. They followed her directions to the elevator, and got off on the third floor.

When they entered 317, he was lying on his back, his head wrapped with layers of gauze. Sylvia stooped down and kissed his cheek tenderly, then his closed mouth. "Andre, it's Sylvia. I'm here and I love you."

She stood there holding his hand. A nurse came in and informed them that the blood on Andre's bandage was nothing to be concerned about.

"There is an antibiotic dripping through that IV drip to make sure no infection sets in. He'll be okay. Doubt if he'll be here more than a few days."

"Thanks for all your help," Jim told the nurse.

"Jim," said Martie, "I swear he has a smile on his face even now."

"Yep, he sure does."

Jim and Martie stayed for a good hour or more, and then

the night nurse assured them Andre was in good hands and it would be best if they went home and rested and returned during regular visiting hours tomorrow. But Sylvia refused to leave. She pulled her chair close to Andre's bed, held his hand, put her head on his arm and fell asleep.

As soon as they reached home, both Martie and Jim had a glass of wine while trying to relax on the couch.

Martie asked, "Jim, what will you do about Ed Bristol? He has no idea any of this has happened. I'm sure he's tried to reach Charles on his cell phone. Will Romeric arrest him?"

"If we arrest him, we can't charge him with murder because a body hasn't been found. We can arrest him for larceny as far as Saint Paul's Church is concerned, but I'd like to nab him for murder, in fact, several."

"And what if no body is found?"

"Well, we'll just keep hoping. What else can we do?"

"Tomorrow should be an interesting day for Ed Bristol," said Jim. "Andre won't show up for work. If Ed calls Brother Charles, he won't be able to reach him. If it breaks on the news about the fire at the retreat cabin, and the strange death of the brother, that is if he's identified, Ed Bristol will really be freaked out.

"I think we should just stay quiet about the whole affair and wait until we see what's dug up at the landfill." Martie slid down on the sofa so that her head rested on its back. She closed her eyes and soon dozed off. Jim moved further down on the sofa then rolled to one side, placing his head on Martie's lap. He pulled up his feet and fell asleep.

35 A Silver Cross

March 5, 2003—Wednesday
7:45 A.M.

It was Father Kerr's day to celebrate morning Mass. He went over to his cubicle about twenty minutes early to hear any confessions so he could be finished and ready to vest for Mass that started at eight. He was sitting in his cubicle in his usual manner when the door to the penitent's side of the confessional opened, followed by that uncanny silence which made the hairs on the back of his neck stand on end.

"I'm back again, Father, to make a confession, but this time I need some cash in case I have to leave town. Here's what I want you to do."

The shaken padre remained silent in a stupor of hate and disgust.

"My next victim will be Martie Meyer. I've picked her because I think she's the one who's fouled things up. She's next unless, of course, you do what I say, today. Do you hear me? Today. Are you there Father Kerr?"

"I'm here," he rasped.

"I want you to get sixty-thousand dollars in cash. One-hundred dollar bills will do, and put it in a nice suitcase and take it to 135 Natrona Street. You must do this by three o'clock this afternoon.

357

"The house on Natrona Street is empty and the front door is unlocked. All you need to do is put the money-filled suitcase inside the front door and leave. Don't hang around because I'll be watching. To prove to you I mean business, I just may have to scare Martie a bit today, but I won't kill her if you provide the sixty-thousand dollars. Did you hear me?"

"I've heard every word, but I'd still like to help you. You can stop doing these terrible things. The Almighty will forgive you and help you. There are people who like you and will help—I can absolve you."

"Don't lecture me, priest. It's too late now. Just see that the money is there by three o'clock at 135 Natrona Street." This time, The Voice did not ask for a blessing.

Father Kerr sat shocked. His feelings, his mind, his spirit were panicking. Getting the money from the bank should be no real problem, but there might be a lot of questions asked. Knowing that Martie would be hurt was the real issue. Once again, the vomit began pushing its way up from his stomach. He could not go on like this. This would be the final blow. His mind could not function under this much pressure.

8:15 A.M.

Yet Kerr immediately became distracted because he knew there wasn't much time. He must get the money and somehow warn Martie so the Evil One won't keep his promise and injure her in some way. He left his confessional cubicle, walked to the front of his church where he turned and explained to those in attendance that there would be no Mass today.

"An emergency has arisen, which must be taken care," he explained to his puzzled parishioners.

Without worrying about the seal of confession, he phoned

Martie's home. The phone rang and rang, but Martie had already left for the middle school. He dialed the school and asked to talk with her, but she had not yet arrived.

"Would you have her call me the instant she arrives?" asked Kerr. "This is an emergency."

When Martie entered her building, the secretary relayed the priest's message, but when Martie tried to dial Kerr, she continued to get his voice mail. In his panic, he had either forgotten his cell phone, or forgot to turn it on.

By nine o'clock in the morning, Kerr had called the bank president and told her exactly what he needed; he must have the money by two o'clock that afternoon. She started to ask a lot of questions when Father Kerr stopped her.

"Please, I hate to be rude, but don't ask me for an explanation, none. I need the money and I need it now, today. It's the church's money for me to use as I see fit, so please save your questions. Will you have the sixty grand ready by two o'clock?"

"Why, yes, Father," she said in amazement. He had never been so curt before—almost rude. "I hope you are doing the right thing."

"Listen," he said bluntly, "I'm doing what I have to do so please, don't let me down; and, make sure you tell no one about my withdrawal. Do you understand?"

"Yes, I do. Is there some way I can help you?" The woman was now very puzzled after the priest's statement.

"No, but thank you. I'll stop by at two and won't have time to chat, so please have the money ready to go. This is a life or death situation. I'll bring my own suitcase."

"I'll have everything ready, Father," she said. Her voice inflections and pallid stare revealed her hidden feelings. She knew something was dreadfully wrong.

10:15 A.M.

When Kerr could not reach Martie by phone, he drove over to the school to warn her not to leave the building. At her classroom door, he said, "I can't tell you why, Martie, but your very life may be in danger. I tried to call your home earlier, but missed you."

"What on earth is this all about? Who is after me?"

"Martie, I can't answer that, but promise me you'll call Jim to take you home today—do you promise?"

"Yes, I'll call him right away, and you call him, too. Please?"

"I'll try, but I don't have a lot of time. There is something I must do, but whatever you do, please call Jim and stay inside here until after three o'clock." Then Kerr turned and hurried out of the school building. He felt better that he had warned Martie because he knew Jim and other police would make sure she was safe.

Martie had been in the middle of a science lesson. A bit shaken after the upsetting warning, she decided to finish her lesson and then call her husband. There were just a few minutes left in the period.

She was teaching her class about different types of levers and how they help make work easier. She had taken a six-foot long, two-by-four and placed it on the floor over a common house brick so that one foot of it was on one side of the brick, while the five foot section lay on the other side. She stood on the short end. This forced the longer side high up in the air.

"See, Class, I am the load, the board is the lever, and the brick acts as the fulcrum. Benny, come up here and push down on the end sticking up."

Ben hurried to the front of the room and pushed down.

With one hand, he could lift the entire weight of Ms. Meyer off the floor.

"Now, try one finger."

Doing what he was told, Ben lifted Martie up off the ground by pushing down with one finger.

"Class, if I had asked Ben to come up here and lift me in the air with one finger could he have done it without this lever?" The students started to giggle.

POW—Before anyone could answer, there was the unmistakable crack of gunfire that shattered one of Martie's classroom windows. "DOWN! Everyone down! Down on the floor," she screamed. "Right now! Get down on the floor! Don't even think of sitting or peeking out a window."

She didn't have to repeat herself because the terrified students got down and made every attempt to hide under their desks.

"Stay down!" she ordered while she crawled along the front of the room to her intercom. Up on her knees, she could just reach the wall phone. "Don't even think of sitting up," she said looking out over her students. She explained to the office that someone had shot out one of her classroom windows, but she and her kids were okay because all were down on the floor below window level.

Within seconds, an announcement came over the loudspeaker telling all students and all teachers to get down on the floor lower than any windows. She could hear the students in other classrooms obeying the announcement. Within a few minutes, all heard the wailing of many police sirens. They parked helter-skelter outside the building, blocking the street.

Along with the police came an EMS vehicle and several fire engines. Some of the students lay in tears wanting to know what was happening. Some were pretending it didn't bother them, but they were equally afraid. About an hour later, after police had searched the inside and the outside of the building and the neighborhood around the school, all was declared secure. Another announcement from the principal came over the PA system saying the police had everything under control.

Jim walked into Martie's room, which thrilled her students, each wanting to tell him about what had happened. Jim put a finger in each ear to show that it was too loud and he couldn't hear anyone. Then when the students began to quiet down, he turned to the blackboard and wrote: "When everyone can hear, each of you will have a chance to talk."

When they quieted, he pointed to the last person in the first row and asked, "Tell me what you think happened."

As the student told his story, Jim put a "1" on the board then wrote beside it: 1. A shot was fired and broke the window. Then he went on to the next student, and the next, writing down each comment until they were mere repetitions of what had already been written. It didn't take long to debrief the entire class because many students would pass when they realized what they had to say was already written on the board.

The only information Martie could add was that Kerr had been there prior to the shooting warning her to be careful. She tried to explain the gist of their conversation, but it had been very short. They decided to discuss the warning later when they were alone. Right now, she needed to calm her students.

Forgetting herself, she said, "Officer Jim, we were all scared shitless."

Her abrupt statement made her students laugh. Jim assured them that the police would be watching the building and the grounds to make sure it didn't happen again. Then he left the room, and Martie let the students gab, making no attempt to finish what had begun as a fascinating lesson. Because of the incident, the police suggested that school be dismissed around eleven-thirty, and the principal agreed. Many parents arrived at the school to walk or drive their children home.

Of course, the incident made the news within a short period of time. Mrs. Pierce heard it on TV and hurried to tell the priests about the shooting. Kerr shook his head withdrawn into his own mental agony. Lucifer had kept his promise. Now, he had to be absolutely sure the sixty grand was delivered by three o'clock.

12:45 P.M.

Although Martie knew that the police would be patrolling the streets around the school, she still felt anxious about returning there tomorrow, and wondered how her students felt? She knew how lethal a rifle could be from quite a distance. She entertained the idea of taking a leave of absence to protect herself and the students until the shooter had been arrested. She convinced herself the shooting was not random. Out of all the classrooms in the building, she believed hers had been selected for harassment after Kerr's frightening warning.

Jim was miffed. He immediately phoned the rectory to talk with Pastor Kerr but neither Pierce nor Walsh nor McKelvy knew his whereabouts. The pastor had told them he "had business to attend to." When Jim asked the whereabouts of Ed Bristol, Mrs. Pierce stated that she had talked with him over coffee for a few minutes earlier in the morning, but then he had gone over to the church like he always did. She said she was sure he was still working over there because she could see his repair truck in the parking lot.

"Has his truck been there all morning?" asked Jim,

"I don't miss much," said Pierce. "I don't remember him leaving. Besides, he always stops in before he goes anywhere."

Since school had been dismissed at eleven-thirty, Martie and Jim went to visit Andre. They arrived at the hospital fifteen minutes before visiting hours began, Martie had called the nurse's station on the third floor seeking permission to visit early. "Sure," said the nurse, "but don't get him too excited." They walked into Andre's room sheepishly, expecting to see him lying semi-conscious, or if awake, in a lot of pain. What they saw was Andre lying very stiff and very straight on his back with his eyes closed, draped with a white sheet looking much like a corpse. His two dark-skinned arms, however, were folded on his chest.

"Good grief, Jim, I hope he's all right. It looks like he's unconscious."

"Or dead," added Jim starting to grin.

"Oh, don't say that; oh the poor thin—" Then they both started to giggle when they noticed that in his folded hands he was holding one daisy upright by its stem.

"That nurse must have put it there, Jim, What an awful way to joke. Poor fellow, he was so brave. But he does look like he's peaceful."

"Or dead," added Jim a second time, catching on to Andre's joke. Martie stooped down and kissed Andre's forehead.

"More—more—"

"Jim, he's trying to say something, maybe he wants more pain medication."

"Pain medication?" said Andre loudly as he opened his eyes, swung his dark legs over the bedside and sat up laughing himself silly. "Pain medicine? You've got to be kidding. I was saying 'more, more' I wanted you to kiss me again."

"Oh, for heaven's sake," chuckled Martie. She walked over, put her arms around his neck and planted a long, tender kiss on his cheek. When she let go, Andre fell back on the bed. "You were right, Jim, I'm dead. After that terrific smooch, I'll never be the same."

"So, who brought the flowers?" asked Jim.

"Mom sent them. She insisted on coming up to see me, but I told her to wait a day or two so she could visit me at home and meet Sylvia. The doctor says I'm A-okay and that there's no reason to stay here provided I don't do anything to knock open the stitches or cause internal bleeding."

Martie said, "You sure had me fooled."

"Or dead!" said Jim teasing for the third time. "By the way, I like your gauze halo. It adds saintliness to your natural good looks."

"Gee, thanks. You know I'm the angelic type. Here, I'll turn around and show you my wings. You don't mind seeing a black ass-crack do you?"

"That's okay, Andre. We believe you. And we're glad you're feeling better," said Martie. "That was some experience you had up at the cabin. It's not one you or Jim will forget."

"My mom keeps phoning to ask me all kinds of questions. And for the life of me, I can't imagine how I'll ever explain what happened when she does visit. I mean, it is a tale straight from the crypt."

"Poor Sylvia. She was upset," said Martie shaking her head.

"Do you know she spent the night here, right there in that little chair sleeping beside little ole me, holding my little hand? She is a gem if there ever was one. She was going to stay here today, but I told her I'd be fine if she went to work."

"Sounds like you're in love, big fellow," injected Jim.

"You know, I think I am. That woman turns me on. I just like to be around her and I love touching her. I'm glad you gave her my name, Jim. I think I'd like to marry her. I don't want her to go away, ever."

"Did she happen to say how accurately I described you?"

"Yes, and I'll do the same for you someday, smart ass."

"By the way, did you call Ed?"

"Yes, I told him I had been in an accident and was hospitalized, but would be going home today and would be back to work in a few days."

"Don't you think that's pushing yourself a bit too hard? You need to get your strength back," declared Martie.

"I've got my strength back. Jump in this bed and I'll wrestle both of you!" he teased.

"Guess what, Andre?" said Martie stifling a grin.

"I missed my period three weeks ago."

"What?"

"I think I'm pregnant."

"Well, hot days in Hades, congrats and all that. Have you tested with one of those pregnancy kits?"

"Yes."

"And?"

"It turned out positive."

"Well, there is no such thing as being half pregnant."

"Well, the first twelve weeks are so critical that I'm just trying to be very careful."

"You mean careful like getting shot at in your classroom?" teased Andre.

"Here's another surprise."

"Lay it on me."

"You tell him, Jim."

Jim could not say it without grinning. "Martie has—has used the ironing board a number of times."

"Hot damn! I told you it would work. My Mama says it never fails."

"Well, at any rate, something worked, and we're thrilled to death."

"Wait till I tell Sylvia. She talks a lot about having kids and raising a family."

"You two are that serious?" Jim asked.

"Let's just say I love that woman and I hope she feels the same about me. We've talked about marriage, but I haven't asked her yet. I'd love to have a family with her."

For a while the three of them talked about living together, marriage, babies, careers, but then Jim had to get back on patrol. He steered the conversation back to Andre's job at the appliance store.

"As far as we know, Andre, Ed knows nothing about you and me visiting the retreat lab. I'm sure he's heard on the news that the place burned to the ground and that a victim had been found burned beyond recognition. Since he told Charles to torch the place, I'll bet Ed's assumed that the brother was killed trying to light the fire. The man was brilliant but not always practical. When the monastery reported Brother Charles missing, I'm sure that convinced Ed that he died. The media reported a gun had been found, only adding to the mystery."

"When I phoned him," said Andre, "he mentioned Charles had died in the fire, but didn't give any specifics. He wished me well. He wanted me to return to work as soon as possible. He asked me if I needed anything. Can you imagine that?"

"No." said Martie. "But Jim told me about some of the experimental gadgetry Brother Charles had been working on,

367

especially the different kinds of cylinders and orbs. It would be interesting to know if and how they operated. Sounds like a prototype for the Oculi."

"The apparatus we saw was clever indeed," replied Andre, "but it worked if I connected and disconnected a row of batteries. Jim told me about the scans done at Saint Paul's and assures me there are no batteries."

"That's for sure. Brother Charles must have perfected some other gadget that includes a power supply. Imagine the mind that man has, or had," sneered Jim, "And it was wasted. What worries me most is, he was going to kill to protect his secrets in that backroom so I think we were close. It's too bad we didn't find our answer before he burned the place."

"There were a number of experiments set up on that long, middle table, but you and I checked out only one of them—the one that looked so much like eyes. I wonder if Ed Bristol knows Charles' secret?" asked Andre. "'Cause if he does, he might just kill to keep it hidden."

"Frightening," said Martie. "I've grown to dislike that man and not just a little bit, either."

"I'm not sure I want to go back to work at the appliance store knowing what I do. But I need the money, and it's best if he thinks there is little suspicion of him."

Jim added, "That's what I was hoping you'd say."

"Any luck finding a body at the landfill?"

"No, we haven't found a dryer, or a washer."

"Well, maybe Charles did the killing and disposed of Anthony; that is, *if* he was actually murdered. It just may be that Ed Bristol's only involvement is pilfering lots of church money."

"Well, without a body, your theory could be correct," added Jim. "Right before you were shot at the cabin, I remember

Charles saying something like 'I don't know about Ed Bristol's involvement.'"

"I distinctly remember that even though he vowed to kill us, he still wouldn't incriminate Ed. Talk about loyalty!"

"Why would anyone be shooting at my students and me?" asked Martie.

Andre added, "I'm sure it was a scare tactic so the two of you would stop your investigations. This scam may involve more people than you think."

He may be right, thought Jim. *Somehow, I just can't imagine Ed shooting out the school window, but I'm sure Andre's right about the scare tactic. Problem is—what proof do I have? I just can't walk up and accuse Ed because of a priest's warning. Besides, Mrs. Pierce said she had seen his truck parked out in the lot all morning.*

They talked for a while and, typically, Andre, who they had come to cheer up, lifted their spirits. When an aide carried in his lunch, the two decided to leave.

"We'll keep tabs on you, Andre, and thanks. You saved the two of us. Driving into that fire was heroic. I kept waiting for my chance to do something, but never got it. I don't know that I'll ever be able to repay you. I had no idea you'd crawled inside that truck."

"You'll repay me right now if you just leave because before I dine on my banquet, I have to take a leak, and I don't want my butt showing when I walk across this room. See you two later!"

2:00 P.M.

Father Kerr phoned Marty to apologize for disturbing her science lesson.

"I just had to warn you," he said. "When I couldn't reach

you at home, I just had to come to your classroom. And I'm glad you're okay. Is Jim with you?"

"Yes, he's here, but both of us would like more information."

"I'm afraid I've disclosed all that I can."

"But, Father, you are abetting a killer. We need your input."

"That's all I can tell you. Please, please understand. This is not easy for me." Jim reached over and took the cell phone.

"Father Kerr, I think I understand your dilemma. Thank you for the warning. We are working hard to get the information we need. I'm going to drop Martie at home, then stop over to see you for just a few minutes. Is that okay?"

"Sure, why not, but I have some important business to attend to later this afternoon." *I'll bet he's going to drop off money. I'll just bet that's it!* When Jim arrived, the pastor was terribly dejected that no body had been found. He was sickly looking, and overwrought with dread and grief. He knew he would have to continue the blackmail payments.

He kept telling himself, *once a body has been recovered, Lucifer can be arrested. That will stop further killings and end the blackmail.* At least, he felt reassured that Jim and Martie knew about the money, but he still felt so helpless—even evil because of his silence. He stood up to let Jim in the front door.

"Afternoon," said Jim. "How are you today?"

"Down."

"I could've figured that."

Mrs. Pierce stuck her head into the parlor where the two men stood chatting, and said, "He hasn't had a thing to eat all day today. He says he feels like throwing up and can't eat. Just like that time when he threw up in his confessional."

370

As Mrs. Pierce continued down the hall, Jim jumped on her comment, "Father, did you hear confessions this morning?"

"I did!"

"Interesting, Father, and I'll bet you've looked sick ever since then."

"It's that obvious?"

"Well, we didn't find a body, and I've surmised that whatever you are being told in confession must be forcing you to use Saint Paul's money. Am I correct?"

"Jim, I know I'm repeating myself, but I can't reveal what's been said in confession. It's a canon law of the church."

"But Jesus never made that rule. Am I correct?"

"Jesus said, 'Whose sins you shall forgive, they are forgiven, and whose sins you shall retain, they are retained.' In order to decide, a priest must know what the sin is and that revelation, by its very nature, is sacrosanct according to my church. I'm not one to argue with it."

"Well, let me approach this a little differently, then"

"I'd rather just change the subject."

"Remember when I asked you if you were aware of the church fund's password change?"

"Of course I remember. I don't have Alzheimer's, yet. Do I—Sam? Is that your name? Now, what was it that you wanted to know?" teased the priest.

Jim did not feel like joking. "Are you the one who changed the password?"

"Yes."

"Can you change it back to what it was?"

"No."

"Why not? Tell me, why not?"

"I don't wish to, Jim."

"Are you being blackmailed?"

"I can't change the password."

"How can I help you if you don't tell me anything?"

"Jim, let me tell you how you can help."

"I'm all ears."

"Last Saturday, you and Martie told me that you suspected Brother Anthony and Sister Lucy were murdered. Right?"

"Correct. At least that was a strong suspicion."

"Are you any closer to proving your suspicion?"

"Not without a body." Kerr's face saddened. His shoulders slumped.

"It would be such a relief to know whether your suspicions are right or wrong. But I've got to run now."

Puzzled over Kerr's remark, Jim said, "Can I take you somewhere?"

"No, thank you. I must do this alone."

2:15 P.M.

Kerr drove to 135 Natrona Street. The Voice had been correct. The house was uninhabited. Turning the doorknob, he found it unlocked. With no hesitation, he set the fat briefcase, filled with six-hundred one-hundred dollar bills, just inside the door then turned, walked back to his automobile and drove away. This neighborhood had wide streets and large homes, but no one was around. He was sure no one had seen him come or go, except his God.

Yet, through his binoculars, Jim viewed Kerr's delivery from a safe distance. He stayed long enough to watch a second person drive up, retrieve the suitcase, and leave.

5:00 P.M.

Romeric explained to Jim that so far neither a washer nor dryer had been found buried in the section of the landfill Leslie indicated. Since she had no suggestion on another place to dig, the chief decided that any further excavation was a waste of time and money.

"Jim, does that dump have a night guard?" inquired Romeric.

"Leslie said 'Yes' when I asked her the same question, so I called the guard's home from the dump's office."

"And?"

"The guard said that he noticed nothing suspicious while he had been on duty the past few nights."

"Jim, there's no reason to doubt Leslie's word or the guard's. So if the dryer had been dug out and moved after our operator left at four o'clock, then there would be telltale signs."

"But just the same, what do you say about you and me driving down there and doing a little snooping around."

"So you're not convinced. You still feel it's worth digging?"

"Something just isn't right here. How could Leslie be that wrong? Besides, the dump did hump out a bit in the area she pointed to."

For a final time, the two policemen arrived at the dump, signed in, then drove out to the area where the bulldozer had been digging earlier.

"Jim, I can't imagine Ed dragging a washing machine or a dryer up this steep embankment without leaving some kind of trace. I know he's a strong man, but he isn't The Hulk." The chief walked at least seventy-five yards to one side of the dump above the dig site while Jim walked in the other direction. Neither man saw anything peculiar.

Although it was winter, the side of the dump was overgrown with crown vetch, which would have been trampled, or ripped out in places, if any heavy equipment had been scraped over it. The two single tracks made from the bulldozer's descent down the dump's steep side were the only visible marks.

Romeric hand motioned to Jim that they should descend to the dump's bottom to continue searching. At the bottom, they worked their way toward one another, walking back and forth, looking for any indication of ground disruption. Soon they met each other at the parked bulldozer.

"Nothing, Jim. Nothing at all. Sorry."

"Same here, Chief. This must not be the right spot—"

"—or the right theory," interrupted Romeric. We can't dig up the entire dump. Leslie says it's foolish to dig back into the hillside any deeper. I'm going to call off the digging in the morning."

"You know, Chief, I feel really bad about all this. Somehow all of it made sense to me. All the threads tied together—the Oculi, the presumed murders, the stolen money—but it may be nothing but a string of coincidences."

"You mean about the deaths, Tim?"

"Exactly."

"But you do have proof that Ed Bristol is stealing from Saint Paul's?"

"Just his money cart! That's all we have. I have no proof that he shot out the school window." Jim remained quiet about witnessing Kerr's suitcase delivery and subsequent pickup. He would tell the chief on their drive back to Latrobe.

5:30 P.M.

"Well, we can bring charges against him for larceny. That's

it." As they readied themselves for the very steep climb to the top of the dump, Romeric noticed a shiny object stuck in the mud of one of the bulldozer's caterpillar cleats.

"Here's a safety pin for you, Jim. Consider it a souvenir gift."

"Great. Just what I need. Should I stick it in my ass." The chief reached down in the dirt directly below the tread where the safety pin had lodged.

"Look at this, Jim, a few pennies, one quarter, a broken pencil an earring and a few beads. Obviously, someone or something was here."

"Hm. Not long ago when I cleaned out our dryer these are the kinds of debris that fell through the tumbler and ended up on the bottom housing. I sucked them out with a vacuum."

"Mm." Romeric walked along the bulldozer looking for similar debris. Then he spotted what looked like a tiny silver square, one-half inch on each side, embedded in dirt just under the front of the bulldozer tread where it met the ground. He stooped down and tried to pick it up.

"It's not just a square, Jim, look." He scraped at the dirt with his fingers. "It goes down into the dirt an inch or two." Jim came over and watched Romeric kick the mud where the silver square was embedded. He wiggled it back and forth.

Jim said, "It looks like a small, silver bar of some kind standing on end."

"And it doesn't want to come out easily. The ground under this bulldozer is tamped down from the machine going back and forth over the same area many times." He continued to wiggle the object vigorously, until it popped free in his fingers. "It's a silver cross with no corpus on it."

"Holy shit, Chief, you don't suppose it belon—"

"Look here on the back where my thumbnail has scraped

the clay off. There is an inscription."

"What does it say?"

"It says, *Suscipiat vitam meam Deus.*"

Both men stood there staring at one another. Romeric spoke. "Do you know how to drive one of these things?"

"No, but I know someone who does. Ed Bristol drove one for a construction firm before opening his appliance store."

"You're shitting me, Jim!"

"Not at all."

"I think he's been driving this one. That's the reason we haven't found the evidence we've been searching for."

"I'm not following you?"

"I know where the dryer is."

"You do?"

"We're standing on top of it, Jim. "

"What?"

"We are standing on top of the evidence."

"What do you mean?"

"Ed Bristol buried it." Jim still had a clouded look on his face. "Ed dug the dryer out and buried it under where we are standing."

"No! You really think so?"

"You just said he knows how to drive one of these machines. You just said debris like this came out of your dryer when you cleaned it. If this is a sterling silver cross, it fell out of the dryer when Ed Bristol came here and moved it. I'm betting he buried it right under this spot. How else would he get rid of it?"

Astounded, Jim said, "Well, I'll be damned forever and ten days! You mean he dug out the dryer, then dug a hole, buried the dryer, and then drove over it leaving the bulldozer parked as he found it."

"That's what I'm thinking," said the chief. "It would take a very keen eye to notice any change in the digging area because of the number of times the bulldozer has dug into the hillside, backed up, turned a bit to the right, dumped its load. You follow?" Jim nodded. "All Ed Bristol had to do was drive the bulldozer forward then backward moving to the left each time to leave the same type of tracks he saw when he arrived here."

"But wait, wouldn't the guard have noticed an intruder driving through the entrance gate?" asked Jim,

"He didn't enter through the gate."

"No?"

Romeric went on, "Look up there." He pointed to a place where the creek ran under a high cyclone fence that cordoned off the dump in that area. "I'll bet he slipped under that fence right in that spot. See that abandoned access road on the other side? I'd wager my job that we'd find tread marks to match those on Ed Bristol's truck tires."

"I can't believe this. I won't let myself believe it."

"Just my guess."

"I'd like to come here tomorrow, Chief, to watch the digging."

"I—will—be—right—beside—you. I wouldn't miss it for a strip show."

"Can you bring one of our forensic people?"

"Sure," answered Romeric. "I'll have whoever comes bring Anthony's dental records. Something tells me we'll need them."

On the way back to Latrobe, Jim phoned Kerr after remembering how bad he looked earlier in the day.

"Father, this is Jim, I'm driving back from the dump with Chief Romeric."

"Oh," was the only comment Kerr made.

"We've, we've—found—him, Father. We're almost sure we know precisely where to dig. We found a silver cross that may be his."

Complete silence!

Finally Jim quietly asked, "Are you there Father Kerr?"

Jim could hear muffled sobs coming from the other end. "I'm sorry, Jim, I—"

"Don't talk. I understand."

Finally, Kerr pulled himself together and whispered, "Thanks be to the Lord on high for both of you," said the priest his voice breaking. "I'm, I'm here. I just don't know what to say to you for being so persistent. You are one good man, a very good man. But I won't allow myself to believe it until you've made positive identification."

"I can understand that," said Jim. "Maybe your suffering is over." He did his best to read the Latin. "The cross is inscribed, *Suscipiat vitam meam Deus*. What does that mean?"

A long silence!

Kerr was obviously battling his emotions. The complete realization of what the two officers had discovered overwhelmed him. His battle was over. His conscience had won the day. After several moments he regained composure. Then he said, "Jim, those words mean 'May God accept my life!'"

36 The Funeral Pyre

March 6, 2003—Thursday
2:00 P.M.

The bulldozer operator agreed to meet Jim and Romeric at the dig site. He had been working elsewhere for a private contractor who allowed him the afternoon to help the Latrobe police. Everything was set. A forensic pathologist had come with the chief and Jim from Latrobe, because they were so certain a body would be uncovered.

Both men were very edgy thinking they had been misled once before and could just as well have made another misjudgment. Jim entertained the idea that Ed Bristol might have dragged the machines by himself along the creek bed to hide his tracks, then pulled them under the cyclone fence, where he hauled them away to heaven knows where. But he remembered seeing the wire fence undisturbed and rusty when he and Romeric looked at it yesterday.

The chief also suggested that a body reduced to bones would not be heavy. Ed Bristol might have carried the dryer on his back up the steep embankment. "He wouldn't care about the washer." They also discussed the possibility that the dryer might be unearthed and found empty if the robed skeleton had been taken elsewhere.

First, the bulldozer operator turned his powerful machine

parallel to the dump's bottom. He began digging fifteen yards from where Jim and Romeric found the silver cross. Scoop by scoop, he lifted out the dirt in front of the bulldozer and placed it to one side as if digging a roadway down into the earth. When he reached the five-foot level, he continued digging straight ahead.

Romeric, Jim, Leslie and the forensic woman stood watching as each scoop was lifted up and out of the hole. When the next scoopful was lifted, they heard a metallic scraping sound. Jim was standing on the edge of the hole above the operator when he spotted the white enamel paint of a large rusted appliance.

"Yes," he said out loud. "Yes, this may be it."

Romeric, who had been standing beside him, stood with fingers crossed. The next scoopful lifted two feet of dirt off of the dryer, which was lying on its side. Finally, the bulldozer operator scooped in below the appliance and lifted it and the surrounding dirt and rocks high into the air. He backed up the slanted path he had dug, turned the bulldozer, and set the scoop down on solid earth as gently as possible. He had been told of the dryer's possible contents.

Romeric walked over first and said, "Well, the moment of truth is here. We should know in just a few seconds."

The door was still bolted shut. The dozer operator handed Romeric a crowbar. It took little effort to pop open the rusting dryer door. Peering inside, he could see the remains of a brown burlap material and one skeletal hand. There was no odor except that of damp earth. Body tissue had long since disappeared providing a myriad of underground creatures with a sumptuous meal.

"Let's set it upright, Jim, and slide it out of the scoop."

As Romeric had surmised, the dryer was not heavy. They

turned it and slid it out to level ground. The skeletal remains of Brother Anthony could be seen inside in somewhat of a heap, intermixed with the folds of what once was his monk's robe.

Leslie wouldn't come near the dryer, but Ms. Brady, the forensic specialist, walked over and looked inside. She took out her folder containing Anthony's dental records from a briefcase.

"Can I have a few minutes by myself here, fellows?" she asked.

All stepped aside. Brady put on her gloves and reached inside moving the remains around until she could find and view the skull and jawbones. Opening her folder, she took out a sheet and set it inside the dryer to compare dental features. Within a very short time, she stood up, took off her gloves by pulling them inside out, and tossed them into the hole from whence the dryer had been lifted. All watched and waited.

"I'd like to take the remains back to the lab for further testing, but as far as I'm concerned, this is Brother Anthony."

Now that the truth was known, everyone grew silent. There was nothing to say. The long haunting search had ended. Chief Romeric walked over to the dryer, put his hand on it, bowed his head and stood there for a moment.

Then Jim did the same. "Good man, holy brother, dearly missed friend—sleep on!"

6:30 P.M.

The six o'clock news revealed that the mystery surrounding a monk who had disappeared from Saint Vincent's Monastery was solved. A body had been recovered from the Turtle Creek Landfill and identified as that of Brother Anthony, who had mysteriously vanished seven years ago on a Sunday evening in August of 1995. The short report mentioned that police were continuing to investigate, but gave no details about their suspicions.

Ed Bristol knew differently. His mind was racing once again. He knew it was just a matter of time now, before he'd be arrested and charged with murder. Since the corpse had been found in one of his dryers, he knew that the MS operator, Leslie, could identify him as the person who had transported the dryer to the landfill and dumped it. But he had plenty of money now.

He'd leave Pennsylvania and drive to a remote town in some distant state. He always liked colder climates, so he would lose himself in the backcountry of Minnesota. The state had uncountable isolated lakes where he could fish in the summer and hunt during the cold, winter months. He was thankful Brother Charles had provided both of them with fake IDs to open the Homeless Relief Fund. Now, he could withdraw its money and establish a new life wherever he wanted to go.

6:45 P.M.

Martie phoned Father Kerr saying she wanted to see him, but he had already heard about the unearthing of Anthony's remains on the evening news. He told her to come over anyway. Upon arrival, they discussed the positive identification of Anthony's remains and the charges that could be brought against Ed Bristol.

She then explained in detail what had happened to Jim and Andre this past Tuesday. She explained what she knew of the horrible events leading up to Andre getting shot, and Brother Charles' hideous death by being burned alive in the retreat cabin fire. But then she mentioned the prototype of the Oculi suspended on a ring stand and how Jim said Andre somehow connected the wires to batteries to make them work.

"That's incredible," Father Kerr said, "But the sad thing is, Martie, the prototype that they saw works by batteries right? We've examined that cross with powerful scanners. They would've seen batteries."

"Yes, that's the disappointing thing. That was Andre's contention also," sighed Martie. "So that shoots our theory, unless there is some other device or power source."

"Well, there must be some way the crucifix gets its power," said Father Kerr, trying to make her feel better.

"I'm fascinated, Martie. Can you tell me once again what they said the contraption looked like?"

Martie did her best to explain even though it sounded very vague. "All I know is that Andre spotted this long line of nine-volt batteries all lined up with their terminals soldered together. He said he connected the line of batteries to some dangling wires and after a short time, one tiny droplet of water began to form. That's all, just one drop."

"Just a drop? But each eye drips more than that. So, that just can't be right."

"Well, Jim said that after the batteries were reconnected many times, only then did the droplet form. Jim said it all seemed so simple; the circuit was a very simple loop—just a primitive loop." Neither person spoke for several moments. Kerr seemed to be thinking deeply.

"Martie," said Kerr. "Say—that—again."

"What?"

"What you just said about the loop."

Martie repeated herself. "When Andre saw the dangling wires, he connected them to the batteries to make a loop."

"A loop. A loop! *A giant loop*," repeated the Priest, "Giant loop. Giant, g-i-g-a-n-t-i-c," he said, "emphasizing the word by spelling it out while making a large, sweeping, loop motion by extending both hands above his head and bringing them down to his sides in large arcs.

"Maybe that's it, Martie. They've made one gigantic loop."

"You've lost me."

"Remember how the Carnegie team said it was unusual that the crucifix had real nails in addition to the bolts?"

"Yes."

"And didn't both scans show support wires as a mesh within the plaster throughout the entire corpus?"

"Yes, but they said those would be for support, and you more or less told us the same thing when you showed us that statue in the basement."

The dark brown skin of Father Kerr's face began to glow, almost as if he were blushing. "Listen to this theory. Imagine that just two of those wires were not for support at all, but instead they were connected to the eyes. How would one know from a scan? You'd probably have to take the corpus apart to check for sure."

Martie was perplexed, "Go on."

"Suppose the wires were connected to cylinder orbs just like those Jim and Andre saw at the mountain cabin."

"Okay."

"Now picture this: the nails through the hands are long enough to touch those imbedded wires and the large suspension hooks in the arms of the cross."

"I think I'm still with you."

"Martie, how is the crucifix suspended?"

"By two long cables connected to the hooks."

Kerr said, "Repeat what you just said."

"By two long cables! The crucifix is suspended by—two—long—metal cables." Then it registered. "Father, the batteries! The batteries are in the attic!" she said.

"I'll bet you're right; the suspension cables complete the circuit. That's why the scan couldn't see batteries. They're not in the cross at all."

"Oh, it can't be that simple. It just can't be."

Kerr replied, "That's why the area above the church ceiling is sacrosanct; the batteries are hidden up there with some kind of remote device that is radio controlled, just like the two doors you told me about in the Offerings cart." Father Kerr stood up and grabbed his flashlight.

"Where are you going?" asked Martie.

"I've got to know. I must know. I'm going to find the batteries."

"Now?"

"It will put the last of my demons back in Hell. I must find out, now! Right now." He grabbed a flashlight from a drawer in a parlor lamp table on his way to the side door entrance. He dashed through the breezeway and bolted through the sacristy door into the church and disappeared. Martie tried to stay behind him.

He didn't bother turning on any lights since all the flickering candles were so bright. This was a man without fear. All his fiendish thoughts were about to be exorcised, and he just couldn't wait. He bolted down the side aisle, and then began fumbling with his ring of keys until he found the old skeleton key to the spiral staircase.

Martie finally caught up with him. She had such terrible memories of these steps that she wasn't sure she could climb them. In a flash, Kerr was gone past the first spiral, leaping two steps at a time. She started up after him.

"Wait, I'm coming with you."

"Hurry," he said. *"Veritas me liberabit"* (The truth will free me).

She was not sure she could do this. She imagined herself falling like Sister Lucy. She could still remember the sound of her horrible tumbling, her first few screams, her spurting head wound—

"Martie, come on, we haven't got all day—er, all night!"

But she knew it was different now. She was safe here helping this holy man solve a mystery he never believed in from its inception. She just knew everything had to be okay. She kept climbing, climbing and holding on to the railing.

She kept her eyes peeled on the steps directly in front of her trying not to think of Lucy dashing up around the spirals ahead. And then she was there at the top with Kerr. And it was very dark. There in front of her stood the murderous door.

"Damn," said Kerr, "why didn't I bring you a light?"

Martie reached into her purse and took out a small penlight attached to her key chain. "It's small," she said, "but it may help a bit."

Father Kerr didn't remember the hasp on the inside of the attic door when he and Jim had been up here, but then he hadn't paid close attention either. Martie could not remember ever being in a place so dark. There wasn't a hint of residual light. Once through the door, they crept along the narrow wooden walkway while Kerr aimed his light straight ahead. "We are on a catwalk," he said. "You can hold on to this railing, but watch out for splinters."

"This place is huge," Martie exclaimed. "How will you know where to look?"

"Just follow me," he said without answering her question.

They crept along for quite a distance before stopping. Martie figured they must be near the end of the center aisle that was far below them.

"Now, you stay here, Martie. See those planks, they go from one side of the church to the other. He shined his light directly on them. I'm going to climb over onto those boards and hunt. They'll hold my weight because they are sitting on top of the stone arches. At least that's what your husband told me.

"I don't know that the old lath and plaster will hold much of anything. Somewhere along this arch, or the next one over there," he pointed the beam of his flashlight, "there must be a large hook of some kind coming up through the archway."

"I understand what you're saying, but I'm thinking that if someone had been up here, wouldn't there be tracks in all this dust?"

"This attic is closed. Surely, there would be some dust, but once it settled, that would be it, just cobwebs and spider webs. However, I do suspect there is more dust here than nature would provide on its own. In fact, it smells like many a sweeper bag was emptied up here. I'll bet this is where the dust from the rectory sweeper gets scattered to hide any telltale tracks or marks. When Jim and I were up here, we both wondered about that odd smell."

Kerr was now about twenty feet out from the catwalk. His black trousers and white shirt were covered with dust. He found nothing suspicious. He turned and began to crawl back toward the catwalk, checking in the dust with his hands. Nothing.

"You know, Martie," he said, "if I had perpetrated this magic trick, I certainly would've put the batteries in a place that was easy to reach."

"Makes sense to me," said Martie, shining her light down on the catwalk floor. "Is there any crawl space right under here where I'm standing?" she asked.

"Let me see," he said coughing and sneezing. "Gads, I've got to get out of here before I choke to death."

By now, he had crawled under the catwalk and was about to come out the other side, thinking he'd hop back up on the catwalk and move to the next archway. Martie shined her tiny light downward through the slits in the catwalk.

To keep from banging his head, for one brief instant, he aimed his light on the support that held up the catwalk—and there they sat. Lined up in a long, neat row were fifteen nine-volt batteries on a makeshift ledge. All were connected in parallel so that in spite of their number, they produced exactly nine volts. The sheer number of batteries would insure that replacements would not be too often needed.

Connected to the wires was some kind of receiver. The priest could see a long, bare antenna wire nailed parallel to the catwalk bottom.

"Martie, that's it," said Kerr. "A push of a button on a transmitter connected the batteries through the suspending wires to the crucifix below. It is that simple." Kerr followed one wire down into the dust with his fingers and gave a slight tug upward.

"Look, Martie. Watch over there." He shined his flashlight and lifted. Martie could see the dust move. Then he pulled a bit harder and a red wire appeared above the dust. He made no effort to hide it.

He crawled a few more feet, stood up, grasped Martie's outstretched hand, and pulled himself up onto the catwalk. The look on his face was one of absolute triumph.

"The great mystery is over! I've found what we were looking for, Martie! The flashes of light you and Sister Lucy saw came from a flashlight when Ed or Brother Charles came up to replace, or check, those batteries."

"So, all they had to do with the remote is turn the circuit on and off until a few tears fell."

"Yep, it's that simple."

Martie tried to dust off the priest's clothing, but it was no use nor did he care. But in the darkness, they heard a soft—*click!*

Aiming their lights back toward the attic door, they could see the back of a giant figure that had just padlocked the attic door hasp.

Father Kerr said, "Get behind me, Martie. *Diabolus venit*" (Lucifer is coming). When the large, hulking creature turned, it blinded them with an extremely bright light so they could not see a face. Martie was terrified. Closer and closer it came toward them, saying nothing, nothing at all. It just kept coming and coming. Then, about eight feet away, it stopped.

The Voice shrieked, "Paul, I want to make a confession."

Kerr recognized the horrible sound. It was that shrill, faked voice he had heard in his confessional cubicle, that same voice that had so sickened him that he puked out his guts. It was The Voice that had forced him to blackmail his own parishioners.

"They've told me what you've done," said Father Kerr. "It's time to stop now. It's over! Your mind is sick, Ed. You need help, and I'll help you get it. You need it right now."

"Ed Bristol doesn't need your help, Paul. He hasn't come here for you. I've come here for that bitch hiding behind you. She's the one, she and her boyfriend. They're the unwed bastards that ruined my plans." He began to walk toward the priest. "I have no weapons. I have no rifle. I carry no knife, no grenades like in the war. All I have is my bare hands. I want to kill that woman behind you."

He took another step then Kerr put up his hand and commanded, "Stop, Ed. Do you hear me? Stop!"

In one fluid motion, Bristol stuck the narrow back end of his powerful flashlight into his rear pocket, reached out with both hands, picked up the priest, turned one-hundred-eighty degrees and threw him down to the catwalk. Martie screamed as loud and long as she could, hoping someone would hear her.

"Martie, dear, that hurts my ears so STOP IT," Bristol shouted. "I locked the door, so you can't get out. I locked the church door by the sacristy, so no one can get in. There is no one to help you now. NO ONE!" he bellowed.

Kerr was crawling up behind Ed. He knew he was no match for the hulking man. But he couldn't just lie there and witness a murder. He had to do something. He crawled closer and closer until he grabbed Ed by the ankle and twisted, attempting to topple him. Bristol merely took his flashlight and hit the priest so hard on the side of his head that he fell to the dusty boards, unconscious and bleeding.

Watching this, Martie gasped. Terror seized her entire being. Ed Bristol gave her a vicious smile then started after her again.

Putting both hands on the handrail, she coiled her legs and sprung up as if mounting a horse, but went all the way over to land on the planks that Father Kerr had previously been crawling on. At their widest, the boards were ten-inches.

"Martie, you fool; you can't get away. There's no place to go. You're my enemy just like in that awful war. I've got to kill, and I can do it quickly or slowly. I'll use my hands. I'll make sure you feel more than just a little pain after what you've done."

He climbed up and over the handrail and got down on all fours to crawl out after Martie on the narrow plank. Martie extended her arms for balance and inched her way toward the far wall.

"The wall is coming up, Martie dear, and then it will all be over for you, just like it was for—"

There was a long moan on the catwalk. Father Kerr was regaining consciousness. "He can't help you, Martie, he's way over there in the darkness. But I kill enemies like you and those Vietnamese goons who killed that little GI."

Regaining his senses, Kerr slurred, "Stop, Ed. Please! Stop! Do it for God's sake! Come back. God will forgive you. I'll give you absolution right now, right here. Just leave her alone. Come back."

Ed continued crawling inching closer and closer. Martie had reached the side wall. There was no way over to the next archway except across the plastered lathe ceiling.

Ed reached for her ankle, but she yanked her foot free leaving him an empty shoe. Wrathful, he tossed it wide into the vast darkness. Then his fingers wrapped around her bare ankle.

"Don't struggle, Martie, it will all be over soon. I can't wait to hear you scream for as long a time as you want." He grabbed her lower leg firmly and started pulling her away from the wall. Martie shrieked in horror. "Getting your neck broken very slowly could be very painful. I'll make sure you scream nice and loud. You can fight and kick all you want, but, you see, I'm much bigger than you. Then I'll have to take care of Paul back there, too," said Bristol. Feeling her body being pulled away from the wall Martie squealed like a person being tortured to death.

"NO-O-O!" she screamed. "NO— let me go!"

Kerr took his flashlight and with all his might, threw it, hitting Ed squarely on the neck. For that brief second, he released Martie's ankle to maintain his balance on the narrow board. "You slimy bastard excuse for a holy priest. You used to be my best friend, Paul. I almost got you once—for sure, now, you'll be next. But wait till you hear her yell! That should make you suffer all the more."

He turned again to reach for Martie. She had but one option and that was all—and she had to do it quickly. There was no other choice. She kicked off her other shoe then stepped off the planks and darted over the thin wooden lath and plaster ceiling, knowing plaster alone would not support her weight. But it did, although she could hear it cracking with each quick step. She reached the safety of the thick boards above the next archway.

"Why, you are one bitching little freak! You must not like me. Is it because I killed Brother Anthony? Do you know he wasn't supposed to come over where Charles was working, but he did. It was his own fault. Or is it because I knocked Lucy down the staircase? Is it because I jerked Phillip's ladder, or maybe because I shot McCarthy? Why that man almost saw my face; now, what would you have done?"

Seeing that Martie had crossed the plastered lathe, Ed stood up, and carefully placed one foot down, and then the other. It seemed strong enough but Ed was much heaver than Martie. He knew he had to step on the lathe strips, not the plaster. "You know Father Phillip deserved to die. He was one of those boy-like adolescents. The ones who killed American soldiers; they erased the little GI that ran beside me. They destroyed my manhood."

"Oh, Christ," screamed Martie aloud to Kerr. "He's coming after me." At the same time, Kerr started crawling out along the board above the archway where Martie was standing.

"Father, he's coming, go back, I can't get around you. Stop! Can't you hear, go back," screamed Martie, "Oh, please, please turn around."

She knew it was hopeless and stood there whimpering, her voice getting softer and softer, "Please! Oh, please, go back, both of you! I don't want to die."

Now, she was terrified to step off the planks around the crawling priest after hearing the ceiling crack very loudly.

Closer and closer crawled Kerr. He was now only two feet from Martie. Ed Bristol, too, was almost upon her. He had placed his feet as carefully as possible, testing with each step, making sure he placed his weight on crisscrossed lathe and not just plaster. Closer and closer he approached. Two more steps and he could easily grab her then torturously take is time snapping her neck.

Kerr stood up and took both of Martie's hands in his. He stared directly into her petrified eyes and said, "Martie, hold me *only* if you can. And may the Almighty give you strength."

Immediately, Kerr jumped up and backward, pouncing hard on the ancient, plaster ceiling with both feet. Ed Bristol stopped to watch not understanding. All three heard a loud crack. The priest stepped back onto the planks of the archway and then jumped even higher up and back down on the plaster again, stomping harder as he landed.

A long, wide crack opened under Kerr's feet that ran over to where Ed Bristol was standing. The demented man saw dim light from candles far, far below and panicked. He teetered forward and took one giant step to reach the planks on the arch where Martie stood. The toes of his heavy work shoe touched the catwalk, but he had pushed off much too hard with his back foot. The weakened plaster Kerr had been stomping on broke.

At first, only Ed Bristol's foot slipped through the crack. The jagged plaster lacerated the skin of his ankle above his heavy boot. He waved his arms desperately, trying to throw his balance forward. But, as the plaster continued to crumble under his weight, his body slipped farther and farther down through the hole so that one outstretched leg and his torso remained above the ceiling. He could watch and feel the ancient plaster disintegrating around him.

By now, both men sank to their shoulders. Sheer terror seized both Ed and Kerr when they realized what was happening. Chunk after chunk of plaster cracked away and plummeted downward. But Martie still gripped the priest's hands firmly. It took all of her strength and his, to flop Kerr's chest up and over the safety of the planks on top of the archway, while his legs dangled into the chasm. Even then—even then when the holy man saw the agonized look on Ed Bristol's face struggling for life, even then Kerr turned and reached for Ed's huge outstretched hand, but just their fingertips brushed one another for the briefest of seconds.

With a thunderous roar and volumes of choking dust, the aged plaster and the thin dried-out lathe collapsed around Ed Bristol. His huge body disappeared through a gaping hole many, many times his size. Martie and Kerr heard a loud, wailing scream of the huge man falling—falling—falling, and then a sickening thud, accompanied by the sound of hundreds of pieces of broken glass.

Far, far below them, The Voice's body had landed on its back atop the rows and rows of vigil candles it used to maintain so carefully—the candles whose offerings it had so cleverly pirated. Long shards of broken glass penetrated the fallen being. The metal fleur-de-lis that once decorated the top of a vigil light stand in the side aisle, had completely penetrated one leg and now protruded from its other side.

Martie and Kerr looked down helplessly on the victim

impaled eighty-five feet below. On first impact, many of the candles had blown out, but just long enough to allow their liquid wax to seep into the outer and under clothing and hair of the impaled man. Those candles that had not blown out licked at the wax-soaked clothing, igniting it. But the creature was neither dead nor unconscious. The horrible thing could lift its head and arms in wrathful agony, but—but not far. Its neck was broken about two inches below the shoulders.

It shrieked and screamed pitifully trying to get off its burning pyre. Both Martie and Kerr held their ears. But soon, every part of the fallen creature became one huge, burning wick. Its rage grew louder as the flesh below the clothing started to sear, then cook, the flesh that the charred arms and hands could not reach.

The hair was now on fire; the legs, the chest, and then finally, the flesh of the face began to pucker and burn. Its agonized cries raged on and on, but as the being cooked and blackened even more, their volume grew fainter and fainter until the dead thing made no sound—no sound at all. All noise in the church stopped except for the crackling, popping sound of burning skin, muscle tissue, and fat.

A foul smell reached the opening in the ceiling, but Martie and the priest had long since crawled to the safety of the catwalk. There was no need for light, now. The vigil candles and the human torch below cast a wicked, eerie glow up into the dark attic. Marty and Kerr had hastened to the attic door, but could not remove the heavy padlock from its hasp. Both slid to the floor far away from the ruptured ceiling with their arms around one another, waiting to be rescued. Father Kerr said, "Lucifer has returned to Hell!"

No longer an unbeliever, aloud Martie said, "Father, your God is here. Indeed he is here with you and with me. He is real!"

37　The Oculi Miracle

March 8, 2003—Saturday
10:00 AM

The monastery held a solemn ceremony for Brother Anthony in Saint Vincent's Basilica. The abbot himself conducted the funeral with the honor and dignity due this holy monk who had been so cruelly taken from this world, albeit seven years past. Several monks gave short but fitting testimonies to the goodness and godliness of their deceased brother. Old Father Martin had asked Jim to give a short eulogy since he and Brother Anthony used to be best friends.

Greensburg Bishop Joseph Mallory attended, along with many of the priests from the diocese that had known Anthony and thought highly of him. Of course, Fathers Kerr, Walsh and McKelvy were there along with the Sister Margaret from Saint Paul's Parish and even Mrs. Pierce. In addition, Chief Romeric attended along with Martie, Brother Anthony's sister and Dr. Troft.

The ceremony lasted about forty minutes. It had always been the tradition at Saint Vincent's Monastery that a deceased monk was placed in a simple, wooden coffin that stood in the center aisle during the ceremony. Following this same tradition, Brother Anthony's closed coffin stood front and center even though it contained nothing more than a decayed robe, sandals and bones.

When it came time for Jim's eulogy, he knew there was little he could say without becoming emotionally upset. Instead of words, he walked to the center aisle, placed both his hands at the head end of the casket and stood there while tears streamed down his face. After a moment or two of silence, he stooped, kissed the coffin and then returned to his pew.

When the funeral was over, everyone present walked in procession to the cemetery where Brother Anthony's bones were finally laid to rest. The abbot presented the cross Anthony had worn to his sister who wept uncontrollably. Old Father Martin and Jim were the last two people to leave the graveside. Although Martin appear sad he stood a few moments with Jim and then said out loud, "I'll surely be joining you soon, pal, so have the cards shuffled and ready." He took a used deck from under his robe, placed it on the coffin, smiled then walked away beside Jim.

Father Kerr had decided to withhold information about the Oculi cross until Father McCarthy returned from Rome. They could then sit and decide the best way to break the news about the fake miracle to the public. The news media had already jumped to several false conclusions regarding Brother Anthony in their efforts to grab the public's attention and sell their tabloids.

One theory suggested that the brother had been abducted at the monastery and taken into Latrobe where his deranged captor, suffering a psychotic episode, murdered him. Since Monday was garbage pickup day in parts of Latrobe, the murderer found a discarded dryer sitting on a street along with some other garbage, and stuffed Anthony inside. This theory explained why his skeleton had been found in the Turtle Creek Landfill. This assumption was made after extensive interviews with the monks at Saint Vincent's monastery, not one of whom could think of a single enemy the holy brother had at Saint Vincent's other than one disgruntled monk, a Brother Stephen, who did not like losing card games. It was a known fact, however, that Stephen was present in the recreation room when Brother Anthony disappeared.

Another theory suggested that the brother abandoned his monastic profession leaving Saint Vincent's of his own free will. Then, unfortunately, he died of a stroke or heart attack either on, or near someone's private property in Latrobe. The owner disposed of the body in the dryer via regular garbage pickup rather than get involved with any kind of police investigation.

The media focused more on the horrifying "accidental" death of the faithful custodian at Saint Paul's Church, Mr. Ed Bristol, rather than on any possibility of wrongdoing on his part. Reporters assumed that Father Kerr, Martie and Officer Jim, were the ones who discovered Bristol's barbecued remains since none of the three would disclose anything more specific about his demise, other than the fact that the old plaster ceiling gave way and he fell to a hideously tortured death.

Then, too, since a gun had been found at the charred remains of the retreat lab where Brother Charles pursued his scientific work, newspapers theorized that Charles' death was one of self defense. Thinking that the retreat lab might contain drugs or money, a druggie or thief attempted a break in, but was thwarted by Charles with his pistol in hand. The angered person then rammed the porch to kill Charles as tire tracks showed, but gasoline stored under the front stoop for a lawn tractor ignited on impact setting the entire building ablaze, including the truck which the intruder somehow managed to back out of the inferno. Additional tire tracks indicated that the invader had escaped in a second parked vehicle.

2:30 P.M.

The group sat in Father Kerr's front room attempting to determine the best way to handle the revelation of the startling faux miracle. Father McCarthy had flown from Rome that morning and had reached the rectory by early afternoon. Kerr briefed him on the entirety of the bizarre happenings at Saint Paul's and its connection with the monastery. By the time of the evening meeting, McCarthy was well prepared to enter the discussion.

"'Tis good to be back, it is, but I'm a bit sad about the miracle. It all seemed so real, did it not?"

Father Kerr interjected, "I must admit, at times it seemed authentic. If none of those awful things had happened, eventually I might've been convinced."

"You're right about that," said Martie. "I was certainly taken by it."

Jim spoke up. "What on earth will we ever tell Bishop Mallory? He was so convinced God had chosen his diocese for divine intervention when he could've chosen any other place on earth."

"What worries me most," said Kerr, "is the negative impact this scandal will have on good Catholic believers as a whole. They have been beleaguered with uncountable sex scandals among the clergy. Not only have priests been involved with child molestation, but bishops have attempted to cover up those crimes. It's like the corporate corruption within the giant companies.

"Once one company CEO was proven corrupt, others toppled from high positions like dominoes. In our church, after the first priest admitted his guilt, those molested by other priests spoke out, bringing down not only the offenders, but the higher ups including that cardinal who was forced to resign."

Then Martie expressed her feelings. "Father Kerr here is the finest example of a manly, realistic priest I've ever known. Indeed, there is such a thing as holiness, and this man has that aura about him." Kerr was embarrassed by Martie's praise.

"But now," she went on, "because of two scheming, dead men, Father Kerr, as pastor of this church, could be looked upon as a participant in all of this. You know how the media will react. They'll slant stories just to make headlines, and in Father Kerr's case, that would be worse than any crime committed here. This man deserves more than that. He has been opposed to the reality of this miracle since it began back in August."

"Martie's right," agreed Jim. "This church will plummet from a place where people came, thinking God visited it in a special way, to a building that people will either avoid altogether, or visit just to see the damnable place. Yet, Father Kerr and the other priests, and certainly Margaret here, had nothing to do with any wrongdoing. Somehow it just doesn't seem fair to allow that to happen because of two demented misfits."

"And what about your Bishop Mallory, now? He believes in the miracle cross, does he not?" asked McCarthy. "'Twill surely be a terrible blow to his mind I would surely think."

Andre, who had said nothing at all up to this time, finally spoke up in his usual, straightforward manner. "I've been listening to you speak of all the negative effects that could result by revealing the truth about the cross. In my opinion, we should just let it die of its own accord. You know, just let it—poop out— so to speak."

With a twinkle in his eye, McCarthy said, "Now, could you explain yourself a little more, Laddie, would you, especially the pooping part?"

"Here's what I mean, plain and simple. I don't want to live a lie. None of us do. But do we have to tell the truth about something we played no part in when it would do more harm than good? Why can't we just let the mystery poop out by itself?

"The cross will stop shedding tears from this day forth. None of us started the mystery, and we couldn't control what happened, so I for one feel no obligation to reveal what we've discovered."

"But generations will go on believing that a miracle occurred here when in fact it didn't. Don't we owe a truthful explanation to my parishioners," asked Kerr.

McCarthy spoke up. "Fawther Kerr, I can see your point of view, I can. But when I think of all the harm it would do, I tend to agree with Andre here. None of us need to lie. When asked meself, I'd just say, 'No, I'm certain it wasn't a miracle at all.' Whether people believe me or not would be their business, but my answer would be truthful, would it not?"

Jim added, "I have a feeling that even if we gave a detailed explanation of the entire debacle, people would still go on believing. To protect Father Kerr and his church and this parish, I agree with Andre that we should just let the mystery poop out of its own accord."

"You mean we wouldn't even tell the bishop?" asked Martie?

Again, McCarthy spoke. "I think both Fawther Kerr and I should talk with Bishop Joseph and tell him honestly what has happened here so he knows every detail, mind ye, every last one. We can show him the actual transmitter and explain how it worked, even though Fawther Kerr has smashed it beyond repair. But in the end, I have the feeling, I do, I truly do, that he'd agree with our decision to let the mystery of the Oculi incident die on the vine so to speak or poop out."

There was a long, thoughtful pause in the conversation when no one spoke. It was a weighty matter, but it did seem that revealing the deception involved with the crucifix would be devastating. It sickened Martie to think of what Kerr might suffer—an honest pastor who had saved her from certain death.

"I feel obligated to agree with Father Kerr's decision, whatever that is. But I'm hoping you," she looked at the pastor, "will at least carefully consider what Andre has proposed."

Jim agreed. "I know you've been under a lot of strain this past year, and this might very well be the worst stress of all, but in the end, I'll support whatever you'd like us to do."

Kerr looked carefully around the group stopping to gaze at each face. He was overwhelmed by the genuine concern this group had for his well-being. They loved him. Immediately, a slight grin began to appear at each end of his lips that grew into an ear-to-ear smile.

"First, we must talk with Mallory," said Kerr, "and then go from there."

True to his nature, Andre added the last words to make everyone chuckle. "Now, if anyone here gets into real financial trouble, just call Father Kerr to see if someone can repair or duplicate that transmitter."

3:30 P.M.

That meeting ended the matter, at least for that day and that time and that place. Kerr and McCarthy would talk with the bishop and abide with his decision. Seeing that the conference had ended, Mrs. Pierce opened the parlor door and said, "Jim," there is a Brant Hardy here to see you. He's been waiting for a while. I didn't want to interrupt the meeting."

"Oh, thanks, Mrs. Pierce, I've been expecting him."

Jim walked across the front hall into the opposite parlor room and welcomed Brant. He wanted to make good his promise to disclose to Brant, why he had come to Pittsburgh asking about Ed Bristol's background. Hardy had insisted on driving to Latrobe after hearing about the death of both Ed and Schaler. He also wanted to see the mysterious crucifix.

"Well," said Jim, "why don't we walk over to the church so I can show you the cross and the deceptive donations cart Ed and Schaler invented. At this time, there is no guess as to how much money was stolen, but after all these years, it would be a sizable amount."

"I can just imagine," said Brant. "Those two were always up to something."

Jim planned not to disclose their involvement with the actual crucifix unless the bishop so directed.

Upon reaching the church, Pastor Kerr and Papal Delegate McCarthy stood staring up at the cross. A look of disappointment seemed to cross Kerr's face. McCarthy just shook his head.

"Ah-h, Fawther, it seemed so real, truly it did. It did so much for me soul and me faith standing here under it!" And with that soulful comment, a tiny droplet of water, then another, fell to the floor between the two priests.

As Jim and Brant walked up the aisle from the back, they could see the look of disbelief on the two priests' faces. Kerr and McCarthy were staring at the floor and then up at the cross. Jim's eyes followed theirs. Then he saw it; the tiny wet spot that had formed on the church floor between the two priests. Jim's mind went numb. Brant just stood there with his mouth open—

CPSIA information can be obtained at www.ICGtesting.com
Printed in the USA
267166BV00005B/27/P